THE CROWN OF COLUMBUS

THE CROWN OF COLUMBUS

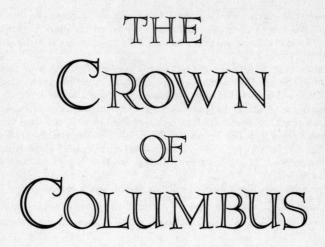

Michael Dorris • Louise Erdrich

HarperPerennial

A Division of HarperCollins*Publishers*

Excerpts from the Blessing Way poem reprinted with permission from *Blessing Way* by Leland C. Wyman, copyright © 1970 University of Arizona Press.

Excerpts from Christopher Columbus's diary reprinted with permission from book #60660 "The Log of Christopher Columbus," by Robert H. Fuson. Copyright © 1987 by Robert H. Fuson and published by Tab Books, a division of McGraw-Hill, Blue Ridge Summit, PA.

Excerpts from *The Diario of Christopher Columbus's First Voyage to America, 1492–1493.* Abstracted by Fray Bartolomé de Las Casas, transcribed and translated by Oliver Dunn and James E. Kelley, Jr. Norman: University of Oklahoma.

Letter of the Admiral to the (quondam nurse) of the Prince, John, written near the end of the year 1500. *From Select Letters of Christopher Columbus, with Other Original Documents Relating to His Four Voyages to the New World* (London: The Hakluyt Society, M.DCC.L.XX, 2nd ed.), pp. 72–107. Translated and edited by R. H. Major, Keeper of the Department of Maps in the British Museum and Hon. Sec. of the Royal Geographical Society.

Parts of this book have appeared in slightly altered form in *Redbook*, *Mother Jones*, and *Caliban*.

A hardcover edition of this book was published in 1991 by HarperCollins Publishers.

HarperCollins books may be purchased for educational, business, or sales promotional use. For information please write: Special Markets Department, HarperCollins Publishers, Inc., 10 East 53rd Street, New York, NY 10022.

First HarperPerennial edition published 1999.

Designed by Cassandra J. Pappas

The Library of Congress has catalogued the hardcover edition as follows:

Dorris, Michael.
    The crown of Columbus : a novel / Michael Dorris, Louise Erdrich.
      p. cm.
    ISBN 0-06-016079-9
    1. Erdrich, Louise.   I. Title.
PS3554.0695C76   1991
813'.54—dc21   90-55964

ISBN 0-06-093165-5 (pbk.)

03 CC/RRD 10 9 8 7 6 5 4 3

For our bouquet of Violets

ACKNOWLEDGMENTS

We are grateful to the research and interlibrary loan librarians of Dartmouth College for their ideas and assistance, and especially to Charles Rembar—friend, fine writer, and tough critic—whose good counsel and stalwart enthusiasm kept this book afloat through every storm.

. . . *Columbus presented the Log to Queen Isabela. With very little delay, she commanded a scribe to prepare an exact copy for the Admiral. . . . The holograph original has not been seen since the death of Queen Isabela in 1504, and it is only presumed to have been in her possession up until that time. There is the remote possibility that it may be discovered someday, somewhere.*

—*The Log of Christopher Columbus*
by Robert H. Fuson

That which grieves me most is the seizure of my papers, of which I have never been able to recover one; and those that would have been most useful to me in proving my innocence, are precisely those which he has kept most carefully concealed. Behold the just and honest inquisitor! But whatever he may have done, they tell me that he has now bidden good bye to justice and is simply a despot. Our Lord God retains His power and wisdom as of old; and, above all things, He punishes injustice and ingratitude.

—Letter of the Admiral to the (quondam) nurse of the Prince, John, *Select Letters of Christopher Columbus*

FOUR
DISCOVERIES

1

1.

In the warm pink-gold of a Caribbean afternoon, something marvelous washed up from the sea. The island girl who found it, Valerie Clock, was known as a good-for-nothing child, the type who lazed about when her mother sent her down to rake the beach. Soon everything would change.

That afternoon Valerie was doing exactly what she was best at. Nothing. The five o'clock sun was so cool and high—why not let the tide roll up everything it was going to, and then use her rake? Way out there, she could see a small dot, yellow, of some piece of trash she'd have to haul.

Long swells, an opaque turquoise, pushed heavily in. Valerie had all the time in the world to wait, as long as the wind was strong enough to keep down the sand fleas. She scratched her ankle, hooked with her toe at a bit of rubber—a thong drifted smooth, maybe kicked off a foot in Florida or who knows where. Valerie tried it on her own foot. Not a bad fit.

The yellow dot was a little larger now. It looked, in fact, like the kind of raft bonefishers anchored out beyond the reef to carry

3

their bounty. The size of it faintly piqued Valerie's interest, and she rose to rake a while, until it was almost close enough to reach by wading. It was a raft, indeed, and she threw her rake high on the beach and approached waist-high into the surf. She pulled the sagging gunwales to her chest, craned herself to see over the edge, and froze. She'd been cautious, ready for a half-rotted catch, but what she saw was so surprising she couldn't register the sight at first. That was the day the people began to call her the Pharaoh's daughter.

Valerie stared and could not stop staring into the bottom of the boat. She stretched out her hand, touched the baby, but the little rose-cheeked child slept on, lulled by the surge and hiss of waves.

2.

The Admiral went ashore in the armed launch, and Martín Alonso Pinzón and his brother Vincente Anes, who was captain of the *Niña*. The Admiral brought out the royal banner and the captains two flags with the green cross, which the Admiral carried on all the ships as a standard, with an F and a Y, and over each letter a crown, one on one side of the † and the other on the other. Thus put ashore they saw very green trees and many ponds and fruits of various kinds. The Admiral called to the two captains and to the others who had jumped ashore and to Rodrigo Descobedo, the *escrivano* of the whole fleet, and to Rodrigo Sánchez de Segovia; and he said that they should be witnesses that, in the presence of all, he would take, as in fact he did take, possession of the said island for the king and for the queen his lords, making the declarations that were required, and which at more length are contained in the testimonials made there in writing. Soon many people of the island gathered there. What follows are the very words of the Admiral in his book about his first voyage to, and the discovery of these Indies.

I, he says, *in order that they would be friendly to us—because I recognized that they were people who would be better freed [from error] and converted to our Holy Faith by love than by force—to some of them I gave red caps, and glass beads which they put on their chests, and many other things of small value, in which they took so much pleasure and became so much our friends that it was a marvel. Later they came swimming to the ships' launches where we were and brought us parrots and cotton thread in balls and javelins and many other things, and they traded them to us for other things which we gave them, such as small glass beads and bells. In sum, they took everything and gave of what they had very willingly. But it seemed to me that they were a people very poor in everything. All of them go around as naked as their mothers bore them; and the women also, although I did not see more than one quite young girl. And all those that I saw were young people, for none did I see of more than thirty years of age. They are very well formed, with handsome bodies and good faces. Their hair [is] coarse—almost like the tail of a horse—and short. They wear their hair down over their eyebrows except for a little in the back which they wear long and never cut. Some of them paint themselves with black, and they are the color of the Canarians, neither black nor white; and some of them paint themselves with white, and some of them with red, and some of them with whatever they find. And some of them paint their faces, and some of them the whole body, and some of them only the eyes, and some of them only the nose. They do not carry arms nor are they acquainted with them, because I showed them swords and they took them by the edge and through ignorance cut themselves. They have no iron. Their javelins are shafts without iron and some of them have at the end a fish tooth and others of other things. All of them alike are of good-sized stature and carry themselves well. I saw some who had marks of wounds on their bodies and I made signs to them asking what they were; and they showed me how people from other islands nearby came there and tried to take them, and how they defended themselves; and I believed and believe that they come here from* tierra firme *to take them captive. They should be good and intelligent servants, for I see that they say very quickly everything that is said to them; and I believe that they would become Christians very easily, for it seemed to me that they had no religion. Our Lord pleasing, at the time of my departure I will take six of them from here to Your Highnesses in order that they may learn to speak.*

> —The Diario of Christopher Columbus's First Voyage to
>   America, 1492–1493, abstracted by Fray Bartolomé
>   de Las Casas

3.

Professors Hilda and Racine Seelbinder rose early, without much hope, and went to search the beach on the Atlantic side of the island. To distract their worst thoughts, they filled their pockets with small fluted mollusks. Racine bent to the sand, displayed a polished horsebean for his wife's inspection. She took it from him, turned it over, then dropped it. As a professor of geography, she ruled on flotsam. Racine, a dedicated medievalist, was indiscriminate in his quick fascinations. It was up to Hilda to keep their baggage below the weight limit, to decide what was unusual enough to bring home to the children. In succession, she rejected his offerings of a battered whelk shell, a four-armed starfish, and, with exasperated disdain, a tar-encrusted orange toy sand bucket. Racine, slightly wounded, walked on ahead, outdistancing her, determined to pick up nothing else she might refuse or belittle.

And all the while they searched the ocean for clues. In the distance, walking toward them from very far away, the sleepless boy did the same.

Because Racine had promised himself not to cry out no matter what was discovered, he made no sound when he spied the shape. He did, however, accelerate his walk to a near jog, drawn by what he hoped at first was a small tree, uprooted, tossed forward by the pound of waves. But as he neared, the tree took on a human configuration. In the slanting shadow of the sun, the torso breathed with each surge of the sea, and limp, branchlike arms rose and fell. The head sank beneath foam as the undertow threatened to suck the whole thing back.

Not until he was nearly upon it did Racine completely admit to himself that this was in fact a man's body, naked in the ankle-deep swirl of tide.

In the next moment, Hilda stood behind her husband.

"Then it's true." She was so sure.

He stepped aside and back as, with nearsighted thoroughness, Hilda crouched to see more clearly.

In the procession of relief, then shock, that followed, he repented and went to his knees beside her.

"But this is an *old* man," she said aloud. Even in her own ears her statement sounded foolish, so she tried to rescue the moment by doing something that would have been still more foolish had it not found success. The ABCs—Airway/Breathing/Cardiac—of her first-aid training fixed in mind, Hilda performed a two-fingered check on the carotid pulse, and was surprised to detect a slow inner thump. The next step was resuscitation. Quick: the brain had four crucial minutes. With a jerk that startled Racine, Hilda dragged the man to her and tried to pry apart the clenched teeth. Failing that, she hesitated until she recalled the nose-to-mouth variation. It was unnecessary. The eyes blinked open, a flooded blue so watery that the morning sea seemed to have welled within them. They peered at nothing, but their fierce intensity indicated that the man was conscious.

Working together, Hilda and Racine carried him onto dry sand. From a half-mile away, the boy saw and began to run.

The old man's body was long, lean-muscled, and pale. His hair was white, the wisps plastered to his head so that he looked to Racine like one of those patrician busts of Roman senators, the eyes large-orbed and marble.

At last, his limbs as rigid now as if the cold of the ocean had drawn the muscles to their full excruciating length, the man focused on Racine's face. In the searchlight of that gaze, Racine was riveted. The eyes spoke questions the way a baby's do, mute but with a frowning wonder that moved Racine to explain who he was, and so he whispered his name. "Racine."

At once, the man's face grew terrible. It flushed with such speed that the skin seemed to blacken. The eyes shimmered within the pits of their sockets, the tendons of the neck brightened and stood out, taut cords, with the effort he made to unlock his jaws.

"He's in shock," Hilda announced. She stroked the man's brow but when he strained toward Racine again, she stood nervously.

"There's nothing I can do here. There's not much time. You stay. I'm going to keep looking, but I'll send Nash for help. He may know for sure who this is."

Racine nodded. He was caught in the moment, in the suspense. He continued to hold the man, to watch intently, when suddenly the lips unsealed with a tiny snap, like the breaking of a rubber band. Racine bent near. The man's jaws relaxed, opened, and between his teeth Racine saw a crumpled wad of clear plastic.

Nothing could have been more certain than that the man wanted Racine to remove it.

So he did, gently pulling at the edges of the small bag, the kind of wrapping used to keep sandwiches fresh, until he'd worked it free. The man closed his eyes, breathed. Racine eased the edges of the little sack apart, removed a folded scrap of paper, and smoothed the page on the wet sand. The ink was heavy, blotted by water, but somehow the script was familiar, not hard to make out.

> Wondrous are the tumultuous forces of the sea.
> Wondrous is God in the depths.

Racine studied the man's face, anxious to read in his expression some understanding of the note, but the man was sinking away, half-conscious now, his body trembling in fatigue. Racine put the paper into his pants pocket and then, when the deep shivers didn't stop, he drew the old man close and cradled him in his lap like a child. His skin was cold, so cold that it drew the warmth from Racine, and for the next twenty minutes, the two sat shuddering in one another's arms, waiting for help, alone together on the beach.

4.

VIVIAN TWOSTAR

Nothing seems important when you're waiting for labor to start. Certainly not research. Shoving my way into the library, I spun the revolving door with such force that I ejected a surprised freshman in my wake. She stumbled outside, onto the lush, late summer grass with a small cry of outrage. I stopped just inside the door to marshal my temper. In my ninth month of pregnancy, I had grown strange in my moods, in turn belligerent and stupefied.

By day I was Assistant Professor Twostar, hotshot lecturer in anthropology, an authority, a professional woman as well as the decent, responsible mother of a provoking and eccentric sixteen-year-old son. Most evenings I was simply Vivian, sitting at home with the grandmother who raised and now lives with me, grading uninspired papers on the sun dance or "Custer's Last Stand: A New Perspective." Near my left hand I kept a bowl of cheese popcorn, near my right the controls to the satellite dish I had trained on the Nostalgia Channel. I would glance up from time to time at the black-and-white movies while Grandma grimly stitched together a baby quilt.

Today had been especially taxing, so I tried a relaxation technique I had learned from my midwife, Sara Thompson. I held my breath, let it out slowly. *Flow,* I told myself. *Lower your pulse rate and remember that your heart is beating for the baby, for the two of you.* Everything passes through the placenta, from beer to rage. Sara's words. At my first prenatal visit she had also demanded that I hand over my cigarettes. She had thrown them into her office sink and turned on the tap full force.

So now I was disgustingly healthy, and mad as hell.

Why mad? It was the fault of Christopher Columbus. Five months ago I had been asked—no, *ordered*—to submit a professional article on Mr. Navigator, and I hadn't made much headway.

Despite my heritage, a mixed bag of New and Old Worlds, I have other interests in life, and besides, I had seen the quincentennial of the discovery coming from a long way off. My primary urge, the same as every other sensible person of full or partial American Indian descent, was to duck it. I was also pissed off because the only thing that fit me anymore was a denim jumper as big as a pup tent. I was mad because I was just . . . mad.

I looked at the clock on the wall above the checkout desk, registered that it was after five, then let my eyes linger on the No Smoking sign. As always, that warning afflicted me with a deep longing, and I desperately wanted to light up. Throughout the first three months of this by-the-book pregnancy I carried an emergency plastic filtered cigarette behind my ear, to soothe me at times like these. In a tense moment during a lecture I'd tap it against the side of a cardboard cup, as if to knock off the accumulated ash, and somehow that simple act gave me confidence, made me feel in control . . . until the day my son, Nash, told me he would have to go to school all summer if he wanted to enter his senior year next fall. Then I snapped the cylinder between my teeth.

I still wished for it, though, still yearned to inhale that fake minty taste and give the anxious fingers of my right hand something to do, but I told myself I didn't need a crutch. I had to rise above minor dependencies, to float, go forward undaunted by the sand traps of my life, the wash of my hormones, and my own plodding and ridiculous size.

I tilted toward the stairs, took them one at a time. Surging through the lower library corridor toward the rest room, I tried to affect a benign expression as students made a wide path before me. I passed along the wall covered with the murals José Clemente Orozco had painted while unhappily exiled from Mexico to New Hampshire in the mid-1930s. They were a jaw-dropping, nightmare gallery: conquistadors and peasants, Aztecs and Jesuits. The only major female figure in the whole damn epic was a vicious-looking schoolmarm with her hair pinned back in a bun, yet Orozco somehow spoke to me. Vivian Ernestine Begay Manion Twostar. Coeur d'Alene-Navajo–Irish–Hispanic–Sioux-by-marriage. I liked to think a version of American history was contained in that logjam of names.

The ladies' room was located beyond the image of a tigerish and jaundiced Christ, who had chopped down his own cross and still brandished the ax. I reached my destination, a comforting small lounge with beat-up furniture, bathroom stall, sink and paper cup dispenser. I collapsed on a chair and let my thoughts catch up with me. There was, actually, one other woman character in the Orozco saga. She was pregnant too, a skeleton wearing a black gown, or actually, she was in the throes of delivery, her head on fire, watched by an unimpressed row of emaciated, gray professors. Her chitinous offspring—fetuses packed in bell jars—wore mortarboards. Outraged alumni still protested that Orozco bit the academic hand that fed him, and some straitlaced parents looked askance at the scene, but as far as I was concerned, it was a glorious, cathartic, absurd inside joke that lightened my load whenever I passed it. Ahead of its time, it could have been the emblem for Native American Studies, my so-called discipline.

I banged my hands on my knees, pulled my face into the supercilious mask I had wanted to assume an hour ago, when an associate editor of the alumni magazine summoned me to his carpeted office and asked about the article.

"Vivian," he had fussed. "We still hope you'll write something fresh on Columbus in time for the 1991 graduation issue. You know, from the Indian, uh, Native American Indian, perspective."

"I've been preoccupied." I gestured to my considerable lap, but his gaze did not dare follow.

"We're very anxious to see a few pages, Vivian."

We'd had this conversation before.

"You know you're perfect," he continued. "Come on—what's your first line, the opening?"

"How about 'There goes the neighborhood'?" I was sour, but of course he laughed politely, still pleased with himself for remembering the "native" part of my sobriquet. I had grown used to the variations that well-meaning colleagues attempted: "North American Indian," "Native Indian," simply "Native," or occasionally the flat, pedantic "Amerind."

Thank you, Christopher.

"But I'm from Idaho," I pointed out. "Part Navajo by odd

way of a Coeur d'Alene Lothario. Columbus never got near us. He was busy kidnapping Arawaks to bring back to the Spanish court, muzzled like dogs."

He actually clapped his hands. "Precisely! That's exactly the sort of revisionist approach I'm looking for." Then he saw the expression on my face.

"Well," he tried again, with mock sincerity, "seeing as how we don't have any actual unmuzzled Arawak Native Indians on the faculty . . ."

What a joker.

"It's a year of mourning for American Indian peoples," I informed him, not smiling.

"Superb!"

I was getting nowhere. He was being cheerfully, though not aggressively, obtuse. I would have to beg harder.

"Look, you know it's my tenure year. I'm behind on the deadline for my book and, well, my due date is this month too."

Finally, we both regarded the mound of baby beneath the tent of washed and faded denim smock. Having a child is a surprisingly public act. I've had strangers stop me on the street and ask if they can touch my stomach, as if I'm some sort of lucky charm. But venerable Mr. Associate Editor was of a more delicate sensibility and, horrified to realize his gaze had lingered, he retrieved his composure with a brisk shuffle of folders.

"Then you'll no doubt be free on maternity leave. Ideal timing. We'd be so very pleased if you'd get the piece to us in the next few weeks, Vivian. No one else could do the subject equal justice."

I floundered for more excuses, but we both knew I would surrender. Even the house organ was a publication, and in this year of career decision, everything counted.

Mine was not an orthodox promotion case, as the dean of the faculty had reminded me. My *curriculum vitae* was top-heavy with teaching experience at four different schools but light on what he termed scholarly productivity. This worried him no end, even though he made my excuses for me before I could open my mouth: a single mother; not my fault the programs I had founded at other institutions had fizzled for the lack of soft money before I had time to fragment my Ph.D. thesis into a book or at least into several seminal articles; and of course there was the matter of the special counseling roles I had to fulfill for the Native American students— let's not forget how much time that took. The "community service" portion of my résumé bulged at the seams—I was a natural double bull's-eye for every college committee that lacked either a woman or a minority—but when it came down to it, the dean and I both knew that good works didn't get you tenure. He hoped I'd use my time away from the classroom judiciously, he really did. It would be no picnic for him to fire the only aboriginal assistant professor.

And, I admit it, I bought into the idea of tenure. It seemed to me a kind of dividing line that I was overdue to cross. My life to date had been what you might call free-lance, at loose ends. I took things as they came and trusted that for every disappointment there was an equal and balancing good fortune. But at forty and with this baby about to make its debut, I could stand a little security. A lifetime contract struck me as a nice big barge to loll upon while I finally got myself organized. Tenure was worth some struggle, worth feeling pressured, but the effort it demanded had to pay off. So when Columbus knocked, I had no choice but to answer the door.

At the entrance to the library stacks, however, the little gate did not click open. I was rejected. "No Admit" flashed at eye level in green liquid crystal, and an angry buzzer sounded, summoning the attention of a firm-lipped young sentinel I didn't recognize, a graduate student type in a limp black dress with a collar of startling lime green. Her eyeglasses, worn like a necklace on a stretchy cloth band, bounced as she let go of them. She indicated that I should try again. There was both question and challenge in her nod, and her attitude made me bristle. I counseled myself, *Don't make a problem of everything.* I pulled my ID out of the slot, checked to make sure that my photograph was faceup and inserted into the mechanism neck first, as the printed instructions directed. I shrugged for the watching woman's benefit, forced a smile, tried again.

"Open sesame," I said aloud.

No Admit. You'd think I was trying to break into a bank. The woman extended her palm and I surrendered the card.

"Ah," she said, satisfied. "You must not have used the library this summer, Professor . . ." She squinted to read. "Twostar."

"Yes, I have," I lied, on the defensive. "I used it just the other day."

I looked in vain for a familiar face, someone to vouch for me.

"I wonder how you managed to get in." She didn't believe a word. "Your card lacks the credential we've required all term."

"Well, I did. The sensors know me and spring the gate automatically when they see me coming." I felt cast into the role of a defendant in an old movie—Ida Lupino cross-examined on the stand. I mentally scrambled for an alibi, for the title of some volume I might have checked out last week, but the woman didn't press the point. She had already established that she owned the books and that I was a deadbeat professor.

"At any rate, you need a new certification." She reached into a drawer and found a self-adhesive bar-code sticker. With what struck me as unnecessary force she pressed it two-handed across my signature. "There," she said, "now you're up-to-date."

"More than I can say for some." We both looked at her dress, but even as my words spilled I realized that I was making an argument out of nothing, venting leftover spleen. The baby kicked, hard, right under my rib cage as if to shut me up. The librarian's eyes narrowed in exasperation, and the student behind me drank in every detail, an unspoken "Some People!" ready to fall from his pursed lips the moment I was through the gate.

"Thank you." I took the card and examined it, my back to the desk. The photo was made on my first day at Dartmouth College, and I was dressed for what I correctly assumed to be my role: gradient shades rather than contacts, hair carefully parted in the middle and pulled to each side with beaded clips, an orange calico powwow shirt with white satin ribbon piping. My expression was stern, an attempt to mirror that of the Indians found in ubiquitous antique Curtis portraits, Indians who were posed to look the way the world expected—wistful for a lost past, distant and harmless.

But I had failed in my effort. Instead, my face resembled more than anything else the round creation of a child's drawing, a child who was angry, who drew straight slanting bars for eyebrows, parallel lines for lips, who wasn't much good at noses, and who misjudged by several extra inches the desired thickness of a woman's neck.

And now, half across my mouth, in chartreuse fluorescent: "Good Thru '92," followed by a series of black slashes.

"It should work now," the librarian prompted.

It did, and I would have been history except for the minor problem of my size. I didn't fit into the library anymore. The gate was smaller than a subway turnstile and it was clear that I'd lied: I *hadn't* tried to fit through now for weeks. My tormentor, instead of gloating, shrugged and took pity. Without a word, she gestured me around the corner, in through the exit, a door of a more accommodating breadth.

Once in the stacks and enfolded by the sudden quiet, I anticipated that when I reached the cluster of call numbers listed in my notebook I would find a gaping absence: every book I wanted was always checked out. And the worst thing was, I knew where they were.

There's something missing from the picture so far. Woman. Baby. This wasn't an immaculate conception, and Roger Williams hovered just beyond the frame. Yes, the same Roger Williams, well-known narrative poet, critics' darling, Byronic media star recently featured in *People* magazine brooding on a plaster bust of his subject, Columbus, and poising a Mont Blanc pen against his handsome chin.

That was where the important books were, the ones I really needed—with my baby's father. This fact aggravated the nuisance quotient of my nagging article. Even from the first, this essay was a giant step onto Roger's turf, a claim on his other baby—the one he publicly acknowledged. My former boyfriend had been hard at work for years on an unrhymed monologue about Columbus—a reconstructed voice as in Browning's "My Last Duchess." Roger planned to finish his masterpiece in time for the five hundredth birthday party of the initial landing.

Now, having located in the lower stacks the Library of Congress numbers written on a paper I clutched in my fist, I saw that although as usual Roger had hoarded most of the first string books, he'd left me a few old dogs.

And there they were, thick and thin, bound in everything from mellow golden oxhide to cheap mottled cardboard. I put down my knapsack, activated the timer light, settled into picking and plucking among Roger's rejects, a dispiriting task. At least I couldn't be counted as one of them. Technically, I had been the one to break up.

Two skinny flights of stairs had been no picnic to descend in my condition, so I rested and restored my oxygen level. I had my grandma's build—small-boned, lean—and even though I'd always smoked too much, did everything too much, I'd never gained weight or felt real weakness. But this pregnancy had not been easy. I'd had to cut out every pleasurable vice, stop doing most of the things I liked, and still I grew rounder, sleepier, bigger. My feet were so chubby I couldn't fit into high heels anymore and had begun to wear sensible shoes, which look ridiculous on a short, pear-shaped woman. Some days I felt like a gnome—a tubby wonder from a fairy tale, unbearably benign, apple-cheeked. I wanted to get wild, but had to sublimate.

Maybe I hadn't punched in as often as I should have, but in my years at Dartmouth this building has been a personal cathedral of sublimation, the most soothing remedy available for choked exasperation, intellectual panic, for both large-scale problems and the small everyday violences endured by the human heart. Baker Library's interior, dry-aired, and gray, perennially temperature-controlled at a bland San Diego cool, with an ambience of aging paper and leather and glue, was itself a compelling reason for craving tenure. Open stacks.

I picked up the *Columbus Memorial Volume*, a rich, red tome with heavy gold-stamped lettering and thick pages that smelled of slightly scorched cotton, as if every one were ironed into place. It had been published by The Catholic Club of New York in 1893, which was no doubt why Roger had spurned it. As a Protestant, he would have expected this book to be predictable and parochial, and boy, was he right. But as an obscure relic of the four hundredth anniversary of the first voyage, it stood for a whole genre and served as a humbling reminder. If there were eventually a sixth centennial of 1492, if the world lasted that long, some wretched drone might again visit this precise spot and pull my presently assigned article, by then fixed in a small brown cardboard folder, from its place among the E119s.

I was born a Catholic, raised a Catholic even though I no longer practiced, so I understood the thrust of this book—all about how unequivocally Roman the entire exploratory enterprise was, from the first funding by the Catholic sovereigns Ferdinand and Isabella to the Catholic eye that first saw land, the Catholic foot that trod it, the wooden cross that was immediately erected. Those nineteenth-century Knights of Columbus—who else?—transported me back to my fourth-grade class at the mission school in DeSmet, Idaho, back to the days of Catholic arithmetic (God's order of things), Catholic geography (two chapters devoted to Ireland as opposed to five pages for pagan Asia and Africa combined), Catholic history (ask me anything about the Crusades), and Catholic science (the jury was still out on Galileo).

Next, I discovered a copy of *The Log of Christopher Columbus*, in what was hailed on the dust jacket as an acclaimed new translation. I knew why Roger had left this one. It was too close to his own idea. He was supposed to be inventing a poetic version of a journal and probably hadn't wanted any authentic words to intrude. To be thorough I snagged a couple of amateur biographies as well, and before long there were almost too many selections to lug up to my sixth-floor carrel in one trip.

The very thought made me tired. I was overwhelmed by the convergence of the shelves, the books, the subject, Roger. My eyelids burned with the exhaustion of late pregnancy, and then, as often happened, my body simply did what it wanted. Without my actual consent, it lowered itself onto the cool, refreshing tiles.

Cushioned by my extra weight, the floor didn't feel hard. Reposing in that comforting subbasement gloom, I thought of food, especially junk food with many calories. To my relief I remembered that I had stocked provisions, anticipating just such an emergency. I struggled onto my side, fumbled with the catch on my book bag, closed my hand around the foil container of honey-roasted peanuts. I tore it open with my teeth, then poured an avalanche of nuts directly into my mouth.

It was, of course, strictly forbidden to eat in the library, so I didn't neglect a single incriminating peanut. After the bag was dispatched, I compressed the evidence into a ball, and licked every grain of salt from my fingers. I continued to rest in the dusk, though I was no longer particularly tired. I had to pick up Nash at nine P.M. from his evening detention study hall at the high school where he was repeating calculus in summer session, and it was not even six yet.

The library corridor grew darker. No other visitors came to this level, activated ten-minute lights, searched for answers. My baby rolled, some angled joint—an elbow or knee—raising a wave beneath my hands. I had no premonitions, no desires, no preferences as to gender, not even a name picked out. I was bearing a child because I wanted the company.

In certain tribes I've read about, the Maker was a lonely heart like me, tired of being abandoned, discouraged, bad at keeping friends. So the poor thing sat down, made a few human beings, and foolishly expected them to be grateful.

With this baby, all I asked was ten good years together. Nash has taught me to keep my aspirations modest. The thought of him, after our many battles of the past week, made my heart pump faster, and I rolled to one side, thrust a knee forward. I grappled to assume the all-fours position from which I could rise safely in slow stages. I found myself facing the bottom shelf. It occurred to me to peruse the books I wouldn't later be able to stoop low enough to see, so I nudged over, squinting in the near darkness, and managed to choose and reject a few more titles.

Columbus: The Man with a Dream I passed over, but *The Secret of Columbus* hooked me, as did *Colón: First Ambassador to the Heathens*. Then, from the place where one particular volume was supposed to be, I removed a book-size block of wood. I have a fondness for these oak rectangles that Dartmouth on rare occasions uses to indicate an absent holding, one that's stored in a special case or in the antiquities room. Their presence triggers an instinct like the challenge of the hunt. The small typed directions, taped to the spine, are often obscure, formally precise yet imbued with the spirit of New England bibliophiles—that is, absolute authority and rectitude. At the end of the quest which they invite, a book of some unusual value, size, or content is promised. Once I followed out a trail of clues to discover Ptolemy's mapped universe, a volume bound in supple yellow pigskin, as tall and wide as myself, sitting on its own tin shelf.

I removed the wood with a sense of anticipation, hoisted myself, and switched on the light again in order to read what I'd netted.

This block, however, was disappointingly smooth and blank, perhaps a mere space keeper. Still, I did not give up. I looked it over until I found a rough spot, vaguely tacky, on the end where a label once had been glued. The message had fallen off or been removed, and not recently, for the square was black with dust and dirt. I scanned carefully along the floor anyway, just in case, and when I crouched down laboriously to replace the block, I moved the other books on the shelf from side to side to see if the label had been stuck somewhere else. There was no sign of it.

I was, as Grandma says when she is frustrated—which is ninety-five percent of the time—"bent out of shape." I hate not finding what I'm looking for, even when I don't know what I'm after in the first place. The presence of the wooden marker was as bothersome as a name on the tip of my tongue, tantalizing, so I gathered the block in with the actual books I was toting to my carrel. Maybe I'd turn it in at the front desk, or use it as a paperweight, or just kill time by imagining what fascinating oddball of a book it had been meant to point toward.

My assigned study, a glamorous higher-level sublet, was a small room at the end of a deserted corridor, protected by a floor-to-ceiling chain-link fence. It was a hard place to enter with my arms full—I was forced to rummage for and remove two keys, one to the hallway itself and the other to my office door. I sank into the folding lawn lounger I'd smuggled in last spring. I can't concentrate when I'm uncomfortable, but when I'm propped in my sturdy, plastic-webbed chair with an afghan and pillows, I can read and write happily for hours, a sort of backyard-barbecue Colette. I pulled the cord on my standard-issue gooseneck reading lamp, then reached down and picked the top book off the pile.

Christopher Columbus, Mariner is the popular version of Samuel

Eliot Morison's two-volume, very detailed biography, *Admiral of the Ocean Seas*. Roger had the heavyweight version of course, so I had this abridged paperback. It was a quick skim and gave me what I needed—an outline of my subject's life, a kind of mental sieve through which to sift the denser flow of texts to come, the ones I'd get if I broke into Roger's English Department office, or perhaps if I put a recall on everything he was using.

There apparently wasn't much to say about Columbus for the first ten years of his sandy-haired, freckle-faced life, so Morison ruminates instead on the name Christopher, how it proved uncannily prophetic and apt. First tip-off to the future: Columbus was named after Saint Christopher, patron saint of travelers. This was a tangent I could relate to. As a magnetic medal on the dashboard of my family's car, Saint Chris protected us from flat tires through our regular route from Idaho to New Mexico and back. As such, he was always one of my favorites, and I took it personally when he was kicked out of the Catholic Legion of Super Heroes a few years ago. Holy Mother the Church suddenly had doubts as to whether or not he ever even existed. Now here was a mind-boggling fact: In the "legend" of Saint Christopher, the kindly old porter carried the Christ Child across a stream on his back. For this feat he got nicknamed, as did Columbus years later, "the Christ-Bearer." *Quel coïncidence!* Of course, Columbus should have been The Wool-Weaver—that's what he was meant to do. His parents were solid, middle-class cloth-makers in Genoa. But instead of joining the family concern, the boy was drawn to the ocean. He worked with his dad on the trade end of the business, made a few long Mediterranean voyages, and served on a battleship during a war between King René II of Anjou and the king of Aragon. He was twenty-five when he survived his first shipwreck, just off the coast of Portugal. The Flemish vessel *Bechalla* sank, blasted by French lombard fire, and Columbus was forced to grab a floating spar and kick his way back to the European mainland.

If only he had pointed himself in the other direction *that* time around.

In those days, Lisbon was the center of exploration and discovery, a regular Cape Kennedy, a haven for chart-makers, entrepreneurs, and would-be mariners. It was there that Columbus learned to read, and eventually got his big idea. Whether or not the average Portuguese thought the earth was flat, Morison doesn't say, but he is clear on the fact that most of those in the know were quite sure that they lived on the surface of a sphere. The size of it was the point of contention: How large a circumference? How far around? Columbus, however, was a recent convert to this concept, and once his brain locked onto the problem, he was a bulldog, unable to let go, increasingly obsessive. He employed every bit of biblical, apocryphal, nautical, or homespun wisdom he could muster to prove to himself—and then to persuade potential financiers—that the earth was a great deal smaller than in fact it turned out to be, much smaller than most respected geographers of his age calculated. Columbus was positive that the fabled Cipango—read "Japan"—of Marco Polo, the Gateway to Spiceland, lay just over the horizon, a mere twenty-four hundred sea miles to the uncharted west.

Of course, he was dead wrong. By air, as Morison points out, Tokyo is over ten thousand miles from the Canary Islands, the jump-off of Columbus's magical mystery tour. But no matter how much evidence to the contrary hit him over the head, Christopher would never as long as he lived quite accept the fact that he had bumbled into a whole new continent. In fact, he drove himself and everyone around him nuts on his last voyage, trying to prove that the coast of Venezuela was but a short step away from the riches of the Orient.

The scenic route, no doubt.

I marked my place with my index finger and rested my head against the soft netting. Linda George, my friend and counterpart in the American Indian Studies Program at the University of Washington, had called me from Seattle last week to see how the baby was coming along.

"Slow," I told her. "Slow and big."

"Did they call you from the National Endowment?" she asked.

"What are you talking about?"

"Quincentennial advice and helpful hints. It finally dawned on the folks in D.C. that Indians might have a role to play next year. They asked me what I thought they should sponsor in order to give proper honor to the Native American point of view."

"And you said?"

"I told them to advertise on reservations for a series of 'Discover Spain' tours. Twenty-eight days, flamenco included. I said the government should erect a huge neon sign near Samana Cay that flashed morning, noon, and night: 'Wrong Way to Calcutta.' "

"They must have been so glad they phoned you."

"I told them the one good thing as far as nomenclature went was that Columbus didn't think he was heading for Turkey. Get it?"

"Are we having fun?" I asked.

"Just promise me one thing," Linda said before hanging up. "If it's a boy, name him Innocent. He's the pope that finally decided we were human beings."

I reopened Morison, kept reading and jotting down notes. For six years Columbus dogged the Spanish court, a place already notorious for red tape, bureaucracy, delays, and soon to be Inquisition-Central. Queen Isabella somehow got distracted from Moor fighting and showed him some sympathy, but the Talavera commission, set up to advise her on the issue of round worlds, turned Columbus down cold.

Christopher repaired to the Franciscan friary of La Rábida near Palos, and in 1491 one of the local priests, Juan Pérez, asked the queen to reconsider her rejection. Summoned to court again, this time with a new wardrobe and a mule, Columbus was officially refused again. Something about him must have made a good impression, though. Isabella privately made a deal with Luis de Santangel, keeper of the king's privy purse, and then sent a messenger to fetch Columbus back. Third time proved the charm.

I closed my eyes and thought, "What if . . . ?" but when I read on, Morison had the answer. If it hadn't been Christopher it would have been somebody else at about the same time—perhaps even somebody worse. It turns out that an expatriate Nuremberger by the name of Martin Behaim had developed a globe based on the same set of false assumptions as Columbus, and in 1493 he hit on John II of Portugal to finance his own exploratory voyage. The Portuguese actually had a leg up on the Spanish at slavery and murder, since they had already begun to exploit the west coast of

Africa. King John was teetering on the point of giving Behaim the go-ahead just as Columbus returned with the news of a landfall.

And if not that scenario, then there's the French alternative. It was Columbus's intention, on leaving the Spanish court after his second rejection, to go to Paris and join his brother Bartholomew in petitioning Charles VIII to underwrite the proposed voyage. I considered it: Amérique discovered by Christophe Colomb, and decided it was a better prospect altogether. Once they got here, after all, the French engaged in no twisted debate over whether or not Indians possessed souls. Huron Indian women clearly had what counted with French trappers, and those ladies turned a lot more Frenchmen into Indians than the other way around.

Columbus's first crossing was not, as I had heard in grade school, an operatic *Sturm und Drang* saga. He was clever enough to find the trade winds, a breeze so balmy, yet perfectly steady, that the three ships made speeds considered respectable for yachting to this day. No doubt the crew grumbled a lot, but during the month the trip took, nobody actually threatened to toss the captain overboard. Frequent signs of land—birds, weeds, bits of wood—drifted past. It was almost an anticlimax. And then the night arrived in which land was sighted. I copied Morison's own portentous words into my notebook:

> On rush the ships, pitching, rolling, throwing spray—white waves at their bows and white wakes reflecting the moon. *Pinta* is perhaps half a mile in the lead, *Santa María* on her port quarter, *Niña* on the other side. Now one, now another forges ahead, but they are all making the greatest speed of which they are capable. With the sixth glass of the night watch, the last sands are running out of an era that began with the dawn of history. A few minutes now and destiny will turn up a glass the flow of whose sands we are still watching. Not since the birth of Christ has there been a night so full of meaning for the human race.

Give me a break. I indulged myself in a fantasy of that fateful event from the alternative perspective.

On the tiny island of Guanahani, a few families of Lucayans are asleep, swaying obliviously in their hemp hammocks. They're a healthy, pleasure-loving group, laid-back beach bums and surfers, with absolutely no aptitude for destruction. If they and their neighboring Carib rivals fight at all, they throw wooden fishing spears at each other. There's not much to argue about anyway, since they share a land with plenty of food, great weather, and fabulous scenery.

There's not even anything very big to hunt, and if there were, these people would probably rather take it easy and dive for fish, gather conch, grow yams, and dig up starchy roots. They live on cassava bread, throw pots, spin and weave cotton though they don't wear it on themselves. Nature lovers that they are, they prefer to go au naturel. Life's a beach from one day to the next. People grow up, make love, give birth, eat, die. The sun sets. The sun comes up. An endless summer of surf and starry nights: a tropical rhythm appreciated even to this day by the paying customers of various Caribbean Club Meds.

Then one particular dawn, there's a novelty. The sails of three Spanish caravels appear on the horizon of the world. It's a new entertainment, and just as you'd expect of a people who never had much to worry about before, they all run down to the shore to wave hello. They've got no reason to expect it's not more good news.

2

VIVIAN

I remember putting down the book, perhaps even pulling the chain on the lamp. I remember drifting off, having confidently set my own internal alarm clock. I usually snap to, alert and refreshed, after twenty minutes, but slumber during pregnancy plays tricks. My body, my timing mechanism and level of control, had become unreliable. Sleep was a magic cave, an underwater place too deep for dreams. It seemed that the element I breathed there was so replenishing and vital I couldn't get enough of it. For whatever reason—the day's frustration, the prospect of dealing with Nash, labor's imminence—this was one of those times. I did not surface completely for a very long while. Then slowly, like a diver avoiding the bends, I circled upward, shedding the dark and humming weight of unconsciousness, clearing my head. I think I went back down several times, sank with a sudden outstretched nervelessness, before there was a jolt, a small shock, as if the dark line of oxygen had crimped.

Nash. I was supposed to pick him up. I shook off the afghan, lunged for the watch I had laid upon my desk and blinked at it, more in disbelief than in surprise. I think I even pressed the little clockface to my ear like a character in a silent movie. It was impossible—half past twelve. But my watch had never skipped ahead before. As I gathered my bag's contents and fumbled into my coat it did not strike me as odd, not yet, that the library was still open at this late hour.

It wasn't.

The hall was utterly dark outside my carrel. I brushed my hand along the wall until I came to the switch next to the grate, used my key, let myself out into the stacks. I left a trail of timered lights all the way down to the exit door beside the circulation desk, where I remembered having seen a telephone. Locked. Then, as if my dream had extended itself, as if this time I was ascending through layers of books, pages, meaning, I stood with my hand cupped to a pane of heavy glass. As I waited there, not thinking, absorbed in a silence that yawned behind me, I heard each light switch I had activated on the way buzz to the end of its allotted minutes. And so the dark came on, landing by landing, until the last bulb, just behind me, went out with a click. In the moment it took for my eyes to admit more darkness, I felt a touch of alarm; then the gray gloom expanded in the part of the main hallway I could see beyond the desk.

All I had to do—*locked in*, as I now acknowledged—was to stand by the door until nighttime security passed on rounds. Then I'd beat on the windows, turn on the lights, get the guard's attention and be on my way. I was surprised that I hadn't been found already. After all, the time I had been stranded in town by a blizzard and had decided to sleep in my departmental office, I soon found that I had attempted the impossible. Every hour on the hour I was awakened by an unapologetic campus policeman whose mission it was to make sure, for insurance purposes, that no one dozed off in a building that was not a designated dormitory.

Where was that nocturnal zealot now? He had seemed so eager to rap on my door with the handle of his flashlight, to broadcast his cheerful greeting, his torment. By morning, I was ready to weep, to confess, to answer any charges. My will was gone. Now I switched on the knob behind me. One A.M. At one-ten on the dot, the light went out. I continued to stand behind the small, thick panes. I kept my mind occupied, listening for footfalls, willing someone to approach.

My thoughts were filled with Nash.

Until three years ago, we were so close that I would have had trouble describing him, but lately I valued any objectivity I could muster. Where before I simply accepted and approved of everything about him, I now had to figure out my son. I could still list qualities anyone would admire: humor, charm, curiosity. He held grudges, though, and tended to be impatient. He liked to take things apart to see how they worked, but rarely put them back together. He was tenderhearted about certain objects around the house. As a small boy, he had preferred a large, black, battered muffin tin to his stuffed animals, and dragged a small footstool everywhere he went. Brooms, plungers, pails, mops, and sponges had to be coaxed or bribed from his stubborn hands. Not that he was precociously neat—these practical utensils simply held more meaning for Nash than conventional toys.

He was an unorthodox though lovable child, with strange enthusiasms and a passion for his great-grandmother. He took food preparation very seriously, and at age eight cooked alongside her every night while I set the table. He collected matchbooks, shells, feathers, bottle caps, shoelaces, wrapped sugar cubes, and, in a burst of normalcy, little steel cars. He constructed labyrinthine Lego cities, but refused to tie his own shoes. For a long while, he believed in a serene white-bearded Caucasian God and in angels with harps—not a word of my exasperated agnostic coaching made a dent. When he said the Rosary with Grandma, he preferred the Glorious Mysteries, she the Sorrowful. He believed in ghosts good and bad, yet could tell you exactly how electricity was generated and fed into a light bulb.

He held my hand a lot, begged off school as often as he could—pretending to be sick, eating Jell-O and learning every word of Navajo Grandma would teach him. She took the instruction seriously, and he started memorizing some of the old chants while still in grade school.

At twelve, Nash impressed himself by becoming coordinated. At thirteen, he grew. Suddenly huge, built like his Dakota father in fact, he was recruited onto the football team in ninth grade, and changed from a pampered seventies child, famous for his oddball tastes, to a teen heartthrob who tucked a ponytail beneath his football helmet and kicked ass for cheering crowds. High school sports did wonders for the swath he cut in what he liked to call "the world of mirage." But increasingly, it was the world he regarded as "real" that made me nervous.

Nash's male friends talked too fast or shaved their heads, sweated profusely on cold days and smelled like burnt rope. His anorexic blond girlfriend had dangerously empty eyes—spacey as an MTV hostess—and wore a little silver clip attached to her nose. Still, she was *decent,* insisted Nash. He tried to help her out of an adolescent slump, and together they became anti-fur activists. Yet just when their relationship had deepened, it suddenly dissolved and she started going out with all his other friends—at once. Nash grew morose, turned to his own heritage for comfort, embraced deep ecology. He went native, and by fortuitous chance he *was* native. But being a boy reared in a college town with only periodic reservation visits had its drawbacks: Nash tended to romanticize, first his own background and then, quite naturally, himself.

He was anxious to encounter his reflection as it appeared in any regular, glossy surface. A walk down Main Street meant his head perpetually swiveled to display windows or to the smooth black stone of storefront trim. The mirror in the bathroom induced a drunkenness of self-regard. He could easily fill an hour practicing expressions and fiddling with his hair, swinging his face from side to side to catch the nuance of his profile.

He was a combination of confidence, innocence, and doubt, and that meant trouble. This afternoon was a case in point: he'd been caught in the girls' locker room with a forged pass.

"The girls' locker room?" I'd tried not to raise my voice. "I thought you were a feminist."

"I blew it," he admitted. "I had it worked out with this woman, Mom, I mean she's extremely mature. Here's the thing. See, she had her period and she didn't feel so good, so she was going to sit out gym class, and she told me she'd be bored just hanging out and studying in the locker room alone. They couldn't put her in the study hall—it was too full."

I looked at him. His face was open, honest. He'd never really lied to me before as far as I knew.

"Just stay away from the girls' locker room," I'd told him. I knew at the time I was ignoring something, not drawing Nash out, and yet he had a right to keep some things to himself. So he'd gone into this evening's detention good-naturedly, if under protest. God only knew where he was now.

According to the chiming clock on Baker Tower, twenty minutes passed and no guard had happened by. One-thirty. I sat on the floor. Another fifteen minutes crept along so tediously that I rose, deciding that the light from my carrel would be noticeable, perhaps, to a patrolling campus police car, and my pillowed chair was an absolute necessity. My back felt as though pins had been driven into it. My coccyx ached and the overstrained muscles of my stomach were painfully taut. When the head of my baby had engaged, dropped into the bowl of my pelvis, I developed a decided waddle that I usually compensated for by brisk, driving motion. But not now, not alone. I fairly duck-walked back to my den, a haven in the echoing tiers of books. I had placed an emergency package of raisins in the back of one desk drawer, and now I wanted that box. Halfway up the last flight of stairs, I stopped for an unusually intense Braxton-Hicks contraction—all that week, I'd been having them: small hints of the inevitable, the body practicing for actual labor. So I didn't think about this one in particular, not exactly, although when I reached the top of the steps and put on the next light I did check my watch. I simply thought I should, that's all. I didn't believe there was anything to worry about. Not one bit. Yet, as I trudged up the stairs I began to whisper one of Grandma's Navajo chants under my breath. "Before me it is blessed when a beautiful one comes into my hands . . ."

Settled into my chair, I reassessed my situation. I thought about Grandma, who would stew all night but never deign to call anyone. Over the years, she'd resigned herself to certain mysteries about my life. When I'd told her a few days ago that I'd seen Roger pass on Allen Street, she had masked any reaction with the precise movements of setting out her dough to rise. I could tell from little things that she was annoyed—the way she tapped the bread when it was done, the acid undertone in her hum. She'd said nothing, but even now I was sure her rosary beads were slipping through her fingers as she lay awake, fiercely insisting to God that nothing come of the reunion she certainly imagined was taking place.

I tore a hole in the raisin box and began on them, one by one. They were plump, sweet, comforting. Anxiety had snapped me wide-awake, and as there was no possibility of sleep, it occurred to me that an academic worth her salt would probably salvage this situation through hard work.

Roger Williams would have. He was worth any mineral you could name, at least in terms of his scholarship. Although he cultivated a languid air, his industry in the library was phenomenal. I should know, as it was his very studiousness that had brought us together.

I had first noticed Roger during one particularly lovely summer on campus. It was impossible not to—he was low-key, yet ubiquitous. His favorite haunt that late August was the wide green apron of lawn just in front of the English Department building. There, leaning against a tall and romantically doomed elm tree, he sat reading Spenser, his thin legs stretched before him, his toes pointing naturally like a dancer's, his classic profile effectively displayed against the grain of bark. Sometimes he parted his brown hair to one side and combed it back, like a polo player in a Ralph Lauren ad, a man just showered, brooding, carving another notch in the handle of his mallet with a silver penknife. Roger did in fact possess a penknife, and a pocket watch, too. I found out later that he hung his jackets on cedar hangers. And there was a code to his dressing: he refused to let a synthetic fiber touch his body, or, indeed, enter his house except upon the exotic and therefore forgivable skin of an ethnic or midwestern person. His clothing could be old, even torn—never mended—as long as it was made of the heaviest cotton, the thickest wool, the supplest leather.

Late summer had frosted over, the earth turned, and in the course of the following year I took note of the habits of Roger Williams. With the changing season, his autumnal range shifted south hundreds of yards to the welcoming porch of the Hanover Inn and, on blustery days, the pretty furniture in its lobby, where tea could be had, and cream pastries, in late afternoon. During warm weather, he stayed outdoors as much as possible and kept his eyes lowered to the pages of his books. Winter made his gaze lift.

His look became keen. His ears smoothed back like a springer spaniel's. On his head he fixed a beautiful tweed cap that matched, but not precisely, the texture of his sweeping overcoat. Around his throat he bundled a long thick muffler with a buttery, lanolined nap, a scarf knit by old ladies in the Channel Islands. Against the grunge, in the classroom and out, he wore boots constructed of real India rubber and leather mesh. When the air was cold he craved society, and he spent his time sitting in the open, plant-lit, garden-green snack bar of Hopkins Center, talking to students and fellow professors, gesturing with the odd, two-fingered hand position Christ used in Bible story illustrations.

It was only in early spring, when the outdoors was too depressing and the Hanover Plain a wash of mud and gray snow, when all conversations were rehashed past bearing and the students' comments seemed inane rather than full of youth's promise, that Roger Williams, at last, came fully indoors.

Where by the next year I was waiting, or not exactly waiting, but curious, I own up to that, since I'd heard rumors that Roger's library carrel was directly adjacent to the one I had been temporarily assigned.

I had not yet caught a glimpse of Roger in the narrow corridor, but I occasionally detected a rustle from the other side of the wall. Because I keep a daily reminder—a simple catalog of days, events, nothing elaborate or literary—I know that it was nearly the Ides of March, close enough at any rate, when, seated at my desk of gray-green metal, I sensed his presence. It wasn't that I actually heard anything, but I felt potential noise, the way you are aware of another person in the dark. I turned the pages of my books without sound, restraining the scrapes of my shoes. I was suddenly self-conscious, though technically alone. It was, I suppose, my utter quietude that led Roger to assume that the wall between our study nooks was insulated. He forgot himself. Within the hour he began to mutter tonelessly and softly as a monk. Was it prayer? I had no way of knowing, at that point, that Roger liked to just slightly mutter the words he was writing, to try them out ahead of his pen—a B-movie convention he had made his own. There was something, for me, of the confessional box in the situation, the low voice heard beyond the grille, veiled lubricious sins recounted and absolved. I couldn't help it. I began to listen for sense.

He was in residence almost every afternoon and so was I, entering silently, settling so carefully at my desk that he never suspected that I could pick up his movements and voice. I'd work—sometimes I couldn't avoid it—but more often I would find myself imagining that Roger was positioned at his desk, almost my mirror image. His lips were moving, mine were not. He was petitioner, I was priest, or God, for I was conscious of him in a way that he could not be conscious of me.

That's the danger of a fantasy relationship. For instance, what I basically concocted in Roger was a Catholic, while in fact he was as staunch a Beacon Hill Episcopalian as one was likely to find in academia as opposed to philanthropy or finance. Roger was not a Brahmin of the highest order, but the money he came from was old enough to qualify him for some sort of upper-caste status in Boston. None of this was apparent, or even of real interest to me at the time, although it should have been. I was naive, egalitarian, a westerner. I was ignorant. Roger Williams seemed smart, romantic, accessible, not to mention famous. I was lonely: that simple. His plumage fooled me with its drab colors and its rumpled, lived-in elegance. I grew accustomed to Roger's mumblings and to the shuffling of his papers. Once, I smelled the surreptitious, strictly forbidden aroma of brewing coffee, and swelled with power. I could have him banished for cooking, kicked out! But I did nothing. No action offered itself, in fact, until the afternoon late into April when Roger Williams coughed.

I'd had a cold myself the week before. Had he caught it somehow? I'd countered mine with vitamin C, orange juice, a couple of saunas at the gym, and many cartons of little black throat lozenges. My cough, however, had not been as bad as his. He had a sharp, hacking bark, annoyingly periodic, irritating and distracting. For a while, I endured with indulgent sympathy, but that soon wore thin. Why didn't Roger Williams *do* something about it? Like strangle himself? Where did he get off thinking that poets, or full professors, could impose their afflictions on other people? He was thoughtless, I concluded after an hour, even arrogant. The self-absorption of art! I felt invaded. What did disturbing *me* matter to him, after all? What was *my* work, compared to his?

I put down my pen, and in a state of stalled fury I regarded my famous unpublished book on pan-Indian religion, a masterpiece of scraps contained in a cardboard box labeled Banana Nut Muffin Mix. Other cartons of notes were stored at home, underneath my bed. But there, right there in my carrel, I had the makings of a dynamite first chapter. Dynamite! Yet with that blast of sound ready to disrupt me at any moment, I couldn't think. How would I ever begin *my* Pulitzer Prize–winner? I sat motionless through ten, maybe twelve, more hacks—I don't know how many throat clearings—before I jumped up. What right had he to keep me from my work, what right to clutter my consciousness at this crucial juncture, what right at all?

"For Godsake, shut up!"

I clapped my hand across my mouth. Stunned silence reigned behind the wall, and I was instantly contrite. I felt ridiculous and small and foolish. I rummaged in my purse, drew out a half-gone packet of lozenges, opened my door, knocked on his, then barreled through.

He stood, eyes rounded, a cloth pressed to his lips. His face was red, strained with a withheld explosion. I thrust the cough drops at him.

"Thanks," he said automatically. And then, "I beg your pardon. I had absolutely no idea."

"I should have more sympathy. I had the same cold last week. It was rotten." I went on and on, unable to stop talking.

"Yes."

His face was so pale, so meek. His plaid handkerchief looked starched and scratchy, and his hair had flopped over, revealing a cowlick. He seemed harmless, especially without the gamekeeper's boots and overcoat—who could tell? Still . . .

He ushered me into the hallway, no-man's-land.

If this had been a movie, we would have stared gravely into one another's eyes, taken a step forward, a step backward, in and out of the magnetic field, then moved irresistibly close. Instead, as this was Dartmouth, we glared suspiciously at one another and then mutually turned away and shut our doors. But not before I had said far too much. I heard no more coughing after that, just the careful uncrinkling of waxed wrappers. A couple of times there were gargling, muffled noises, averted coughs that struck me with pangs of guilt. But I got over that feeling.

Embarrassment made me suppress my former interest, so I was unprepared, a few days later, as I picked my way along one of the muddy paths across the large square green in the center of the campus, when Roger Williams fell into step beside me. He could do so easily, shod as he was in his rabbit-stalking all-weather boots. I on the other hand was wearing a favorite pair of pumps to make myself taller. One foot had just plunged to the ankle in an icy pothole. I skidded, plowed a wedge through the turf with my other heel.

"Would I insult you if I offered assistance?"

I retrieved my balance, stood straight. My three-inch heels sank with a pop into the mush. More water seeped in through the points of the toes.

"Insult me," I said, and took his arm.

It was impossible for me to forget Roger's telephone number. Literally impossible, because complete with area code it was almost the exact duplicate of my social security number. Every time I filled out a health insurance form or punched my automatic teller ID into the bank machine it leapt at me.

When our walk across the green had yielded no further intimacy, I hadn't dared to disturb Roger again in his study. But one night I looked up his name and address in the faculty directory—just out of curiosity—and the amazing concurrence announced itself. Naturally, I took it as a sign and dialed without hesitation.

"Yes," he answered emphatically, as if already in the middle of a conversation. His voice was so even in its tone that I thought I had reached an answering machine.

"Yes," he said again. He didn't pronounce the word as a question.

"Uh, Professor Williams?" I realized that I had nothing casual to say and no work-related excuse for calling. If, right off the bat, I confided the news that he was my social security he might find it a bit strange.

"Yes," Roger said for the third time. "The same."

"This is Professor Twostar. Vivian? On the faculty? Your

next-door neighbor in the library carrels?" I forged ahead, in order to forestall a fourth "Yes." "You won't believe this, but—"

"No!"

"No?"

"Oh. I'm sorry. Truly. It's the pure coincidence. Not thirty seconds ago you were on my mind, and then here you are."

I stared into the mouthpiece as though expecting Roger's face to materialize through the tiny holes. Neither of us spoke, but we both became aware of the silence.

"What are you thinking?" I asked.

"I'm afraid it was not a very scholarly thought," Roger warned.

"I can take it."

"I . . . umm . . . was wondering if there were a Mr. Twostar in the picture."

I was a sucker for pretentious syntax.

"Only my son, Nash, aged sixteen."

"Only Nash. . . ."

"Only Nash." I pictured Roger's rather small, neat mouth curved into a smile.

"Well, I see. Well, that answers *my* question," Roger said. "Now tell me how it is that you came to ring me up."

Ring me up! "That can wait. I'd rather hear your next question." I was in no hurry. I imagined a moment, not too far into the future, in which I would idly drop my social security number into Roger's lap and he would find the arrangement of numbers less an oddity than a confirmation. I'd bring it to him one day like flowers and chocolates: our entwined fate bestowed upon me at birth by an indifferent government, and upon him by Ma Bell. For now, I'd let him make the next move.

He served an ace.

"Would you by any chance be free this evening?"

Now, back in the cubicle where all of this had started I tried to see myself as victimized, as one of the holy martyrs. It didn't work. I knew from the beginning that to fall in love with a handsome man who knew a lot about the world, but very little about himself, was to ask for trouble. And yet I came out the better, because for me the affair included this kicking baby—of whom I would be the sole support. Spurred by that thought, I returned to the consolation that if I had to be trapped overnight, there was probably no useful place than Baker Library, in the middle of an unread pile of material on Christopher Columbus.

My mind had been wandering as I drummed my fingers, rationed raisins, tried to divert myself from the two questions that loomed largest: First, where had Nash gone when I didn't collect him? And second, would I have more regularly spaced contractions?

Just at the twenty-minute mark, when the next twinge tightened deep in my pelvis, I firmly decided that Nash, tired of waiting, had walked over to visit my friends, Hilda and Racine Seelbinder. I pictured him now, sleeping on a futon mattress by the tiny woodstove in their newly slate-floored basement family room. The contraction hung on for a minute and a half, during which I persuaded myself that my failure to show up for Nash was a positive learning experience that he would one day come to appreciate. He depended too much on me to always be available, to take him seriously, to be his straight man. Wasn't it time that he discovered how it felt to be left in the lurch?

I stood up. I had to stop this, take some form of action. I practiced a few stretches, a couple of hip rolls to get my blood moving, walked over to my desk and picked up the smoothly varnished oak marker I had found in the library stacks. I turned it over in my hands. Perhaps the book it pointed to had been misshelved, perhaps it had fallen through a crack in the wall, or lain abandoned for decades underneath a steel bookcase. I jotted down the call numbers of the texts I had found on either side of the marker. What else could I do with myself but search? I went back down the stairs, as far as they went.

I started with the logical places, the outsize-book shelves and side cabinets pushed along the whitewashed brick walls on the first level. Some were too heavy to pull aside, but I managed to peer behind the ones I could budge and to grope in the slots beneath and behind. Nothing was unaccounted for. I crisscrossed the entire floor, lights ablaze, certain that at any moment I would be discovered, but one hour and two slightly less intense contractions passed before I exhausted my first plan and tried the next, which was considerably more ambitious.

Determination seemed to slow the contractions, even make them less noticeable. In the space of the past sixty minutes, I had become old friends with the Library of Congress filing system. With an air of pious fortitude, I began a slow sweep behind the steam pipes, in the netherworld of books, among the rows of worn-out Pliny, the frayed primers of Latin grammar. I walked my fingers along every book, comparing the numbers to my mental index. I had nothing but time after all, and too much adrenaline to allow for rest. Driven by the fear of labor, I went from Anaximander to Plutarch to Seneca to Zeno. I didn't stop to muse, to puzzle out or to open any of the dry, rich titles. I didn't have another contraction, either. That is why at around four-thirty A.M., when I had scanned the very last shelf and then stood at the stairs to the second floor, I did not hesitate. I did not let myself picture the vastness of the tiers and tiers of books that rose above me, deep in cool dust. I simply mounted the steps as though my monomania were entirely normal. At the landing, I turned to the right and switched on the lights all along an aisle that led to a wall of looming cabinets.

Maybe it was a kind of stubborn inertia. Or perhaps I was gearing up to have the baby, shifting into physical overdrive. Whatever it was, I didn't quit. I inspected the tabs of the first case of oversize books. Then the second. It was there that I made a find.

Not a book but a thin brown portfolio of cardboard, glossy and brittle with age, labeled with the name Cobb, but noticeable for its lack of any library markings. Wedged at the very end of a row of outdated atlases, uncataloged, it had apparently been overlooked, perhaps because of its resemblance to the pock-grained wood itself.

Slightly dizzy, I tugged the thing out, unknotted the fragile pink ribbon that bound it together, and pulled something at random from the interior. I held a pamphlet composed of paper so thick it looked handmade. The title confirmed my theory that this was where the mystery block had pointed. "O Mariner! A Poem in Twenty Parts Commemorating the Passion of Christopher and Beatriz," by Harrison Cobb II. I wedged the thing back and drew out "In the Shadow of the Mizzenmast: A Freudian Analysis of Christopher Columbus' Diary of the First Voyage."

After the initial thrill—that is, to actually have found what I didn't know I was looking for—my head cleared and I wound down. Pains shot from my ankles up the backs of my legs, my shoulders were cracked boards, and my eyes itched. I felt swollen and confused, almost stunned with expended energy as I slunk back up to my carrel desk. What I'd knocked myself out to find, was no treasure but a stray part of one of those special gift collections donated to the college by housecleaning Dartmouth alumni. Some of these bequests are marvelous and valuable, but most are worthless. What I carried in my arms was in all likelihood the assembled jottings of a crackpot.

All the same, I couldn't help but feel a pang of sympathy. My own unfinished manuscript had for years maintained only an immanent unity. No library in creation would accept my muffin boxes. That put Mr. Deceased Columbus Freak one up on me.

The Cobb name had a familiar Dartmouth ring. There was the Cobb Room, where poetry readings were held; a freshman dormitory; the Cobb Memorial Pool in the basement of the gym. A gaggle of Cobbs had graduated from the College, one or two about every twenty years, and they all seemed to maintain strong allegiances both to the place and to preserving a wide-sweeping commentary on Christopher Columbus.

I closed my eyes. The folder slid down the slope of my baby, and when I slept this time it was with a hard, whole mindlessness during which I may have had contractions, I don't know. Nothing woke me until I heard the rattle of metal wastepaper baskets emptied and banged against the side of the first-shift janitor's cart.

3

ROGER WILLIAMS

The only victory over love is flight," was a prescription attributed to Napoleon, and one I had myself employed more than once. If indeed "love" was what I had been in those times I fled. Love had always struck me as one of those hypothetical sentiments, like the acceptance of death, which could only be positively identified in retrospect, but for which there is never, by definition, the opportunity for an epilogue. Love, if it exists, is a constant state, at rest and stable, the very antithesis of passion—with which it is often confused. Love is solid, connected without fissure to the planet's core. Passion, on the other hand, is volatile, molten, ever ready to erupt and spill. It requires energy and attention and, in my experience, supports a brief half-life. From that I've escaped, and gratefully, with the same disregard of repercussions as when, in each instance, I had initially pursued its obvious pleasures. Passion was a bell curve, or rather a series of them. When the *mal de mer* became too intense, a sane man sought dry land.

A sane man was what I had not been since the day Vivian

Twostar had pounded on the door of my study. I was fighting a winter cold, trying not to succumb to it. Concentration on work was the best antidote to illness—I still believed that. I had been in midthought, eyes closed, mind casting for a verb to fit into the rhyme scheme of my poem. It needed to be an active verb, of two syllables with precisely the right accent, and it needed to mean something like desire, though milder and more colloquial. I whispered possibilities aloud, experimenting with emphasis on the past tense: want-*ed*, long-*ed*, lik-*ed*, hop-*ed*. Nothing worked. Each sounded too mannered, too . . . poetic, like something from the Metaphysicals, which is no wonder since Donne is one of my emphases. Why this tyranny of first syllables? Surely in the grand lexicon there must be the word I sought, the precise meaning for Columbus's yearning for a favorable reply from the court upon his petition for funding. I had him firmly fixed in my imagination, seated at the rude boards he used as a desk at La Rabida, staring at the cracks in the plaster of his wall. In those pre–Age of Reason days all men placed a disproportionate faith in luck and in their ability to affect it. Superstitious, I would go so far as to say. If I do this—wear a hair shirt, put pebbles in my shoe, prostrate myself before the altar during the Offertory—then X will happen. Or, conversely, if I don't do something—consume animal flesh, speak, move any of my limbs for a designated period—then a predictable consequence will ensue.

I had some difficulty in projecting the Admiral's psyche in this instance, for, truly, I personally craved nothing. Oh, to be sure, I was not without my wish list. I sought a good publisher, the respect of my peers, a degree of material comfort. But all those things were within my power to command, with sufficient effort. My failures, therefore—be they what they were—proceeded more from a scarcity of this wanting-longing-liking-hoping than from an unfavorable roll of the cosmic dice. As a modern man, I regarded fate as mine to influence, if not control. Events evolved from history, not the reverse. I was a devout disciple of the Super-organic theory: there were no "great men," but rather simply the right man at the right time. When the culture was ready for change, it spewed forth several catalytic candidates, any one of whom, under propitious circumstances, could and would succeed.

Man was not the agent but the carrier. A culture's destiny was sui generis.

Columbus, of course, being pre-Enlightenment, could not have comprehended this. He thought that what he did or didn't do mattered. He failed to construe that if he lacked royal sponsorship some other European seafarer—Venetian or French or Portuguese—would, at around the same time, sai! west and encounter the remains of the world. He thought that finding the short way round to the Indies was up to him alone, and so indeed he lust-*ed*, burn-*ed*, aspir-*ed* . . . *hankered*! My *Roget's Thesaurus* once again had saved me, but was "hankered" too contemporary? Columbus, it could be argued, was the first legitimately Western man, but was he *that* western? "Hankered" scanned perfectly, but it somehow connoted the tinkle of spurs, the vision of red-checked shirts, the scent of sagebrush.

I indulged myself, tried out this alternate version of "Diary of a Lost Man," and did so aloud.

"Well, ma'am, Ah've got a powerful hankerin' to git to Japan and git me some of them spices."

"SHUT UP!" a female voice thundered. I heard a slam, very close by, and then a drumming at my door. I almost fell backward in my chair, so absorbed was I in my own fantasies, in my internal conversation. Without thinking, I slid the bolt, turned the knob, and revealed what looked to me at first like a lunatic. Her eyes were wild. With one hand she grasped a sharpened pencil like a dagger, and the other shook a box of throat lozenges in my face. I took the packet as she virtually fell into my room, propelled by a knock that now met no resistance.

A study is a small space, intended for one person only. As a result of the woman's rude invasion, we suddenly found ourselves at close quarters and both instinctively recoiled, our eyes locked in dread and surprise; then by common unspoken consent we moved into the hall. Immediately we spoke at the same time.

"I beg your pardon?" I managed. I *had* been coughing. Had she heard?

"I'm sorry," she gasped.

It was not an auspicious introduction.

"No, really," she continued. "I'm inexcusable. I should have more sympathy. I had the same cold last week. It was rotten. I don't know what's wrong with me. Blame hormones, blame tenure anxiety, blame it on the bossa nova."

I held my tongue, suppressed a tickle in my throat, waited for further information.

"I'm Vivian Twostar, Professor Twostar, your next-door neighbor." She gestured to the left with a tilt of her head. Her hair was black and curly, her skin flushed with embarrassment.

"Of course," I replied. "I've seen you at faculty meetings." I had noticed her, but had kept my distance. She had struck me as a hummingbird—small, bold, gaudy, absolutely fearless, and very quick. "You're in . . . sociology, is it?"

"Close. Native American Studies. The point is, I'm sitting at my desk alert for any excuse not to concentrate—total intellectual avoidance, you know?" She looked at me for some sign of agreement, but found none.

"Well, maybe you don't know. You're a full professor. You didn't get that way for nothing. You've paid your dues, written your book, published your refereed articles." She nodded while speaking, confirming her observations, which were, after all, quite correct.

"But me! I'm close to forty, still an assistant, under the gun. Did you read Maxine Hong Kingston's *Woman Warrior*? No? Well, that's me. In the trenches, attack at dawn, and staring at a blank page. No ammo in the gun."

I was completely mystified, but fascinated all the same. The woman had presence, but she didn't know when to turn it off. I stepped a bit closer.

"So anyway," she went on, "these walls are thin, which you wouldn't expect in such an old building, but there you are, they're thin. And sometimes you talk to yourself, or you cough, like today, or you clear your throat. I mean, there's nothing wrong with that, it's fine, it's your right. It's me. I require silence—otherwise, good-bye concentration. *Adiós.* So I get fixated. I sit there and wait for you to move your chair, to breathe! And then when you do—I mean naturally, of course you do, what choice do you have?—I freak. This time, when you started mumbling, loud enough that I could hear, but not loud enough that I could make out the words . . . It's my problem. You're blameless. Really. I beg *your* pardon. Forget I said anything."

She took a step backward, pulled her study door closed after her, and I was alone except for the trace of her perfume, the echo of her monologue, the vacuum left by her absence. Nothing but the hush of green tile, spackled walls, serenity. I returned to my work, but all that afternoon I was subject to a persistent fantasy that simply would not leave my mind.

This often happens to me—a replay of action in which I do what I should have done, say what I should have said. In this scenario, there Vivian was, her head bent against the wall, her shoulders shaking. I sought to comfort her, to tell her that she need not castigate herself, and I gently touched her arm. But then, the turn of my imagination surprised me. The plot changed. It was not humiliation that inhabited her body, not suppressed tears. She buried her face in my chest and laughed. What could I do? I put my arms around her, embraced the soft knit of her sweater, drew her to me. Her hair brushed my chin, our bodies elided at every crucial juncture, and I felt myself irresistibly infected, incapable of not joining in.

"So what was it?" Vivian gasped in my daydream, her voice muffled by my tie. "What was it that was so important you had to say it out loud?"

" 'I hankered,' " I endeavored to explain, but covered my mouth so that next door she would not hear.

Vivian claimed me in body a few weeks later, on my Jackson Pollock print rug, before my leather couch. She was so sure of herself and of her apprehension of my own intentions that when she said, "I've got your number," I took her word for it. But when one enters a relationship a step behind one's partner, there persists a lack of balance. Communication is slightly off, like the hesitant delay experienced in a phone call from a colleague in Budapest or Helsinki—just a fraction too much time elapses between question and answer. You're never sure that you shouldn't be listening when you're talking, and so tend toward the staccato, the telegraphic mode, in all vocal utterances. Oddly enough, this dyssynchronicity did not extend into the physical realm. There, Vivian and I harmonized perfectly and often, rarely commenting on events as they transpired. I had previously been accused by women of being too cerebral, a "head tripper," as a fellow graduate student had put it, but in the first six months with Vivian my brain seemed not at all involved, except to delight. I forgot to analyze or worry. I anticipated, I remembered fondly, but *in medias res* I simply existed, functioned well enough to be labeled "a pleasure machine," and thought, when I thought at all, in colors rather than in words. One experience was orange, another green, another pale blue, another, positively crimson. I ricocheted through the spectrum, never dipping my brush twice into the same hue.

Until one rather purple afternoon in February when Vivian leaned across my chest, kissed my shoulder, and told me what was going to happen next.

"Time to run," she whispered.

I assumed she meant she was late for a meeting of some kind, and so I nodded. "Where are you off to?"

"Not me. You. I've missed two periods and I figure this is probably the last child I'm going to be offered. I've scheduled an amnio, and if everything is okay . . ." She sighed, patted my arm, and sat up. "I know this isn't on your agenda, and that's okay. I can't see you changing diapers either. No problem."

She swung her legs off the bed and began to dress with her back toward me. I was confused, as if I had failed to hear my part of a crucial conversation that was now over. Vivian was announcing two things at once: her pregnancy and the termination of our affair. There seemed to be no doubt in her mind that the events were inextricably connected, and I asked myself why. We rarely discussed anything to do with our future, much less the possibility of children. I inquired of myself about the matter and found that I had no formed opinion, and Vivian did not seek one. My response seemed irrelevant to her, and but a single angry explanation for her attitude flashed into my brain. I spoke before I thought, and I asked the most wrong thing.

"Who is the father?"

She answered with a sad, tight smile, and left.

I was blameless, but blamed all the same. My capital crime had never been judged except in Vivian's mental courtroom—where I had been summarily convicted—yet I was sentenced to solitary confinement for life. She was convinced that, given the chance, I would bolt, an impregnating dragonfly, all mate-and-run.

"I will not allow myself to be deserted again," she said, deserting me. Weeks had passed, and we sat unreconciled over decaf in the dining room of the Hanover Inn, finishing what I had assumed was a reconciliation, as well as a celebratory dinner in my honor. An avant-garde literary journal had shown some interest in a section of my poem in progress, and when I called Vivian with the news she had seemed as gratified as if it were her own work, and invited me out.

"What desertion? I haven't gone anyplace." I protested her verdict, trying with my eyes to reestablish the recent mood created by our not-inexpensive lemon scallops for two.

"You will. You know you will."

"Don't tell me what I know." I glanced wistfully one last time at the dessert menu. In a devil-may-care moment of abandon, condoned by the journal editor's enthusiasm—he had even mentioned the promise of *pay* for my verse—I had all but decided on the mud pie. Now that was clearly a lost cause.

"Roger." Vivian's answering look was positively forgiving, maddening in its acceptance of my anticipated perfidy. "Tell me you want this baby. Tell me you want to be a father." She gestured toward the inn's tasteful lobby as if I had decorated it myself, refurnishing it in her mind as she spoke. "Sesame Street on the parquet floors. Crayon marks on the walls. Unmatched socks."

I must have winced, for she nodded. "It would drive you crazy, so let's not waste time. Let's avoid the ugly scenes. No lingering hard feelings. This way is best."

"You're depriving me of my paternal rights," I argued. "It takes two to conceive a baby, unless I missed something in biology. I am entitled to a say."

"You don't—"

"Stop putting words in my mouth." The vehemence of my objection, partly inspired, I must confess, by a sense of chocolate unfairly deprived, momentarily startled Vivian. She folded her arms and regarded me calmly.

"Okay," she said. "So what is your 'say'?"

Now it was my turn to be at a loss. "I didn't even know I was fertile," I offered, backpedaling.

" 'Fertile' doesn't begin to describe you," Vivian countered.

I looked at her suspiciously, but her gaze was secret, bland. I didn't know whether or not she had planned this pregnancy and I felt oddly shy about asking, as though it were something I should inherently know. But I wanted to understand my function, to comprehend Vivian's attitude, so I dared to inquire further.

"You're a marvel of fertility, the producer of supersperm," she answered, her voice dipping sarcastically. "Out of the millions, one jolly Roger scaled all barriers and hit a home run."

"You're mixing your metaphors," I corrected, but felt a bit like Ulysses all the same.

"If you think *I* am"—Vivian smiled without humor—"just think of our kid. Beaded herringbone, the look for the nineties."

The words "our kid" produced a curious reaction in me, a confusion of pride and terror. I had never even held a baby and regarded them as a kind of pupal stage, ever moist and spindly until at last they blossomed into being literate. I had no real conception of how long that process took or what was demanded of a father during its metamorphosis. Would it expect me to sing to it? To select its clothing? Would it expect me to play baseball?

As though she could read my mind, Vivian reached across the table and covered my hand with hers. There was something patronizing, irritating, in the gesture, and then I realized it was a typically masculine ploy. I had seen men reach across the table in similar situations, pinning down the hand of a spouse to hold her attention.

"Let's face it, Roger," Vivian said. "You and Nash haven't exactly hit it off."

"You're being premature," I objected, removing my hand from underneath hers. "Communication is improving."

"You're trying, I recognize that, but you're not going to win him over with expensive gifts."

"There's nothing wrong with—"

"The Cross silver pen and pencil set, Roger. It's simply not Nash. And the green silk necktie embroidered with little tennis rackets . . ."

"He likes tennis. You told me he played."

"Not in a tie. He uses your present as a sweatband to hold his hair back from his face."

"No!"

"And the books. Your heart is in the right place, but do you really expect Nash to sit still long enough to read *Persuasion* or *Bleak House*?"

"*I* read them," I insisted, but I knew she was right and I hardly cared. Her son was unreachable, a hopeless misfit full of harebrained theories, a mumbling oaf who watched television for hours a day and ate his meals with ambidextrous indifference. He mocked my name at every opportunity, sneered at my affection for his mother, forgave us no privacy.

"But a son of mine would necessarily be different," I pleaded.

"This son of yours"—Vivian drew my hand back and covered it again—"happens to be a daughter. I got the test results. She will also eventually become a teenager. Then what would you do?"

A daughter.

Before I could explore the notion, the waiter brought our check—exactly half of which Vivian insisted upon paying now that in her mind we were no longer a romantic couple. Always before, either she or I had treated the other, but now her credit card next to mine on the white tablecloth was a statement more final than a "Dear John" letter, and we both knew it.

"Are we not to see one another again?" I asked. "Do you intend to go through your pregnancy and delivery alone?" The question conjured the inescapable stories of shared labor with which I was constantly regaled by my younger, domestically oriented male colleagues—tales related with lines like "*We* pushed for sixteen hours" or "*We* didn't lose much blood at all with the placenta."

"I've already talked to Hilda and Racine," Vivian said. "They'll be my tag team partners. It's okay."

"You told them I wouldn't stand by you?" I was horrified. These were my oldest friends at the college. What would they think?

"I didn't have to say anything. They *know* you, Roger. They accept your weaknesses along with your strengths, as I do."

It was insufferable to endure her superior condescension. All right. Good. If I was collectively judged such a sniveling coward, so be it. Let Vivian present her baby to the world as the product of parthenogenesis, let her titillate the Women's Studies Program with her brave unmarried motherhood, let her unpaired body evolve into an increasingly emphatic statement of female power, with its subtext of male ignominy.

"What will you say when this . . . girl . . . asks about her father?" I demanded. "Isn't that rather inevitable?"

Vivian answered with by far the worst and most unforgivable thing she could say: "I'll tell her the truth."

I threw myself into my work, scanned Latin texts for mention of Columbus until my eyes hurt, read every book known to have been part of the Admiral's small library—Sir John Mandeville, *Imago Mundi*, Pliny, Esdras, the Bible—discovered brilliant and subtle denominators for disparate events, chose time and again the perfect word of poetry. Vivian began wearing maternity clothes in her sixth month, and the *raison d'être* for her condition was the subject of much faculty speculation. Various candidates were proposed and dismissed, and if I was among them, I never heard. We had been clandestine, apparently successfully so. Except for the annoyingly understanding Seelbinders, no one at Dartmouth identified me with the cause of Vivian's expanding proportions.

After a reasonable interval, I brought up the issue with Hilda.

"But Vivian never consulted me," I protested. "It was simply presented as a *fait accompli*. My thoughts on the matter were never solicited!"

"And if they had been?" Hilda inquired. We were in her lablike kitchen, all dull metal cabinets and butcher block, and she had made a pot of tea. Now she raised a china cup to her lips and waited for my reply.

"Well, I don't know," I said. "I would have had to weigh the options, consider the implications."

"So what was stopping you?"

Nothing, I realized, except my own reluctance. I helped myself to more tea, added milk and pollen honey, stirred slowly, and tried to project a future in which a small female person would refer to me as "Daddy." I could not, and looked up at Hilda in some helplessness.

"You see?" she affirmed. "That's the expression that Vivian chose not to see on your face, and who could blame her? She's not really angry, you know. In fact, she rather misses you. But somehow, Roger—no offense—none of us could quite cast you in this movie."

It was all very civilized, very postmodern. I had been discussed, found wanting, and dismissed. Well, fine. They were probably right, my Grand Inquisitors. Biology was not destiny, and my sperm had gone where my brain could not follow. All right, I washed my hands. I accepted who I was, who I was defined. If I could not be domesticated, I would delve further into art. I attacked "Diary of a Lost Man" with a vengeance, with a mission of paternity. Columbus would be my child, his exegesis my midnight feeding. I awoke with whole stanzas ready for transcription, and the epic grew, surpassed my most optimistic ambition. Content followed form and I bent the facts to my will. Posterity would be thankful for the man I would create.

To say I retreated into my work, submerged myself into it, gives too little credit. My poem, as the response of the journal critic had attested, was no mere diversion. However, it is true that when I sat at my desk, turned my composition book to a new page, and wrote a line, I left behind the twentieth century. Eyes closed, ears listening inward, I hovered in some netherworld of pure form, a Plato at the cave's gaping door, more alert for shadow than for substance. I was not after the facts—those were as known and as mulled over as they needed to be—but rather I sought their fresh interpretation. Here was a man, this Christopher Columbus, whose very name—fictitious or not—connoted so much more than an individual life. *Nominae temporis pulvis.* Names are but the dust of time. Graveyards are full of names, the only remnant of souls whose acts and years are not only forgotten, but also of no import to the present. Anonymous antecedents, flesh become bone become dust, they are at most the blazes on a trail, the itinerary of a trip whose only remarkable events were departure and arrival.

I do not entirely disassociate myself from these sorry masses. Indeed, within a hundred, two hundred years' time, most of us will join them—our collection of ambitions and deceits, successes and failures, condensed into the letters carved upon a piece of granite, if that. This insight is not original, but I suspect that modern man is more aware of its implications. Lay the blame on telecommunications and the census. In a small hamlet, each life seems worth commemorating. Genealogies live and become entertainment, recounted around dinner tables, gouged into totem poles, or worshiped in ancestral shrines. Cemeteries flourish in little towns. Each plot is the destination of a pilgrimage, the trigger for a feud, the waiting, yawning resting place for a surviving spouse or child.

But now, can we help but know better? When the globe is visually revealed each night as a seething anthill, its inhabitants packed tight as Tokyo subway riders? There are too many names to know, too many faces, too many stories. And the conclusion is inescapable: If they don't matter to me, these flickering images of mobs and war casualties and starving masses, can I matter to them? Little wonder that cremation has become the rage, sanctioned even by the Roman Catholic Church. Sprinkle me upon the waters, let me fly and scatter into oblivion with the wind. Why not? The mind billows at the apocalyptic vision that used to be at once so consoling and so terrifying: the assembly of all who had died, now returned in corporeal bodies to eternal life. As a child I worried about that Last Day, when everyone would know my sins, and care.

Now, that egocentric cringe is beyond my ability to conjure. In place of those clustered familiar faces, aghast at my small thefts and lies, of those grandparently hands clapped over mouths that once had smiled at the sight of me, I see different scenes: a shopping center at the starting bell of a post-Christmas sale; the opening mile of the Boston marathon, the field jostling shoulder to shoulder across a six-lane highway; the floor of the New York Stock Exchange at an hour of busy trading, everyone shouting at once. Better to be a neat package of ashes, a mote in a blinking eye, or to populate an urn decorative on a shelf.

Yet some escape this fate. Their names become emblem, immortal, part of the working vocabulary. They, and their retinue of biographers, shine like lighthouses, like streetlamps seen in a rearview mirror. Carl Sandburg's Lincoln. Virgil's Aeneas. Shakespeare's Julius Caesar. Christopher Columbus, currently on loan to Samuel Eliot Morison, was still up for grabs, and he would be mine. Once rendered in my poem, his name would be forever linked with mine, and we would travel down the ages arm and arm. I might be only the barnacle on his whale, but who ever thought of Johnson without Boswell, Brontë without Gaskell, Satan without John Milton, Moby-Dick without Melville?

Was the fear of death my engine, my motor? Was it that simple? Had I no thirst for Truth? I didn't know, and though mildly curious, I didn't care. Zeal cannot be manufactured or found at the end of a rainbow. It was for me, as an emotion, sufficiently rare that I did not question its source. Some say lust rules the species, others argue for hunger or greed or power. If mortal awe was my driving force, so what? My script still fed into my hard-bound ledgers. The number of stanzas built toward a satisfying edifice. I had even experienced my allotted fifteen minutes of fame, appearing in *People,* listed as that rare species, a poet to whose future work readers could look forward. Let graduate students in the coming decades debate my muse—they would never guess Vivian, whose superficial Columbus promised to be mere regurgitation, served up as filler between real estate advertisements and endless columns of class notes.

I had heard from Racine that she was at work on an article for the Dartmouth alumni magazine. An editor, ever anxious for controversy, had invited her to submit an essay. I knew the man, and guessed his aim. He assumed that Vivian would pen a vitriolic lament, an excoriation blaming Columbus for all the Indians' troubles. I had more faith in her than that, but what could she hope to learn in so short a time? Her baby and her submission were due in the same month, and she was not a diligent worker. In an effort to avoid encountering her, I arrived at my carrel early, stayed late, and was therefore a sentry over her neighboring cubicle. I heard when she entered—seldom more than two or three times a week in the beginning, and then almost not at all in the end. I checked my watch when she exited for the day. Her average endurance was less than two hours, and toward the sixth month I began to feel pity. How hopeless her quest must seem. Who knew better than I how much information there was to absorb, to sift? I debated assistance. She would reject any direct help simply because it came from me, but perhaps there were other means.

Early in the morning I prowled the stacks, trolling for the most useful and succinct introductory sources. These I pulled out, ever so slightly, from the surrounding volumes, thinking that the oddity might draw her attention. But when I would check at the end of the day, these good books were rarely disturbed. Instead, Vivian had browsed among the sensational titles, the fantastical theories, the improbable speculators. I came to know her method, and it was a disappointment. She was apparently attracted to the odd, not the reliable, and I could only imagine what silliness she was concocting.

I yearned to counsel her, to advise as a friend, to act as rudder of her course, but naturally I could not. Instead, I was forced to rely upon the erratic stream of recall notices I received from the library. I had stockpiled the most esoteric and erudite of the collection's Columbusiana, and now and again the circulation desk would request that something be returned. I knew who wanted it and, following these footprints in the dense forest of data, I attempted to reconstruct Vivian's stumbling path. She wandered here and there, never pursuing a lead to its conclusion, an idea to its source. There was no method that I could discern, and I was tempted to slip a helpful note into a book she wished to read.

"Ignore the pabulum about Majorca," I could have written about one otherwise useful analysis, or, "Skip the chapter on Savoy, it's redundant." But I resisted the impulse and feigned ignorance of the whole project. I was scrupulously quiet when Vivian inhabited her study, holding my nose when a dust allergy made me sneeze and sitting for hours without altering the position of my chair so as not to alert her to my presence. I knew how keen her vigilance could be. Now I was the listening board, the silent eavesdropper, the other side of a one-way mirror. At the expense of my poem, I became an expert observer of Vivian, while she in turn dabbled in history. I half awaited an exploratory knock, the Cressida tap of a pencil against our adjoining wall as we sat like convicts in exclusive confinement, but I determinedly did not anticipate my response to this summons. I was simply ready for any step—fully prepared to be humble or gracious, contentious or oblivious. But I hid myself too well and never had the chance to take it.

Hilda and Racine were my link to Vivian, and of course, to me much more than that. They were well suited to each other, matched in their intellectual reach, their European roots, their taste and sensibilities. Of the two, Hilda was the more irreverent—at least that was her self-presentation. Her asides were famously unpredictable, as likely to produce a laugh as an insight. She possessed what is called "survival humor," and a lucky thing that was, for she was the sole remaining member of a distinguished Slovakian family annihilated by the Nazis. Somehow as an infant she had been spirited first to England, then to Australia, and finally, when she entered college in Georgia, to the United States. It's no wonder she gravitated toward geography. Raised and nurtured by a succession of brilliant refugees, she spoke several languages—Slovak, Czech, French, German, Yiddish, and a rather self-consciously southern-accented English—with complete fluency, and somehow she also seemed to incorporate into her personality the kind of worldly wisdom, almost ennui, that would be less of a surprise in a much older woman. Despite it all she professed a fascination with popular culture: network television, microwavable food, sports scores.

Hilda was eminent in her field, with a specialty in intercontinental plates and faults. She was not oblivious to fashion though. Her hair was collected in a blondish knot that perched on her head at a jaunty angle. She favored oversize clothing, big-shouldered coats and long skirts, cut from bolts of raw cotton dyed deep shades of red and purple. Her signature scent was musk, an overpowering sweet aroma that encompassed her like an aura, a halo that radiated from her person in spikes and shadows. She invariably wore long and complicated earrings that chimed subtly when she moved, providing, during the meetings of faculty committees of which she was a member, a warning gong just before Hilda emphatically registered her thoughts.

Racine, on the other hand, was as reticent and contained as his wife was exuberant. His smile, enigmatic and refined, was expressed more by his eyes than by his lips. He was known for kindness, for empathy, for withholding his opinion until it was sought—which guaranteed that his observations were in constant demand. Slight of build and rather dapper, Racine was a man who would clearly age well, becoming an ever more perfected version of his younger self. He was an unobtrusive companion, a charming host, a careful if not groundbreaking medievalist. His presence was a reassuring, leveling influence in any setting, and together he and Hilda provided a kind of yin and yang that seemed complete, a unified whole.

It was therefore disconcerting to see them split and at odds in their reactions to Vivian and me. They had thoroughly approved of our relationship, had facilitated its progress by inviting us to intimate exquisite dinners, by extending the umbrella of their easy domesticity to shelter our tentative movement toward public exposition. They even reassured me about the loutish Nash.

"Remember what you were like as a teenager," Hilda had exhorted. And I did. In the summer of my fourteenth year, I had received a dictionary from the library in reward for having read a book each day. About the same time, I attempted to compose a play in verse based on the first section of Genesis. I found the title in a glossary of foreign quotations, a Portuguese saying: *Esa la herencia d'Adan* ("It is the legacy of Adam"). Our family cook, an expert baker from Martinique, taught me the secret of crusty baguettes. I wrote but never mailed love letters to a neighbor, Harriet Wells, two years my senior. I was no stranger to hormonal rebellion, either. At twenty I went alone to Florence and stayed at the youth hostel. Built for Mussolini's mistress, it was festooned with rococo cupids and fauns. I shared an interlude with a Swedish cyclist, her thighs inflated by her journey through the Alps. And I often exchanged tense words on the subject of politics with my parents. They voted for Nixon while I canvased for Kennedy, a fellow Massachusettsite to whom they objected, I was certain, on the basis of his religion.

None of these activities, however, seemed remotely analogous to Nash's surly indifference. When Vivian introduced us, I extended my hand in friendship but he merely snorted, shook his head, and went to his room. When, in subsequent efforts to win him over, I would ask about his day, his interests, his preferences, he would tap his lip with a forefinger and regard me as if I were a curious specimen, something unappealing from, say, his botany lab. And yet if I ignored him he seemed equally nonplussed. Nothing about me, in fact, engaged him.

"Don't be insulted." Racine, as usual, was conciliatory. "He's in a difficult stage and even at his best he is . . . hard to know."

"Perhaps that is an inherited trait," I offered. "The grandmother . . ."

Hilda swung her large head from side to side, filling the room with the clank and jangle of her earrings, on that day twin replicas in miniature of the masks of comedy and tragedy. "Angeline's affections must be won, and over time. The woman is deliberate. She is forming an opinion. She's seen Vivian hurt before and is naturally wary."

"It's more than that," I said. "Whenever I hang my coat in the closet she takes it out and puts it on the chair by the front door. She clears my dinner plate before I've finished eating and then she goes to bed, announcing that she can't sleep until the house is quiet."

"Have you tried bringing along a gift when you arrive?" Racine asked. "Some token to soften her heart?"

"The first time, it was wine," I said, "and she poured it down the drain. She stated that her house was dry. Fair enough. The next weekend I tried flowers, a lovely bouquet which I presented to her with some ceremony—I thought perhaps she expected a certain deference due to her age and foreign status."

"She's not foreign," Hilda pointed out. "We are. You are."

I could have contested that point, marched out my cross-hatched New England pedigree dating back to the seventeenth century, but I took her meaning.

"How did she respond to the bouquet?" Racine at least approved of my intention.

"She took it into the kitchen, I assumed for water and a vase," I told him. "Then she returned to her chair empty-handed. She rocked and glared, rocked and glared, turned up the volume of the television when I tried to talk to Vivian. I kept waiting for the flowers to reappear—I even stole a look into the dining room, but they were nowhere in evidence. I think she threw them away."

My voice was strained, indignant, but Hilda suppressed a laugh. "The grandmother is a character," she said. "You see, she's told me that where she comes from, the woman is the king. Perhaps she's testing you."

"Then I failed." It was no exaggeration. Vivian was bounded on either side by generations positively hostile to my existence, and my enthusiasm for winning them over had weakened. Who were they, after all, to regard me with such miserly attitudes?

And now, months later, Hilda herself seemed to have joined the select club of Roger-bashers. Though she never spoke the words, I could tell she disapproved of my alienation from Vivian, even when she knew very well that it was neither my choice nor my fault. Racine was typically neutral, and the result was a kind of alliance split along male-female lines. The boys versus the girls. I remarked to Hilda on this unenlightened posture—it seemed so lacking in originality.

"You're right," she nodded. "Lucy and Ethel on one side and Ricky and Fred on the other."

It took me a minute to catch her reference, and then I rejected it.

"Ricky was a Cuban," I said. "A musician."

"Don't be so literal. Maybe you're Fred."

I thought of the man, bald and fat, a former vaudevillian. He was even worse. He and his blond wife were the supporting cast. But before I could object, Hilda corrected herself.

"No, you can't be Fred. There is, let us not forget, the impending arrival of Little Ricky." She fixed me with a stern look, then laughed out loud.

"Roger is quite upset, my darling," Racine said. "I think you should be more empathic."

"Perhaps you two should go hunting or something, *mon petit chou*," Hilda answered. "Make the male bond complete."

4

ROGER

For a teaching scholar, the fall is a time of rebirth. In nature, of course, Persephone exits the underworld in April or May, and bons vivants, in reflection of the ancient rites of winter solstice, pop their champagne corks on January 1. But not the breed of pedants. Since kindergarten, the commencement of school has marked my new year, the turning of a clean page. All is potential, the only given my syllabi—those ultimately flexible outlines of the lectures I expect to present and the reading and writing assignments I will require of my students. The rest is chance, never twice the same. When my preliminary class lists arrive in intercampus mail, I match the students' names with their faces in each freshman book, curious as a blind date. They have chosen me—or at least my subject—and so have an initial advantage. They have a week to shop before committing to a final schedule, and if I disappoint in any way, they can transfer out of my domain without penalty or ostensible hard feelings. But if they elect to remain, the balance of power shifts. Then *they* must please *me*.

Within the department there is an unspoken rivalry that surfaces in the first several days of a semester, when enrollment printouts are circulated. Who's up, who's down. There's endless speculation regarding cause, and as with so many elements in life, unobtrusive moderation is ideal. A large subscription is suspect: Why is Professor X suddenly so popular? Are the grades inflated? Are the tests too easily graded? Trends are carefully monitored: Have students enrolled in blocks? A surfeit of football or hockey players is probable cause for tittering in the faculty lounge. Professor Y has clearly pandered to the masses. Standards must perforce have been sacrificed.

Underenrollment, on the other hand, is not necessarily all bad. Like a slightly frayed cuff, a poverty of students can be genteel, honorable, as long as it does not constitute a trend. "Tutorial" remains a kind of holy benediction, a faintly Oxbridge designation reserved for the most exclusive, and thus the smallest, of eclectic seminars. The longer and more specific the course title, the adage goes, the more "limited" the appeal. My offering, "Flora in the Lesser-known Verse of John Donne," for instance, is notoriously underpopulated, as well it should be, whereas the fast food of one shamelessly crowd-pleasing assistant professor—a course on classic and modern mystery writing known in the vernacular as "Books for Crooks"—teems with Goliaths fresh from the gym.

Naturally, a good thing can be carried too far. It is tedious to devise a brilliant lecture and then deliver it to three sophomores who couldn't get into their first-choice courses because they were last in line at registration. And there's no denying that any dip in one's collective student/teacher ratio that exceeds ten to one is cause for alarm and a stern chat with the chairman. One's "service" courses—normally having to do with composition—are chaff that protect the wheat. My own such purgatory is the abominable "Beowulf to Byron," a predictable potpourri, and I save it for spring when I am as fatigued as the material. In autumn, enlivened by the summer's respite, I say, enrollments be damned.

Now, as I returned to my house I looked forward to the beginning of school and to the first meeting of my experimental seminar "Heroic Couplets, Heroic Couples: The Art of Human History as Rendered into Narrative." As a prime example of the process under investigation I would share samples of my own work, a daring departure. Students would grapple with the living word, the evolving corpus of a poem. As a final paper, I promised in my course description, each member of the class would be asked to submit fifty lines of original work. I had no real hopes of discovering a budding Milton or Virgil among the sons and daughters of Winnetka, Scarsdale, and La Jolla, but stranger things had happened. Look at me. Without a daunting challenge, what was education for?

I turned the key in my lock, opened the door, switched on the ceiling light, and paused. When one lives alone, there is a feel to one's domain that is particular, almost palpable. Each item has its special spot, its specific juxtaposition, its unique place in the symmetry of the whole. Solitary animals have this sense about their caves, I'm sure. It is an intuition both protective and protecting, a translation of territoriality into an internal radar through which each irregular blip is audible. The place one sleeps, where one lies unconscious and vulnerable, must above all else be secure from invasion or unwelcome intrusion, and now, as I surveyed my premises, something, some subtle but unmistakable alteration, felt . . . wrong.

Ostensibly, all seemed as it should be. The pendulum swung in my antique corner clock, but otherwise the air was still. Nothing appeared to have been moved. There were no telltale dents in the cushions of my couch, and my baskets of mail—correspondence/business, correspondence/personal, bills—were as neatly organized as I had left them. The sideboard drawers that contained my grandmother's cutlery—arguably my most valuable material possession—were flush with the cherry wood frame, and my television set rested securely on its mobile stand.

Still, there was something. Goldilocks had been here, as surely as if she had left a bowl of half-eaten porridge. There was no unusual odor in the room, but ions had been disturbed. Was that throw rug too far from the chair? Had I uncharacteristically left that glass on the counter? Was the door to my bedroom, visible at the top of the stairs, a bit more ajar than usual? I advanced slowly, stealthily into the large room, my gaze flitting over the rows of books on the built-in shelves, the arrangement of canisters in the kitchen area, the display of my collection of cloisonné horses on the mantel. Everything was right, properly aligned, unstolen. Yet . . . yet . . .

The telephone rang, its jarring noise the more grating because I had been listening so intently for evidence.

"Put Vivian on," cracked the grandmother's distinctive voice.

Only minutes before, I had contentedly anticipated my nightly routine: my comfortable chair, a snifter with two fingers of brandy, my Tensor reading lamp tilted at its most heuristic angle for glare-free reading, a book open on my lap. Now the evening was a lost cause, the last straw a cranky interruption from a woman who had never liked me in the first place.

"Did you dial correctly?" I retorted. "In case you missed the past few months, your granddaughter and I are no longer an item. Try the women's center."

"She's not with you?" There was a new tone to her words, an uncertainty that instantly made me regret my rudeness. She sounded . . . I strove to identify the emotion, and then it penetrated: worried.

"I haven't seen Vivian to talk to in a long time," I said. "What's the matter? Are you ill?"

She didn't answer me directly, but did continue to speak. "Not with Hilda and Racine. Not in her office. Not with you," she ticked off. "Where then?"

I glanced at Great-grandfather Williams's clock. Ten-fifteen. Not an alarming hour unless the party in question always checked in when she was going to be late. Not unless the missing person was extremely pregnant.

"The movies?" I suggested, modulating my timbre to its most helpful resonance.

"She doesn't like to go alone," Angeline replied absently. Her responses revealed to me what I secretly wanted to hear: that Vivian's solitude had endured.

"What about Nash?" I inquired.

"She was supposed to pick him up downtown. Hours ago. He called twice but now I can't find him, either."

I understood the concern. Hanover, New Hampshire, was a far cry from a danger-filled metropolis, but a boy like Nash could find trouble anywhere and so he was kept on a tight leash.

"Don't tell her I called you," Angeline said, and hung up. I held the receiver for a moment, then punched in Racine's number.

"What's the story with Vivian tonight?" I asked when he answered.

"Roger. Have you seen her? Did you two have another argument?"

Terrific. Now Vivian's disappearance was also assumed to be my fault. And what did he mean, "another"? We had never once raised our voices.

"Her grandmother called me. That fact alone suggests some emergency."

"Roger, what's going on? Is she with you? Don't you two know people are worried?" Hilda had wrested the telephone away from her husband and her annoyance was evident.

"She's not there," Racine calmly intervened in the background. "Angeline called him."

"Called *him*?" Hilda's voice swelled. "Oh, my God!"

"Vivian is a grown woman," I said. "It's only half past ten. This isn't Istanbul."

"*Istanbul?*" Hilda exclaimed. "What does *Istanbul* have to do with it?"

"Nothing," I said. "It was just a joke."

"He's joking," Hilda confided to the hovering Racine, who then took back the receiver.

"This isn't funny, Roger," he said.

"I'm not saying it is," I insisted. "I just—"

"She could have gone into labor," he continued, "but we contacted the maternity ward and she has not been admitted."

"Hang up," Hilda demanded. "She might be trying to call us now."

"Let me know," I shouted into my mouthpiece, but before the words were out the instrument went dead. I reached for my brandy, paused, thought better of it. One should keep a clear head in a crisis, and suddenly I felt sure Vivian was upstairs. She was obviously the presence I had sensed, and I crossed the room, ascended two steps at a time. Of course, of course. The door had *not* been left open. My pulse raced in anticipation. This was just like her, this surprise. I could foresee the expression on her face: half-abashed, half-defiant, awaiting my reaction. I would not disappoint her this time.

"Vivian!" I said just before I entered my—our—bedroom.

It was unoccupied, the coverlet neat, its military corners un-ruffled. I was as deflated as if I had been knocked to the ground from behind. Then I was overtaken by anxiety. I imagined Vivian, alone in the woods, stared at by the gleaming eye of wild beasts, as she gave birth to our daughter unattended. I considered alerting the town police, but then imagined how stupid I would appear if Vivian were simply lingering over a cup of cocoa with one of her less obvious friends. But all the same, I couldn't sit still and do nothing. I set my briefcase on the floor, moved to my bureau, and put on a sweater. Then, with a last look around my room, almost as if I expected to find Vivian hidden in the closet or standing as she had so often by the window, I rushed downstairs and out of the house.

Late on moonless nights the darkness of northern New England is near absolute. There are no large cities to cast a glow into the sky just beyond the hills' horizon, and Hanover is well known enough to its inhabitants so that the occasional streetlamps are more decorative than necessary. A student traversing the green might pass by suddenly an arm's length away, preoccupied with nocturnal thoughts or still pondering the screening of a foreign film.

Tonight the air was damp, unusually heavy, with the feel of river fog. I had wandered for hours, and Main Street was deserted. Once again, from a new direction, I approached the Dartmouth campus proper, and was pleased to hear opera drifting from the window of a dormitory room—*La Bohème*, I instantly identified, second act. The music was reassuring, a welcome companion, and my pace accelerated though I had in mind no clear destination. Because of the seclusion we had practiced, I didn't know the public Vivian, her favorite spots. It would be a striking coincidence if I happened to encounter her, and yet I could not return home. Too many what-ifs tangled in my imagination. I let myself be guided by the romantic notion that if Vivian needed me I would find her, and so I paused at every corner, sensitive as a dowser, alert for the slightest inclination.

The sign, when at last it came, was not ambiguous. To my left a door slammed with the force of an explosion, and somewhere before me the sound of running footsteps broke the even rhythm of the night. A light came on in a third-floor room, but there was no pursuit and the noise abated as abruptly as it had begun. Yet there was still someone nearby. A panting breath, swallowed though not altogether concealed, rubbed the silence. I strained to catch the fugitive's outline, but saw only the deeper black posts of trees, planted at regular intervals. The solitary light was extinguished, the panting became more regular, then finally it, too, disappeared.

"Hello," I called into the void. "Is everything all right?"

I was answered by the whisper of a sound so distinctive, so irritatingly familiar, that there was no denying its origin: only one person I knew was capable of producing an autonomic snort that conveyed, in equal parts, disdain, churlishness, and inarticulation. It was an involuntary reaction, dredged up from some primal, obtuse core, and it functioned as a barrier between him and everything that smacked of wit or grace. Out there, within my easy earshot, up to no good and unwilling to identify himself by name, Nash lurked.

Like two uneasy denizens of the veldt, we froze all motion and blended into the environment. But in this true-life adventure, who was hunter, who was hunted? Did he recognize my particular voice, or was his tongue-tied antagonism distributed neutrally to all humanity?

He shuffled—tentatively, I was sure. The movement was the equivalent of tossing one's hat to the far corner of a room, a ruse intended to seduce the stalker into betraying his position. I was not that easily duped and held my ground. He took a step, flat-footed in his perpetually unlaced shoes, and when that, too, produced no reaction he expelled a louder version of his derisive sneer, this one formed around the word "Shit." Against all logic—a normal person would not assume that the source of my "Hello" had evaporated—the boy believed he had outsmarted his pursuer and now bore that anonymous presence—me!—nothing but contempt.

I fought an urge to knock the knees from under his cockiness. "You have the right to remain silent" came to mind, but I resisted. If anything, clever words would only frustrate him, fire at random the synapses of his brain and make his response even harder to anticipate. I bided my time to see if he would relax his guard still further, and he did not disappoint me. A match flicked three trees away and his furtive, unpleasant face was led by a cigarette into the circle of light. He could have been, in this incarnation, Fagin's protégé, the inheritor of the thief's mantle.

Ah, yes. And not just any cigarette. The cloying odor of marijuana smoke stained the watery air. Was he celebrating a misdeed previously committed, or finding courage for the next? Vivian, wherever she was, could not intervene and so I had to be her agent, her camera. I flipped a page in my mental notebook and dutifully recorded the growing list of offenses—surely smoking pot was a misdemeanor even for a juvenile. What did they call it on the TV cop shows? A rap sheet? Loitering, illegal possession, trespass, failure to respond to an officer of the law. I had more than enough evidence to justify a citizen's arrest, and yet I hesitated. If I officially found Nash, took him into my custody, I would have to turn my attention once again to Vivian's inexplicable disappearance, and there I hadn't a clue. I decided it was better to wait, to keep the son under close surveillance. I trusted in a mother's innate ability to locate her imperiled young. If Vivian was able, she would eventually home in on Nash as though he wore a genetic beeper whose frequency she alone could decipher. I would find her by letting her find us.

Even as I adopted this plan, however, I disapproved of it. Why was I invariably so passive, especially in this relationship? Vivian led, I followed. She proposed, I objected or reluctantly assented. More and more, I treated Vivian as though she possessed the only map of our future. She was Sacajawea and I was Lewis, or Clark, guided through unknown territory by a stranger in quest of God knows what. Certainly I was self-aware of this pattern, but the knowledge did not seem to liberate me.

I asked myself all the hard questions: Did I have a mother complex? Was I intimidated by Vivian's ethnicity? Was it simply the hypnotism of sex? All of the above, no doubt, but what else?

Did it have to do with my age? I had sailed across the moat of my fortieth birthday so smoothly that everyone had commented upon the trick. I had attained the stage described as "midlife"—statistically I was unlikely to live longer than ninety or so—but need that instigate a "crisis"?

I noticed no diminishment of physical vigor, no special grip of gravity against my muscles, and in terms of mental health I was at full throttle. I was respected, perhaps revered, in my profession and had grown more into the natural contours of my face. With your bone structure, Roger, Mother had said from the time I was very young, you will improve with age. If anything, Vivian's attraction to me had justified this prediction.

Why, then, was I not a more commanding fellow? Why did I skulk in concealment instead of taking Nash by the scruff of his neck? Was I afraid to offend him? To annoy Vivian by acting in too precipitous or presumptuous a manner? After all, what was I to him, or to her, for that matter? The "boyfriend"—an absurd role for a full professor, for a man whose *curriculum vitae* ran to eight modest, single-spaced pages.

And then, undeniable, stinging, and utterly prosaic, it came to me: I had lived too long at a distance from life. The dynamic I observed, critiqued, wrote about, was past and fixed on the printed page. My major experience was with code, not fluid context. I dealt in retrospect, *re*examination, *re*search, reason, *re*collection, not in events unfolding. In the present tense I floundered, unable to act until I saw what happened. Vivian and her whole unruly entourage had me by a lead that pulled too insistently for me to ever find a footing.

The experience was, I suddenly thought, like being young. And now, as though compelled by a force of nature that one neither liked nor disliked, chose nor could defer, it had taken me over completely. So, when Nash flicked his last ember and, emboldened by narcotics and arrogance, moved back in the direction of the dormitory from which he had so recently fled, I had no option but to pad softly behind.

It was odd, but in all my years on the Dartmouth faculty, I had never entered a student residence. Dormitories, sororities, and fraternities were foreign countries last visited when I myself had been an undergraduate at Chicago. They connoted, therefore, a reminiscent mixture of frustrated, rampant hormones and accumulated clutter, bad mattresses, discordant roommates, a constant deprivation of privacy. And as I tentatively broached the unlocked, wooden door to the first floor the faint smell of the place—dirty laundry, disinfectant soap—evoked a spate of memories. The indignity of group showers and rows of sinks, the noisy all-nighters pulled by students improvident in their preparations until the day before a paper was due, the buzz of clock-radios not one's own. Each step I took was progress backward in time to a period of my life with few highlights. I had been a serious student, the stalwart, conscientious, assignment-on-time, anxiety-prone plodder. I had been neither brilliant nor popular in my first four years at the university, and my B's were less gentlemanly than hard-won. It was not until graduate school, under the mantle of a demanding adviser who saw promise in my work, that I finally took intellectual flight.

And thus it was with a certain vestigial cloak of alienation, that I mounted the stairs on Nash's trail. At one-thirty A.M. on a Sunday night the building was quiet, asleep, and so it was easy to keep track of the sounds he made in the hall above. It was impossible, however, to determine his purpose. He would walk, stop, tear at something made of paper, then repeat the process, over and over. I let the distance between us build, and waited until I heard Nash climb another flight before I explored the first dimly lit corridor he had visited. Initially, nothing seemed disturbed—a series of closed doors, uniformly the same—but then I did notice an unusual feature. Taped at eye level, above each knob, was a note filled with handwriting. My first thought was Luther's Ninety-five Theses, nailed to the door of the Wittenberg church but that was absurd. I approached the nearest sheet, leaned close in order to read the message, and stopped breathing. The penmanship turned familiar a split second before the words. I stared at a page ripped ragged from my own journal.

I snatched it free, clutched it to my chest. I had read only a few words, ". . . has no kindness," but I recognized with sick horror the context—self-pity. My humiliation was absolute, my private weakness exposed, and then a siren went off in my brain and I looked down the long highway of the building. Like Burma-Shave advertisements aside a country lane, equally excruciating pages hung at regular intervals, awaiting the light of day. I knew what they contained: diary entries and snatches of my poem, the inspiration of odd moments, *pensées* and copied aphorisms, telephone numbers and grocery lists. And copious hypothesizing about my unborn daughter. My journal was the jumble of my mind on paper, incautious, self-important, cruel and petty, and, worst of all, nakedly lovesick.

Slowly at first, then peripatetic and manic, I zigzagged from door to door. Snatching back my words, stuffing them into my pockets, I crumpled the days I had not meant to relive until the fervor of their disparate events had been tempered by the passage of years, of decades. From above I heard the swish of a closing door, the tap of Nash's feet climbing a third flight of stairs. I could catch him now and leave my pages to be discovered, or I could gather them up and allow him to escape.

There was no choice to be made. My secrets, small and ridiculous as they might seem to the eyes of anyone else—perhaps precisely *for* that reason—took precedence over justice. The ledger he had stolen from my desk drawer—the current volume and therefore the only one not stored in my safety-deposit box—comprised two hundred and fifty days, starting last January. It took me four large sleeping buildings in order to recover them all. At the exit of the last one I found discarded the mutilated remains of my leatherbound 1990. The blank autumn was left whole and untouched, its hopes and further disappointments yet to be learned.

When I finally made it home, I opened the bottom drawer of my desk as if to confirm what I already knew. My diary was the only thing missing, and bitterly I realized that my estimation of Nash had increased in both directions. He was at once meaner and wiser than I had guessed. Somehow, from our few grinding conversations, he had gleaned my most vulnerable area and systematically trod upon it. Was it revenge? Retaliation? Regret? Was it hurt or cruelty that inspired his target? Or was it, simply, most important, to attach my name to his mother's baby?

My impulse was to shred my violated pages, to incinerate them in the fireplace, but I knew I couldn't strike the match. However I might at this moment feel about them, they still constituted the only record of my life's progress. They could not be lost, and yet in their present form they could not be saved. No amount of smoothing and pressing would restore their freshness, no roll of clear tape could reaffix them in their proper order. Absently I picked up my Mont Blanc pen, the instrument I used with such pride whenever I had something significant to write, and then replaced it. I would not retranscribe each line, much as the sight would soothe me. What had once been found could be found again.

My glance passed over my desk and stopped. There was an alternative, a means by which I could both preserve and conserve in portable form. I pushed the button for power and the screen of my computer turned a bright sky blue. I opened a new file and typed the first date, even before I sat in my chair. Then I re-created my year, pressing "Save" at the end of every week. By the time I caught up with the present, August 26, I could legitimately have typed a new entry—the day was already that old—but I didn't. Let there be an intermission to mark the boundary between myself as I was and myself as I would be. I ejected the disk and slipped it into my shirt pocket.

Finally released from my compulsion, I glanced around the room. The ruby eye on my answering machine was blinking. How could I have missed it? The two messages told a complete story. The first call, from Hilda, had come in shortly after midnight.

"Roger, are you there? Pick up," she instructed, then waited for me to obey. When I failed to answer she became irritated. "Where are you?" she wanted to know. "Vivian's still lost and Nash isn't back either. Angeline is frantic in her own way. Too quiet. Too serene. Call me. *What are you doing?*"

There was a beep, an interval, and then the second call while I was still patrolling the campus.

"Roger, Racine. No word from Vivian. Are you all right? Roger? If you want, come over and wait with us. We've given up on sleep."

There was nothing further, but the machine ran on, the whispering grind of its turning wheels the only message. I let it revolve and switched off my desk lamp. The tape would coil into itself until there was no more room for messages, and then it would answer all calls on the fourth ring with a long mournful wail that promised no hope of return. If Vivian tried for me—and who could be sure she would not?—she would have no choice but to proceed to the next-best number, the Seelbinders' private line, and I would be there, waiting.

Hilda's face fell when she saw it was me. She was dressed in a blue plaid flannel robe and her light hair had been allowed to dry uncombed after a shower. She looked younger, less imposing, than usual.

"Racine called," I offered by way of explanation.

She nodded, stepped aside, then looked for a moment into the night after I had entered, as if expecting to spot Vivian or Nash concealed in the shrubbery.

"Nothing?" I asked.

She shook her head. "Racine's in the kitchen, baking something. He says it's therapy. Me, I take my anxiety straight up."

I sniffed the air, gave her a puzzled look.

"Right," she nodded. "Some kind of peanut butter thing out of a West African cookbook. Kuchen à la Kano. Every pot in the house is dirty, but it keeps him sane. Go. Hold his hand."

Racine was peering into the glass window of his oven, watching the batter rise. Bowls were stacked to overflowing in the sink, and the floor was dusted near the counter with a fine sift of flour.

"Smells good," I said from the door.

"It better. You wouldn't believe what the recipe called for. Jasmine. Lemongrass. Coriander."

"Peanut butter."

"Well, not exactly, but it was the closest thing. I hope it doesn't overpower. Do you think?" He seemed to consider, then asked, "So where were you? Out looking?"

"On campus." I hesitated, reluctant to admit having encountered Nash. The memory was too fresh and too painful.

The bell on the stove rang and with a pot holder Racine gently rotated the baking pan and eased the door closed. "How do they do this in a clay oven?" he wondered aloud. "What if animals are close by? The instructions are very clear: it cannot be jarred."

Hilda joined us and sat at the table. "I called the campus police," she announced, "but they were gone. They'll call back." She pinched the bridge of her nose, squeezed her eyes shut, and exhaled.

Racine pulled up a chair and we three sat in silence, each kept company by private thoughts while we watched the oven door as if it were a television screen. We waited for a signal, for some push that would move us from this late-night ditch into the business of a new day. In time, the cake was done and set upon a rack to cool. Eventually, after testing it with a probing finger, Racine cut three slices, set them on matched plates, dug into a drawer for dessert forks and napkins. The first bite was a shock—the taste exotic and delicious, a rich blend of improbable flavors.

"Too much of the peanuts?" Racine inquired. He wanted compliments.

"Superb, my angel." Hilda strained to lighten the mood. "You are the Julia Child of the jungle, the James Beard of Bamako, the Escoffier of Kumasi."

I held up my fork in a toast to the chef, who bowed in return. We each ate a second piece. It was almost dawn.

"Roger, your face is gray. Racine, you look like hell. We don't all need to exhaust ourselves. Women are stronger. We have endurance. You two get some rest—you on the futon in the family room downstairs, Roger. I'll clean up this mess and sound the trumpet when I hear something." She held up her hand, palm out, the universal sign of peace, to still our protest. Her mind was made up and I was too tired to argue. I used the railing to steady myself as I slowly descended the steps, but even so I stumbled, caught myself, stumbled again—the model for Braque's painting. The futon, covered in brown corduroy, was piled with books. I set them on the floor and fell face forward onto the cushions. Their embrace was more comforting than that of the softest bed, the refuge I needed from the fear for Vivian, and the thought of Nash, loose and hostile and beyond my grasp in the dark.

5

VIVIAN

I t was still too early for most of the library staff to have appeared and so, in the end, there was no drama or climax to the long night. By the time I awoke, the janitors had unlocked the doors and propped them open with rubber wedges. I simply gathered my books together, folded the afghans, and shoved off, walking out the fourth-level doors as I had a thousand times, encountering not a soul.

I arrived to a damp clear morning, to air that was almost food, rich with water and oxygen. As I walked three blocks to the lot behind the hospital where I had parked my car, I felt revived, prepared to find Nash and bring him home.

I dumped everything I'd carried from the library into the backseat of the Subaru and registered the small shameful fact that I'd unintentionally brought along the Cobb folder. Either the beeper alarm had not yet been activated for the day or the collection had escaped the library's infrared marking system. I told myself I'd return the whole mess eventually, but not now.

It took the full extension of the seat belt to fit around me—no slack—as I drove straight to Hilda and Racine's house on the outskirts of a quiet Hanover neighborhood. They lived in one of those forties-vintage bungalows that predate Ozzie and Harriet or the Cleavers and suggest a more hand-hewn and eccentric American wholesomeness than the fifties ranch styles. The bay windows in the children's third-floor bedrooms were the perfect nooks for reading in window seats, for suspending collections of model airplanes. Of course, Hilda and Racine's offspring, Mark and Rachel, the ideal children in the world, actually *used* the window seats, shifting the piles of books they read. Their perfection was an affront, a daunting reminder of who Nash was not.

The Seelbinders were already up, spooning a healthy-looking mush into themselves when I came to the side door. Mark, the son from Hilda's first marriage, was home from his brilliant freshman year at Georgetown and let me in, his face excited.

"Mom," he shouted at the room behind him. "Here she is!"

He put his arms around me, patted the baby. There are kids like this, I reminded myself, kids who aren't completely self-dramatizing. I tried not to hold it against him or his parents.

"Where's Nash?" I asked Mark, hopeful that I'd willed my son to this door.

"What do you mean? Where were *you*?"

Sheer exhaustion kept me numb.

Hilda stumbled into the kitchen dressed in a plaid robe, her sharp, foxlike features bleary and testy. Like me, she was no morning person, for which today I was especially grateful. She put her hands on my shoulders, and her grip was not gentle.

"You worried us to death. Call Angeline, and then you have some explaining to do."

She handed me the phone, pointed to the coffeepot on the table, and shambled from the room with an abruptness that was almost rude. There was a strained air of hesitation about her, something held back quite apart from her obvious annoyance. It was unlike her to be inhospitable, even when stressed. I sat down anyway, opposite Mark. Rachel poured a bowl of Familia for me and pushed the milk close.

Grandma answered on the first ring.

"Don't say anything," I said. "I've been locked inside the library all night."

"Who with?"

"Bruce Springsteen."

That temporarily stopped her, but she would now be relieved that her rosary beads had at least successfully averted the imagined reunion with Roger.

"Did Nash come home?"

"He's not with you? You lost him?"

"Maybe you bolted the door and he didn't want to wake you. He could have climbed in the second-floor window. Go check his room. I'll wait."

She put down her phone. I had gulped half a carton of orange juice by the time she returned.

"No."

I shut my eyes. A tight red nothingness drummed behind my lids. My worry regarding Nash, a dull black bludgeon, hung near, ready to fell me. I sensed the wind of its passage beside my cheek. In the past two years I'd learned to guard myself, to try not to step into the arc of its range.

"Well," I said, "he must have stayed over with a friend."

"Or been kidnapped by a maniac," said Grandma, all quivering accusation.

"The same thing." Several of Nash's friends were currently barred from the grounds of the school for crimes the newspaper could not publish because they were still minors.

"Don't panic," I counseled Grandma, and tried to believe myself.

Hilda came downstairs dressed in knit pants and a sweater of snake yellow. Her outfit, which would have looked atrocious on anyone else, brought out the startling green of her eyes. After she got Rachel through the door to a baby-sitting job and Mark followed, promising that before playing soccer he'd check the places where summer school students hung out, Hilda turned her high beams on me.

"What's going on?" I demanded. "I just spent nine hours locked in the library, where I could've gone into labor, for Christ's sake. And then there's this thing with Nash. He's been out all night, maybe at a party, maybe lying in a ditch, maybe high somewhere in some kid's basement. And all you do is stare at me."

Hilda's face took on a glaze of uncertainty. She turned away. Her uneasiness unnerved me. "It's about Nash, right?"

"Compared to Nash it's nothing. Put it out of your mind." Her mouth indented with guilt.

"What?" I demanded loudly.

"Okay. Roger's here, asleep downstairs. He was out looking for you, walking the town. We made him come over."

The image of Roger's bright face caught me off guard.

"Who cares?"

Hilda stirred sugar and milk into her coffee. She was one of those people who blush at anger, who never say a censorious word if they can help it. She was, above all things, a woman of unqualified tolerance.

"What are you, a Sister of Mercy?" I said. "The bastard left me."

She looked at me very steadily and seriously, knowing better. "You're going to upset the baby."

There were too many loose ends to the morning. Roger's worry, at this point, was just something for *me* to worry about.

"Let me call the school and I'm out of here."

Hilda curled her hands tightly around her empty cup, and bowed her head, revealing a tough-looking grizzled streak in her fine blond hair. The sight of it touched me, restored some balance.

"It's not your fault." The bite was gone, my words flat. Roger had been their friend first. Hilda and Racine had assiduously refused to become involved in our breakup, had not taken sides or tried to play counselors.

"I must be having some sort of ninth-month hormone attack," I continued, groping in my bag for a Kleenex. "I need to get centered before I scare the principal."

Hilda reached behind, grabbed a roll of paper towels and set them down on the table. I read the label.

"Super absorbent. God, I need that." I started to laugh, which was the only thing that saved me from the next moment, in which the father of my child opened the door from the basement, rubbing his wet hair with a towel. He looked so calm, fresh, and immaculate that my mood instantly changed to an irritation raw enough to render me speechless. But then, so was he. If I ever needed confirmation of the imposing nature of my size—and I didn't—his face registered it. His jaw actually did drop, as they say jaws do. His blue eyes went blank, and his hand froze in the folds of the towel. We'd managed to avoid each other almost completely for months, and he'd last seen me up close at a svelte 118, polishing off the cavalier farewell dinner to which I had invited him.

That meal, like all those that followed, had collected on my hips, and now, thirty-five pounds heavier, here I sat, the cartoon figure that I'd seen in his anticipating eyes when I announced my pregnancy.

Then the bludgeon swung again, and this time it connected.

"I'll be on my way now." I spoke in a tone of such cold-blooded mildness that Hilda retreated with her coffee cup to the safety of her bedroom. I pictured her in that cozy place decorated with framed posters and expensive Marimekko pillows. She'd wake up Racine, and together they'd let the storm below them bluster and wail.

How safe.

The phone rang.

Roger shifted his weight, hung the towel around his neck and tucked in his shirt. He always neatened himself as he prepared to conduct an argument, smoothed back his hair, removed imaginary lint. The trick to bushwhacking him lay in cornering him when he was badly groomed. He once revealed to me that in order to write, he had first to dress meticulously from underwear to cuff links. Now he had found a chance to gather himself, and it wasn't fair. Hilda shouted down the stairs that the phone was for me. I could tell from her voice that it was Nash. I drew in a breath and picked up.

"Where are you?" The parent's first question, from which the whole situation is measured.

"School."

I breathed out.

There was a long silence from his end, then a nonchalant, almost self-righteous, "Well, I've got class."

"I know."

"So I better get going."

"Nash, where did you stay?"

"At a friend's."

"Whose house?"

"You don't know him."

"The name?"

"What are you going to do, call his mother? Where were *you*, anyway."

I hung up. And although Roger hadn't said a word, everything had changed. In the interval in which I talked to Nash, I had lost my advantage.

"What did he say?"

"The usual runaround."

Roger looked relieved, but couldn't let it go at that. Affecting a wistful tone, he asked how I felt.

I didn't answer.

"How *are* you?" he insisted, as if he had the right to know.

I looked at him evenly. He remained promising genetic material. The planes of his face fit together with clever precision, but the tremulously even smile was, I suddenly suspected, the product of expensive orthodontia. I'd have to keep my job in order to pay for this baby's braces.

"Who's your dentist?" I asked.

Roger looked wary, took a gulp of air.

"Please," he said. "You sent back all my letters. You've crossed streets to avoid me. By now, you must know I would have—"

"You would have what? Married me? We're not teenagers, and besides I don't have a father to hold the shotgun to your head."

The coffeemaker ticked and breathed as it passed through another cycle. A bird hopped on the windowsill feeder, pecked at the plastic dish.

"Did you sleep well?" Hilda loudly entered the room, quizzing Roger as if there were nothing amiss. She had reverted to her role of perfect hostess. She put on her coat. "Vivian didn't. She was locked in the library—can you imagine?—and it's bad for her to endure any sort of strain. I'm driving her home."

Her brown windbreaker had big flaps on the pockets. Her books were packed, her keys in her hand.

"I could do it," Roger offered. "I'd be glad to," he added to me in an private voice. "You shouldn't be—"

"Driving in my *condition*?" I completed his sentence and heard in my voice the beginning of an uncontrollable fury. I was determined to remain calm. "I can and will drive myself, thank you both."

They each stood still as I rose—and rose, for what seemed like forever. I opened the door, turned, and forced a smile.

"Don't be Superman," said Hilda.

"Absolutely not."

I waved, then stepped carefully down the front walk, and not until I was safely behind the wheel with the motor running did I let go. I knew I shouldn't cry, that it was bad for the skin, that I'd get a headache, that my baby would somehow feel sorrow too, that it wouldn't help anyway. I put the car in reverse, backed out of the driveway, and took aim at Dunkin' Donuts. Bavarian cream. Better *Schlag* than angst.

The night's contractions had long since ceased, and by the time I got home I was convinced that anxiety had brought them on. My due date was still ten days away and I had the last class of the term to teach, or rather host, for it was scheduled to be a student potluck at my house.

My home is a comfort, and I craved its deep quiet. It's an old place, painted white, with a tin roof and sagging black shutters decorated with cutout, slivered moons. I turned into the yard. Grandma was in front watering a burst of morning glories she had trained to grow over the door. At seventy-nine, she was a fierce gardener, hoisting plants from the earth by the irresistible force of her expectation. Now she stood waiting, a short, fine-boned woman as perfectly proportioned as a doll, her soft tan skin creased in graceful lines radiating from the corners of her eyes and mouth. As soon as she saw that I was all right, a scowl carved her face more deeply and her black pupils gleamed like creek pebbles. I was relieved to see her drop the shears into her pocket. She angled her head, cocked to one side to accommodate the unadmitted deafness in her right ear. We exchanged our usual pleasantries, with her commencing in Navajo for added emphasis.

"You have only yourself to blame if you miscarry."

"Good morning to you, too."

Yet she was relieved to see me. I could tell by the way she

yanked the bookbag from my hands and pushed me through the doorway.

"Take it easy!" I tried to make a joke but my voice scraped. She slammed the teakettle onto the stove.

"Nash is at school," I said. "I already ate."

"I can see the sugar around your mouth. Poison." She thrust a dish towel to my face, chose pinches from her various tea tins and sprinkled them into the pot with a sorcerer's flourish of the wrist. She set the steaming cup before me, and I sniffed the fumes before committing myself. It was the vile brew that she claims tones the uterus. The bitter taste would linger for hours, but negligent mother that I was in her estimation, I had to lift my mug. Her eyes dared me not to swallow.

"Now if Nash will just stay straight for a few days, I can have this baby," I offered.

Grandma peered at me, then remembered her glasses and fumbled them out of her pocket. Through the thick lenses her eyes looked huge and wondering, inescapable. I knew she was examining me for signs of fatigue. They were there all right, impossible to miss—my baggy lids, my hangdog look, my hair straggling loose from its quilled clip.

"There's that party tonight," I reminded her. "My whole class is coming, and each one is supposed to hand me a thirty-page term paper."

She sat in disapproving silence. I was doing too much, to her way of thinking. Too much of some things and not enough of others, as always.

"I can't get out of it," I said defensively. "We don't have to cook either, because my students are bringing the food. God knows what they'll show up with: a hunk of Vermont cheddar, a couple jugs of cider, and a package of stoned-wheat thins. Maybe if the vegetarian contingent gets ambitious, a big casserole of ratatouille."

Grandma thumped her hand on the table.

"Do you plan to sleep?" At least she was back in English now.

I hauled myself from the chair, and she accompanied me like a prison guard to the foot of the staircase.

"Don't worry," I said, turning to look down at her from

halfway up. "A couple hours and I'll be a whole new person."

"Good," she said.

It was a lively seminar, one of the best all term, and if I hadn't been so tired I actually would have enjoyed meeting that night. But I was still wiped out even after my nap, and Nash wasn't home yet. I tried not to worry. Precisely at seven, punctual and cheerful, my students piled out of three cars, bearing their politically correct foods, including organic grapes and a meatless meatloaf made from crushed nuts. The class was the mix I regularly drew, including a few skeptical, sharp-eyed economics majors who had enrolled in order to fulfill a distribution requirement. Their contributions to the dinner were six kinds of chocolate cookies. Then there were the solemn five or six students who were truly interested in pre-contact civilizations, and finally, the one or two zealots who henceforth vowed to make Indian rights their life's cause.

One of my fanatics this term wouldn't last long—he was too sweet, too heart-on-his-sleeve, with the angel face and white-blond curls of Art Garfunkel and the conviction that he should attend a Lakota ceremonial gathering. He carried *Black Elk Speaks* against his heart. The Sioux would eat him for lunch. On the other hand, Kate, a no-nonsense redhead from Tulsa, intended to go to law school and specialize in water and mineral cases. She was the one I tried to hook and hold on to.

At the table Kate immediately fell into an intense conversation with Grandma, while the others clumped around the food. Black Elk looked bereft at the lack of traditional fare. He had clearly hoped for roots and berries.

My course was a survey of pre-1492 tribes but I always use the final class to introduce the impact of the Old World. Without writing systems, it was impossible for North American Indians to preserve precise accounts of their initial meetings with Europeans, and so I had to rely on hearsay, to read between the lines of the often pompous and fatuously self-serving Spanish or English accounts. Some of my hypotheses were pure logic: What would have been the reaction of people who were known to bathe several times a day when they found themselves closely quartered with a ship's crew who had not washed for months, for years, who did not even *believe* in washing? European chroniclers regularly assumed that the first Indians they met had bowed their heads and clapped their hands over their faces out of deep respect, but my guess was that they were holding their noses.

Bad news was another reason for waiting to discuss contact. I had just spent ten weeks conducting a tour of ancient America's greatest hits: ingenious exchange systems, subtle and complicated religions, thriving agriculture, political equity between men and women. The students had been an appreciative audience, wowed by ethnoscience, impressed by traditional arts, fascinated by the richness and beauty I revealed. "Why didn't we know this?" they had asked time and again. "Where did it all go?"

Now I had to tell them.

After the food was gone I began by dealing out some "Discovery of America" cartoons, culled from various magazines and newspapers. In every frame, Columbus is a naive innocent craftily observed by a couple of unseen, jaded Indians. Christopher is lost, confused, wrongheaded, and the Indians are wiseasses—not like in the old social studies books, where they fall all over themselves to worship the ships with the cloudlike sails.

"Do you have reservations?" a supercilious Native inquires of the Discoverer in the first illustration.

"Contact was a different type of experience for Indians than it was for Europeans," I said. "Over here you had hundreds of societies, millions of people, whose experience had told them that the world was a pretty diverse place. Walk for a day in any direction and what do you find? A tribe with a whole new set of gods, a language as distinct from your own as Tibetan is from Dutch— very little, in fact, that's even slightly familiar. The one common ground is how odd you and they appear to each other, so you figure, okay, different strokes for different folks, and let it go at that. There're too many of them, and no two tribes are the same. Forget sending out cultural missionaries, forget insisting that everybody agree which end is up, except among your own group. So when Indians met the boys from France or Portugal or Spain for the first time, it was just, "Great, another set of weirdos in an unpredictable world. No big deal."

"But they traded with them," Kate insisted. "They were interested."

"Naturally," I said. "Europeans had great stuff for sale. Do you know how long it took an Arawak to fashion a nail out of shell? Then what do you do when it breaks? And mirrors! *You* try fixing your hair in a complicated do with nothing but a puddle of water to go by."

"You're saying technology," one of the budding economists noted. "European inventions were attractive."

"It was a two-way street," I countered. "Indians gave as much as they got, though they rarely received credit. What's a hamburger without fried *potatoes* and *tomato* ketchup?" His expression suggested that I had just named his ideal food. I didn't let up.

"A third of the medicines we use today were developed over here long before the fifteenth century. Not to mention the Iroquois concept of representative government or the Equal Rights Amendment."

"If the Indians were so smart, why aren't we sitting here speaking their language?" The salivating economist was not quite ready to concede. Thank God for a straight man.

"Languages," I corrected. "Thousands of them, which created a certain problem with internal communication, for spreading the word from tribe to tribe about what was going on. But really, it boiled down to just a few things. Number one, Europeans were organized and self-confident. After hundreds of years of fighting among themselves, they had developed a whole system of weapons that were superior to anything the Indians—whose 'armies' rarely consisted of more than a bunch of cousins out to raise hell—could throw back at them. Plus the fact that European powers had not only the *will* to win but the belief that it was their *right*. One god, one family from which all their languages originated, one creation story, one agenda: to rule the world. Never underestimate the power of chutzpah and positive thinking. They absolutely believed that the earth was their oyster."

Black Elk was woebegone. He, dressed in his sandals and Nicaraguan shirt, had resisted the charms of the Old World, so why did Indians succumb?

"Why couldn't they fight back?" he said, chagrined. "Why did they surrender their lands so easily?"

It was time to drop the real bomb.

"It wasn't the cavalry," I said. "It was germs. The assault

began invisibly, even accidentally, airborne, conveyed by touch, fleas, blood, a handshake. The first European who stood on the North American continent and coughed probably indirectly killed more Indians than George Armstrong Custer ever imagined in his favorite wet dream. It's estimated that more than a hundred million people lived in the Western Hemisphere in 1491, and nineteen out of every last twenty of them died from things like smallpox and measles and other infections imported from overseas. They didn't know what hit them. There was no precedent, no medicine that worked. The world came to an end, almost. A few people, by genetic chance, had a natural immunity, and they became the ancestors of today's Indian people."

I paused.

Perhaps it was pregnancy, the size of the baby pressing up against my lungs, but I began to feel slightly dizzy. In the silence of my students' breathing, of their note taking, I heard a car stop down the road, followed by the hollow thump of a slammed door. Then the car roared off. It had to be Nash.

My class watched me, their pens poised to record testable facts, their brows knit in concentration, some of it real, some for effect. At any moment, I knew, Nash would appear just behind me and frown into the window, try to figure out what was happening.

"Shut your eyes," I instructed in a fit of inspiration.

I faced a roomful of calm, closed faces. I suddenly wanted to sneak out the door, to run upstairs and crawl under the covers.

"Now imagine yourself in another time," I suggested. "You're part of a community, say the place where you grew up, populated with people like the ones you knew there. People in love. Married couples fighting with their in-laws. Children sneaking outside at night to look for shooting stars like you used to do. People planning revenge against their neighbors for an insult. People who expect tomorrow to be an improved-on repeat of the day before. Then for no reason, they start getting sick in ugly ways. Scabs on their bodies. High fevers. Madness. They try every medicine they know, medicines that have usually worked, yet no matter what cures their trusted doctors attempt, they still keep dying. Old people and babies go first, then the strong. Almost everybody dies. Those who don't die right away are so lonely that they wish they had."

The well-tended young faces looked sad, sorry for themselves. I heard Nash approach, rattling the dry bushes as he craned to see into the house. I could almost hear his brain click as he saw the students in their meditations. The cogs would whir as he tried to figure out a plausible explanation. Had we become Buddhists in his absence? I mentally signaled him to enter, say hello, and walk to his room, to not make any sort of scene.

But there's a sense a parent has, not so much a tangible connection as an awareness of a child's timing, and something was off with Nash. He stood at the window a beat too long, hesitating. It wasn't just the roomful of zombies—he needed to hide something and was not sure just how to do it. Before any of the students peeked, I began to talk.

"When all your medicine fails, your science, people begin to search for religious or political explanations. God is angry, fate is cruel. Some assume it is the work of enemies, witches of some kind. Get them before they get us. Yet when you attack your neighbors it only spreads the diseases. Everything that you try to do makes things worse."

Nash's feet scraped the bark of the tree that grew beside his window as he hauled himself into its branches. A twig snapped and the baby kicked. Then he was on the roof, then heavy footsteps above my head.

I had listened too long, and the students had opened their eyes. Their faces were upturned, listening too, and they looked at me in alarm when Nash fell onto the floor of his room. There was a series of crashes and I pictured a domino effect as each book, computer terminal, pottery bank, lamp, radio, sent the neighboring object toppling.

Grandma rushed past on her way from the kitchen and up the stairs. Then she banged on his door. My students still had their notebooks ready and, helpless, I looked into their eyes.

What could they possibly think? I wondered as I mounted the steps. Black Elk would opt for some sort of closet shaman, an Indian poltergeist. If only that were all it was—but Mrs. Rochester was closer to the mark: the dope fiend in the attic.

"Go home," I called down to them. "Term's over. Papers due on Monday. Have a good break." It was useless to explain the situation. These were the law-abiding teenagers, the ones who had compiled adolescent dossiers that had gained them entrance to Dartmouth. Motivated, upstanding homework-doers. The progeny of proud parents, reminders of my failure.

Grandma was standing outside Nash's shut and locked door, her head bowed.

"He won't answer," she said, defeated.

I asked Nash, perfunctorily, to come out. No response.

"Wait here," I said to Grandma and went to find my tool chest in the bathroom closet. Once back in the hallway, I put the screwdriver to the hinges, hammered once, and the metal gave easily. There was no sound from within.

"Nash," I warned. "Stand clear."

I pried the pins free, and then with Grandma's help I lowered the door and stepped over it into my son's room. He was half on the bed.

"Nash?"

He didn't move. My voice sounded normal, but a thin tremor of fear swept down my arms and clenched in my stomach, behind the baby. Then Nash opened his eyes and focused.

"Oh shit, Ma."

My dread turned to anger, a wave of relief mixed with rage so powerful my legs buckled and I had to lower myself onto the edge of the mattress. Nash smiled dreamily and turned from me, wedged himself into a gnarled lump of blankets. He dropped instantly into sleep, breathing deeply. I grabbed his ankle, gave his leg a savage jerk.

"What's wrong with you!"

"Wha . . . ?"

I pulled his foot toward me, shook it again.

"Hey Ma, knock it off." His eyes were still shut. "How can there be anything wrong with me if I'm asleep?"

I dropped his damn foot, got up and looked down at him. His long hair was caught against his cheek; he had flung a corner of the bedding over himself and looped his knee around the outside of his comforter. He slept like a child, but his body was a man's, broad-shouldered and strong.

"He's on some kind of drug, I think," I said to Grandma. "Ripped."

His pulse was regular, his breathing even, but his sleep was too deep and sudden. Grandma turned off the light and we stood on the fallen door, just outside his room, looking in. There is a first time to everything, a threshold that's crossed. A chill flooded from the cracked window. Nash gave off the musty animal odor of dirt and dope. Broken things cluttered the floor, his boyhood was smashed among them. His future hung dark above us, and I was swept through with emotion, too weak to stop the rain.

"It'll be all right," I said to Grandma, touching her elbow. She put her hand on my arm for a moment, and for once said nothing.

I tried to put the incident into perspective. Even if Nash had been drunk, stoned, high, it was the first time I'd come face-to-face with it. I told myself that these things happened, that this was a late twentieth-century rite of passage. But at midnight I was still wondering whether to check Nash's breathing for the tenth time, to wake him up and scream at him, or to just give it all up and cry into my pillow. *How could he do this to me, how could he, now?* I was so consumed with resentment for his self-absorption that, at length, the only viable option seemed to be the pint of Cherry Garcia ice cream stashed downstairs in the freezer. I was seriously considering the steps I'd have to take—leaving my cool sheets, walking the hallway in the dark, softening the ice cream in the microwave—when I must have drifted off. Eight or nine hours later, I woke in daylight to a strong and rhythmic dragging sensation, a real contraction, and I knew for certain that my body was at last serious about the business of having a baby.

Before labor happens it seems as if it never will happen. Once it's happening, it seems as if it always has been in progress. Nash's birth had been long and difficult, lightning flashes of pain and then a fog of anesthetic. He was born rear first with his feet tucked around his ears, a position I've since thought of as a metaphor for his life. Sara had convinced me that this baby was head down, however, and I'd immediately assessed Roger's hat size. I remembered it as average or slightly smaller, and had been reassured. I had done my exercises, the hip rolls, angry-cat arches, kegels, and breathing. So if I didn't call Hilda or Sara immediately, it was, I guess, because in spite of my less-than-perfect level of fitness, in spite of my age and the anxiety of the last few weeks, I was confident and calm.

All fear, all worry had left me. The sun fell through my dusty windows in a magic arc, alive with burning motes. The sky was a sweet, cold blue and a slow wind blew fat pads of clouds through the air. I watched twelve red minutes dissolve and re-form on the digital clock beside the bed. Each number was composed from the same set of straight lines; the only difference between one moment and another lay in which were lit, which were dark. I was still for a contraction strong enough to require a little fancy breathing. I didn't want to leave this bed, this room full of my favorite pictures. I didn't want to turn from the square yard of blue out my window, from the small green pillows of embroidered silk I'd bought in Boston's Chinatown, from the books and the shelf of Rosebud Sioux pottery, from Grandma downstairs with her bitter teas and green chili, from Nash, even Nash, from everything comfortable and known.

I called Sara.

"Take a nice warm shower if you want, and relax while Hilda drives out to get you. I'll meet you at Maternity."

I waited dreamily through one more contraction before I dialed the Seelbinders' number. The phone rang five times. Grandma's mean cat came into the room, looked around, and walked back out. If Roger answered, I decided, I would hang up and have the baby at home.

Racine was on the line. His father's academic specialty was the history of the French theater; his mother is a character actress on television. With their marriage as his setting, Racine had developed a comedic touch. He was also gently intelligent, sharp of tone and perception, the most devoted of fathers and an avid adorer of females in any stage of reproduction. In short, he was the ideal man for my situation.

"Hilda's in the middle of class, so I'll be right there."

This was the backup plan, and Racine sounded so pleased that the spin of the wheel had stopped at him that I almost preened, and then the next contraction slammed into me. This one was strange, like hitting a brick wall, though not painful, just entirely immediate. I dropped the phone. Too stunned to remember my breathing patterns, I made strange erratic sounds so thoroughly impressive to Racine that when I picked up the receiver again, calmly, and said, "Excuse me," all that met my voice was a buzz.

I showered with vetiver soap, using Grandma's handrail stall, then put on a kind of caftan, a dress of thick green cotton that had spoken to me in a Women of Large Sizes store, a dress I'd managed to fill out in front but which I figured, or hoped, I'd fit just right by tomorrow. My bag was packed, and I carried it quietly down the stairs, into the living room where Grandma was sitting upright in her rocker of bent willow twig.

She was dozing as old people do, lightly and evenly, without losing poise or composure. Her feet were placed neatly together on the floor, and her hands rested firmly on each smooth armrest. I sat across from her in the vinyl recliner, watching. We got along best when she was unconscious, when I could pretend she was a benign and gentle elder. Her skin was soft as the touch of water, her dress a recently sewn rose-print flowered shift reaching past her knees. Her small head fit precisely into the indentation in the pillow of the headrest. She looked like stopped time itself, quiet in the warm glow of sun, the soundless rush of wind that moved the maple boughs across the road.

Orphaned at twelve, cared for by Catholic nuns, married at seventeen—eloping with a romantic Irish and Coeur d'Alene railroad worker on a honeymoon trip in a boxcar to Tensed, Idaho—Angeline Begay Manion thought she was wild until my mother blazed up and did her one better, until she got me. Grandma had the forceful mind of an autodidact. Somewhere in the chaos of her life she claimed she had bullied and faked her way through night and college correspondence courses. She had taught school, written for tribal newspapers on every subject thinkable, and she had wandered. She had been to Adak, Alaska, and to Philadelphia, Mississippi. I saw the traces of her history upon her sometimes, in certain expressions, in her ability to handle Nash, in the quick way she came out of sleep—never groggy like a regular person but hostile, like a prisoner of war, like a stray dog, immediately on guard.

She opened her eyes, already focused on me, flexed her hands, saw the hospital bag.

"About time," she said.

Good-bye, kind elder. Hello, Angeline.

"The contractions are still more than ten minutes apart, nothing critical. Racine is on his way."

He was here, actually. He had managed the drive that took me over half an hour on the very best of days, in eighteen minutes. He swept into the house without knocking, so quickly it was as though he materialized through the walls. Grandma, annoyed at not having heard his car, not having admitted him, was fully capable of insisting that he go back outside and reenter properly, but I didn't give her the chance.

"I'm in a window of opportunity," I explained, propelling myself past them. I was in the car before the next contraction. Grandma followed me out, pressed a small bag made of the same material as her dress into my hands. Racine slid behind the wheel and the Volvo, which had been idling, started to move. I waved a little wildly as we turned the corner below the house on the other side of a thin grove of trees. She was standing with her arm frozen in the air, a tiny figure in a blur of green leaves.

"Don't get a ticket," I said. "It'll be hours yet."

Racine's thick floss of red hair swirled around his ears and down over the neck of his jacket. I watched his steering hands, blunt-fingered, square. They could belong to a finish carpenter, muscular and careful.

"Should I put on some music, something calm, Chopin?"

"Sure," I said. "I'm doing great."

But then came the first five minutes of the "Raindrop" Prelude and I felt as though we'd entered a foreign movie with a melodramatic sound track. The monotony threw off my breathing, too, and I had to sink low in the seat, deep into my center, eyes closed, to regain a sense of control. I pushed the eject button.

"You're all right, right?"

"It's weird," I mumbled, overcome by another contraction, which didn't stop but blended into still another. I was rocking against my seat belt, gripping the dash.

"Floor it!" I said when I could catch a breath, and he did. The world whipped by—I could tell although I couldn't really see. I was panting against the flowered cedar-smelling bag, held to my forehead. Trees fused, smoked, houses and barns, smears of white, smears of red, fences illegible as the signatures of painters, and then the town, a kaleidoscope of noise and detail, more countryside. Horns blared as Racine ran a red light, and finally, the car halted at the hooded emergency room entrance.

A young man, a young woman, and a wheelchair materialized. The woman tried to remove Grandma's bundle, but I clutched it. "Okay, okay," the nurse said, soothingly. "You just keep hold of that." Once, twice, I had the nearly intolerable urge to push. I was definitely, consumingly, in pain. "Pain" is a forbidden word to advocates of natural childbirth, but what I felt was far from the preferred "discomfort." I grabbed for Racine.

"Don't leave."

He squeezed my hand. At least I was into the deep part right away, no getting used to the water. There was the door to the birthing room . . . Sara, who introduced the anesthesiologist. After weeks of pros and cons, I had finally requested an epidural. Except I was so far along that it was now out of the question.

I tried to joke, to be above things, and to mobilize myself for whatever came next. But I was beaten down, craven, afraid of the next contraction. There was no space between them.

"You're eight centimeters," announced Sara. "We're having this baby. What have you been up to?"

"Research," was all I managed to say.

Then it was the baby in command, someone else's body taking charge, a lot of drama and a lot of noise, things clanking. As if my body became distracted, then interested in what was taking place around and within it, the contractions slowed.

I concentrated on steadying Racine's trembling fingers, returned the strength of his grip.

"I'm an imposition," I apologized.

Racine leaned to put his arm around my shoulders and held me close, supported me. I was swimming in air, dazzling air that hummed and sang with lightning.

"Dim the damn lights!" I cried out. But there were no lights, and when the contraction ceased I saw the darkness gather, numbing but full of threat.

"You're doing great, almost in transition," Sara said. "Listen to me. Vivian. Short births can be hard. Everything is so sudden. Breathe through."

But the wind was knocked out of me, as if I'd been tumbled to the floor of the sea by a foaming breaker. I tried to climb out of it, to swim from it again, but wave upon wave crested, broke, and dashed me onto the hospital bed. I was like a drowning person with but one point of reference: Racine, his strong grip that a part of me focused upon and clasped with hope. His hand, the simple human weight of it, was a mooring attaching me to myself. His presence meant there was an end to this, reminded me the end was worth anything. Then I lost track, lost bearing, washed free. The blackness swallowed me.

"Push now," called Sara.

I did push. I pushed like hell. Like I was getting somewhere.

"That should do it," I heard myself say wearily, falling back.

There was silence. I became mechanical, spurred to effort to avoid the cramp of my own muscles. I took my sustenance from material things, watched the wall clock when I could. Passing time was my friend. This baby moved by centimeters, but sometimes drew back when the push was over. I was the focus of a small cheering squad.

I remembered the cloth bag that Grandma had sent, and made Racine open it. When he did, the odor of sweetgrass drifted around me, the smoke of sage, the scent of the bark of red cedar. For a moment I left the room and was once again on reservation land, in the close, dark containment of the women's sweat lodge, murmuring the right words of prayer. I saw the glowing rocks, heard the sizzle of water thrown from a dipper, the steam so hot my eyelashes burned on my cheeks and my breath seared my hands. I drew strength from the physical peace of being where I was meant to be, next to earth. I took a deep, clean breath and with the next long, endlessly long push, in which I spent everything I was, in which I felt my body stretch impossibly, a bridge between this world and the next, I let go, and my baby slipped into her life.

She was born ruddy, strong, and plump. Sara placed her on my chest, covered her with a fresh hospital towel. I reached for her and she looked straight at me, focused like her great-grandma, alert as a hobo in a train yard.

"Ms. Violet Twostar," I said. "Hello."

*　　　*　　　*

When Nash answered the phone there was genuine excitement in his voice, authentic emotion. Sometimes we're two batteries in a flashlight case, and it is for the unexpected connection that I fend, foot the bills, worry, front, and struggle.

"You're a big brother," I announced. "The party's over."

"I heard from Racine. She's a Virgo, a tight-ass."

"I'll be home as early as they'll let me out."

"How're you feeling?"

"I love you, Nash."

I respond too eagerly, too fiercely, scare him away when he takes the first step. He hesitated just a beat, then forced out in a low voice, "Me too, Mom."

Grandma took the phone.

I hadn't had the nerve to tell her I wanted to name the baby after my mother, her errant daughter—the passage of years since the day she ran away had not softened Grandma's heart. Now there was no avoiding it.

"I'm calling her Violet."

"Violet *Marie,*" Grandma instantly bargained. "After my mother, too."

In our family there is a random gene, a stubbornly reckless streak, improvident and ruthless, that turns up in each generation. Grandma's father, Grandma, my mother, a cousin now brutally dead, and perhaps Nash, all had the tendency to throw off sparks. As I listened to the lock turn in Grandma's voice I examined my daughter. I was clearly not her only parent.

Her hair, pale fine bristles, stood up straight in places. Her fingers were long and tapered, clenched as if already itching to wrap around their first fountain pen. Had she escaped the runaway gene? Had blue blood prevailed? No. She'd just been dozing. She opened her mouth and filled the room with a blast of sound.

There was no doubt she was Roger's daughter, but fins, chrome, and a threatening grille had been added to the BMW. This baby was turbo-injected.

If he was mentioned at all, when Hilda and Racine came to visit, I knew I'd have to be the one to say Roger's name. What the hell.

"Does Roger know?"

Racine had to turn his head to look at Hilda, which made his hesitation obvious. She always let him put the delicate news, the difficult nuance, into words.

"He's been keeping a vigil at our house."

"You told him?"

"I did," Hilda admitted. "I also told him to let *you* decide when you wanted—if you wanted—to make contact. Was that right?" She was confident she had read my wishes to the button.

"Absolutely." I spoke emphatically, but felt a pang of disappointment. If Roger had been unable to endure being absent from this event, if he'd run into the room and thrown himself down at the foot of the bed, well, maybe I wouldn't have kicked him out. But he hadn't.

"It's irrelevant, but how did he react?"

Again the pause, while my friends took stock of each other's perceptions, compared notes wordlessly.

"He's become stoic," Racine allowed at last.

"What does that mean?"

"Well, he is feeling a lot of guilt," Hilda went on, seeing the expression on my face.

"He doesn't feel guilt. At most he feels ethical failure. Very different." I had told Roger months ago to stay away, but I didn't forgive him his obedience.

Late that night I lay in a kind of stupor, listening absently while the new mother in the next bed sales-pitched the Tupperware she sold for a living. She explained the mysteries of the air lock, the patented "burp," the plastic Popsicle-makers, sheet cake pans and Jell-o molds and the "husband-proof seal." Around one in the morning, all restraint gone and completely wakened, I began to get interested. By two-thirty, I was satisfied that my kitchen could now be organized, that this order would somehow infiltrate the rest of my life, that by a simple purchase of these extraordinary compartmentalized plastic tubs and bowls I could prevail over chaos. If only there were an indestructible product that would keep teenagers unspoiled and safe. By four, we were both nodding off cozily, our babies swaddled tight in their pink and blue waffle-weave blankets, hers appropriately in a Plexiglas cart, mine tucked against me. Violet's breath was light and rapid and nearly invisible. Her heart was no longer united to mine.

There was a part of me that wanted to get out of the hospital and a part that dreaded leaving. When I first brought Nash home he cried hour after hour, interrupting his protest only when he was fed or walked through the house at a rapid pace. By the end of the third month, his father, Purvis Twostar, literally ran out of steam. That was when he had decided to become an emissary of goodwill, had traveled with an international treaty organization to Geneva and never come back. Later, he surfaced in Australia for a conference on Aboriginal rights, where he met the sunburned and adoring strawberry blond Stanford groupie who became his second wife and set him up in Sausalito.

Alone with the baby and trying to finish a B.A. in anthropology, I had dropped, like a winter coat, the weight I gained during pregnancy. In the pictures taken of me that year, I look peaked and desperate as a starved cat. Nash, on the other hand, fattened on every cry and thrived, so that by the time Grandma took it upon herself to live with me he was an enormous, energetic, well-contented toddler and Grandma couldn't see what all my fuss had been about. He was the son she had always wanted, and he adored her.

Nash didn't miss Purvis in the least, or so I told myself at first. But it was hard not to revise my opinion when he'd count the days until his summer trip to California, then talk about his father, Betsy, and the ocean, for weeks after he came back. The invitations slowed down when Betsy started having her own babies. Nash said he didn't care, but I knew he felt replaced and abandoned—that, I could relate to—and I resolved not to let it happen now.

He didn't make it easy.

I couldn't stand the hospital another minute but I was tired of asking favors, so I took a cab. Grandma came out alone to meet me. Her eyes lit with ownership the minute she saw Violet, and I surrendered. This was a battle we would fight later, and often.

"Sit down, no, lie down." Grandma pretended to be shocked that I was on my feet, but I wasn't fooled. She just wanted to get me out of the way so she could examine the baby closely. I lowered myself onto the couch, put up my feet, and waited for Nash to descend from his doorless room.

But he did not descend. Grandma frowned.

"I couldn't make him stay."

The first weeks of Violet's life leave a blur except for the celebratory meal Hilda and Racine insisted on fixing at my house the first Saturday I was home. They cooked in the morning, marinated in the afternoon, then, that night, laid out the feast on small trays by the couch so that I could recline, their godchild secure in the bowl of my lap.

Hilda handed me a small plate with a tiny, hot, open-faced *croque madame.* She poured a glass of iced spring water, spread my napkin, then clicked the edge of her glass to Racine's and ate about three of the little sandwiches in quick succession. She was a formidable eater, and always amazed me with the amount she was able to casually put away.

"Violet is a miracle," Hilda said, awash with sentiment. "A pure soul."

"What about original sin?" Grandma looked sternly at me. The First Sacrament loomed between us. Like Pascal, she hedged her bets and was in favor of Baptism. I was on the fence.

"Maybe there's just a touch of the illicit, around the corners of her mouth." Racine stroked the delicate, crocheted fabric of the blanket. "I love baby clothes."

"One of the few men who'll still admit such a thing," said Hilda affectionately. "The trend seems to have shifted, or rather, regressed. This summer my male students have developed broad chests in place of broad minds. I miss those sensitive Young Werthers with their half-grown beards, I pine for those sexy *fleur du mal* glares. *They* were very much involved in their original sin."

"Hilda, of course," noted Racine, "arrived without stain."

"Jewish babies have enough to worry about."

"Especially if they were born in Bratislava in 1943." Racine touched her arm.

"Saint Augustine believed original sin was passed on through the act of procreation," I said. "S-e-x."

Grandma gave me a look of profound disapproval, and I

thought to myself that if any couple ever had the chance to prove Augustine right, it had been Roger and me. After discovering each other, every one of our sins was original, but our passion had changed, and I wondered whether, if we had stayed together, it would have become a comfortable routine. Perhaps by now we'd have been eating popcorn in bed, watching old movies. I was glad I had quit when we were ahead.

I wondered how long-married couples managed, as they say in glossy supermarket-rack magazines, "to keep the spark alive." Hilda and Racine did not resort to therapy, racy lingerie, or, surely, as I'd read somewhere, such ploys as meeting your spouse at the door clad in only Saran Wrap. Maybe they didn't need to even think about this sort of thing. Or did they? Who knew what other people indulged in behind closed doors? Who among our Dartmouth colleagues would have recognized Roger Williams the time he draped ivy over his ears and made like a satyr on a Greek vase?

And yet Hilda did look wholesome as she carried a tray of iced bowls shaped to resemble the leathery skins of avocados. Inside each one a real avocado half reposed, burnished with lime juice and olive oil, stuffed with a mixture of shrimp, crab, rice, and pine nuts. Tears of joy filled my eyes at the first bite.

"My family grew avocados when I was a little girl," Grandma announced. "My grandma and grandpa fought over whether to christen me. Grandpa was Catholic, and wanted me in the Church. Grandma was a healer woman. Grandpa worried that if I wasn't baptized I'd wind up in limbo, where he said I'd just whirl around forever."

"Carnal bliss for all eternity." I couldn't help remembering my fifth-grade definition of limbo. "Just your cup of tea."

"This was punishment?" Racine asked, genuinely confused.

"I was nine years old before the ceremony." Grandma ignored us, deep in her own story. "Then I had to be good all my life." She looked at me, challenging me to deny it, aware that I knew from her friends, from overhearing their gossip, that she'd cut a wide swath.

"She's pious now," I said. "No carnal pleasure whatsoever."

Hilda made an expectant sound and froze with her fork

raised. But Grandma had momentarily lost interest, distracted by the appetizer. To fill the silence, Racine made a lame joke about having been a womanizer in his youth.

I looked incredulous.

"Of course," he said in defense, "sin as a concept has nothing to do with right or wrong. It has to do with obedience. You have to submit to the transcendent authority, God, the Church, community, whatever. Sin is deviance." He smiled to himself as if in reverie, stacked the empty plates onto the tray, and vanished.

"I expect that about now," Hilda said, reclining dreamily and twirling the stem of her glass, "Racine is carving the leg of lamb, finishing off the cream sauce with a bit of mustard, and crisping up the little potato pancakes we brought from home. I could go and help him, but at this stage he rather likes to dominate the kitchen. I'd be in the way."

"I claim the dishes," said Grandma. "I'll wash up later."

And so, since I was exempt from all duty by reason of Violet, we sat comfortably together with our consciences clear while Racine made loud, feverish sounds with pots and pans. From time to time, puffs of smoke or delicious odors wafted toward us.

"I know you must be worried about Nash." Hilda's tone offered comfort, and I took it. I had told her what had happened the night of the class potluck, but she was unimpressed.

"Racine and I had terrible troubles with Mark a few years ago," she had said.

"The ideal Mark? The Christ figure in a Gap shirt?"

Hilda nodded. "Even him. Adolescence seems to get them all. It's most confusing. What Racine did was physical, I remember. He decided that Mark needed something to truly disorient him, other than drugs. So we were looking in the paper one night and noticed there were all kinds of lessons—voice, belly dancing, tap, horse riding, every sort of thing. We settled on parent-child karate. Instead, Mark became interested in tropical fish."

"A boy who raises Neon Tetras instead of snorting coke. If you ever complain about that kid, I'll kill you."

She changed the subject. "Racine says you're writing an article about Columbus. So what is it? Was he or wasn't he Jewish, as Roger insists?"

I tried to mentally reconstruct the bits of arcane evidence I'd come across in the library. Though collected and presented with such care, they seemed arranged more to carry out the private agendas of Columbus's biographers than to prove objectively one theory or another, and I wasn't about to pronounce Roger right about anything.

"I don't know yet. I can tell you that he left Spain the same year Isabella expelled unconverted Jews, but that could have been pure coincidence. In fact, there's no telling he didn't sail past the boat containing Spinoza's grandfather, bound for Amsterdam."

"Don't believe a word of it," Grandma stated. "In the convent where they sent me, those Mexican nuns used an old book to practice our Spanish. Thanks to them, through me, you can speak and read it, Vivian. I had to copy out and translate parts of Columbus's *Lettera Rarissima* so many times I could recite them by heart. Remember Columbus's letter to Prince John's nurse? 'For one woman,' that is, an Indian, 'they give a hundred castellanos.' Oh yes, that man was a dyed-in-the-wool Catholic. No matter how many girls he sold he started out and ended up poor."

I slammed down the tray to shut her up. I hated it when she was rude to my friends. Here Hilda and Racine had fixed this wonderful meal, and all she could do was make anti-Semitic, anti-Catholic, antisocial pronouncements.

"Perhaps he was Italian," Hilda said. "The Russians claim him, you know. The Norwegians, too. Perhaps he never existed at all."

Grandma rolled her eyes the way she always did at Roger when he talked about his poem. No matter how much an expert a person might be, she knew more. She was so sure of herself, so damn smug.

Holding Violet's small, compact weight against me, I decided I would take on the Columbus project with new fervor, and prove her wrong, even if it meant vindicating Roger Williams.

A baby's arrival puts the world into perspective, gives a person a false assurance that everything is somehow settled. All our future complications looked quite simple compared to the long and rickety bridge of pregnancy, labor, birth. I surrendered to an airy confidence that somehow life would take care of itself. The solitary months had been so arduous and still arched so clear in my mind that it seemed any complication life might toss would be minor in comparison.

I did not, of course, count on my own lack of energy, the need for hibernation. I did not count on the next three weeks passing in a blazing mist, as if I were traversing an actual landscape dotted with deep wells of joy in which I tended my new daughter, a month divided by long plains of penitence from which I tried to reclaim my son. I didn't count on Violet waking to her character and asserting her mercurial sensitivities. I didn't count on missing Roger.

6

VIVIAN

On Violet's six weeks' birthday I found myself dialing Roger's familiar number once again. I had convinced myself he was entitled to hear from me, to receive direct news of our child. I persuaded myself that this was a kind of public service on my part, a onetime gratuity. But as the numbers clicked into the phone I felt weak with power, as if what I was doing were dangerous.

It was.

"Yes!"

Ah, consistency. Still the answering machine delivery. I made my voice light, careless.

"Is this the social security office?"

"Vivian."

"That's right. Old six-oh-three, at your command."

"I've wanted to call, so often. How are you? How is *she*?"

"Possessed of your nose," I said. "Missed it?"

"I've missed you."

I swallowed.

"Would you by chance be free this evening?" I proposed on cue. The invitation had during our months together been a private joke, the code to signal a repeat of our first night, when the eight o'clock reservation Roger had made at the faculty club was allowed to lapse, when we never left his house, when we each managed but one square wheat thin spread with Danish Brie for dinner and then abandoned the pretense.

"All night. All week."

"Me and my little girlfriend," I said. "We thought we might drop over for some cheese and crackers."

I drove past the house, slowly but without stopping. Every light downstairs was on and I caught a glimpse of Roger through a window. He was walking into the kitchen carrying what looked like the Sunday *New York Times.* I circled the block and paused at the corner of his street. I called myself every kind of fool—first, for coming at all, and second, for my indecision once I was here. I made a contract with my future. If Roger did not come out of the kitchen I would go home, write him a postcard with my apologies, and get on with my life. I would leave him in the hands of his Book Review and Arts & Leisure and Week in Review and get a grip on my emotions. I would stop at Ben & Jerry's and treat myself to a fattening double chocolate milkshake. I would challenge Grandma to a tournament of silent cribbage, and win for once. I would write the damn Columbus article, then graduate to something less predictable.

The front door was open. Roger was silhouetted, turned in the direction I would come. He waved.

I honked my horn, and stalled.

But really, who could resist this Roger Williams? What did he have to eat, stored in the refrigerator in case I called? Not just Brie. *Danish* Brie. And on the stereo? Not his usual Bach but the vintage Aretha Franklin record I gave him for his birthday, with the volume turned up to my preferred level.

This was a man screaming "compromise."

Violet, on the other hand, was simply screaming, from the moment I unhooked the safety belt around her car seat and brought her into her father's house. With her eyes squeezed shut, her back arched, her mouth wide, she was pure protest, a raging fury, Old Testament in her wrath. I rocked her against my breast, hummed into her ear, even in desperation gently pried open the muscular lid of her right eye so that she could see it was me— familiar food source—at whom she railed. This intrusion of reality, however, only increased her hysteria.

"It's not you," I consoled Roger, who looked stricken. This was clearly not the meeting that he had imagined with the fruit of his loins.

"What, then?" he demanded above Violet's din.

"The lack of motion," I explained. "She likes the car, the motor rumbling underneath. She hates being still. Give me a minute with her. She's overstimulated."

Nash had been a sensitive baby too, reacting with alarm to all unexpected sound or light or touch. The only thing that worked with him had been total sensory deprivation, a quick-fix return to the womb. Now, standing in the brilliantly illuminated foyer of Roger's house, even I felt overwhelmed. The polished blond wood floors reflected the laser beams of the futuristic chandelier. An Azerbaijani rug on the facing white wall throbbed with dark reds and blacks. Aretha demanded respect, and there was the distinct tang of sautéed garlic and onions in the air.

"I'll just be a moment," I shouted, and disappeared into the hall closet. With the door closed, the sounds and smells and eye-popping illumination of Roger's world were muted by the soft brush of good wool. Coats of all kinds hung from expensive wooden hangers, thickly layered and faintly musty. Despite the dark I could sense neatness, order. A gulf of habit separated Roger's existence from my own. Even Tupperware hadn't helped me. There was no closet in my house in which Violet and I could fit, much less stand upright, without disrupting chaos, without tipping balanced stacks of partially read magazines or stumbling over unmatched shoes. Roger knew the precise location of everything he owned. Nothing broken of his was left unfixed overnight. Unwanted gifts he returned for store credit, old items of apparel he bundled and had collected by the Goodwill, and since Roger never purchased anything on impulse, he used whatever he bought.

Violet was calming by degrees, like a kite descending to earth after a strong blow, and I took the opportunity to prepare myself. The enclosed space of the closet was, compared to what awaited me, a relief. Roger had completely gutted his eighteenth-century house, knocked out all the downstairs walls and created an open arena disrupted only by shoulder-high shelves and furniture that was made to be viewed from all sides. An inverted garden of copper pots hung above his island stove, and the color scheme of his upholstery and throw rugs and metal-framed prints was a descending spectrum, dark to light, from front door to back. There were no extraneous objects, no misplaced books. If the current issue of the *American Scholar* or *Daedalus* or *Caliban* lay across the glass coffee table at an odd angle, it was a sure bet that Roger had a new poem or article in print.

"Shh," I murmured to Violet. "Be nice for Daddy. He's not used to crazies." Her face was more relaxed now, but still wary. One false move on my part, one break in the rhythm of the swinging cradle of my arms, and I would pay.

The first time I had come to Roger's house I was struck by the impossibility of concealment. Ridges of beams were still visible in the ceiling, the evidence of a former maze of small rooms full of nooks and retreats, but now even the front windows didn't have curtains. I marveled at the notion that this man had nothing to hide, that his home was as unveiled as the look in his clear blue eyes.

"A coffee?" he had asked that night, and when I accepted he had produced a thick, bitter espresso in a tiny white cup. Afloat in the dark brew was a paper-thin slice of lemon rind. I lost my head.

"Sugar?"

"No, thanks." I was obliged enough.

Roger indicated a low beige-linen couch, and I sat. "Now," he had said, descending to a pillow on the floor at my feet, "tell me all about yourself."

"Uncomfortable" did not begin to define my state of mind that evening. Roger's handsome thin face was within inches of my knees, not at all my best feature. His eyebrows were peaked expectantly, his mouth was ready to smile, his ringless hands brought together in the supplication of prayer. Our eyes had locked in a private frequency, and their communication raced beyond the limits of our words. I set my cup on the end table and slipped down to Roger's latitude.

"Fate," I had murmured. "You have my number."

"I hoped so." Roger smiled, not understanding at all, but for weeks I didn't bother to explain.

In sleep Violet's face assumed a mask of beatific compliance, the appropriate Child to my Madonna—just the impression with which I wanted to hypnotize Roger. So after her last, conceding shudder I waited a good three minutes to let her slumber settle and become fixed; then I tapped gently from the inside of the closet.

"Come in," Roger said automatically.

I inched the door open a crack. "Kill the lights and turn down the stereo," I whispered, then waited while he carried out my orders. When the room was lit only by the liquid numbers that shone like green, subtly changing candle flames from the VCR, the microwave, the answering machine, I entered. My eyes were already adjusted to darkness, so I could watch Roger clearly as we resolved into his view. Gradually the panic left his face and he stared at Violet. I let him take his time, and finally the level of his gaze rose and he looked at me. His eyes were awed, without their usual knowing, and as the glowing numbers all around us in the room altered their shapes, told their tales, I caught the glint of one extra reflection from Roger's cheek.

I stepped closer and Roger's arms drew me in, our baby between us. Violet kicked and I held my breath, but she only redistributed her weight, leaned into her father's chest, like me.

I don't know for how many minutes we stood together like that. Probably not for as long as it seemed to me who accepted every passing second as grace, probably only as long as it took for Roger to become conscious of and pleased with the classic tableau we made. Somehow I sensed the focus of his attention shift from Violet and me back to himself, and at that point I moved out of his embrace.

"She'll sleep now," I said. "She's exhausted. We can lay her on some blankets in the guest room upstairs." It was one of the few areas of the house in which a door could be closed. Roger's adjoining bedroom was another.

He followed me to the second landing, then fiddled with arranging his great-grandmother's quilt into a nest in the center of the unused but impeccably made-up extra bed. Violet was closed as a locked diary, sealed in that newborn version of sleep that forgets the world completely. From experience I knew she would be out for hours.

"We'd better stay up here," I said after we had eased from her side. "In case she wakes."

Roger nodded obediently and we went into his room, turned on the nightstand lamp, and sat next to each other on a bed carved from New England oak trees by one of Roger's famous forest-clearing ancestors.

"I've missed you," Roger repeated. He took my hand and suddenly I felt nervous, though of course this situation was precisely what I had secretly envisioned. I was not the only one of us who was ill at ease.

"How is your Columbus article coming along?" he asked abruptly. The question popped out as if freed after a long imprisonment.

"It turns out to be more provocative than you'd think," I countered. This was pure bravado: there was nothing I could tell Roger on the subject.

"Perhaps I could suggest some titles."

"No, thanks." I liked this superior role I had devised for myself and embellished it, let my imagination loose.

"You know that night I got stuck in the library?" I confided. "I came across this uncataloged cache of discovery memorabilia donated by an alumni family of Columbus nuts."

Roger had been in the process of reclining and now sat up.

"Surely you don't take such things seriously. The perimeters of Columbus's life are well documented. Your reputation will not be made by resort to amateurs, dilettantes."

The operative word here was "amateur."

"I love it when you talk dirty." I stretched out next to him, and closed my eyes.

"Seriously, Vivian." Poor Roger. How he worried about my reputation.

"I must warn you," I said as I reached to unbutton his shirt. The touch of his skin against my fingertips produced an instant physical reaction in my breasts. "There are both hazards and advantages in making love with a new mother. You've heard of the land of milk and honey?"

"The Promised Land?"

"I was thinking more of Noah. The flood? Can you handle it?"

Roger was stumped by my nursing bra, so I helped him release the clasp and he lowered his head to my chest for a long, glorious exploration. At last he came up for air.

"Well?" I repeated my question.

He ran his tongue over his lips, pondered. "Not a bit over-rated," he said. "High-caloric, to be sure, but I think it will catch on. What about the honey?"

"The evening is young." I smiled. "The world is yours."

Roger thought he wanted me to stay the night, but I knew he didn't. The two o'clock feeding would have been a rude surprise, and the four-thirty an outrage. Roger was a man used to routine: to thirty minutes of National Public Radio news before slipping into a silk robe at seven-fifteen, pressing the button of a West German machine that ground coffee beans and then dripped water through them. If he was feeling racy he ate a croissant spread with some chunky British marmalade he had found advertised in *The New Yorker*. The climax was a soapy shave with his father's straight razor, sharpened six strokes against a dark leather strap. It was hard to imagine Violet as part of this scenario. How would Roger ever select the right necktie when blasted by the shrieks with which she greeted the world? How would he take to the dark circles under my eyes, to the hungry rival, greedy and possessive at my breast?

So, after a reasonable postcoital interlude, I decided to make my good-byes. It wasn't easy—Roger smelled so damn good. The bedclothes, as if trained, had remained smooth and comfortable. As I lay, eyes open, waiting for the impulse to rise, dress, collect Violet and go, I pondered for the hundredth time the alternative life of this place. A land of fresh-squeezed orange juice, Nova

Scotia salmon, Sunday crossword puzzles completed while propped against goosedown king-size pillows. Pedicures. Electronic music. And most of all, long stretches of quiet.

As if she read my mind, Violet trumpeted a challenge through the wall. This was a preliminary salvo, the cry of the half-awake that would rouse her to full, indignant consciousness. I rolled from the bed to my knees, crawled to the bundle of my clothes, carried them to the hallway, and closed Roger's door. My left nipple first muffled, then satisfied Violet's protest, and, seated in a straight-backed Shaker chair while she fed, I counted the parallel slats of light—the effect of the streetlamp filtered through the lattice of tiny venetian blinds. Violet sometimes touched her ear, almost caressed it with her hand. It was a gesture of such self-comfort, such easy grace, such unassuming authority, that I knew it came from Roger.

I left, letting the door lock quietly as I released the knob in gradual degrees. Violet didn't wake as I fitted her body into the seat and tucked in a blanket. I didn't switch on the headlights until the cross street, and instead of a radio or cassette, I let my memory replay the music of the hours just past. There is an appropriateness to being alone, outdoors, in the middle of the night—a kind of primal interflow with the landscape. The cricket calls were strictly etched, the marks of sharpened pencils on white paper, as everything in the world awaited the early autumn sun.

I took Violet to bed with me, and somehow I managed another few hours of sleep by tending to her needs without ever becoming completely alert. At six forty-five I thought of Roger's eyes, opening on schedule, searching for something, realizing that the something was me, then figuring out that I had gone. I imagined him momentarily sad, then, by the time he set his coffee machine in motion, approving of my practicality. Last night's arrangement was designed to fit into his life. I meant it to be thoroughly compatible with the slack of his limits. I hoped he'd build up a tolerance for change, want more, not less of us.

I slept for another hour; then at eight I dialed Hilda at home, assuming she'd be running late as usual.

"Ya?" I could tell she was reading.

I made a loud yawning sound.

"Either this is Vivian or a very tired obscene caller," she said. "Did the little one keep you up?"

"No, the big one did."

There was a pause while she sorted this out, and then a stagey gasp. "Not . . . ?"

"He beat down my door. What could I do?"

"Roger came *there*?"

"Well, not exactly. But the mad, impetuous fool *did* answer the phone when I called him. He *did* open the door to his house."

"Shocking!" Faintly in the background I heard Racine's voice ask "What?" and pictured Hilda mouthing some message. Her face would be full of exaggerated gestures—pursed lips and improvised sign language—and he would answer in kind. They had been expecting this reunion, I knew, and had their happily-married doubts about my sanity. Now they could worry all day about me being hurt again.

"Well, how did it go?" Hilda asked, once her pantomime communication with Racine was complete.

"Oh, I'd give it a seventy-seven," I said. "The words weren't much but he was great to dance to."

"What?" Hilda loved American idiom but sometimes missed the punch line. While I was memorizing the *American Bandstand* rating system on TV, she was probably learning to play the violin in Melbourne.

"On a scale of one to ten," I tried again, "I'd give the evening about a twelve."

Racine was suddenly on the line, unable to control his curiosity. "You're out of your mind," he pronounced. "Are you happy?"

Was I? I looked around my room, arched my back, felt the weight of Violet on my shoulder, saw last night's clothes in a heap at my feet.

"Yes," I said. "Today I'm happy."

As the weeks passed I didn't know how long I could manage the orchestration: nurturer and available energetic lover, dutiful researcher, mental health dispenser—but somehow the balance held. For whole days at a time, everything was as it needed to be.

Grandma had Violet to pacify her, and Nash was temporarily daunted by my female ability to reproduce. He'd kept regular hours ever since he'd been confronted with the actuality of Violet. Her physical presence had relieved something in him. I caught him staring at her instead of himself, studying her hands and feet, watching her face for long moments. This, I decided, was the time to strike. Without consulting him, I enrolled us in a family karate class at the local Grotz Academy, figuring that, like Grotz's advertised promise, the family that kicked together would stick together. While I regained my muscle tone we could chop our way to mother-son harmony.

As for Roger, he was relieved to have me back with so little adjustment required of him, and for once I asked for nothing I didn't get for free. I counted my blessings, and there were many. A baby who was healthy. A grandmother who took her role as live-in childcare provider as a divine right. A teenage son who was not noticeably on drugs. A single boyfriend who found me attractive. A job that paid the bills. Even Christopher Columbus, who was turning out to be a regular Chinese puzzle.

"What do you know about Columbus?" I put to Nash one evening as he ate a bean burrito for dinner.

He regarded me cautiously. Was this a test? Had a history teacher from his school called to complain? Was my question a setup for some lecture he didn't want to hear?

"The man or Ohio?" he asked.

"The guy who sailed the ocean blue." I kept my voice neutral, disinterested, but I was genuinely curious about his answer. When you begin to become an expert on anything, you forget what people ordinarily know. You lose track of the starting point.

Nash put down his burrito, a light dawning in his eye. He thought he knew what was coming now: the Indian stuff. Me making him aware of that part of his heritage. Yah-ta-yah-ta-yah-ta. "Give me a break," his expression seemed to say, but because Violet was in my arms he indulged me.

"He thought this was *India.*" Nash rolled his eyes at the sheer stupidity of such an assumption. "That's why he called us 'Indians.'"

Oh, he was being kind to me!

"Anything else?" I was the essence of nonthreatening.

"He found a lot of gold, right? And that made him a hero." He glanced at me, decided something.

"Columbus," he stated categorically in a different, more serious voice, "is the reason we're in this mess."

I sat down at the table. He propped his elbows and pushed his plate aside, fixing me sternly—almost accusatory—in his gaze.

"Mom," he said. "I know you've been working on some article, and I didn't want to sidetrack you or anything, but as long you brought this up, here's the scoop."

In the sudden bite of his response, the pleasure Nash took in expounding on something he had troubled to read about, I recognized myself. He began again, this time listing the things he did *not* believe about Columbus: that the man was Spanish, that he was the only one who had thought the world was round, on and on.

I stopped him. "This is the scoop?"

"Yes, well. What I'm going to say now is off the record."

"My lips are sealed," I assured him, but at full tilt he was as impervious to sarcasm as Grandma.

"Columbus was a slave trader, Mom. My history teacher knows all about it."

He waited. When I didn't fall off my chair, Nash picked up his burrito again and spoke between swallows.

"A lot of kids said 'No way,' but I said I believed it. 'Look at me,' I said. 'I'm an Indian. Columbus would have wanted to make a slave out of *me.*'"

"Not geographically likely," I said. "Lucayans, Arawaks, Tainos, yes. But your teacher's right—from the very first entry in his diary it's clear Columbus couldn't visualize anything but a slave-master relationship between the people he met and Europeans like himself."

"He didn't find enough gold, so he sent back slaves the next time he came over to the United States."

"The Bahamas."

"Right." His outrageous fact verified, Nash was satisfied, but he wasn't finished. "See, to go back to what I said about this mess we're in being Columbus's fault . . ."

"Yes?"

"It's because he came here with an *attitude,* a power attitude, and he imposed it. First on Indians, then on the land. It was like 'I'm it. You're shit,' and that's the way it's been ever since. I think different, see? Anglos aren't 'it.' *We're* not even it. *Human beings* aren't it."

"What is?"

"Nature. We're all part of it together." Nash laced his fingers. "That's why I don't eat meat anymore."

"I hadn't noticed."

"You never notice what I eat. But Grandma has."

He made this statement without obvious malice, but I still flinched.

"Mammals dream," he said. "I won't eat anything that dreams. That's my philosophical position. And too, people are using up the aquifers out west to irrigate grazing pastures to feed cattle so we can eat *steak*!"

"Fine. No hamburger either."

"No steak."

He sounded wistful, but his voice was firm. We nodded at each other, a pact made. There was a pause while Nash searched his memory banks for further data, but he came up blank. End of Columbus file. From the next room Grandma's voice cut through the air.

"He went crazy," she volunteered.

"Hark," I said. "The traditional speaks." I resented her intrusion in my moment with Nash. Couldn't she content herself with paying attention to his diet?

"They brought him back to Spain in iron chains," she continued. "He had a *mistress.*"

The last was said in a tone of scandal, as if Nash's dreaming cows, drought, and untold other environmental catastrophes were a direct result of illicit sex. I did not miss the reference, the pointed finger of her accusation. *I* was a mistress, as evidenced by my late nights.

"Was she lucky enough to have any children by him?" I called back. "Were they the light of her grandmother's life?"

In response I heard only the determined creaks of the rocking chair, and scored major points for myself. Roger as Columbus. Me as Beatriz Peraza. What a casting concept.

*   *   *

It was four-thirty P.M. two days later, after school, before dinner. We had paid our registration fee and had been admitted to the Grotz Academy of Karate. The place was touchingly makeshift, located on the premises of a bankrupt men's clothing store in Claremont, a town south of Hanover. The blue paint was peeling back in flakes, and the shelves were empty. There was a basement mildew smell—the air seemed both chilly and wet.

Nash and I had been placed in a standing formation with shoes off. I was uncomfortable and felt ridiculous, on display to passersby through the plate-glass windows.

"This is our dojo," said Grotz, entering from the dressing room, sweeping his hands to all sides. "I am Phil Grotz. You may call me *Sensei.*"

A short, solid man in a white outfit—everything had a name— he beamed and began to explain The Way of the Empty Hand, as he called it. Over the next fifteen minutes, as I was barraged by unblushingly facile pseudomystical gunk, I felt my resolve wilt. Could I go through with this, even for Nash's sake? I sneaked a look at my son, and had my answer. His lips were parted and his breathing was quick and shallow. Completely hypnotized.

"As for drugs," Grotz said in conclusion, "they block awareness. You won't do them if you want to come near our dojo. Our work is the search for true awareness, and that can only come from intense physical and spiritual training. If you take drugs, you give up control, self-mastery, which is what karate is about. Is that clear?"

Crystal and wonderful, as far as I was concerned. Sixty-five dollars well spent.

Over the next weeks, as I attended Grotz's dojo faithfully, I continued to think that the ersatz philosophy might benefit Nash, but for good measure and to bring us close, I added my own ritual. Before each session we recited a portion of the Navajo Blessing Way that seemed to fit. "Earth's feet become my feet, thereby I go through life. Its legs become my legs, therefore I go through life. Its moving power becomes my moving power . . ." it began. Yet it was still a struggle to endure. Who had time for this? My work sat undone. Roger felt neglected. Grandma glared at the strange-sounding phrases Nash tossed off at odd moments. And on the purely physical level, for me it meant practicing the basic kick until I thought my leg would drop off, plunging my hands in and out of pea gravel to harden their edges, and bouncing in place like a basketball. Even with my specially ordered and expensive combination jogging/nursing bra, I was pushing myself to do all this so soon after labor. I was still heavy, always tired, but if we didn't try this now, I was afraid it might be too late for Nash. The unhinged door to his room had eventually been replaced on his insistence, and it was usually locked from the inside.

Violet gradually, reluctantly, settled into a routine. She rose with a howl just before five A.M., dozed after her breakfast until eight o'clock or so, and then confronted the day with clenched fists and a mistrustful expression. She usually deigned to perch on my chest, supported by a Snugli, while I went about my business, but she hated to be out of physical contact. As if she were more marsupial than mammal, she nestled close, assuming the reverse of the approximate position she had occupied within my body. She had become the kind of baby who took her time, assessed each new step until she understood it, mastered it in her mind. Her approach was not so much tentative as deliberate. Unlike Nash, unlike me, she looked before she leapt, and she then rarely made a mistake.

I was the box seat from which my daughter viewed the world, and because all was new to her, she was content to accept and scrutinize whatever vista I allowed. Some mothers tote their offspring through swirls of color and shape and sound: cacophonous outdoor markets, city streets blaring with honking horns and barking dogs, verdant jungles full of the odor of earth and flower. Their babies must quickly learn to filter out the extraneous, to seek the single thread within the woven tapestry, to create for themselves a passage through the din. To compete. They develop protection, ears both sharp and deaf, eyes at once piercing and blind. By the time they discover their own legs, they're ready to run.

Not Violet. With me she spent each day in the dim and hushed hallways of Baker Library. The spectra she beheld were muted, arranged in horizontal rows of book spines. Each footstep was audible, each voice a whisper. The pace was slow, the air still.

She translated her life one page at a time, sought meaning from the evidence at hand. She came to expect, to depend upon order, and, hungry and curious, she cultivated a wide frequency to catch every variance. In those quiet halls my daughter became so sensitive that when she found herself in a normal context—a grocery store, a restaurant—her systems overloaded and she went off like an alarm, baling a wall of her own creation for protection. With the strictures of my work as her guide, she forged a preference for solitude, for the company of her own undistracted thoughts. While I pursued the secret life of Columbus, Violet adjusted, honed contemplation. In a quiet place she learned to be invisible, and in a noisy place she made the loudest sound.

Sometimes I talked to her, my constant companion, as if she understood my words. "Imagine," I said softly, her ear the microphone to my thoughts, when I uncovered some previously unanticipated fact. "What do you *know*?" I soothed if one obscure source contradicted another in their analysis of my subject's motive or origin. "How about that?" I stage-whispered to keep myself awake when an author, galvanized by minutiae, asserted a minor theory. My voice attracted Violet's attention, and for an instant she and I would become conspirators. Her face would radiate delight, complete accord, and fueled by the flattery of her approval, I would take the extra note, consult the unlikely source.

Of course, the portfolio of articles I had stumbled upon during my long night of early labor was especially meaningful to me. It was the first thing I owed directly to my daughter's influence, her initial, inadvertent gift, and I was determined that it would prove valuable. With more patience than I normally possessed, I sifted through the sludge of iambic, rhymed heraldry, the souvenir programs from small-town tributes, the reproductions of romantic portraiture in which stylized versions of Columbus, usually faintly bilious, squinted toward a shore that only he could see. The Cobb family had assembled over the last two centenary anniversaries of 1492, enough kitsch to paper the Smithsonian, and sheet by sheet I put it behind me. And then, stuck in the back of the portfolio, I found a library memo that read: "For more Cobb cf. Correspondence File, Treasure Room." I figured that as long as I had gone this far, I might as well take the search to the end.

7

ROGER

Beatriz Peraza, Columbus's mistress, was not a woman to annoy. The story goes that when a man questioned her virtue, in retrospect not such an outrageous accusation after all—she had him hanged twice, once indoors and a second time outside. Her subsequent lovers, shadowed by this double jeopardy, presumably kept their criticisms to themselves.

I took a lesson from this tale and avoided whenever possible the temptation to comment upon Vivian's life. We were, I reminded myself in private, different people, both adults, free to organize our respective existences in whatever ways we chose. It was not my province to suggest additions or subtractions from her wardrobe, to mute the colors or to soften the edges of the geometric designs of which she seemed so fond. I had no authority to advise that she be more assertive in her dealings with her grandmother or that she pay more attention to solid scholarship and less to tangents. She marched to her own drummer, and the beat had gotten her this far. She was her own person, and rationally I knew that it was her very idiosyncrasy that attracted me, that made her quite the most intriguing woman I had ever met.

Still, now that we had reestablished our relationship, I found myself devoted to her improvement. I was not Professor Higgins to her Eliza Doolittle—it was not nearly so extreme as that—but there were any number of ways in which I could be helpful, if only she would permit me. Granted, I am no paragon. I can be stuffy, set in my ways, loath to act until every option has been carefully weighed. Vivian joked me away from these solitary tendencies—to my benefit—and I was anxious to return the favor. She added the element of surprise to my daily repertoire, but her life could stand more predictability, my specialty. Between us, the sum of our habits, good or bad, divided by two, could only bring us greater harmony. Television was one arena: I was, at best, PBS. Vivian was network.

If we spent a weekday evening together I would turn off the television set after the *MacNeil/Lehrer Newshour* so that we could visit with each other in peace and plan for our next classes.

"I like *Murphy Brown*," Vivian protested one Monday.

"Better than *me*?" I chided. "Better than the satisfaction of a lecture well executed?"

She grit her teeth, shut her eyes, and I prepared for a storm of retaliation. Vivian would accuse me of trying to dominate, and I would counter by ticking off all the adjustments I had made to accommodate *hers*. Who owed whom a concession, and of what magnitude? Would *Murphy Brown* be her Maginot Line, or would she make her stand over a more substantive issue? In the end, Vivian found a middle road.

"We'll tape it," she announced. "Then watch it *together* on Friday."

I nodded, but not in real victory. I knew she would collect.

The main ongoing bone of contention between us was the overindulgence Vivian showed toward her children. I had promised myself never to bring up, to anyone, the indignity of Nash's theft. I was silent, and cynical. The boy's rehabilitation was a long-term project—if in fact he was redeemable at all as a civilized human being. I even stifled the urge to critique the absurd classes in Oriental self-defense, though, to my mind, not only did the dabblings increase Nash's already considerable self-regard, but the lessons might also render him actually dangerous.

Furthermore, the time Vivian spent in these pursuits was, of necessity, time spent away from me, time I could not help but resent losing. About that, I did complain.

"Life is short and art is long," Vivian had replied in mock solemnity. "That's the philosophy of Sensei Grotz. You can relate to that, Roger."

"Do I take it, then, that you are not altogether a devotee of this Grotz, a man who spends his days as an exterminator?"

" 'Pest consultant.' " Vivian smiled. "He works with local organic farmers, and this is therapy for Nash. I suppose it's harmless enough for me, too, though I'm the worst one in the whole dojo, the least proficient. All I get to do is kick. I've been kicking imaginary opponents for the past month. Grotz says I'm a 'small universe' and that I should try for complete tranquillity in my kick. I told him that was not my usual mode, but I keep watching the others, preparing for the day I am allowed to graduate to a chop."

Still, I was not persuaded. Nash's recalcitrance and rudeness had endured unchecked for too long and had penetrated his very character. No oversimplified Eastern regimen, in fact nothing short of complete psychoanalysis, was likely to alter the egomania with which he approached the world. I kept waiting for some sign from him of repentance, of honesty. Surely, I told myself, the mutilation of my diary, the violation of my private life, however unspoken, must weigh upon what shred of conscience he possessed.

I was apparently wrong—he seemed a stranger to mercy. It was as if I'd done something so terrible, so unforgivable to Nash that he felt justified in taking what revenge he could.

I spent no little time trying to identify the nature of my crime, but finally, I concluded that it was not a complicated question. I *was*—and that was ample enough reason. What's more, I was romantically involved with Vivian. Biological father or not, this was a Sophocles ground zero, a classical triangle, the stuff of high tragedy.

Violet, though, was still a tabula rasa. She was reachable, possibly malleable, and I felt sure she was capable of responding positively to direction if it was delivered clearly and firmly. Genetics counted for something, and she *was* my daughter. On some level she must yearn for order, structure, consistency. I empathized with her confusion and inability to communicate her true desire when Vivian strayed from this regimen.

No wonder Violet spent so much time in hysteria.

"She's testing you," I groaned late at night when Vivian bolted from our bed at the baby's first muffled wail. "Remember that book said a schedule was important even in the first two months?"

"Remember Orestes' nurse?"

I myself had quoted to Vivian Cillissa's passage, "Children's young insides are a law unto themselves."

"Roger, she's just a newborn."

Rat studies, reprints from *Neonate Psychology*, logic itself, held no sway against Vivian's faith in brute maternal instinct.

In her own fashion, she tried to shelter me from discomfort. She asked for very little help, but in return she expected that I would leave all developmental decisions to her. My role was limited to that of an appreciative audience member always willing to clap when Vivian held up a sign that said "Applause" and struck deaf and dumb when I had an opinion contrary to her own. I was encouraged to proclaim a rapport with my daughter as long as it did not translate into a program of action or, as was more often my inclination, inaction. Countless experts agreed: a baby need not dominate the lives of its parents. But let them try to convince Vivian, for whom holy motherhood was sufficient excuse and justification for any excess.

Naturally, under such license, the baby began to evolve into a creature at once foreign and irritating to me. We became mired in adversarial roles, I advocating the golden mean and she demanding baths of rose petals. Out of respect for her inherent intelligence, I refused to speak to Violet in pidgin language, would not insult her with a falsetto voice. The sooner she grasped the conventions of normal conversation, the sooner she would find solace in the light of reason. But, encouraged by a world of indulgence and crooning murmurs, my daughter rebelled against my lonely pressure toward progress. She chose to reside in the land of the lotus-eaters and threatened mayhem if her every passing whim was not instantly met.

It is not surprising, therefore, that when my thoughts were perpetually interrupted, when my beautifully presented meals were left to cool uneaten, when my rest was deprived and my advice unasked for, I felt some resentment. "Violet," I could not help but privately note, had the same root as "violence," and emotional violence was the crime of which I was the hapless victim. Perhaps this child was misnamed. Where were Shelley's *"violet paths of pleasure"*? How did Richard II, in Shakespeare's version, manage to say: "Welcome my Sonne / Who are the *Violets* / That strew the green lap of the New-come Spring?" Was not Athens called the "City of the *Violet* Crown" *after* the Furies had been banished? The *violin* is a soothing instrument. Under Vivian's permissive tutelage, my daughter should be retitled Cymbeline.

The fact was, when given half a chance I proved to be capable. The first time I was granted the honor of changing Violet's environmentally approved biodegradable disposable diaper, I began by reading the instructions printed on the side of the package. Vivian mocked my thoroughness, protesting that the procedure was perfectly obvious, but I had no intention of struggling like one of those bumbling inept males, the slapstick fools of television situation comedies and Hollywood cliché.

I noticed on one occasion that Vivian had to control a mild annoyance when, against all her expectations, Violet responded well to my calm and monotonic mode of address, ceasing abruptly in midcry, her expression poised for further woe, yet listening transfixed as I beseeched her to be tranquil.

"Tears will do you no good," I advised, not unkindly. "We are all sometimes hungry or thirsty, and I can appreciate your frustration: you cannot put a name to your want."

"Roger!" Vivian hovered protectively close to Violet's crib. Of course I knew the child could not comprehend me word for word, but something, if only dignified empathy, if only companionable reassurance, was being communicated. The baby and I locked gazes, and by an act of will I held her suspended between curiosity and her previous ululation. Vivian, however, insisted that our communion was coincidence.

"She's not one of your students," she said. "To her, at this stage, you're just a vague extension of herself."

All the more reason, I thought, to offer an unperturbed harbor. If there was no boundary between me and my daughter, why should I not do the thinking for both of us?

8

VIVIAN

I belong to the lost tribe of mixed bloods, that hodgepodge amalgam of hue and cry that defies easy placement. When the DNA of my various ancestors—Irish and Coeur d'Alene and Spanish and Navajo and God knows what else—combined to form me, the result was not some genteel, undecipherable puree that comes from a Cuisinart. You know what they say on the side of the Bisquick box, under instructions for pancakes? Mix with fork. Leave lumps. That was me.

There are advantages to not being this or that. You have a million stories, one for every occasion, and in a way they're all lies and in another way they're all true. When Indians say to me, "What are you?" I know exactly what they're asking, and answer Coeur d'Alene. I don't add, "Between a quarter and a half," because that's information they don't require, first off—though it may come later if I screw up and they're looking for reasons why. If one of my Dartmouth colleagues wonders, "Where did you study?" I pick the best place, the hardest one to get into, in order to establish that I belong. If a stranger on the street questions where Violet gets her light brown hair and dark skin, I say the Olde Sodde and let them figure it out.

There are times when I control who I'll be, and times when I let other people decide. I'm not all anything, but I'm a little bit of a lot. My roots spread in every direction, and if I water one set of them more often than others, it's because they need it more. To the college I am a painless affirmative action, to Roger I'm presentably exotic, to Nash I'm too conventional, to Grandma I'm too Anglo, to Hilda and Racine I'm the romantic American friend. To Violet, at least for now, I'm perfect. No wonder I enjoy her company.

I've read learned anthropological papers written about people like me. We're called marginal, as if we exist anywhere but on the center of the page. Our territory is the place for asides, for explanatory notes, for editorial notation. We're parked on the bleachers looking into the arena, never the main players, but there are bonuses to peripheral vision. Out beyond the normal bounds, you at least know where you're not. You escape the claustrophobia of belonging, and what you lack in security you gain by realizing—as those insiders never do—that security is an illusion. We're jealous of innocence, I'll admit that, but as the hooks and eyes that connect one core to the other we have our roles to play. "Caught between two worlds," is the way we're often characterized, but I'd put it differently. We are the *catch*.

I could relate to Columbus, stranger to stranger. There he was, no matter what version of his life you believe, pushing and pulling at the city limits of wherever he found himself. An Italian in Iberia. A Jew in Christendom. A *Converso* among the baptized-at-birth. A layman among Franciscans. He spoke all languages with a foreign accent, and his sight was always fixed away from the heartland. He didn't completely fit in, anywhere, and that was his engine. He was propelled by alienation, by trying to forge links, to *be* the link, from one human cluster to the next. It's no wonder he positioned himself in the Atlantic, on the western horizon. He *had* to think global because the whole world was the only context in which he was unambiguously a full member.

As I became more and more immersed in my research, far in excess of anything required for a house-organ puff piece, I justified the time spent away from other things: The more disparate and contradictory the facts I accumulated about Columbus, the more I understood the man, both identified with him and hated the failure of understanding he'd come to in the end. Far from being frustrating—the perpetual complaint of so many scholars who had sifted the loose threads and false leads of his life—Columbus's paradoxes, his impossibilities, attracted me. He couldn't be all he said he was, yet I recognized the fiction that he had constructed and presented, never twice the same. He was a certain kind of man in court, another in the Caribbean; a mercenary, a saint, a scholar, a fanatic, and, of course, a slave trader. The New World's first importer. The paradigm. He affixed a cryptic symbol to one signature and scratched out another with such agony that it seemed to corroborate his contention of recent literacy. His lies added up to truth, but only if viewed at an angle, only if weighed by a fellow liar. He was a nexus of imaginary lives, of stories with but a single foot in fact, and when by accident he was at last truly a part of the greatest, most farfetched tale of all, he didn't know what to make of it. Could he believe himself, after so much deceit? He had stumbled into the unthinkable: A world in which there was no other was a world without bounds. By touching the rock of America, Columbus made Europe forever smaller.

At first I was alone in my enthusiasm but for Violet, who approved of everything except delay in the satisfaction of her needs. Grandma regarded my nightly progress reports with suspicion, as if I had gone over to the other side. "Why can't you study an Indian?" she wanted to know. "A woman Indian?"

Roger, who had built a career on poeticizing history, was no fan of anyone else's revisionism—he thought he owned the patent. Right on his guarded shelves, he had lined up more than enough material with which to conjure—the writings of Las Casas and Díaz, of Columbus's descendants and detractors, Simon Wiesenthal's *Sails of Hope*, Peter Martyr's *De Orbe Novo*, the translated snatches of the Mayan *Chilam Balam*, the body of literary interpretation: Milton, Shakespeare, and his beloved Donne. The last thing Roger wanted was a reinvented past, a new almanac for 1492 that would render his precious iconoclasm obsolete. Though he never said it directly—we were, after all, technically reunited lovers lost in the marvel of each other's very being—I could tell he regarded me as an annoying interloper in his scholarly domain, a bull in his china shop, a dangerous amateur whose every gain would be his loss.

Hilda, on the other hand, worried that I was neglecting, during the precious, fleeting weeks of my faculty fellowship, the work that would gain me tenure. Columbus was a much-plowed field, she counseled at every opportunity. The likelihood of my coming up with something new, much less the required-for-promotion *book*, was slim. I could dally in esoterica once I was an associate professor—God knows that was more than many on the faculty did—but for now I should pad my *curriculum vitae* with evidence for the Committee Advisory to the President—that august make-or-break evaluation body that stood between me and a lifelong paycheck—to justify my elevation to the ranks of the elect. The members were known to be sympathetic to my case—who wanted to fire the only Indian on the faculty and a woman to boot?—but standards couldn't be bent. Of the three official hurdles, my dossier easily cleared "teaching" and soared over "community service." Only "scholarship" remained, and there I needed a fat file of reprints or accepted "forthcomings."

In fact, the only real encouragement I received in my efforts came from a source easily discounted: one Henry Cobb, Dartmouth class of 1950, latest member in the club of discovery-obsessed Cobbs, most recent contributing author to the file of letters I had finally tracked down in the Treasure Room, where rows of green metal cabinets housed the collected opinions of the college's sons: gratitude and recrimination, petition and denial. The Cobbs had a whole drawer to themselves.

I did a quick skim. For seventy-five years a parade of Cobbs had repeated basically the same complaint: Find what we lent you and send it back!

Oddly enough, given the reams of correspondence, I couldn't get a clear idea of what "it" was supposed to be.

A *New York Times* profile appended to Henry Cobb's folder by a thoughtful librarian portrayed the man as a mover and shaker on Wall Street, a trader of bonds temporarily exiled by reverses in the market to a longtime family retreat in the Bahamas. It was not hard to grasp why Columbus might be a project more to his liking than his much-postponed but impending date with the Federal Trade Commission.

In his most recent letter dated only weeks ago, Henry Cobb demanded that a Dartmouth official of the highest rank contact him immediately. Otherwise his alma mater would lose its chance at greatness, its opportunity to be the source of an earthshaking announcement, to become the ultimate repository of "a time bomb that's been ticking for five hundred years and is set to explode."

The Dartmouth alumni directory revealed that Henry Cobb's son Carey, '73, was an investment banker in Boston; Vernon, '76, was an executive vice president of a textile firm in Raleigh, North Carolina; daughter Melinda, '85, was an environmental engineer currently employed in southern California; and Avery, '88, had a Fulbright fellowship in Taipei. None had added so much as a P.S. to the family epistolary harangue. It seemed that Henry, unlike all the Cobbs who had come before him, had failed to pass the family fixation on to an equally zealous son or nephew in the next generation. No wonder he was determined to detonate.

His letter of October 10, 1989, read ominously and tantalizingly: "I insist for the sixth and last time that you locate and return all materials pertinent to Christopher Columbus sent to you in good faith by my father and grandfathers. Unless you comply I will be forced to make knowledge of the original documents in my possession a matter of public record. Only by pooling our resources may we open the past. Have no fear that your assistance will go unrewarded, but don't delay. Time is of the essence." The return address was, "The Bight, Box 18, Rock Sound, Eleuthera, The Bahamas."

I copied the address into my notebook. Had I missed something amid the dreck of the Cobb portfolio? Later, in my office, I couldn't resist: I wrote Cobb a deliberately ambiguous letter of inquiry.

DEAR MR. COBB:

I am Professor Vivian Twostar of Dartmouth College. While doing research for a scholarly article on Christopher Columbus, I came upon your family's lengthy and very provocative correspondence, as well as a collection of memorabilia that had inadvertently been uncataloged. I would be most interested to learn more concerning your theories. I am on deadline—isn't it always the case?—so your quick reply would be appreciated.

With best wishes,

Sincerely,

I expected an answer, though I didn't know how long it took for a letter to reach Eleuthera. I anticipated that Henry Cobb would be relieved to finally catch a fish, even a small one. I would not have been surprised to receive a thick packet of photocopied articles, a ten-page handwritten exegesis, or an anticlimactic pronouncement that Columbus was by nationality Portuguese or West African.

But I could not have predicted what I heard when I answered my office telephone early in December, less than a week after I had posted my note.

"Professor T*w*ostar?" a woman said.

" 'Two' like 'too,' not like 'tw,' " I corrected, pronouncing the two syllables of my name with equal weight.

"Is this the professor speaking?" the woman demanded.

"The same."

"Western Union calling. I have a message for you from a Mr. Henry Cobb of the Bahama Islands. Shall I read it or mail it?"

"Read it," I answered automatically, amazed.

" 'I await your arrival. STOP. Advise flight number and date. STOP. Guesthouse at your disposal for duration of stay. STOP. Bring with you originals of all loaned Cobb family items, including missing page of letter. STOP. You will not be sorry. STOP.' "

I blinked, letting the command sink in.

"I have a money order here as well," the operator continued. "In the sum of one thousand dollars. How do you wish to collect it?"

"A thousand dollars?"

"You can receive the cash at the nearest Western Union office, which would be White River Junction, Vermont. Or I can have it paid into a bank account, though that transaction will take a day. Which do you prefer?"

"I could get to White River." I was stunned.

"It will be available after one P.M.," the woman concluded. "Have a nice day."

For a long beat I simply stared at the receiver. My first impulse was to refuse the cash, to wrap the experience into a funny story to tell Racine, but then as I gazed out my window, I heard the spit of snow against the pane. This was Eleuthera we were talking about. An island in the tropics. A goddamn house at my disposal.

Nash's Christmas vacation started next week. Roger would finish correcting his exams and turn in his grades at about the same time. I calculated: one thousand divided by three. If round-trip tickets cost anywhere near three hundred and fifty dollars we could swing it—Violet could still fly for free. I'd have to endure Cobb for a day or so, and I probably would disappoint him by not being bowled over, but what the hell? He could clearly afford it. Nobody had twisted his arm. And a couple of afternoons' worth of phony nods was a small price to pay for escaping winter in New Hampshire, for providing a quasi-romantic-*cum*-family-vacation.

I had no idea what Cobb wanted with all the Columbus memorabilia, but mine was not to wonder why. I called the travel agent, and then walked across campus to Roger's office. He was seated behind his immaculate desk, his fingers poised above the keyboard of his computer. He looked up expectantly, mildly jolted by this breach of routine. Had he forgotten an appointment with me?

"Ho, ho, ho," I said, locking his door behind me. "Say hello to Santa Claus."

Now that I was going to meet Henry Cobb, I went back to the green file cabinet and examined the earlier Cobb correspondence with greater attention, starting with the present and working my way back in time to where it ended, in 1915. Henry himself had indeed written six angry letters, each more insistent than the previous, to demand return of various unnamed objects, some of which apparently the college once claimed to have lost. It was clear that he regarded these items as having great value and bitterly resented that access to read some of them and to reclaim the rest had been denied his younger children, Melinda and Avery, during their undergraduate years.

Was this joker crazy, or what? The stuff I had was third-rate schmaltz. It occurred to me for the first time that what I found might not be what the Cobbs were looking for.

The college librarian had answered Henry's mail with polite photocopies of standard user regulations: "In order to protect against damage or loss, uncataloged or donated material is available only to authorized personnel, such as faculty and administrators, until such time as it is absorbed into the regular collections of Dartmouth College." What these letters did not specify was the time frame in which such a condition might come to pass, and no wonder. My midnight packet had been lost, and if more was still missing, it would be in the museum's storage room, a huge slush pile repository of legacy and will.

This was getting to be a regular scavenger hunt, but I was hooked, and figured a little poking around was the least I could do for free tickets. The next day, I went to the basement where all objects of dubious worth contributed by alumni were warehoused. The rooms were packed with an assortment of stuff that ranged from the boringly good to the wonderfully awful: suits of armor, New Hampshire botanica carefully pressed between rectangles of glass, souvenirs of the St. Louis World's Fair. There was a lifelike rubber head sitting on a platter, Salomé's John the Baptist, a stage prop. Shields, maps, a kayak, the carefully recorded minutes to a million meetings. There were theater programs for the Ziegfeld Follies, and, in daunting abundance, stacks and boxes of articles and memorabilia pertinent to Dartmouth's own past. Sports trophies. Nineteenth-century commencement addresses. Endless volumes of earnest faculty resolutions now entirely forgotten.

I used two crates of World War I uniforms as steps to reach the remaining Cobb stash, squeezed high in a remote corner, gathering dust. Every shelf was stacked double, an outer and an inner assortment of junk—too much trouble, too hurtful of alumni feelings to reject, yet not worthy of the time it would take to sort, list, and curate. Assignment of worth is the most subjective of measurements, fluid and fickle. Objects and papers that had, to one or another of Dartmouth's sons, been of incalculable worth, the things first saved in case of fire or flood, were to a basement receiving clerk like so many unwelcome bundles of autumn leaves. Yet extraordinary care had been taken with much of what entered. Fresh, carefully typed labels were affixed to cardboard crates. Manila folders guarded precious scraps.

For all of its purported lostness, the Cobb box didn't take long to find when viewed from a new angle. The looking just took ingenuity and a sense of creative filing. Roger, with his innate sense of order, would have been stumped for longer than I. He would have expected a name beginning with "Co" to fall between "Ci" and "Cu," and when it didn't he would have given up. I, however, was not nearly so optimistic. Given my own haphazard system of organization, I assumed I'd be lucky if even the "C" proved useful—I've been known to file correspondence under "L" for "letters," although I always keep my reading neatly alphabetized. I started with the boxes at the beginning of the "C" shelf, and there it was: "Cabb." The original clerk must have had a Boston accent.

I spoke to an assistant curator and was permitted to bring home whatever I wanted.

"Keep it as long as you like," she said as I signed a receipt. She was engaged in the quixotic task of removing potentially rusty metal staples from precious pages, replacing them with plastic clips. "And while you're at it, can I interest you in a fabulous matched set of vintage Coca-Cola bottles?"

When I laughed, she raised her little hooked tool and shook it at me. "Just promise that if you get famous and donate your papers here, you'll take out all the staples yourself."

"If nobody's interested in this stuff, and nobody really wants it, why does the library keep it at all?" I asked Roger as we sat in his livingroom. It had been a long evening of sneezing my way through crumbling newspaper clippings. I seemed to be highly allergic to the disintegrations wrought by time.

"The Vinland Map," he replied, and went back to reworking a line of his poem.

"What do you mean?" I was interrupting his creative muse, but I was entitled. He had barely spoken to me since dinner.

"Yale," he said. "Some years ago a scholar stumbled onto a forgotten document that has since been authenticated as Old Norse. It showed the first mapping of Greenland and the Labrador coast. The man's career was made. There was a whole conference held around him at Berkeley. Since then libraries don't throw anything out, just in case."

To forestall further inquiry, Roger bent low over his desk and turned on his computer screen. Within the tight, bright circle of his Tensor lamp the delicate Yankee bone structure of his face was evident. The curve of his nose, seen in miniature on Violet's face, was elegant and patrician. His nostrils flared in the intensity of his thought. He held his breath, waiting to be inspired, summoning the next line he would type.

"I get a perverse thrill out of watching you think," I whispered.

His fingers curled into his palms, then tightened into fists. Knuckles pressed against his teeth, he leaned to his work, caught his breath, then madly entered a line or two. Blipped it out. Typed in another. I turned back to the box of collected Cobb—more quadricentenary pamphlets, red-white-and-blue banners, and various artists' renditions of Columbus's face. Blond was apparently big in the nineteenth century. Under the script of a play titled simply *Hark!* I came upon a large yellowed envelope labeled "Letters Before 1900."

These actual epistles as opposed to the supporting documents and mishmash made fascinating reading, at least as much from a psychological as from a strictly historical viewpoint. Taken as a group, they constituted a record of obsession, unfolding back more than a hundred and fifty years. Self-importance seemed to be a Cobb genetic trait, the common denominator that bonded one generation to the next. But it was narcissism of a very particular strain: Cobbs regarded themselves as endowed not for who they were but for what they, and only they, claimed to know—or to know about. Cobb upon Cobb, fathers and sons, preached on a single theme, the family secret they were desperate to reveal. There were recurring buzzwords: "Columbus," of course, but also

"Eleuthera," and *"corona."* The farther back from the twentieth century I delved, the more elusive references became, with *"diario"* dangled more and more frequently.

"These guys were monomaniacal," I said to Roger, but when he sucked in air and leaned even farther toward his keyboard, I allowed him to ignore me. God forbid I should lure him from the path to the *mot juste*.

And anyway, there was no lack of Cobbs to keep me company. Henry, my recent pen pal, was just over sixty. I tried to imagine how he and Grandma would get on—this American wheeler dealer who had nothing better to do than rave about his lost legacy, and the woman who even now sat at home, watching the clock, willing me to return. She accepted that Roger was Violet's father, but she refused to acknowledge him as my lover. Paradox was her stock-in-trade, a talent derived from her mission education. In her unshakable universe, there was ample room for Navajo chants and Jesus Christ, for directly competing—even conflicting—truths. It all came down to what she needed to believe at any given instant, and in my particular case that meant something akin to virgin birth.

I thought of Henry's paternal uncle, Harrison Cobb, an erratic correspondent up through the years of the Great Depression. What would this man, who railed in long asides against unions, whiskey, and suffrage with equal fervor, have made of my Irish great-grandparents, part of the very "immigrant rabble" that he so abhorred? "Micks" got the occasional unfavorable mention, sandwiched between diatribes against Jews and Poles. "This fair continent was not intended for such," Harrison had complained. From what I had heard, Pat Manion, Grandma's father-in-law, would have been unimpressed with such arguments. To him any Cobb would by definition have been just another Black and Tan apostate.

Carefully I shook a fragile-looking letter from the yellowed envelope and unfolded the stiff paper. The elegant brown-inked script was initially hard to read, but I could make out a date—November 12, 1876—and a name: Dr. Elijah Cobb, Sr. Veteran of the Civil War, 1st Connecticut Volunteers, wounded at Antietam in 1862. He wrote with bluster and impatience. Why had not

President Asa Dodge Smith replied to his last two letters? What was the unconscionable delay in locating "the packet"? Was the college not interested in treasure, in glory? Had he lost an arm in defense of the Union only to be spurned by his alma mater? With his cooperation the *corona* itself was within the college's grasp, and wouldn't that make upstart Princeton sit up and take notice?

He made no mention of the Little Big Horn, though it must have still been front-page news in that centennial year. By November the word would even have spread to my mother's mother's mother, Sweet Whistle, in her northern Idaho village. How would the story of Custer's defeat be expressed in Coeur d'Alene, and would it be the source of celebration or anxiety? She had left no record of her thoughts, no parallel to Elijah Cobb's cavil, and yet she occupied the same country, lived and died within the shadow of the same events.

Some conscientious librarian had preserved Eleazer Cobb's letters between sheets of waxed paper, but the effort was made because of the antiquity, I suspected, rather than the contents. Eleazer unnecessarily reminded the "Sir" to whom he addressed his six letters, sent each year on Independence Day, that he was named for Dartmouth's founder, Eleazer Wheelock. This Cobb, too, was a soldier, and from the Mexican campaign. His tone was no less strident as he recounted a "pilgrimage" made to "the isle itself," but without success, thanks to the college's "carelessness." He strenuously objected to "Sir's" lack of response and cooperation, "despite my most ardent admonitions." "Sir" must bear full responsibility.

I thought of Porfirio, the single non-Navajo in Grandma's lineage, the first entry on the tree in the center of the ancient Spanish Bible she kept in a woven basket that she swore would absorb all dangerous moisture. I had no idea whether or not Porfirio had been in combat under General Santa Anna, but as a result of Mexico's defeat he had lost his land and his nationality. He was from a family of traders near Ship Rock, the residue, according to legend, of a group who had followed Coronado north from Compostela in search of the Seven Cities of Cibola. Their cattle, pigs, and mules died. Their horses were slaughtered for food, and when they finally reached Cibola—no great city with walls studded in precious stones but a peaceful adobe pueblo—the men were said to have deserted; some settled down to raise squash and pumpkins and beans while others went on to engage in commerce. Was it possible that Porfirio and Eleazer had met across the sights of guns? Not likely, but nevertheless the one life had an impact on the other, a chain of drastic consequence that I, so much later in the march, could regard with mere curiosity.

The earliest Cobb letters were protected by cardboard binders. Within was more paper, brittle with age. It was by now nearly midnight and Roger, satisfied with his progress and my regard for his requirements, stretched to signal his availability. But now I was the one with loose ends to tie.

"I'll be up in a bit," I said, and used Violet as my excuse—my work alone would not have seemed to Roger enough reason for me to make him wait. "I'm going to let her wake naturally, then feed her. That way maybe she'll sleep until six or so."

Roger cocked his head, considered this logic, weighed the immediate pleasure of my body against the anticipated comfort of uninterrupted sleep, then nodded but didn't speak. He didn't want to disturb the baby prematurely. He closed his eyes in pantomime. He was going to sleep too. I got the message. When I came up the stairs, I would step quietly.

As soon as I was alone, I moved to Roger's desk and eased the sheaf beneath his light. The very antiquity of these pages merited them a place among Baker's rarities, and when I finished I would bring them to the attention of the head librarian. The first item was from the college to a Mr. Cobb, and was signed by the second president of the school. It apologized profusely for the grievous loss of something Cobb had sent. Apparently in the construction of Moor's Indian Charity School a "youth of the Mohawk"—naturally an Indian would be blamed—had mislaid a package "of ancient value." The president offered his sincere regrets, but it seemed irretrievably lost, though not destroyed, he felt sure.

There were two letters from an earlier Henry Cobb. The first asked the perpetual family question: Why has my letter gone unanswered? The second, a reply to the Dartmouth president, expressed outrage at the imbecilic loss of a gift whose worth was beyond measure. He had waited half a century. Would that which had been entrusted to the college's care by the late Samuel Cobb never be found?

It was a puzzle all right, and I have to admit that the procession of Cobbs had reignited in me a sense of business unfinished. I was still bothered by that damn block of wood that I had found on the Columbus shelf the night I was trapped in the library. In my imagination, when I thought of it, it had come to stand for utter mystery, for the hazy goal that each of us pursues without knowing what it is we're seeking or whether or not we've ever attained it. I might well have been after the same object as all those Cobbs, but their letters about it weren't much help. If only they weren't so enigmatic, as if they feared to say too much, to tip off some unprivy reader who would claim the prize for herself. What were they—were we—after? And, whatever it was, where was it? I combed my fingers through my hair: too bad that careless Mohawk student wasn't handy so that I could ask him. But he was long gone beyond my reach.

Or was he? I sat up straighter in my chair at the thought. There hadn't been that many Indians around Hanover back in the 1700s—at least I should be able to come up with the guy's name. He was the bane of generations of Cobbs' existences, and so even if I had nothing concrete to take along with me to Eleuthera, even if I proved to be yet another in the line of disappointments and recent setbacks in Henry Cobb's life, I could perhaps at minimum provide him with the m.o. of the kid who had run the family train off its track. It wasn't much to exchange for a thousand dollars, for a honeymoon taken without benefit of marriage, but it was something, and as I arranged the pillows on Roger's couch and made a nest for myself, I composed a research strategy.

Old libraries have wings like attics in houses where families have lived for many generations. My destination the next morning was the Samson Occum repository, named for that jewel of jewels in the college's early crown: its very own American Indian preacher/recruiter/fund-raiser, the first in a procession of salaried aboriginal tokens of which, I had to admit, I was the current model. By all accounts Samson Occum was an intelligent, articulate Christian, albeit of a dusky hue. Eleazer Wheelock, knowing a good thing when he saw it, had dispatched him to Scotland to successfully raise the core of the college's first endowment. His hook, the reason why Edinburgh philanthropists were supposed to shell out for Dartmouth rather than for, say, Harvard or Yale, was that this was an *Indian* school, founded to bring enlightenment to the heathen as well as to the sons of up-country Anglo-Saxons.

And there *were* a few Indians at the beginning—not at the college itself but at the trade school attached to it. They came from throughout New England, and most of them didn't last long. Either they got homesick and left or they caught smallpox and died. I remembered hearing that some of their letters were preserved with Samson Occum's records, and after shifting through a few labeled cabinets and files, I found what I was looking for. Some were collected in makeshift binders, and others—the more extensive correspondences—were packed in individual slipcases. But which one, if any of them, came from *my* Mohawk, the boy who lost Samuel Cobb's treasure?

I have a belief that what you're looking for is never easy to find, never the thing on the very top of the pile or on the bottom, so I started my search in the middle. Violet slept in her stand-up harness and I had the whole afternoon free. I'd browse in one box, read a few paragraphs of self-deprecation—"Doctor Wheelock, my black soul is not worthy . . ."—then push on to the next. The essays, regardless of their author, had in common a theme of abject apology. Their authors were all sorry for who they were, for what they hadn't done right. Nobody was deserving of the kindnesses he had been shown.

Totally brainwashed.

After about an hour I opened a heavy case bearing the name Peter Paul and fished out a stiff page at random.

"I do not beg," it began. "I do not forget."

I blinked, leaned back against the wall to ease the ache in my shoulders. Peter Paul was a troublemaker and I was very glad to meet him.

"Your Lord Jesus Christ is here and I bow to Him as you instruct. But He knows not the path to my mother's longhouse. In her lodge He has no sway. In the north the fires yet burn."

I gave this Peter a lot of credit. Such opinions would not have been welcomed by the Moral Majority of his day. I got to my knees and bent over the box, shifted among its contents: a single hide moccasin, thin and quilled; a worn copybook with various passages from the New Testament reproduced in arduous script; an animal tooth of some kind; a flat leather pouch affixed with rawhide to a lidded and tightly woven basket, gray with age. Inside the case was a small sheaf of papers. The first I drew out was very old and bore a notation in Peter Paul's distinctive script.

" 'The secret things belong unto the Lord our God.'—Deuteronomy, XXIX. 29."

Beneath this he had written: " 'That which hath been is now; and that which is to be hath already been.'—Ecclesiastes, III. 15."

And beneath that, simply: "I take back that which was taken from me. (Signed) Peter Paul, of twenty-two years."

The words made sense to me, even though I didn't know what they meant. I set the basket and the packet on the floor next to me, rested my face in my hands, and was wrapped in a blanket of grief. My fingers were cool, and when I lifted my head I found that tears had mixed with their fine coat of dust. In that quiet room of forgotten lament I mourned Peter Paul and all his brothers and sisters. I envied him the home he had come from and trusted to remain intact. He was a link, the last generation to be born without the foreboding of domination. I didn't romanticize his mother's life in a tribal community. It would have been hard work, often dangerous, terribly uncomfortable. But nevertheless, it completely belonged to her. She had borne a proud son, sent him out of her village to learn new ways. Maybe he never came back. Maybe he was buried at Dartmouth in the little cemetery behind the observatory. But if he had returned home, he would have been changed.

I was born changed, dropped running into the current of events with no rock for bearing. It seemed sometimes as though I had spent my life reacting, a silver sphere in a pinball machine flipped against one brightly lit obstacle after another. For years I gathered speed, slowed down, rolled on, but found no resting place, aimed in no direction by my own will. But that was history. I chose Violet, even if it had been unconscious. This time I had done more than let fate happen to me: I dared it, and I won. It was a step, and others would follow. I would find a purpose to my career beyond the recitation of atrocities in fifty-minute doses. I didn't care what specifically I did with the rest of my life as long as I had some sense of what it entailed in advance, as long as I gave more than I got, as long as I made some difference.

Peter Paul had left me a metaphysical message and it was received loud and clear: make trouble and you stand out. I don't know how long I sat there thinking, resolving, consolidating. It could have been a minute, it could have been an hour. But it was enough.

Inside the packet, the several other pages seemed different, on heavier paper. The ink was faded but from what I could tell, the writing was the product of a different hand. And there was something else inside as well. Another, smaller folder of some kind. Before I had a chance to extract them, however, Violet awoke, startled to find herself upright and alone. Her legs, suspended through canvas openings, kicked furiously and her cries exploded into the silence of the little sterile cell. I had obtained in advance permission to borrow overnight whatever I wanted from this collection, and so without guilt or any real intuition of what was to come, I replaced Peter Paul's quotations, carefully fit the whole case and its basket into my tote, and got out of the library before we were asked to leave.

My afternoon was full of errands: an immunization shot for Violet, a routine visit to Sara's office for me, grocery shopping for Grandma and Nash. I ate supper with them, watched television for an hour, then gave the baby a bath, put her to bed in Grandma's room, took a shower myself. I dressed in the outfit I would wear the next day, and finally, about ten o'clock, I drove to Roger's.

The house was dark but he had left the front door unlocked as promised. He had warned me that he planned an early night. I was not yet tired, so before I joined him upstairs I sat down and gently extracted the leather pouch and basket, whose contents clacked softly as I lifted it. The top was closed with a slender tie that snapped completely at my touch. I opened the mouth, tilted it, and spilled the contents onto Roger's immaculate blotter. A pile of oyster shells lay jumbled before me, blackened and crusted. Peter Paul was a real comedian.

I eased out the papers I hadn't yet seen, and looked at the last one for the identity of their author. To my surprise, the signature penned with a flourish at the conclusion was that of none other than Samuel Cobb himself. I was looking at the root of all the combustion that followed: the very first words from Cobb to college.

Dear Reverend, the letter began.

Into my possession has come a marvelous and astounding Document. Yea, a Document of such Awful Import that I am of Torn Mind. Shall I Destroy or Preserve? Shall I Close my ears or Open my eyes?

The Answer, Gracious Master, must come from You, for it was in Dartmouth's Hallowed Halls that I first met Truth and became forever more her Humble Servant. Was Cassandra wont to Shield her Prescient Gaze? Did Socrates shy from Bitter Truth? Did Aeneas remain in the supple arms of Dido, or did he make for Rome?

It was Fate herself who brought this Burthen to my possession, who Entrusted me with its care. I paid for it with a hundred lives, yet still there are those who Doubt. The Book from which this page is Torn reposes Safe in silk, within a carved Chest. It came to me from an Impeccable Source, from one too desperate for my services and good Graces to lie. The Signature on the Letter is of the same Origin, as are the Shells herein enclosed. They bear Marks both Curious and Familiar, surely the Manufacture of a Human Hand.

I appeal to you, Kind Sir: Come to my Aid. Add to my poor chorus your Esteemed Voice. Surely one as Learned as Yourself can determine the Veracity of these Treasures, or at least will want to Inspect the Whole. Summon me, and I shall bring it.

Even now with the War done and Victory to the Just, I place no faith in the safety of the Messenger to whom I entrust this Packet, and so I send but two pages of the Scrawl. I cannot help think, Kind Sir, that they will be Sufficient to convince you of the Worth of the Whole, and of that which it Portends. I await, therefore, your Wise Instruction.

With Sincere Prayers for your good Health, I remain, your ever-faithful and indebted Student,

SAMUEL MARTIN COBB

I turned back to the case. I couldn't help it, I was as excited as if I had identified some germ, some pirate virus long dormant except for a strain that survived in the tenacious Cobbs. I had read enough mystery novels, seen enough whodunits on television, that I was a sucker for the drama: yellow parchment, unfinished sentences, portended treasure.

The shells were, indeed, decorated on their smooth undersides with odd raised markings. I would save examining those for later. The last thing in the case was a slender folder closed with a small lock that disengaged as I grasped it. I located the two promised pages, so frail I worried that they would disintegrate with much handling. Before doing anything else, I carried them carefully to the ell of Roger's high-tech home office, and carefully laid them—first one, then the other—onto the glass surface of his copying machine. A pressed button, a *whrrr*, the procedure repeated, and into the tray slid two copies. The image, fixed now on standard bond, duplicated in grays and white the withered print, its pattern impressed with even parallels of writing. At first I thought the chirography was unreadable. I stared hard into the curves and cuts, yet no meaning answered. I followed the trails of clustered letters, left to right, left to right, awaiting enlightenment, until at last one spoke to me: "Colón."

I stared, absorbed, my only company the hum of the machine and its green light, blinking to signal "Ready." At last, I allowed my gaze to retrace its path, and this time saw what I had previously missed. The cramped language I beheld was not English. I knew its shape before I found its sense. I had seen this pattern, this particular slant and spacing, almost every day for the past two months. There was a chance. It could be his hand.

Roger was so unused to being awakened by other than the familiar voice of Bob Edwards, host of National Public Radio's *Morning Edition* show, that it took him a moment to regain his equilibrium.

"I will," he said to my insistent shaking, as if assenting to some dreamed invitation.

"Come on, Roger. This is important. This will blow you away."

"It's on the table by the back door," he said in some irritation.

"Roger, snap out of it. You just went to sleep."

"I was *not* asleep," he asserted indignantly, then rolled onto his side and mumbled into the pillow. "Just shut my eyes."

"Well, open them. I've got something to show you that you won't believe."

Roger, at last aware that he was not alone, squinted over his shoulder in my direction. His look was not friendly.

"Trust me. Come back downstairs."

His face contorted into a mask of shock, of betrayal, of petulant regret. He had enough self-control to remain silent, to not voice what he thought of me. He waited for my request to be politely withdrawn, for me to let him be, but finally he relented. Summoning all his patience, he dropped his legs over the side of the mattress until his toes found the rug, then let his weight settle into his feet. I handed him his robe and watched while he put it on, automatically adjusting the collar of his pajamas so that it spread evenly over the shawl.

"What could be the dire emergency?" Roger addressed the universe, not me. "What crisis could not wait until morning?" Then he became momentarily alert. "Not something wrong with the baby?"

I shook my head in reassurance. "You'll see," I promised. "You'll be glad I got you up."

"Want to bet your life on it?" Roger asked with a steely, unforgiving look, but found his slippers and followed me down the stairs into the light.

On the kitchen table, I had arranged a display of everything except the shells. Those would wait. The copies of the two documents were set out, framed by reference books opened to samples of Columbus's signature and script. I made no further explanations, but watched Roger's face, followed his eyes as they at first moved slowly, began to compare, then darted faster from one thing to the next.

"What are these?" he asked finally. "Where did you get them?"

"They're what all the Cobbs have been fuming about for two hundred years."

"They're only copies."

I had anticipated this objection, and opened a new manila

folder to reveal the originals. Roger stood very still, licked his lips, gently rubbed the tips of his fingers together.

"If these are genuine . . ."

"They are," I said. "I feel it."

Roger turned to me. His countenance spoke neither question nor denial. It was that rarest of all visages in a late twentieth-century agnostic intellectual male: pure awe.

I moved to stand by his side, took his hand. Together we stood in front of his table, like supplicants at an altar, like bride and groom awaiting blessing.

DIARY?

~~took~~ me by the arm in the most ~~amorous~~ way   "friendly", PLEASE!
and brought me to his own house where he
had a (plat form) and chairs set higher and
apart from the rest of the ~~assembly~~ ~~court~~ } ← He took
the Crown
                more a dais

Knowing at this moment that my men depended
upon him for their lives, I made certain
to bind this king to me in fellowship ~~under~~
the eyes of Our Lord, who has shown ~~His~~   in the gaze of
goodness. ~~From~~ my own   ?
and bloodstones. ~~Also~~ a fine-woven cape and   agates
~~tied up~~ shoes. On Guacanagari's head I placed   boots? laced
a silver ring of the ~~type~~ he had
admired on the hand of a sailor.
a marvel   ? (Grandma   ↑
              can't read this part)   Someone did
                                                  her homework!

I have described to your ~~Highness~~. By God's
Grace you have forgiven.

Vivian — This is very close to Las Casas.... Too close?!

Part of a letter?

one bearded man of the colony bound by rope, ~~lifeless~~ dead,
and the GRASSY? graves of others, I write to you
the eternal God, Our Lord, who gives (grants?) those ∧ who
walk in His way peace and mercy.   men

                    ↳ FACT: we know This from Morison!
At the counsel of our priest, I considered ordering the
execution of the cacique. But before deciding either
in favor or against, it was shown (by signs?) to
me that Guacanagari ~~requested~~ my presence, in order
to explain the calamity. ← "begged" is more Like it!
                    ↑
        makes it sound like
        the murder was an Act of God!
In his burnt hut the king   signs of extreme° pity   what?
and by weeping his sorrow. Guacanagari caused a
basket to be dredged (pulled on a line) from the sea
and I am convinced from signs ? ?   entrusted
these oysters, which he further indicated that his
courtiers would steam open, then boil, keeping the
juices for flavor, to make a thin soup flavored
with herbs. ↖ EARLY VERSION of chowder ?!

              Here - what - can you make anything of this?
broad leaf. Sir, my son, you can see for yourself the
message ⟨written in pearl.⟩ I understand the way
back to the Crown but I chose not to follow, and
the gift ? ↳ broken finger of land between everything
and nothing ↳ I read: " the brother redeem
              I could not embrace"
        Given in the settlement of Isabela on the
twenty-eighth of January in the year fourteen hundred and
ninety-two.
                    COULD IT BE ? → COLÓN

Vivian —try er
Don y try:
poetry: —
RW

9

VIVIAN

Columbus wouldn't leave me alone. Less than a week later, Roger and I awoke at six forty-five A.M. to the coaxing of the now-familiar radio voice of Bob Edwards.

"How does the National Geographic Society justify spending millions of dollars on an expedition to the Caribbean? Does it really matter where Christopher Columbus landed?"

Bob was being his usual provocative self, baiting the expert into betraying enthusiasm. His tone, full of gravelly insouciance, invited a horrified response.

"National Geographic is after the *truth,*" Bob's guest interjected, his speech strained and high-pitched in indignation. "Our members expect answers and our job is to provide them. As the society's information officer I am privileged to convey the results of years' worth of research. Happily, in this case, we have a definitive answer: Samana Cay. There now remains absolutely no doubt that this was the site of the Navigator's first Western Hemisphere landfall."

Bob, the spirit of a skeptical America, was unpersuaded. "What about Watlings Island—San Salvador?"

"*That* is a hard belief to eradicate! But we've used computer simulation."

I jabbed Roger with my elbow, and reached across him to turn up the volume. Whatever he had been about to say was squelched by my look, by the jerk of my head toward the clock radio.

"Admittedly, there are problems, minor inconsistencies," the information officer conceded. His public relations role was to be balanced, fair, but with the full weight of the society behind him, he was also confident he was right. "I think you will agree that the Las Casas version of Columbus's journal is the only reliable source we have, that we will *ever* have. Unless someone knows something that the National Geographic does not!" *Fat chance,* his inflection implied.

As the show's theme music came up I stared at Roger. His face was white, grim, and his mind was closer to home.

"They didn't even mention my poem."

Was it jealousy I heard? Resentment? Would Roger never get over his mention in the *People* forecasts?

"Aren't you forgetting what we've just found?" I demanded.

"My conception bears discussion too."

His competitive myopia never ceased to astound me. No matter what the category, no matter how obscure the contest, Roger had to be the superlative, had to win or lose the most.

Violet, roused further into consciousness by the sound of our conversation, began to cry, demanding that all attention be directed to herself.

"Your conception calls," I said in exasperation, pushing back the quilts and picking up the baby.

Authentication. Roger was correct. In the world of scholarship, nothing is valid unless an expert says so, and before I confronted Henry Cobb, I wanted answers of my own. Was I in possession of clever, terribly old fakes, or could the impossible be true and the pages be the real thing?

Whenever I was overtaken by this thought, which seemed to be hourly, I experienced a pang that could only be described as pure *want.* The most tantalizing feature about those two pages was not even that they might have been written by Columbus himself, but that there was no record of their contents in any of the books I consulted. If they were genuine, then they were, as far as scholarship went, absolutely *new*. And if they had survived, perhaps there was more. I couldn't forget a phrase from one of Henry Cobb's letters to Dartmouth: "only by pooling our resources . . ." Every word Columbus wrote, every thought he recorded, had enduring importance to Indians—either as a record of our world as it had existed before contact, or as evidence we could use to seek overdue justice.

Curiously, I got little help from Roger, so I had to start at the beginning. What did I know about parchment, the composition of fifteenth-century ink, or even about handwriting analysis? For safekeeping I had placed the documents in my Tupperware sheet cake carrier and burped every breath of air from the interior. I sat watching the red plastic rectangle as if intensity alone could solve the riddle of what it contained. I had no idea whom to consult. I searched the room for a clue, a direction, an inspiration—and there it was, within my reach: the Yellow Pages.

The Hanover, New Hampshire, region is sparsely populated. Its telephone book is not thick enough to elevate a small child to the dinner table, but it did have a category called "Maps—Antique" squeezed between "Maple Sugar & Syrup" and "Marble—Natural." There was a single entry: The World Is Round, located on the second floor above my hangout, the Ben & Jerry's ice cream store on Main Street. I dialed the number, and a man answered on the second ring.

"Can you tell me how I could ascertain the age of some old handwritten papers," I asked, trying to sound knowledgeable.

"How old do you think they are? Who wrote them?"

"Five hundred years?" I suggested. "And they are possibly by Christopher Columbus."

"Oh." I could tell from the man's pause that I had lost him. "Been hearing a lot about the anniversary of the discovery, have you?"

I didn't appreciate his patronizing tone. I could have been anybody, as far as he knew. How dare he jump to conclusions.

"As a matter of fact, I have." I was haughty, formal. "I'm a

Dartmouth professor and I've come across a rather *interesting* fragment." I stressed the password of all academic investigation. One didn't spend one's life in the library tracking down arcana because it was compelling or profitable or even bizarre. No, the facts had to be *interesting*, which implied both a superiority and an air of some indifference. "I'm so smart that my life doesn't depend on this, buster, amazing as it is," was the subtext of the message.

"Ah," he said. "I see."

"Yes," I encouraged. "So . . . ?"

"Well, of course the ink could be carbon-dated. There are more precise radioactive methods, but that should give you a general ballpark. It would be a start."

"Is that something that can happen around here?"

"No, but Boston, yes. Perhaps the Peabody at Harvard. It's an expensive procedure."

"How much?"

"Depending on the size of the fragment, the condition, I should say, roughly, seven fifty?"

There went the plane fare. But wait! I remembered the existence of a faculty development fund, available to be tapped at short notice. It meant a proposal, an application to a collegewide committee. But how could they refuse?

"Where do I call?" I asked the man, and, after the sound of many small pages being turned, one by one, he gave me a contact.

The Development Committee met, as luck would have it, a week later, and my one-page petition was on their docket. I had debated how much to say, what to reveal. I didn't want to make promises I couldn't keep, and I worried that if I claimed to have a holograph of Columbus's writing, I'd be laughed out of the oak-paneled conference room. I couldn't afford a misstep. Roger had urged brevity laced with vagueness, a quality at which he personally excelled, and I took his advice.

The committee's three arbiters could have been appointed because of their propensity for internal disagreement about virtually any topic. One fancily named professor was more self-impressed than the next, and each was accustomed to being paid court within the smaller sphere of a department, used to having a hush fall over an assembly whenever he or she entered the room. Now, clustered at one end of a long wooden table, they constituted—within the universe that was Dartmouth College—an almost cosmic revolving pecking order, an array of supernovas waiting to happen.

My case was third on the afternoon's agenda.

The committee chair, James O'Brien, the portly Esther Hadley Holcomb Professor of Human Biology, was a man recently renowned for having put aside tobacco. Two years ago he had tamped his mahogany pipe for the last time, made his declaration of abstinence at a full faculty meeting, and been applauded. With much philosophical musing and discussion of revitalizing internal organs, he had weaned himself from the "evil weed"—at which reference he had managed to nod ceremonially at me, as representative of the Western Hemisphere societies that first cultivated the scourge—but he had not yet managed to divest himself of the need to grasp something hard between his teeth.

Now, as I watched him open the top folder, he sucked air in little, audible gasps through the empty chambers of a carved meerschaum; I missed my fractured plastic Winston. When he finished the page he looked carefully on the reverse side for any further evidence, then blew an imaginary puff of smoke through the bowl. Something clearly bothered him. He raised his eyes above the level of his half-glasses, regarded the first candidate—a film studies instructor who wanted to attend a conference in Iowa—and read the request aloud.

"Correct me if I'm wrong," Humanitarian Biology, feigning confusion, queried the artistic-looking young man in a bomber jacket and wooden clogs, "but you have already attended one out-of-town meeting this school year."

"Yes, but—" the specialist in the lighting of Busby Berkeley musicals began.

"If we approve this grant, worthy as it *surely* is," purred the Abraham Stein Professor of Belles Lettres ominously, "we open the door." Signaling a forecast of distress, she wrung her hands gently, as if applying cold cream. Though the most senior of the women faculty, her hair was cut in the severe style of a little girl's first trip to the barber. Scorn of fashion was one of Belles Lettres' trademarks, and I anticipated no sisterly support when my turn came. I was dressed to the nines in a blue linen suit with a short tight skirt. I tugged it down my thighs and flipped the edges of my favorite scarf under the lapels.

"How important *is* this conference?" smiled the Lawson McGill Pike, Sr., Professor of Music and Art. His long, sad face was all sympathy, ready to champion any underdog cause, but his pale eyes held no promise of victory. He knew how it felt to lose, to be regularly outvoted.

"It is *crucial*," the instructor insisted. "It represents the chance to liaise with lighting scholars from all over the world. There's going to be a special festival of Minnelli outtakes. My students will benefit enormously from what I will carry back." The young man lowered his eyes, awed at having mentioned the magic word "students," the official, precipitating cause for all that transpired.

"No doubt true," nodded Humanitarian Biology. He smoothed his hair, combed like a fringed curtain on his domed forehead. "But we can't risk the precedent of underwriting two meetings in a single academic year."

"I'm sorry," condoled Music and Art.

"Perhaps they will publish the proceedings," suggested Belles Lettres, who had once famously edited a Modern Language Association journal.

The disappointed instructor made a show of donning his black gloves, of slowly, dramatically zipping his jacket, of sighing deeply, but the committee's attention had moved on. Already Music and Art was summarizing the next request, this one submitted in discreet absentia by Roger himself. There had been no avoiding the coincidence of our making petitions at the same session, but Roger had been philosophical.

"Yours looks ahead, mine behind," he had said, then added, "Apples and oranges."

Music and Art always dragged at least one syllable in the key word of each sentence, as if this practice alone bestowed intellectual ballast.

"What we have here is a simple matter of reim*burse*ment." His tone was defensive, prepared for the unjust judgment that clearly lay in store. "Professor *Wil*liams . . . in the noble spirit of enlightened *ped*agogy . . . hosted his "Flowers in Donne" class in his own home, serving a menu culled from his reading of the Meta*phys*icals. The bill comes to forty-eight dollars and twelve cents, and he would like us to assume the *cost*."

Humanitarian Biology was not comfortable with this idea—in fact, it caused him to shift meaningfully in his chair—but Belles Lettres was first into the fray.

"How large is this class?" she demanded.

Music and Art scanned the page. "It is a seminar of six *soph*omores," he confessed.

"But that comes to more than eight dollars per head!" calculated Belles Lettres, the human adding machine. "What did he cook, lobster thermidor?"

"Prime rib?" Humanitarian Biology was outraged.

"No, *no*," defended Music and Art. "Let's see, it was the flying hart. *Ven*ison."

"Venison!" exclaimed Belles Lettres and Humanitarian Biology in rare concert.

"*Wine*," continued Music and Art.

"Wine!" his colleagues harmonized.

Music and Art laid down the paper in defeat, but he made one final effort. "People did drink wine in the Renais*sance*," he said with the superiority of one who, by the nature of his field, knew about such things and how to pronounce them in French.

"Were these some rare breed of sophomore who were twenty-one years old?" asked Humanitarian Biology. "Or are we being asked to subsidize the shattering of the laws of the state of New Hampshire?"

"*I* should have an eight-dollar meal," shuddered Belles Lettres, who seemed ready to reveal a diet of bread and water.

Reimbursement righteously denied, they turned to me, the smiles of the just playing on their faces.

"Why, Professor Twostar," said Belles Lettres. "I thought you were on leave. I thought you had previously been granted a faculty fellowship for your research."

I discarded the tactic I had planned to adopt. If I told them I wanted to go to the Caribbean to investigate an unlikely lead, they might have lost consciousness. Here they would be in cold, snowy New England, while I, their junior . . . No, that would never work, so I played it a different way.

"Technically, it's not entirely for me," I said. "It's a long story, outlined in the materials I submitted. But to be succinct, there's a very wealthy alumnus who contacted me about a major donation to the college. First he wants to see some documents that need authentication. That's what the money is for: proof."

I didn't give them time to react.

"He mentioned the possibility of a building. Maybe . . ." I let their imaginations roam in the silence, and when each of their expressions registered that this hypothetical gift had been individually spent, I continued. "I think he would be receptive to a personal visit." I didn't mention where he lived.

"You want to articulate with him on this matter?" Humanitarian Biology clarified.

I nodded. "He's paying virtually all of the travel costs. He wired me a thousand dollars."

That got their attention.

"Just for a *visit*?" Music and Art was in the bag.

"I suppose we could look upon it as a kind of investment. For the college," pondered Belle Lettres.

"I am inclined," decided Humanitarian Biology, "to overlook the unorthodox nature of this particular request."

Anchors aweigh.

To keep my excitement at bay, I made lists. First the easy things: the clothes to take, Nash's and Violet's birth certificates, my passport.

Cobb had written a letter with the telephone number at his club—he refused to have one at his house—and a date and time for me to call for any last-minute instructions or special requests. When he was summoned from the bar by the manager, his tone was coaxing, practiced in technique, oiled with a salesman's sincerity and solicitation. He had a low voice, a beautifully cultivated voice through which there washed small bits of gravel.

"Bring everything you found," he repeated twice. "In all honesty, I don't even know what I'm looking for. I just want to close the chapter."

Chapter Eleven, I thought, as in illegal trading and phony securities. Roger had taken time away from his own work in order to accumulate an extensive clipping file of the various shady operations of Cobb's businesses. Stories dating back to 1986 mentioned high-yield bonds, possibly indexing. Takeovers. Troubled companies and "fallen angels." So far, no charges had stuck on Cobb, who in any case remained steadfastly out of the country. *Mene, Mene, Tekel, Parsin.* Did he see the writing on the wall?

"I'm not going to vote for the guy for president," I had told Roger. "Why are you so determined to turn me against him? On the one hand, he's nothing to me but a free vacation and, if he's lucky, a footnote in the alumni magazine. On the other, what if he has more pages like the ones I found?"

"Highly unlikely," Roger sniffed. He had gathered himself since the night I showed him the photocopies. By morning, he was skeptical, by noon full of scoffing jokes, and by the end of the next day he had become peculiarly antagonistic to the possible existence of unknown Columbus materials, as though displeased that anything could come to light without his being the one to initiate the event. I told myself that he couldn't comprehend what finding the documents would mean to the Indian world. For him, they were just more history that I should already have returned to the library. I didn't try to explain. We were on different quests and I feigned dispassion.

"I simply want you to be prepared," Roger had said. "I know his type. He doesn't give tickets away for nothing."

"It's quid pro quo. He gets what he wants and I get what I want. Where's the problem?"

"You only know what he says he wants. You don't know what he wants."

"I know what he's going to get, and that's not an inch more than I want to give. I'm not even going to take the actual pages, just copies of the translations that Grandma made and we corrected. I'll play the negotiations by ear. Who knows? Cobb may really have more. I don't want to scare him off and go public with this discovery until I know."

Roger underestimated my ability to see through people, to handle myself. You didn't survive for forty years as an Indian woman without a sixth sense for bullshit. Besides, this was the new me talking, the charter of her own course.

And now, as I made small talk with Henry Cobb, I listened to his description of the extraordinary view from the club bar, and parried his questions about what Cobb material I had unearthed. I had complete confidence.

"Surely there must be some little personal thing I can bring down," I interrupted Cobb. "I hate to show up at a place empty-handed, especially when I'm a guest."

There was a pause—was it contemplation or annoyance, did he think I was ingenuous or as crafty with indirection as he?—and then he took the hook.

"I trust your hands won't be empty. But yes, perhaps a *Wall Street Journal*," he suggested. "Even at the club it arrives a day late."

As an anthropologist I had learned one universal law of culture contact: a kind of reciprocal obligation for decency went into effect once hospitality or kindness was accepted. The trick was to be the first one out of the gate in this exchange. The Dow Jones averages were an inexpensive ticket to fair practice. Hell, I'd deliver the newspaper. I'd bring him two copies.

The next names on my agenda were Hilda and Racine, and they turned out to be a piece of cake. In the rush of things to do, I prevailed upon Racine to take the original pages to Boston for dating. He, of course, was intrigued with the whole business. Watching him stand there by my kitchen table, I could tell that he loved to even touch the old paper, to let his eyes trace ink laid down so long ago.

"And then there are these," I said, pushing across the Tupperware pie server, stuffed with cotton, that contained the oyster halves. "Maybe you can make some sense of them. Put them in their proper medieval context."

He took out one shell, turned it over, took off his glasses to peer closely.

"I agree with you," he said at last, nodding. "These lines of mother-of-pearl cannot possibly be pure chance. They're too uniform, too similar from one shell to another."

"I've got an idea of how they got there," I said, rather proud of myself.

I told Racine that I had spent an interesting afternoon with the research librarian gathering books on conchology and malacology, tips pertaining to bivalves. I found that it was possible to produce designs on the inner shells of live oysters by irritating their linings—sand laid down with a needle like a tattoo was one way, and then there was the method that the Chinese developed in the thirteenth century. They cultivated beads in freshwater mussels by inserting small tin outlines of Buddha between the core and the mantle, then left the mussels to dangle in bamboo cages underwater for a year. After that, the tiny, nacreous, raised Buddhas were sawed out. Marco Polo might easily have brought back news of this technique. Something of the sort could have been accomplished by implants of gold leaf, the only metal the Lucayans were known to use. A message could have been inserted into the live mouths of oysters for safekeeping, but if that was the case, its language or code stumped me.

"Fascinating concept." Racine continued his examination, then suddenly looked up with an idea. "May I have a piece of paper?"

"You think it might be writing? If so, it certainly isn't shorthand Spanish or any other language I know."

I watched as he copied the marks from one shell.

"Greek to me," I conceded.

"Not Greek," he said. "But possibly Hebrew."

"You're kidding. How could it be Hebrew?"

How indeed. Roger was of the school that was quite certain Columbus sprang from Sephardic roots. I stared at the cryptic designs, now written in blue with a Bic pen on a piece of Native American Studies stationery. Then I had a thought. Perhaps this was the work of the first voyage's official translator, Luis de Torres. He knew Aramaic, also Hebrew, and was one of those left behind at La Navidad in 1492 when Columbus sailed back to Spain. I thought of the crown whose mention Grandma had laboriously puzzled out and—I'll admit it—visions of lost treasure flooded my imagination. Could these be directions of some kind? Was this what all the Cobbs were so hot to retrieve?

Get a grip, I told myself. If these were words, they were probably just names or cabala or the fifteenth-century equivalent of "Have a nice day."

"Let me take them to a rabbi I know," Racine said. "Naomi's a Talmudic scholar. Let's see what she can make of them."

He made to get up from the table, but I touched his arm.

"One thing," I said, firmly in the spell of my new resolve to play all games close to the chest. "Let this be just between us for now. If you find out anything, let me be the one to tell Roger."

Racine looked confused. "How come?" his expression asked.

"I don't want to get his hopes up and see him disappointed," I continued, providing a scenario that Racine, the most considerate man I had ever met, could not only accept but think well of me for anticipating. Caginess, I was learning fast, had no end of rewards.

Hilda and Racine were so taken with the idea of our trip that they decided to rendezvous with us in Eleuthera over the holidays.

"Like a double date." Hilda was delighted with the idea. "Count us in."

It was that simple. She and Racine had visited Eleuthera together on vacation some years before, and during this break between academic terms they were at loose ends. Their children, Mark and Rachel, had decided between themselves that the combination of materialism and the iconography of a religion not their own was to be avoided, and so had made their own arrangements. He had a job as a cook with a whale-tracking expedition in Baja California, and she had accepted an invitation to visit her grandparents in New York for two weeks.

"How wonderful to travel with friends," Racine had exclaimed when the plans were finalized. "Otherwise we would be all alone."

I didn't laugh because I understood what he meant. He and Hilda were such a matched set that they sometimes seemed to look out upon the world with four eyes and thus see both sides of any issue. There was an unwritten rule on campus that they could never serve simultaneously on the same faculty committee—their votes invariably canceled each other out, and between them they tended to know too much.

With any luck, by the time they flew to the Bahamas, a few days after us, Racine would have proof that the pages were as old as I thought they were. He would also try to bring the translation of the shells.

"The originals stay here," I reminded him. "The climate would be hard on the paper. Once you get back from Boston, put them back in the Tupperware and stick everything in the freezer."

I anticipated that Nash would oppose a trip to Eleuthera—he rarely leapt at any idea that came from me anymore—so I devised an ambush I hoped he would find irresistible: I told him he couldn't go.

"Why *not*?" he demanded, unfairly deprived. He had come home late for dinner—he and his anti-fur gang were engaged in a philosophical debate on the pros and cons of frog dissection in high school, and this required lengthy meetings and endless midnight phone calls.

"It's *work*, Nash, not pleasure. The only reason I'm bringing Violet is that I have no choice. Roger and I are going down there to see if this Henry Cobb person actually has more old pages like the ones I found in the library. You'd be bored to death."

He tried to look serious, self-sacrificing. We both pretended that Eleuthera was not a tropical vacationland loaded with sandy beaches, palm trees, and warm weather in December.

"I could help you, Mom," he offered generously. "I could scope out Cobb for you. I read about him in the *Valley News*—he's clear-cutting old-growth redwood forests in California to pay off his debts. A real scumbag."

I looked dubious, so Nash became shameless.

"I could baby-sit, then, while you guys have your meetings."

"That wouldn't be fair to you," I protested. "I can't imagine you want to spend your school break taking care of Violet. But it's nice of you to offer."

He hesitated, started to speak, then stopped himself. For a moment I feared that I had pushed my reluctance too far and that he would agree to stay home. That would be a problem—he was too much responsibility for Grandma.

"Okay, Mom. Let's cut the crap." Nash sat on the couch. "You're not the only Indian in the world. Give me some credit.

Discovering the truth about Columbus matters to me, too. I hear you and Roger talking about the Diary, fighting about what it might say—crowns or secrets or whatever. Well, it's great if there's something new or valuable, but even if there isn't, just finding it would be like making a connection to the past. To know stuff that's been forgotten, to bring it out. I don't want to miss being there."

I looked at my son closely, trying to gauge the degree to which his words matched his feelings, but he was at his most inscrutable. He so articulated my own unspoken feelings that I had to suppress the urge to grab his hand, confide, open my heart. But I held back, determined that for once I would not overwhelm him with an embarrassingly emotional response. This, I sensed, was the beginning of a very long, very important conversation, so I took my time.

"You surprise me," I said. "I didn't know you were that interested in history." Then I changed the subject. "Tell the truth. What else is it about going that gets to you?"

He answered with a question of his own.

"So. Are you going to marry Roger, or what? I was just wondering."

"You'll be the first to hear, when I figure that one out. How do you vote?"

"I didn't realize I got one."

"Give it a shot."

Nash shook his head, stood up, headed for the stairs.

"Hey, it's your life," he said. The old distance flowed between us once again. "It's not as though he's going to be my father. The reason I ask: if Roger will be hanging around . . . well, I could get to know him on this trip. That's a reason for me to go."

"I'm supposed to believe that one? You don't have to worry who your father is. You're Purvis Twostar all over—ninety-nine and forty-four one hundredths percent con-artist."

"That means I go, right?" He smiled.

"I already bought your ticket. And the good news is, the way the reservations worked out, you get to travel down with Roger! Think of all the opportunities for meaningful dialogue you two will have."

*　　　*　　　*

That left only Grandma on my list, and she would not be easy to cross off. In the first place, she thought my project was not merely a waste of time but immoral.

"Let them study their own past," she had argued from the start.

"It's not as if Columbus didn't have something to do with us," I pointed out. "Who's to say what I'll turn up? Besides, I can't just ignore it when this dynamite material falls into my lap. You take advantage of something like this."

I decided to appeal to that sense of the intended, of predestination, with which she so delighted in filling Nash's head—her explanation for the fact that while her grandson might not at the moment be setting the world on fire, it was only a matter of time. "Maybe I was *meant* to find these pages, Grandma. Maybe there's a purpose we can't yet decipher."

"Ha!"

Silly me. Of course she would have already thought this possibility through, and formed her own conclusions. She wasted no time clueing me in.

"I translated those pages," she said meaningfully.

"So?" I had spent a lifetime hearing about the meticulous Mexican nuns of her school days, suffering the consequences of their insistence that she learn Castilian Spanish. I had never spoken a word of that language to her without being corrected, never shown her one of my own Spanish textbooks without listening to her haughty dismissal of its failings. Wasn't I entitled to some benefit?

"Well, the one is just a recipe. How to fix oysters. How old they were. How Columbus liked them so much he even kept their shells. And the rest of that letter's nothing but killings, evil crimes. You're going to spend two weeks, go around the world, and it will all turn out to be salt."

"Come on," I said. "Be fair. What about that crown? And you know it wasn't only spices he was looking for. It was gold. Or souls. Big-time stuff. What about the sign of the cross mentioned on the page from the Diary?"

"We don't need to know about more missionaries."

So much for her prognosis of my potential breakthrough. But

that was only half her argument: in the second place, she absolutely refused to fly.

"I am tied to the earth," she liked to say—so that eliminated any thought of finagling her a ticket. Thank God. Roger felt crowded enough by the fact that Nash was coming. If Grandma joined the party I felt pretty sure he'd head for Mexico with Mark.

But of course I had to ask, anyway. As ever, her lightning response time amazed me: she perpetually had an answer ready in the wings.

"I had a dream," she intoned. "We can't go."

We. I had to hand it to her.

"I'll bet you're going to tell me about it," I said. There is no avoiding a flood when you have just opened the dike.

"A bird," she said portentously, "fell from the sky."

"As opposed to falling from the ground."

She ignored me. "It was a Water Bird." That was an Indian symbol, so it had to be us. She waited for me to foam at the mouth, grateful that her convenient prescience had saved us from our fate.

"I have to go," I said. "It's important to me."

"Then at least leave the boy here. He's so young."

I couldn't blame her for not wanting to spend Christmas alone. I felt guilty about it, as a matter of fact, and I was not immune to the temptation to be Nash-less for a couple of weeks. But the truth of it was, she couldn't manage him on her own. Affection clouded her vision, impaired her judgment. Especially after last summer's brush with the small-time drug scene of the Upper Valley, I would worry about him.

But it did no good to appeal to her empathy—not Grandma's strong suit. The direct approach was the only possible route, save capitulation.

"I can't do that," I said. "There are too many temptations here for him. Besides, he wants to go for the same reason I do."

She sat very still, neither agreeing nor disagreeing. There was no denying my words, but assent meant her defeat. It was one of those terrible moments when the truth of our relationship—Grandma's and mine—rose to the surface. Her power over me came from my willingness to allow it, which mostly I did—out of a combination of habit and gratitude. It was a bargain we had struck long ago and it was an order of things that worked. But the passage of time causes shifts, even in rock. Each generation must claim its turn or lose its chance. It would happen to me—Nash and eventually Violet would follow their own ways and I would hate it. But I would hate it more if I had never done it myself.

Grandma was watching me, and spoke first.

"Go, then. It will be good to have the house to myself for a change, to not be bothered."

I nodded, agreeing to believe her. If I let her send me away, I could go without going completely. Only if she ordered me to leave, could I come back.

She understood, but couldn't completely stop herself.

"This is that Roger's idea."

"He isn't 'that' Roger, he's Roger, and you're on the wrong track. It's me that has to go. Thanks to the late booking, Roger and I aren't even flying on the same plane. I'm going down with Violet one way, and Nash and Roger will come on a different flight." I tried a joke. "It was just *one* water bird that bit the dust, wasn't it?"

Her eyes blazed, thwarted. "Make fun now," she invited. "He probably won't even show up. If he loved you, why would he make you go alone? People who love you don't go away."

Her words, spoken without forethought for their shades of meaning, fell around us like snow. We had entered a private room that we almost always kept cordoned off with a steel chain. There had been a lot of leavings, a lot of not coming back, in both our lives. She looked away.

"I'm not my mother," I said softly. "Roger isn't Purvis."

"Why is this trip so important?" Her chin was tilted up, her lips barely moved.

I thought before I spoke, then listened to my answer. Sometimes you don't know your own mind until you're hit with a question that turns the key.

"There aren't as many chances as we think," I said. "When you're young it seems like there are, but really, you get two or three at the most. Chances that make a difference."

She was with me. I knew because she didn't contradict, didn't put me down.

"I know you think this Columbus thing is a waste, is the

wrong thing for me to be involved in. Maybe you're right. But if I can figure him out, if I can put a face on him . . . Maybe I can put him and all he represents behind me. I want to blow his cover, right before his birthday party. I want a voice in this."

"You think a lot of yourself," she said quietly, oddly, as though her meaning wasn't as biting as her words.

"I'm trying to," I answered. "It's not easy. I had a father I never remember seeing, a husband who left me for a Betsy, a son who . . ."

"And Roger?"

"I know you don't understand. You think he's conceited, talks too much. But I'll tell you something about Roger Williams that I don't think he realizes about himself. He's got a rare heart, Grandma, if he ever learns how to use it. On the Roger question, the vote is still out."

"Don't feel sorry for yourself," she insisted, hanging one of her famous 180-degree turns. "You'll figure it out. And if you don't . . ."

"If I do, I might be able to nail *Christopher Columbus,* Grandma. How's that for a grand payback? Maybe it *will* be salt, but maybe that's the best thing it could be. Without the myth, he's just another man. Not the father of Manifest Destiny. Not the hand of fate. Not the inevitable force. Not some agent of God. Just a man whose good luck was our bad. That's somebody familiar. That's somebody we can handle."

She graced me with a quick glance, but the shades were up. She didn't believe for a minute that I could do what I said, yet she couldn't altogether blame me for trying. I swear she even wished me luck.

10

ROGER

I became obsessed by meat.

"Provisions," my brother, Bart, had warned when I called
him at his house in Del Mar and mentioned my plans to visit
Eleuthera. "None of those out-of-the-way islands have decent beef.
You must import it, Roger, you must carry it on your person to
ensure quality."

I passed on this good advice to Vivian as we sat together over
coffee one late afternoon in the faculty club and she, of course,
laughed. My extended family was a source of unending amusement to her, a kind of diorama of everyday life among the WASPs.
She delighted in describing what she imagined my relatives were
wearing during their various pursuits and activities.

"Bart's the one in California?" she inquired.

I admitted as much.

"Okay, I see him. Pink pants, lime-green shirt. A putter in
one hand, a cellular phone in the other."

"Bart does manage two businesses," I reminded her. "I think
you can allow him to have a telephone, even if your Mr. Cobb
eschews such an instrument."

"A car fax," she went on. "Shoes with tassels. Boxer shorts with tiny crossed golf clubs printed in blue."

"Is this necessary? Do I poke fun at your background at every opportunity? Do I adorn your loved ones with feathers?" I looked around the almost deserted lounge. A senior biology professor, with whom I was currently in high feud, illicitly filled his pipe while grading exams, and in the next room the waiters were preparing the tables for the first dinner sitting.

"I'm sorry," she said. I wanted to believe her but I could plainly see that her mouth enclosed a laugh and her mind was already springing for its next rejoinder. It's true that there's much about me, about all the Williams clan, that could bear a soupçon of deflation, and Vivian can be mercilessly on target. But today I was impatient. This was no game. I had decided to accompany her, partly, I must admit, because I thought I smelled a rat in this dreary business.

Of course, this was not a matter I could explain to Vivian. I couldn't come right out and say something as insulting—but obvious—as: If Henry Cobb actually had any other fragments of Columbus's Diary, he'd want to present his case to a real scholar, someone who had done years of research on the subject. Someone like me, I thought in sincere candor, not a dilettante like Vivian. Clearly, the man depended upon her lack of expertise rather than her possession of it. As a professor, she had a title, a kind of credential, but no depth. We would see, in Eleuthera, if the man dared allow *me* to examine whatever else he claimed to have inherited.

In any case we must not arrive unprepared, overly dependent upon the man. I had taken the responsibility of shepherding Nash to the island, and I reminded Vivian of this gesture on my part. Her face clouded.

"Look, if it's too much trouble, forget it. Nash can just bite the bullet and go with me. *You* can bring Violet. I'm sure she can survive on a bottle for six hours. Besides, Nash has his doubts about your route anyway. Grandma's warned him his silver bird will crash and there's part of him that believes it. It's just some typical teenage self-importance trip. He controls the world. If he's in a plane, it goes down. Forget that he takes you with him. Forget the conflicting destinies of every other passenger. He's the only one that counts. Now I'm supposed to be grateful that his unselfish act spares Violet and me."

"He doesn't say it's going down," I corrected her.

"Excuse me. It 'disappears.' Another mysterious statistic. Nash's name in the *Guinness Book of World Records.* His life cut short before it begins. Why humor him? Isn't an all-expense-paid vacation fate enough?"

We were straying too far off the subject. "I am not lobbying to change the plan," I said. "You and Violet go from Boston to Nassau to Rock Sound as arranged; Nash and I will depart from Hartford and arrive in Governor's Harbour via Fort Lauderdale. We'll join you three hours later. There's nothing unusual about a family dividing itself in transit."

Vivian looked at me with genuine surprise. Her lips remained parted but she abandoned whatever it was she had intended to say next while another thought overcame her, and then, in one of those spontaneous gestures that so disarm me, she leaned close and kissed my forehead.

I glanced to my left. The biologist was staring, savoring his mission to alert his colleagues, to confirm the much-speculated-upon *liaison dangereuse* between two professors of differing ranks. Well, so what? I tipped my head, raised my empty coffee cup in a toast to his smoking pipe, and he looked away, temporarily foiled. Vivian's eyes, however, did not stray from my face.

"So we're a family now," she said.

"You know what I mean."

"I'm beginning to, but I'm not going to completely believe it."

I listened for accusation in her tone. Was this the opening salvo of a reprimand for my absence at the time of Violet's birth, for my hesitations, for what she imagined to be my too-slowly-abandoned allegiance to the solitary life? But I heard nothing of that, nothing aimed at me. Vivian was simply protecting herself, and I respected her caution. Clear expectations were for the very young or the very old. In between you judged experience like history, in retrospect. I determined to type this insight into my journal at the first opportunity, so as not to forget it.

*   *   *

I equipped myself on Main Street. It was mid-December, but the stores seemed particularly attuned to the needs of a would-be beachcomber. I purchased madras swim trunks, two pairs of shorts, two Egyptian cotton shirts, a lavender and a pink, and rather complicated sandals—the thongs conjoined with a series of decorative loops and hooks. At the pharmacy I found precisely the types of sunblock recommended by *Consumer Reports*, and bought a sufficient quantity in graduated strengths, beginning at SPF 15 and ending at 4. In a burst of inspiration I added a tiny vial of herb-scented insect repellent and a bottle of salt tablets. One could not be too careful.

My most satisfying acquisition was a futuristic collapsible case that I found at the Dartmouth Co-op. The clerk assured me that the tote's silvery walls—constructed of the very Thinsulate that astronauts used to protect their perishables from the extreme temperatures of outer space—would preserve a freeze for at least twenty-four hours, even in the tropics, provided that they had been compacted around the contents and that the Velcro seal had not been broken. I observed his demonstration closely and then had him watch me to make sure that I properly grasped the instructions.

Finally there was nothing left but my visit to the supermarket. I chose carefully, balancing the weight I would have to carry with nutritional and aesthetic concerns. I mentally calculated whole menus, dubiously conceding certain staple items to the local island emporiums: salt and pepper, flour, powdered milk, dish detergent. We were scheduled to spend nine evenings on Eleuthera and I assumed that our host would feed us dinner at least twice. Surely we could locate a restaurant for one night. That left six meals, two original preparations and several composed of leftovers. Bart had strongly advocated a leg of lamb, arguing that even served at room temperature, this could make a tasty centerpiece. But when I factored in the bulk of mint jelly, a jar of rosemary, and the various traditional side dishes, lamb seemed a bit *de trop*. Besides, I could too easily imagine Vivian's mocking reaction.

Instead I chose for simplicity, determined to rough it with only the most simple fare. A nice square rump roast, sufficiently marbled and satisfyingly dense. A roast went with anything, I consoled myself as I wheeled past the lamb, and surely the local folk must have potatoes, a carrot or two, perhaps an onion. For the second serving we could throw together a kind of stew, employing native dishes, made succulent with cubes of beef retained from a previous dinner. I was not afraid to experiment. I was not, after all, Bart—no matter what Vivian might think.

To anchor the second pair of meals, I lit upon the idea of a turkey breast and found one shaped like a large, solid white heart. It had heft, low cholesterol, and the second-day makings of sand- wiches or even hash. I could supplement it with a convenient, shamelessly easy envelope of gravy mix, with two boxes of frozen peas, and then count on finding enough bread to make a respect- able stuffing.

Vivian brought Nash to my door the night before our planned departures. She and Violet would go ahead to Boston and spend the night at the Logan Hilton, while her son and I would rise before dawn and drive down the interstate to Bradley Field in time for our ten o'clock flight to Florida.

"Don't encourage him," Vivian whispered in my ear as she kissed me good-bye. She was bundled in a coat of thick black wool, and her wavy hair, half caught back, crackled with electricity in the cold wind. I took a single strand between my fingers.

"Aloha," I said. "I expect you to meet us in a hula skirt with a lei around your neck."

"Wrong island," she smiled. "Wrong ocean, wrong direc- tion."

"Holding a planter's punch with an umbrella in it," I con- tinued.

"Wrong girl."

"Right girl."

"Give me a break," Nash groaned. He was not prepared to accept emotion between adults. He stood on the landing, a lumpy duffel bag at his side, and kicked at it absently while his eyes darted around my living room, carefully avoiding my desk. In this room he was more ill at ease than usual.

"There's a TV in the bedroom you'll use upstairs," I advised him, and without another word he left us, clomping bowlegged, as if the new muscles in his calves were so bunchy, so over-developed, that he could not walk without accounting for their grip and pull. When he sat he invariably splayed his thighs wide, as though only through this uncomfortable pose could he accommodate the bulk of his teenage genitals. I remembered boys like him from my prep school days, remembered how intimidating they could be in their aggressive masculinity. Their very presence tended to close down all topics save the discussions of sports or bra size. When at last I found my niche at the University of Chicago, encountered others with whom I could talk about books and ideas and the larger questions, I had put such boys and their blunt self-assurance out of my head. And now, here I was, the putative stepfather, the live-in Oedipus, the natural enemy.

"Why 'Nash'?" I had asked Vivian early on, referring to her choice of names.

"As in Crosby, Stills, and," she had answered. "Spell it G-n-a-s-h if it helps."

It did.

I looked in on him before going to bed.

"Do you need anything?" I offered pleasantly and was careful to avoid reference to the topic most, I was certain, on both our minds: his unconfessed rape of my journal. I positively refused to mention it. Let him think I didn't know or, better, that it hadn't mattered to me. "A glass of milk?"

Somehow, without averting his gaze from a *Star Trek* rerun, he grimaced at my stupidity. He was sprawled on my favorite log cabin quilt and had not removed his shoes.

"Excited about the trip?" I asked.

"Oh, right," he said sarcastically, as if my naïveté were self-evident.

"Surely you're not worried about flying?" I asked innocently, and watched him squirm.

Nash blew air from his lips in a disgusted puff, but I wouldn't let him off the hook by asking him whom he favored in the Super Bowl. That stock masculine filler I would save for a true communication emergency.

"Well, what then?" I persisted. "Clearly something is disturbing you." I was curious to see how much he credited Angeline's dream.

Nash lay still for a moment, watching as aliens dematerialized. Finally he swiveled his body and glared at me.

"The Bermuda Triangle, okay?"

"I beg your pardon."

"I checked out the route. Did you know this plane flies near the Bermuda Triangle? Where people disappear?"

I shook my head. "I've heard about this . . . triangle, but I'm afraid I'm not altogether up on the theory."

He sat on the edge of the bed and looked at me intently, as if trying to judge whether or not my interest was sincere. I cocked my head to encourage him.

"You know," he began. "There's this area in a certain part of the ocean where strange things happen. People go in and never come out. Or they come out in a different dimension, a different time."

"*Documented* cases?" I made my voice sound concerned.

"There was this army plane from World War Two? It showed up two years ago. It had taken off in 1942 and it landed in 1988, and none of the members of the crew had aged at all."

"Why haven't I read about this phenomenon?" I marveled in amazement.

"The government kept it quiet," Nash confided. "All those guys were put in this special security prison in Nevada. They don't want anybody to know."

"But people fly to Eleuthera all the time," I protested. "I don't think we have anything to worry about. This triangle must be someplace else."

Nash was unconvinced. "They don't know exactly where it is. It might move around."

"Nevertheless, I think statistically our chances are good," I said. There was no hint of mockery in my voice, nothing with which Nash might find fault. He had let down his adolescent guard, made himself vulnerable by confessing his fear. Even I, who made no claim to comprehend the minds of children, could recognize this as a positive step, a potential turning point in our relationship, whatever that might be. If nothing else, it removed his advantage. Now we each knew a bit of the other's secrets.

I watched him ponder my opinion, hesitantly accept it because, after all, I was an adult and that still counted for something, and nod. As he turned back to the television, his shoulders seemed to have lost some of their tension. I quit the room and closed the door, relieved. This was not high school *redux*, with me at a perpetual loss. Nash was, alas, as much an idiot as I had feared, but I was not subject to his cruel whim. He was to mine. So I let him know I knew. "Feel free to borrow any book in the house," I said meaningfully, and closed the door.

The waiting room of the small commuter airlines at the Fort Lauderdale airport was crowded with stalled tourists. Families sat huddled together, surrounded by carry-on luggage. Some transported their possessions in straw bags embroidered with painted shells, the souvenirs, I presumed, of previous visits, which were hauled out for return trips in order to advertise their destinations and put their bearers in a properly rustic mood. Winter coats were piled in mounds, and scattered in their valleys young children slept in various poses of exhaustion. Nash had a tic of tapping his lower lip with his right index finger, and it had been in constant operation for the duration of our two-hour delay. Outside the glass walls the humid weather looked gray and blustery, and showed no signs of improvement.

"I'm going to ask that guy what's going on." Nash propelled himself from a sitting to a standing slump and self-consciously shuffled toward the airlines employee who spoke into a telephone behind the check-in desk. He and the man engaged in a lengthy conversation, a longer verbal interaction than I had thought Vivian's son capable of sustaining. When at last Nash returned to his seat he seemed almost frightened.

"What did you find out?"

He turned to me balefully. "A private plane is missing," he said. "Blown away by freak winds." His eyes were witness to a prophecy come to pass.

"Missing?"

He nodded. "Out there. There's a search going on, which is why we're grounded. And now there's a storm. The guy doesn't think anything's going to fly today. At least Mom and Violet have gotten there by now."

If the stringy white clouds to the east had suddenly resolved themselves into a script that read "Bermuda Triangle" and been followed by an arrow, Nash could not have been more certain of his destiny. I was about to pooh-pooh his gloom when the loudspeaker was activated. The ticket agent substantially confirmed Nash's summary. Indeed the coast guard had mounted a search and had temporarily halted all traffic on our route. And the worsening forecast was not promising. We were to stay in the lounge area to await further bulletins.

"I'm not taking off into the fourth dimension," Nash announced. "No way."

"So what do you want to do?" I asked in impatience. As if spending more time in this stuffy room were not annoyance enough, I had to put up with a reader of the *National Enquirer*. "Do we go home? May I remind you, we have nonrefundable tickets. You're talking about forfeiting two round-trips to Eleuthera plus the return from here to Hartford."

"It's better than . . ." Nash swallowed the rest of his sentence. He had a truly impressive talent for melodrama.

In vexation, I turned away. I would have to formulate some kind of plan, some distraction. I noticed a West Indian–looking man addressing a cluster of our fellow passengers. They listened to him at length with some interest, then finally shook their heads. He caught my eye and moved in our direction.

"Elvis Greer." He introduced himself formally and offered his hand, which I shook. He had a slight colonial accent but was perfectly understandable. His grip was firm, dry, dependable. "Where are you off to today?"

"We have tickets for Eleuthera, but hope fades," I replied. Nash was folded into himself, a pose as close to the fetal position as the seat, his long limbs, and public exhibition would permit.

"The boy is nervous," Elvis Greer observed.

Thank you so very much, I felt like saying. All we need is a fortune-teller.

"I have a boat," he continued. "A strong engine backed up by sails. It is an overnight trip. Very beautiful, very comfortable.

These planes are canceled half the time, so I always check at the airport. I offer passage at a small fee since I am going anyway. I can sleep six people."

My impulse, of course, was to follow my neighbors' example and send this windjammer entrepreneur on his way, but beside me I felt Nash become alert. Apparently he believed his chances of arriving in the same century were improved by crossing water rather than air.

"What do you think?" I asked him.

Unwilling to take responsibility for a decision—God knows I might blame him as we tried to cope in some postapocalyptic society—he remained mute, but I took that as assent. I was no stranger to boats, having sailed in the summers on various Williamses' craft since I was a child, so I quizzed Mr. Greer on specifics: length and motors, the age of his ship, his experience in Caribbean waters. It all sounded quite satisfactory, and to my relief the fee was not exorbitant. I calculated the cost of meals and motel—commuter airlines took no responsibility for their passengers' inconvenience—factored in Nash's opposition to becoming airborne and what toll upon my good humor convincing him might extract. I eyed the glistening rectangle of my Thinsulate case, which even in the temperature-controlled climate of the airport seemed to wilt, to give off a slight hint of steam. The potential lost investment of the meat tipped the balance, made the equation work.

"All right," I told Greer, and for the second time in five minutes I shook his brown, square hand. We would approach Eleuthera in the tried-and-true old-fashioned way, and arrive, Greer assured me, just before the break of day.

A few hours later, Nash and I boarded—the only passengers. Greer hoisted anchor, and soon we had left the overcast Florida coast behind. The weather had at least remained stable: not good but not terrible. An unexpected bonus of this method of transportation was the parallel it offered to the Admiral's own voyage, though of course we debarked from the opposite shore. Interpretation of Columbus's quest was never far from my thoughts, blocked though I had recently found myself. The text of my poem was safely stored in my pocket on a floppy disk, but so far it had not progressed much beyond his arrival in the Canaries.

After a light meal, Nash claimed fatigue and retired below to seek oblivion, though to what time and place he would wake he was no doubt loath to predict. I flipped the cover of my laptop computer and booted up my text. The bounce of storm-swept waves against the hull, the whiff of warm salt air, the sensation of dry enclosure in a liquid universe: all could not help but propel my inspiration. I waited, my fingers tensed to record my thoughts, to give voice, to write as spontaneously as Mrs. Yeats if only the channel could be established. I sat that way for some time, my hands played before the keyboard, my eyes closed—but nothing came.

I considered writing a letter instead, a note to Bart to inform him of my unorthodox mode of travel. He would be slightly alarmed, just the reaction I so enjoyed provoking in all members of my extended family. The backlit screen glowed softly. The stanzas of my already written words were pale turquoise, precise, etched in uniform rows. I scrolled back and read, as if momentum alone would generate new thoughts, as if the inertia of the flow would extend the verse, but when I came to the end, there was only blank space. I had four hours of stored battery time so I indulged my impulse to leave the machine running. Above me the clouds had pushed south and the stars described a wondrous arc. Automatically, like a schoolboy at a planetarium, proud of his accomplishments, I identified constellations. I was partial to the Pleiades, never ceased to delight in the flicker of their shield. I found true north, confirmed our eastern progress, and imagined Africa, dense and green, dead ahead. I listened for the jump of fish above the humming song of Elvis Greer, who stood behind the wheel, indifferent to my presence.

Translate, I willed my brain. Get this down. Let the poem take wing. You can always edit.

But nothing. I stared into the black horizon, searching for some sign, some pillar of fresh thought. Pillar. The word snatched at a poem I had once memorized—Herrick's "The Pillar of Fame"—but tonight my brain could move neither forward nor back. I could retrieve but two lines.

> This pillar never shall
> Decline or waste at all

I found the flash of Venus, lower than I would have thought possible. It seemed almost to swim beneath the waves—appropriate, I reasoned, for a water planet, but if the sharp curve of the earth were so close, if the precipice over which I looked were so immediate, then the globe itself would be too small.

A thought. "Venus beckons," I typed. "To Cathay and Cipango."

"Seasick?" Greer, hearing the click of my keys, noticed me for the first time. Whatever chance I had of discovery was now forfeit.

"Too lovely a night for sleep," I answered with more civility than I felt.

"There is Dramamine in the medicine chest beneath the sink," he replied, discounting my explanation. "No shame in a stomach used to land."

"This is hardly my maiden voyage."

"The open sea is calypso tonight," Greer said. "You have to limbo with the beat or let it lull you."

"We seem to be heading slightly to the north," I noted, showing off my training in celestial navigation. "Why?"

Greer pointed southeast, toward the horizon. "I'm giving that a wide berth. It could be refugees but most likely it's drugs. Running with only the one green spot, low to the water. This passage is full of illegals."

Faint, in the distance, I saw a moving light, tracing a path at odds to our own. It rose and sank beneath the waves, a bobber without sound, its destination and purpose lost in the vastness of the night.

"Lost," I wrote, "in the vastness," and then deleted the words. I thought of Vivian, of the improbability of our mutual attraction. She could be all impulse, all exterior signal, hands and eyes and hunched shoulders broadcasting her thought before it translated into word or deed. Her lithe body was strong, as if each tendon were a stretched band whose snap and pull were irresistible. There was something clean about her physical power, something unmitigated by self-conscious conceit. I never saw her exercise in the conventional fashion—she was a slave to no video regimens, a player on no teams, a member of no gymnasia, unless one counted the therapeutic Pole who taught karate—and yet she seemed never at rest. Each movement had a function beyond itself. When she stretched, she reached for something. When she bent, she returned upright with an object in her arms. When she ran, she had a purpose. When her body rested, her mind worked.

Occasionally, in the dark, too exhausted by the preceding day to endure her nightly litany of indignations suffered or her recitation of upcoming plans, I would feign sleep after we assumed our accustomed positions, back to back. Then suddenly, almost as if a jet of water had infused her spine, I could feel her stiffen with an idea. Alert and hungry for conversation, she would begin to probe my receptivity with tiny pushes and adjustments—each in its own way innocent enough, each possibly a mere drowsy quest for further comfort, but taken together, these twitches and shifts called to mind the noises made by members of a symphonic orchestra, fine-tuning their instruments in preparation for a Wagnerian overture.

Early in the days of our romance, I had answered these summons with reciprocal metalanguage. When her elbow poked my rib, I might lean my leg in the direction of her foot. When she sighed deeply, I might clear my throat. "Not asleep either," this would signal, in preparation, I naively assumed, for a resumption of lovemaking or perhaps only the quiet, postcoital murmuring of a pair of doves whom even slumber could not tempt apart.

I remember the first time this happened, when, rejoicing in the presence of her awakened company, I rolled over and with a single motion embraced my beloved with my free arm. My lips softened and sought her throat, but instead of the compliant, fragrant skin I expected, I encountered a taut stem, rigid with fury.

"Preston says to me," Vivian announced, her head nodding in agreement with herself, "that some of the outside evaluators on my tenure committee question my objectivity. Can you imagine? The fucking nerve of that idiot!"

She propped her torso on one elbow and bent over me. It happened so quickly that I found myself kissing the warm indentation where her head had pressed the pillow. When I opened my eyes, her tousled hair formed a silhouette corona against the faint outdoor light that penetrated the window.

"*Bill* Preston?" I managed.

"Oh, yes, *Bill* to you," Vivian accused in passing. "Torquemada, the Grand Inquisitor, to me. He treasures his little chairman's power, especially over women. 'Oh, Vivian,' he says after the department meeting yesterday—I forgot to tell you—'could you spare me just a moment?' Then, when of course everyone has frozen so they don't miss anything, when every other sound in the room has been eliminated, he drops his bomb. I'll give that bastard 'objectivity.'"

To love, the poets tell us, is to put the needs of the other first, to subvert one's self, and in those halcyon days, I ever attempted to live up to this ideal.

"But surely he must have said more," I whispered, my shocked tone appropriate to the gravity with which Vivian clearly regarded this situation. "Who made the accusation and in what context? Published scholarship? Classroom teaching? Community service?" I noted each of the three tests a candidate for tenure must pass.

"Get serious," Vivian said, and collapsed back into a prone position, barely missing my head. She curled against me, yawned and when she spoke again her voice was heavy, half-unconscious. "The point was . . ." Another yawn, as if I were keeping her awake and she were humoring me. "The point was to make me nervous. To put a knife at my jugular." She pecked my cheek, rested her head on my shoulder, and in less than sixty seconds her breathing slowed into a steady rhythm.

I, on the other hand, lay worried and upset until almost three o'clock. Over and over I analyzed Bill's motives. Were there real concerns surfacing in Vivian's file? What would be the consequence if she failed to be promoted? Would she leave? Would I resign to accompany her to a lesser institution? I projected some dreary scenario in which I was forced to teach three English composition courses in a single term.

When the voice of the radio finally woke me, my thoughts were still woeful, but Vivian was already out of bed and at the window.

"Don't you love rain!" she exclaimed.

"I couldn't get back to sleep for hours," I said. "What are you going to do about Bill Preston's warning?"

She looked momentarily confused. Then she remembered.

"Don't give him the satisfaction," she said, "It's not worth talking about."

It took me a while to learn that, if she was offended in any way, Vivian's mind worked like the San Andreas fault: it had diminishing aftershocks, usually late at night or just before dawn, and then gradually returned to normal. Furthermore, while she enjoyed having an audience—me—for her diatribes, she didn't absolutely require it. If I ignored the beeper signals sent out by her recumbent body, if I pretended to be in a comatose state, she would go through her indignation cycle alone. For a few minutes she would toss from right to left, brutally punch her pillow, sometimes sit up, and once or twice give actual voice to an expletive, but—and this was an important observation for my peace of mind, for I truly didn't want to desert her if she was in genuine distress—she always calmed within the same general perimeters of time whether I rose to the occasion or passively declined it.

But then there were instances where I was more than Vivian's sounding board. There were the exquisite recognitions where she sought not just anyone, not just a handy male, but me, Roger Vandyne Williams. Those piercing looks—demanding, bold, vulnerable—flattered me more than I would have thought possible. To be, how shall I say, the object of Vivian's desire, the source of her pleasure, the main arbiter of her happiness . . . well, that not only was unsettling and new, it was, when I allowed it to be, spectacular.

From the start, she had made the rules. She led, I endeavored to follow, to anticipate her forward step with a backward feint of my own. Escalation built upon escalation, and before I realized the direction we were taking, a complaining knock at my office door had become infatuation. A drop-in visit at my house had metamorphosed into an addiction, a condition in which Vivian in absentia figured as prominently in my thoughts as when she was present. The annunciation of a missed period progressed, as if no time at all had passed, into an actual daughter who in certain light resembled Bart, and this unimagined offspring, this abstraction become three-dimensional, was but a toe in the door. Not two years had passed since that first fateful thud of fist on wood, and now I had a sort of mother-in-law, fierce and unyielding, a Saint Augustine devotee wrapped in a Pendleton blanket who could not even be depended upon to return my greeting when I entered her presence. And if that weren't enough, asleep belowdecks was a cold-hearted interloper, a surly, faddish, superstitious lump who prided himself on being broad-minded about my relationship with his mother.

"Do I call you 'Pappy' now?" Nash had asked at a dinner when I sat, mouth aflame from too much chili powder, at Vivian's table. My expression must have been horrified, for it goaded him to continue. "Mister Rogers? Uncle Bill? Mom's 'friend'?"

"My friends call me Roger," I offered as kindly as I could manage, and took another gulp of water.

"Nash!" Vivian admonished, spooning me a second helping.

"All right, ROG-ER," he conceded. "Nice to meet you, ROG-ER. Tell me, ROG-ER, are you a DODG-ER fan? So, ROG-ER, want to go chase a few pop flies? I just hope you practice safe sex."

"Nash, put a lid on it!" Vivian's voice was more exasperated than irritated. "Ignore him," she implored me. "I never saw this kid before in my life. He's a punishment inflicted by a wrathful God, a long penance."

The grandmother, no more hospitable than the son, spoke up at last. "Chastity," she intoned, as if thinking aloud. "A mother's fervent prayer."

"Meet Saint Monica," Vivian said. "Welcome to purgatory."

According to Milton, purgatory is a temporary state leading to heavenly bliss, yet it was difficult to believe that such was my present course. As I gazed over the dark waters, even the one lone light now swallowed and extinguished, I tried to imagine a future scene in which Nash and I shared the affection of a son and a father. I tried to conjure a hypothetical family outing—to admire Violet as she starred in her high school play, for instance. Lady Macbeth? Medea? One of the maenads? The roles had in common an opportunity for my daughter to emote and shriek, so I had no doubt of her success. Nash would be an adult by then, a peer of sorts, so I dressed him in a suit. Seated next to Vivian in the hushed theater, sunk side by side in red velvet seats, I reached my hand to hers. The pressure was returned, the confirmation of conjugal pride at our progeny's triumph. I sighed at this thought, sighed loudly enough to hear myself, and the sound brought me back to the here and now. In some embarrassment I became aware that with my right hand I clasped my own left. The night cloaked my gesture, made it private as a thought, as a sight I might see only when my eyes were closed, so I did not break the contact. I did not let go.

When the sun rose I was reclining against a bulwark, the light in my eyes, and facing a cloud formation that bunched against the horizon like the outline of a volcanic island. The illusion was convincing: jagged striated spikes, straight as the trunks of slanting palms, poked from the central mass in all directions. The sea was still, the boat's engine quiet, and we seemed to glide forward, pulled by an invisible magnet. There was no wind, no birds called back and forth, no sounds emerged from the cabin. It was a moment of expectancy, the rich pause that sometimes precedes revelation.

I tried to render this presage into words, groped for an adequate juxtaposition of verb and noun. I have found that the best way to achieve this osmosis, this blend of the external exposition with internal consciousness, is to think of nothing and let the phrases materialize upon my inner screen. Not meditation, exactly, but rather precise listening. Somewhere there was a voice demanding to be heard. All I, as poet, had to do was open my mind.

"Jesus Christ!"

I cocked my head, leaned forward, was shocked by the pure clarity, until recognition penetrated.

"How long have you been standing behind me?" I asked Nash.

"Did you see that cloud?" His hand emerged in the right field of my vision, his blunt index finger extended forward.

"As a matter of fact . . ." I began.

"It looks like writing. There's a *C*. An *N*. Do you think it means something?"

Ah, we were back in the land of portents—the hand of God jotting a memo especially for Nash.

"Cable News?" I suggested. "Has Ted Turner bought the Caribbean? MTV?"

"MTV is its own network," Nash informed me with extreme condescension. He wore an expression of betrayal. I had committed the cardinal sin of not taking seriously one of his pronouncements. More than a week lay ahead of us, so I made amends.

"Of course, how silly of me. That's where I always catch Milli Vanilli." I was grateful that Vivian had insisted I become at home with the new music. She had read an article that said a true definition of middle age was when one did not recognize the names of groups who appeared on the "top forty." Nash flashed me a surprised look, clearly impressed. I was afraid he'd quiz me, demand that I identify a song that Miss Vanilli sang. My tutorial had not progressed that far, so I changed the subject.

"Well, today's the day. Are you looking forward to the tropical isle?"

"Oh, right. I don't know what I'll do first."

I tried to be encouraging. "I've read that there are beaches virtually encrusted with interesting shells. The snorkeling on the Caribbean side is supposed to be excellent. And then of course there will be ample opportunity for exploration."

"I don't even know what I'm supposed to be looking for."

"One seldom does. But one tries to make the best of things," I said.

I watched as some dismissive remark seemed to press against Nash's lips, but then perhaps we both saw those thumb-tacked pages once again. He managed to repress whatever comment he had in mind, then to nod his head slowly as if gravely registering my admission. I found myself possessed of a distinctly new attitude toward Nash: gratitude, coupled with the seed of forgiveness. He could have laughed at me, could have dropped a steel wall between us, but he hadn't done it. He was not quite who I had assumed he was.

We sat together in silence, each fearful of upsetting the truce with the weight of even one more word. The day was golden, the sky overhead was still pale, but yet a more vibrant, pregnant pastel than any I had seen before. It was the gray of a backlit curtain, of a lampshade that housed a two-hundred-watt bulb. Its vastness matched that of the ocean, and each in its way seemed the smooth surface of a facing wall urged forward by enormous power. In the isthmus, in the narrow channel that separated their dual grandeurs, our boat moved east. I strained my eyes. For some reason it mattered to me to be the first to sight the land, but I was looking the wrong way. Nash touched my shoulder, tipped his head to the south. And there it was.

11

VIVIAN

The sky was calm and the sea tipped beneath us, horizon to horizon, a silken turquoise so clear the shadows of the clouds made deep and translucent wells in which I caught the shapes of dolphin, the wedge and sweep of shark. Tricks of the eye, of course. I leaned against the airplane's window and stared into the constantly advancing shimmer of waves, the heavy shoals and coral barriers. Violet, mesmerized by the drone of the small plane's engine, slept hard in my arms. I drifted too, in and out of the vibration that filled me slowly with a weighted warmth, but I snapped to at the pilot's voice. Eleuthera's northern islets were beneath us, Egg and Royal, then a thickly vegetated ribbon of land, then just the sea again. If Arnie B. Molander's dark horse landfall theory was correct, we had just passed over the spot where, one night nearly half a millennium ago, some Lucayan had lit a torch which Columbus described from the vantage of his own darkness as "a little wax candle bobbing up and down."

The moon had been in its third quarter on that night. From the *Pinta,* which was running ahead, Columbus heard the cannon fire indicating that land had been sighted. Yet, because of the small light he'd seen, Columbus insisted on claiming the honor for himself. At sunrise, he and the other ship captains, the secretary of the fleet, and the comptroller went ashore bearing the royal banner with the green cross and initials of the sovereigns. "At dawn we saw naked people," he wrote in his journal, the version transcribed by Las Casas.

The image haunts: *dawn . . . nakedness.* In contrast, Columbus's actions were ordinary, bureaucratic, deeds done by full light of day and while thoroughly clothed. He took official possession of all that was before him simply by speaking certain formulaic words—making sure that the secretary carefully recorded and the comptroller duly witnessed what fell from his lips.

Our plane touched down, hopped slightly, and bucked to a halt beside the airport, a low whitewashed building. Inside, the walls were painted the green-blue of pool bottoms. Our faces swam in the light, washed with color. The air was different, thicker, smelling not of the sea but of leaves, bark, mud. There had just been a storm, and once Violet and I were released into the glistening asphalt lot of parked cars, I saw the tattered fronds of palmettos, the scattered petals of some purple flower, torn fencing, a litter of debris.

The two other passengers from the plane were already seated in a low-slung station wagon—the airport limousine, I presumed. Local people lounged against the sides of cars, lost in conversation, gossip. No one approached us, no one held up a placard with the name TWOSTAR. I shifted Violet to my other arm, impatient. She was frantic with hunger, hard to appease.

A tall Caucasian male poked his head from the airport building, pulled it back again. I caught just the flash of his profile, the beaklike nose, familiar from Roger's clipping. Henry Cobb was dressed in a brisk white polo shirt, navy blue tennis shorts, crew socks, and hi-tech Pumas. Creases ran alongside his mouth—not laugh or frown lines but perfect parallels. He had straight, white, thick hair and the lean muscles of a vigorous sixty-year-old. I identified myself, put out my hand. As he spoke, I recognized the curled precision, the Buckley-esque whining frown at the end of each word. In person, his voice was even more commanding—low, modulated, and electric. Cobb's long face—broad and flat-cheeked, a bit horsey—wore a contained expression of annoyance. He touched the tip of his chin like a talisman, and stared into my features.

After the briefest of greetings he got to the point.

"Did you bring it? Everything?"

I nodded. Cobb's handshake was crushing. He pressed my rings into my palm so hard that I winced.

"I'll pick up some food for dinner on the way—not that you can find much that's edible." He gestured to the parking lot, the buildings beyond, with a flap of his hand. "These people don't believe in work. They won't even plant a few seeds. The only place to get a decent meal is at the club, and even there the salads are made of iceberg lettuce." He kept up a running monologue as if he hadn't spoken to anyone in a long time. "I had completely stopped drinking before I came down this last visit. But there are two activities here. Look at the sea and look at the sea. Impossible to do without a drink in your hand. Did you remember my newspaper?"

I handed over the *Wall Street Journal,* and he raised his eyebrows, even granted me a small, pursed smile, then loaded my luggage into the back of a dusty Jeep.

"It's this or walk," he said helping me into the front. There were no seat belts, so I held Violet in my lap.

"What's that?" Cobb looked down at her for the first time.

"*That* is my daughter, Violet. Don't cross her."

"Formidable," said Cobb, loosening up a little as he pulled out of the lot. "My wife had a tough one like that. Melinda."

Violet gathered herself, drawing up her feet, clenching her fingers into fists, wrinkling her face into a red mask. Her mouth opened and her cry was a blast of unalloyed sound, each decibel contained and ricocheting off the Jeep's interior. In response, Cobb half swerved into the other lane, but by the time we reached the main road the rumble of the car's engine had a soothing effect.

The give-and-take of normal conversation had now been entirely eclipsed. Afraid to disturb Violet, Cobb spoke softly. I could see his lips move, and I nodded at what I thought were the appropriate moments, but I couldn't make out much about the occasional sight he pointed at here, jerked a thumb at there, along the way. Occasionally, one of us made an observation directly into the other's ear, but it was too much trouble, so mostly, after a while, we talked to ourselves.

We rode on the left-hand side of a narrow, paved highway bounded by scrub vegetation, sparse and tangled, struggling for purchase in the thin and salty soil. Along the shore, brown banks of dead coral jutted into the sea. The edges looked cracked off, jagged and sharp. I saw no long sand beaches, no royal palms or coconuts, no paradise. Unfinished construction frames, skeletal and hollow, appeared from time to time. The clustered settlements we passed consisted of one store with a gas pump, a small restaurant, and houses of cement block painted lime green, magenta, powder blue, or yellow. No one sat on the iron grillwork porches, no customers walked in and out of the stores, few cars passed us. Farther on, a solitary, tall, thin man stood in a cleared field, just stood there, an attenuated Giacometti figure, burnt expressionless and still beneath the high sun. We looked at each other, then he was behind us.

"This place reminds me of a reservation," I mouthed to Cobb.

And it did. Poor soil, bright colors, dark people, junked automobiles. In the variety emporium where we finally stopped, there were the same kind of long-shelf-life staples that rural Indians depended upon. Macaroni, soup, cereal, and ketchup. Bologna and powdered milk. There was a deep freeze full of beef cut into fist-size cubes. Soft drinks, Christmas cookies. I automatically asked myself whether Violet needed anything, but half my bag was taken up with diapers. Plus I myself was on hand, a kind of voice-activated walking refrigerator, so I didn't have to shop for her. I walked up and down the three aisles, curious, noting the dusty boxes of S.O.S. pads, the packets of hair tonic, banana pudding, saffron rice, the cans of green peanuts.

Once back in the car, Henry Cobb carefully stowed a bag of food on the floor behind the seats.

"This is not exactly my usual routine," he told me. "Before this goddamned exile I hadn't been inside a grocery for years."

"You seem to do all right," I said, rocking Violet against me. There was nothing to indicate the turnoff from the highway as Cobb slowed and bounced onto a nondescript narrow land paved erratically with crushed coral. The sand-gray bed was pot-holed and irregular.

"I've let it go," said Cobb. "Discourages the locals."

The track widened to skirt shallow slashes and ruts, luminous with standing water reflecting the faint pink tinge of the afternoon sky. Not until we were maybe a mile down the road did the surrounding land begin to admit, grudgingly at first, that someone had once hacked it into a semicultivated state. Tattered groves of citrus ranged to either side, and then, as we topped a small sandy escarpment, there were finally tall coconut palms. Around their bases all the undergrowth had been destroyed, so I saw, as we passed slowly through, that the ground was matted with a thick fabric of woody dried-brown fronds, molded and woven into a springy floor. We lurched and rocked over a track of even sharper coral, across a perilous jerry-built bridge, and then the motor cut.

"This is it," Cobb stated. "My own heart of darkness. Time stretches long down here, you'll see. I'm actually glad for the company."

What I'd taken to be a green jungle was really a wall, a garage covered with a tangle of clinging leaves. In the sudden shade, I was surprised at how much the palm grove blocked, how dark the air was underneath, though ahead daylight still gleamed blue and ivory between the bowed trunks. Cobb turned, eager to find me impressed.

"You first," he insisted.

There was no refusing. As we reached the crest of the path the trees parted and the sky yawned to all sides.

And then, it was simply *there*.

Surrounded on three sides by water, the world rose before me. On the rippling troughs of waves, ovals of deep fire were carried forward and then instantly replaced. The sand was rosy, lavender in places, composed of tiny fragments of conch shell. The color and the movement, the constantly exchanging gleam of sky and sea, were so immediately arresting, so silken, unchallenging, so inviting to the eye, that I stopped where I stood.

I remembered what Columbus wrote in his letter regarding the third voyage. Having explored the Gulf of Pearls and the southern strait of a great river, which he named the Serpent's Mouth, he became convinced that he had found the entrance to the legendary terrestrial paradise. As far as I was concerned, Cobb's beach also qualified.

Cobb approved of my reaction and took my arm, leading the way to the house. We entered through a low stucco wall, into a tiled back hall that smelled of powdery brick and mildew. Two or three rooms adjoined an enormous modern kitchen, all beige Formica and copper. The ground floor consisted of huge ceiling fans, tall windows, white pillars, and deep couches—one expansive room facing a vista of water. A grand piano on a simple rug took up a shelved alcove. There was a stone central fireplace and lots of carefully displayed old glass fishing weights, shells, sea fans, and formations of bleached coral. A side stairway led up to the second story.

"Renovated ten years ago, not touched since," announced Cobb. "My mother, then my ex-wife used to take good care of this place." He paused, looked at me, raised his eyebrows. "Know anyone in the market?"

I must have looked startled.

"A joke. We've had an offer from some minor British royalty, just between you and me. Turned her down. Not out of sentiment, I assure you, but one of my uncles, Harrison, originally bought this place because, as legend goes, he was convinced that the crown mentioned in the Diary"—at the word he gave me a conspiratorial glance—"is hidden somewhere around here. The old skinflint had millions salted away in gold brick, but on his visits he lived in the little beach house where you'll be staying. He spent his time walking the island. Never found a thing."

I took Violet upstairs to nurse, and was glad for the intermission. The bathroom was so big it had an easy chair in one corner. A huge gray tub faced the sea.

"Forgive me, but this slipped my mind," Cobb called from below. "I had a message from your . . . husband. He and your son are delayed. They arrive tomorrow morning."

There was nothing overt to make me feel suspicious, but that voice was an expert's tool. I didn't like the situation: me isolated here with Violet, Cobb the only contact. I locked the bathroom door and sat down, feeling ridiculous and better all at the same time. I stayed there for a while, then decided to make the best of things. Cobb was putting the finishing touches on a dinner of canned beans, rice, pâté, grapefruit, and coconut rum. He held up his hands in exaggerated apology.

"Not exactly my line," he said. "I told you."

Five minutes later, we dined at one end of a long table made of glass. Cobb lifted his fork in a toast and smiled at me, his teeth sharp and crowded. There was an almost palpable change in the atmosphere. We were getting down to business, to the real thing, and when Cobb spoke, he had shed the patrician drawl. His words thumped on the table, his syntax turned brutal, simple.

"If a thing isn't smart, it's nothing. Worse than nothing. It's a minus," he said.

"What do you mean by 'smart'?"

"*Smart.* Not dumb. You play the percentages, take your risks. If you're smart you don't lose, at least not for long."

"And you're smart?" Cobb liked talking about himself, that was obvious. He liked to answer questions about who he was.

"With a capital *S.* So are you—which is why I invited you here."

"I'm sorry, I still don't get it." I played dumb, pretending to forget his mention of the crown. "What is Columbus to you? I mean, I know it was a family tradition, demanding these papers that your ancestors sent to Dartmouth, but I would hardly think you had time for that kind of stuff."

"On the contrary," he replied. "The 'stuff,' as you put it, has a direct bearing on my present . . . embarrassment."

Violet had fallen asleep, and I laid her in the baby seat beside us.

"My ancestors . . . not smart," Cobb continued. "And you're right. I don't give a fuck about Columbus. But he's got something that belongs to me, and I need it."

With the word *fuck*, Cobb signaled his willingness to abandon civility. Uncomfortable, I put down my fork, hooked my leg around Violet's carrier, and scanned for the nearest exit, just in case.

"Don't kid a kidder, Professor Twostar. You're no fool. What do you want for it?"

Cobb spread pâté on a cracker, put the whole thing in his

mouth. Even his manners suddenly became sloppy, contemptuous in their careless greed. He waited.

"By 'it' I assume you're referring to the papers I found in the library," I said.

"Screw the papers." Cobb smiled at himself, ate another cracker. I was obviously to be persuaded in the crudest manner possible. "I just want to know what they said," he went on. "You can keep the goddamn papers. Sell them to a collector, make yourself a little nest egg. Buy a Cadillac. You have no idea how to use what you've got, but I do. So let's deal."

His bluntness took me a moment to absorb. It was obviously a tactic he'd employed to good effect in the past, this sudden shift in self-presentation. His words had changed from scalpels to hatchets, but he used them for the same purpose.

"Wait a minute," I tried. "Question one: How do you know what the papers say if you've never seen them? Question two: Why didn't you come and see me in Hanover if they're so important?"

Cobb chewed a few bites of grapefruit, then spoke meditatively.

"I'll answer 'two' first. It's simple. I have reasons for staying out of the country at the moment. Private reasons."

"Legal reasons?"

Cobb smiled a careful smile, and held up his hands. "Let's go back to question number one: how I know what the papers say. Cobbs keep diaries too. The vault at the Boston bank is full of them, right back through the eighteenth century. What the authors did, where they did it, how much it cost. Details, prices, times, dates. Every day saved for posterity. It's all there. How Samuel Cobb traded a shipload of his slaves—half of them sick anyway—to some viceroy in Santo Domingo. In exchange he received two chests of gold bullion—the beginning of the serious family fortune—plus a ship's log that was supposed to be in Columbus's handwriting, along with a two-page signed letter, and a bunch of shells that this Spaniard claimed were the garbage from Columbus's dinner. Sam had the sense to keep the bulk of the diary, but like a fool he sent the second half of the letter, a page of the journal, and the trash up to his alma mater. Not smart. They got lost, or held for ransom. I was afraid they were gone for good until you wrote to me."

"And this Samuel Cobb didn't say what was on the pages?" I was beginning to appreciate my bargaining position. Cobb was bluffing. He clearly thought the pages revealed more than I knew they did, and as long as he continued to believe that, I was in the driver's seat.

"Like I said, not smart. I had a photocopy of the log translated by some jackass at Harvard. The bastard held me up for ten thousand dollars to forget what he'd seen. He'll *wish* I could forget, someday. And the letter: it starts out with a lot of praising the Lord and then just when it's getting interesting, when it says he could not seek the crown where they have hidden it but instructs the reader to follow these steps to locate it, the text stops. To be continued on page two—misplaced in New Hampshire. So where *can* he not seek it, Mrs. Twostar? I'm sure it's here on this island."

"There *is* mention of a crown," I said, "in the fragment I found." His cool eyes fixed on me. "And my page *does* contain vague instructions." Let him wonder. Did Cobb know the significance of the shells? He had only mentioned them once. I wondered if Racine had located someone who could figure out their meaning. "But what makes you believe a . . . crown would survive after all this time?"

"*Your* page?" He cocked his head slightly as he weighed the import of my possessive pronoun, fit it into his calculations, recognized that the ante had just gone up. "If this particular crown had been found, it would have made news. As you well know." Despite his false flattery, Cobb hadn't counted on me to be "smart," and he didn't much like the discovery.

We stared at each other, stalemated. Finally, he turned his attention to Violet, still asleep in the baby seat.

"There are many things she will need," he said pointedly. "What does an assistant professor take home these days? Forty? Forty-five? That won't be enough. What do you think *might* be?"

I caught my breath. I'd never before controlled anything worth a bribe.

"Mr. Cobb, even if the pages contained what you're looking for, they belong to the college, or to the country. They're part of history, not mine to keep or give."

"How high-minded of you." Cobb sounded almost amused. "If you really believed that, you'd have given them back already."

I had no ready answer. Cobb's tone gentled a little. "By the time she gets to college age tuition'll run, what, two hundred thousand? Three?"

He was serious. He was willing to pay me three hundred thousand dollars just to know the little I knew. What surprised me almost as much as the amount was the fact that I felt weak with temptation. It would be so easy, so painless, to comply. Easy come, easy go. What difference did it make? I didn't care about Columbus, not when compared to Violet. Cobb watched me closely, without blinking, saw me waver. Then he did a thing that wasn't "smart": He smiled, and his face became the mask of every crooked trader who ever sold a smallpox-infested blanket to an Indian.

"She'll get scholarships," I said, abruptly taking hold of myself. "She inherited brains from her parents."

His mouth froze and his eyes narrowed. I didn't look away.

"Don't be hasty. Let's have a drink. What can I make for you?"

"I'll pass on the firewater," I said. "Nursing mothers and horse traders don't drink. But be my guest. Have a double of something strong."

My teeth smiled back. Take your twenty-four dollars' worth of beads and trinkets, white man, and stuff them. This time I'll keep Manhattan.

"Professor, you disappoint me." His voice, once again, was smooth as old satin. "I seriously overestimated."

"That's one way to describe it."

I got up, walked onto the veranda, and tried to stifle my anger—I needed a cool head—and the sight that greeted me went a long way toward changing the subject. Only hours before, I had slogged through frozen slush and worried that a blizzard might cancel the flight. Boston had been coated with a glaze of hail that left the air as damp and clammy as a wet towel. And now: bougainvillea blossoms, sand so fine it reflected light. The wind was a fragrant comb. I could stand to live here, I thought. I could barter for this house that he so wants to get rid of.

Cobb joined me. "I wish I had a dollar for every time I've been defeated by this view," he said. "A resort chain offered me a bundle for the property but I told them to get lost. They'd ruin it."

Maybe he wasn't all bad. "It would be nice to keep it just the way it is," I agreed.

He regarded me oddly, as if I were too dense to be believed, then his laugh barked abruptly. "You really don't get it, do you? There's a crown out there someplace that was *the* most valuable single thing in fifteenth-century Europe. It's worth ten resorts. I'm not liquidating an inch of this estate until it's located, insured, and on the block at Sotheby's."

I *had* been wrong about him. He was worse than I thought.

"Ten resorts," I repeated. "My, my. And to find it, you're willing to pay me a whole three hundred thousand dollars. Aren't you generous."

He cast a sidelong, assessing glance in my direction, then said soothingly, "All right. You can't blame me for trying, but don't let yourself become greedy. If what you've got is real, I'll do an eighty-twenty split with you. Off the top. I've got years of investment sunk here. Hell," his features roughened again, "I could take you to court with an injunction. Those pages are the property of my great-great-grandfather. You have no status. Or I could have you thrown off this island. The chief of police owes me a favor."

"Mr. Cobb, I just arrived. At your invitation. And now you're sending me back, missing pages and all?"

That got his attention.

"Where are they?" His look flicked toward the door and I read his mind: my luggage was in his trunk.

"Let us say that I have committed certain rather essential passages to memory," I said, regretting that I had even brought along photocopies, presently stored in an envelope at the bottom of Violet's diaper carrier.

Cobb didn't altogether believe me, but he couldn't be sure and held up his palms in mock surrender. "This afternoon has not gone a bit as I intended," he conceded. "*What* did you say you taught at Dartmouth?"

I smiled, ready to act conciliatory. I could just imagine Roger's face if I told him we were going back home immediately.

"This can't be just about money," I prodded Cobb. "You don't seem to be hurting in the wealth department." I made a gesture with my hand that encompassed the house, the gardens, the view, but then I noticed something my first impression of the place had missed. The drapes were creased in lines of dirt. A few tiles were missing in the hall. The floor was stained and unswept, the straw rug tattered. A few patches on the wall showed water stains. A window, cracked, was left untaped, and it rattled.

"I took a beating in the October dive a couple of years ago," Cobb said candidly. "And let us say the money that I lost wasn't all mine to lose. I've made some wrong moves since: Houston real estate, savings and loans. I bought too many yen and not enough marks. I unloaded my defense-based stocks just before Kuwait. Who could have predicted any of what happened?"

I have always found honesty disarming, probably because I come from a family that doesn't believe in euphemism. Grandma taught me to look life in the face and prepare for the worst. I didn't like Cobb, but he interested me.

"How about if we backtrack a couple hundred years and you go over again how the Cobbs got mixed up with Columbus's Diary. I thought nobody had seen the original since Isabella died in 1500."

"In 1504," he corrected, and noted my surprise. "I think you'll find me well versed in the history. It's been a family avocation for many generations. But fine, I'll tell you. I don't claim it's all true, but it makes a good story."

He steered me back inside, but we sat in view of the sea. I settled onto a wicker chair, tilting my chin to catch the heat of the setting sun through the glass. Cobb laced his fingers, and began.

"All that scholars have of the Diary to date is a partial transcription of the copy of the original. Isabella commissioned a scribe to prepare that copy for her just after Columbus returned from the first voyage—the Barcelona version. Since lost. And the original was lost too."

"I read someplace that the holograph was used with the rest of the Salamanca library to line the stables of Napoleon's horses when he invaded Spain."

"You're ahead of yourself," Cobb said. "Everything has to do with the kind of man Columbus was: an ingenious opportunist. He wasn't even the first one on his ship to sight land, you know—but there was a bonus, an annuity, attached to being first, so as captain he claimed it for himself." Clearly, Cobb approved of this prerogative.

"An Early American cheat."

"As you yourself so astutely recognized," Cobb reminded me, "motivation is rarely just about money."

"What, then?"

"It's about control. Perks. Power. It's about changing the rules when it suits you and about defining the game. It's about staying captain of the ship."

"Even when you don't know where you are?"

"Especially when you don't know where you are. Then more than ever."

"Okay," I said. "So Columbus keeps a diary and brings it back to the queen from his first voyage."

"Columbus kept two diaries," Cobb corrected. "One for his crew's consumption, to convince them that they hadn't gone as far as they thought so that they wouldn't want to turn back. And an unexpurgated version for himself and for the king and queen."

"So which do you have?"

"You mean, which original? I don't know. It doesn't matter."

"What do you mean, it doesn't matter? Only the second version was true."

"The document in my possession is the single one that survived. That makes it the true one."

Cobb's cynicism was so deep-rooted that it verged on the profound.

"Tradition has it that Las Casas lifted parts of the Barcelona copy, probably borrowed it from Columbus's son Diego," Cobb continued. "He used it to support his liberal arguments about the rights of Indians and omitted everything that didn't suit him. But perhaps he had possession of the real Diary, and didn't give it back to the court. Perhaps when he was finished with the journals he deposited them in the Franciscan monastery at La Rábida for safekeeping . . . or to guard them from the eyes of his enemies."

"I never read that." I frowned at the ocean.

"Naturally. We are now into official Cobb apocrypha, which in turn is based upon the rather spotty oral traditions of the pirates to whom Samuel Cobb sold his cargo of slaves."

"You lost me."

"As the priests lost *it*. Someone had the bright idea to bring the original, plus the letter, to New Spain—probably one of Las

Casas's do-gooder cronies who wanted to rub a conquistador's nose in it. But then the whole missionary venture went belly-up and all property was confiscated by the governor of Hispaniola, including . . ."

"The Diary."

"The Diary. Except nobody knew whether or not it was the real thing. Apparently in the years that followed there were lots of fake orders from the king floating around: Mexico belongs to José, Peru belongs to Juan—that kind of business. So the Diary was put into a private library at Santo Domingo along with some other papers of Columbus's that had been confiscated in the early 1500s, and nobody checked it out for another two hundred years, until one good growing season when there was too much sugarcane."

"What does sugarcane have to do with anything?"

"It has to do with slaves. Look around at the people on this island and all the others. How do you think their ancestors got here? They arrived on the one-way trips from Africa, not a few of them on Cobb boats."

"How can you sit there and say that?"

"Professor Twostar, it happened before I was born. What am I supposed to do about it? What's done is done. The point is, the head Spaniard had a slight problem of liquidity. He needed all the slaves he could get, and into the harbor sailed the answer to his prayers, but he had only x amount of gold, which didn't begin to cover the cost per capita. So he thought, Do I have anything else to barter?—and he remembered this legend about some moth-eaten book across town, and put it to old Sam Cobb. The chance of a lifetime. A one-of-a-kind proposition, the next best thing to a Gutenberg Bible. Lucky for him, Sam was a graduate of Dartmouth College, his head filled with books. How could he refuse?"

"Incredible."

"That's what Sam's father said. The story goes, he compared the transaction to trading a cow for a certain magic bean. Nothing Sam could do would persuade the rest of the family that he hadn't been snookered good and proper, and by a greaseball to boot. The rest of his life looked like the butt of one long joke, so he did the only thing he could think of. He shipped off two sample pages to his old college president and asked to be proven right. And, as if the poor fool didn't have enough bad luck already, Dartmouth claimed to lose the damned documents. For two centuries. The only thing a Cobb hates more than to be shortchanged is to be ignored, to not be taken seriously. Frustration drove the family wild. Still does. Oh, they believed in tradition. They kept sending their sons up to Hanover for schooling. They also believed in getting what was theirs. Over the years I'm sure they turned the campus inside out. But Cobbs don't concede, and by God, it looks like we were right. Here you sit. But tell me: How did you happen to find the documents when so many have failed?"

I was not about to be charmed. "You're leaving out something," I said. "Where do you come into it?"

"I told you. I had some cash flow reversals, and like that pirate in Santo Domingo I had to ask myself: What can I put my hands on that's worth something? I went to our vault, hoping to uncover some forgotten stock portfolios—AT&T or Boeing would have been nice—and I started browsing through all the old papers. On every other line of those journals somebody rattled on about the missing pages and how Dartmouth didn't answer their last letter. Finally I went back to the old book itself, wrapped in silk inside a mahogany box. I commissioned a new translation and concluded that the only things that stood between me and balancing the books were two missing pieces of paper. Correction. The only thing, apparently, is you."

I willed Violet to cry, to call attention to herself, but telepathy failed: she slept on quietly. Finally, I pretended to hear her and picked her up. I needed a moment to think, to review my strategy. Cobb only wanted a crown. I wanted America back.

The cornerstone of Grandma's philosophy of getting her own way was: Don't invent, don't overcomplicate, stick as closely as possible to the facts. But hold something back for when you need it.

"I might as well be straight with you," I said. I told him about the blank oak block that had started me off, about the Mohawk student's revenge, about the discovery of the pages, but I kept the shells to myself and Cobb seemed to forget them. He listened attentively as I painted an odd yet credible picture of myself—a picture, I realized, modeled after Roger Williams. Columbus had been forced upon me, I complained, but then when I lugged home research, one tale of Columbus's life more convincing than the next, each containing its own set of details, I eventually started to form my particular unique vision of the man, a composite of all I read. I came to resent it when others differed. *I* knew what there was to know: *I* had figured the man out. I had possessed him, claimed him. That's why I needed the whole Diary, the rest of the story, the missing flagstones to the foundation. Every day since I found the lost pages, I had read them, had pored over the words, memorized each one, considered each obscure and possible shade of meaning. Because I'd made the Diary my talisman, my own future, there was no way Cobb could deny me. My obsession to know matched his to possess.

As I talked, as I stood back from myself and heard my own words spill between us, further recognition tugged. I was close to the bone. The language I used was that of another time, another place. It was the vocabulary of the colonizer. Discovery. Possession. How different *was* I from the construct I fabricated? Cobb's goal was clear, predictable, the logical conclusion of the man. But was mine or Roger's more original?

"So you see," I concluded, dodging my own thoughts, "it's the real Columbus that's so important to me. If you've got evidence, say so. If you don't really have the rest of the Diary, don't tease."

Cobb watched me, his opinion shrouded, every fiber of him gone keen with listening. Was I dumber than he had thought, or smarter? He held himself in suspension—we both did, two adversaries or two allies, it came to the same thing. We crouched in our chairs with our eyes on each other's faces. I hardly dared move.

"The rest of the Diary," I coaxed. "It's here. Say it."

Cobb drew in a breath, his gaze fixed and wide. Then he spoke, almost angry, his voice fierce with the same possessiveness I'd heard in mine, the same emotion near to lust, the same desperate need to encompass, to complete.

"If you've got what I think, then we have the whole damned story."

The papers that Cobb placed on the study table before me were as brittle and desiccated as leaves after snow has washed through them, after they have lain on the floor of the woods for a full winter and a spring—browned, eaten, bitten through, and rusted around the edges. But over the past months I had spent so much time following each curve and whorl, each dot, and each scratched-out mistake of Columbus's distinctive hand that I now knew the low-slung loops, the arrogant and carefully arranged capitals, the precision and repetition of the writing.

I thanked the Mexican nuns for teaching Grandma, and her for teaching me. I could read the old Spanish, though with enormous difficulty.

With my back to Cobb I reached into the bottom of the diaper bag and took two sheets out of the envelope: the copy of the page from the Diary, and Grandma's translation of it—the page filled with gifts. Cobb took them in both hands, frowned at them. It was only half of what he hoped for, but it was a start, a proof that the words existed and that they were not exclusively in my memory. He shrugged and indicated I could proceed to examine his part of the bargain.

He pulled out a chair for me and then hovered briefly, watching for my reaction. He had produced his own set of notes, and his own hand, I recognized, had taken on some of the same eccentricities as Columbus's. *That which we love, we come to resemble,* said the mystic, Bernard of Clairvaux. Perhaps we begin to resemble what we covet, as well. If so, then I saw in this tiny air-cooled room, its cupboards full of chemicals and shelves of data on paper preservation, the closest living human representation of Columbus himself. Henry Cobb was commanding as the Admiral had been, his freckles faded in age, his arms powerful and roped with veins, his legs taut and slender. The stern lines that ran from the flare of his nose to his jaw, the great arched nose itself, the chin and brow, all seemed familiar to me in a dreamy way. His face recalled Sebastiano del Piombo's portrait of Columbus—the shrouded and yet direct gaze, the thin-lipped mouth and somewhat underslung chin. No painting of Columbus done during his lifetime has survived. Biographers develop a feeling for the set of features closest to the portrait in their own heads. For me, the Piombo was the best facsimile.

And now, as I looked down at the ancient text, I was sure that these were Columbus's own words, his own phrasing, recorded directly after an experience, while all was clear in his mind.

Satisfied, Cobb removed the book from the table, carefully put it in a waiting box, which he locked in a wall safe. He set a neatly typed transcript before me.

"Take your time," he said. "I'm going to run over to the club and fax your page to Boston. You won't be insulted if I obtain my own translation. It's been well paid for in advance."

I shook my head, glad to have him go. My eyes embraced the words.

Because it was raining and the sky was cloudy, I read, *we did not depart the island but stayed in that harbor and searched farther to the northwest for another settlement, but found only deserted houses. On a narrow footpath we saw an old man, too weak to run fast, and I sent a man to catch and subdue him and ordered that he should be given a piece of cloth, a few beads, and brass hawk's bells, which I hung around his ears so that he seemed pleased and calmed by this. We did not find the large towns that the glory of the land predicted, but in one house we came upon a loaf of wax, that was so golden and pure to the touch we could almost see through it. I have taken it to give to the Sovereigns, for where there is wax there should also be a thousand other good things.*

I compared what I read with the facts of the voyage that I remembered from other sources. On November 29, Columbus had been delayed in Cuba, in a port now called Barocoa. The wind was unfavorable, and he did not set sail for the next four days, during which time he explored more empty houses, scared four young men digging in their gardens, came across a canoe made of a single tree, marvelously gouged and cut, large enough to hold a hundred and fifty people. At the entrance to this harbor Columbus and his men set up a large cross.

It was all here in this version of the Diary. It all matched so perfectly that the two new sentences leapt out and jarred me. The first referred to treasure: *I knelt with the Crown and dedicated myself once again, Most Serene Princess, to finding the gold which will pay Spain's task.*

I knew the task Columbus meant—the crusade he and half the Christian world envisioned to recapture Jerusalem—but this crown business was not mentioned by Las Casas: Nowhere in the biographies or surviving letters had there been any description or reference to a crown. Just in my pages.

I read on. The wind continued contrary, and on the third of December Columbus and a few armed men decided to investigate the mouth of a deep river which, he said—more overstatement— would hold as many ships as there were in all of Spain. Proceeding along the river, he met Indians, gave away the standard complement of trade beads, and sat in his launch while a few men went up a hill to investigate what was believed to be a large beehive. While Columbus was waiting he had collected an audience.

They began to gather and grouped themselves around the launches where I had instructed my men to remain. There was one who came near, wading to the depth of his waist in the water of the river, drawing near to the stern of the launch where he began to speak in their language which I did not understand. From time to time the crowd thrust their hands into the air and raised a great noise, from which I sensed they were glad to see me. But then I saw the face of the Indian who accompanied us in the boat turn yellow as wax and he seemed to grow ill, shaking and telling us by signs that we must leave because those on shore were readying themselves to kill us. Whether for his own preservation or ours I cannot tell, but this Indian approached one of our men, who carried a crossbow, and he showed it to the others on shore. I believe he told them of its power, how it killed from a great distance, and then he drew a sword from the scabbard of one of our men and he raised it high and spoke some words, regarding its deadliness, or so I could tell from the fact that the whole company vanished sudden as a breath of smoke and there was not a one remaining there. The Indian with us then fell down into the bottom of the boat and would not be raised from there, but I decided to follow the ones who had disappeared.

Columbus must have been crazy. He followed a group of men who painted themselves entirely red instead of wearing clothing and decorated their mud-plastered hair with airy plumes and feathers. Here Cobb's anonymous translator reported that the writing was so fractured and blurred that he could not distinguish some words in the text. Las Casas had reproduced the scene, however, so I knew that Columbus traded for the sharpened javelins of the Indians he followed, then divided among these people bits of a tortoise shell no bigger than fingernails.

They soon give what they have for anything that is given to them, without saying that it is too little; and I believe that they would do so with spices and gold if they had them.

The Admiral was eagerly optimistic. So far he had found, in his own words, "a thousand good things," and yet he hadn't come upon in any quantity the *one* good thing, the cure to his fever, the key to Jerusalem, the guarantee of fame. He hadn't found gold.

I skipped to a new page. On the feast day of Saint Nicholas, Columbus entered a harbor that surpassed all others before it in beauty. His descriptions had the redundancy and desperation of a man whose language has begun to fail him. Holding on as ardently as he could to the maps in his head, he continued to fit everything he saw into the framework of his prior learning, his familiar reference points. But he was beginning to suspect that what he saw wasn't Cipango.

Their king of twenty-one years only, received my gifts with a solemn courtesy and counseled in that language with his tutors and his advisers, who conveyed to him our purpose in searching out the route to the island of Baneque, where there was much gold. The young King, in their language the cacique, showed my bailiff the route to go and said that indeed there was much gold on the island. He indicated to my men that whatever there was that he might give us from his island, he would give us. This king and all the others around him, the women even, walked as naked as their mothers bore them, without any trace of shame, and we saw they were the most handsome people we had met in these islands, and very white. If they wore clothes and protected themselves from the sun, I am certain they would be white as any people in Spain.

And here it was, the second major variation from all existing versions of the Diary, and exactly what I had hoped to find. *He is clearly a King*, Columbus had written, *a Sovereign the equal of Portugal or France, the Lord of all his dominions.*

Bingo! I closed my eyes, blessed Columbus for his big mouth. In one sentence he had by extension recognized every native tribe and nation. Wait till I got this baby before the Supreme Court. The first European chronicler, official representative of the king and queen of Spain, had acknowledged in his own handwriting that native peoples had the full right to govern their own territory— and that was the missing ingredient in every indigenous land claims and repatriation case from Long Island to Hawaii.

I had been reading for an hour, sitting hunched in the captain's chair, my breathing shallow, hardly moving. When Cobb returned, a piece of fax paper curled in his hand, I raised my head with a start. My neck was stiff and my vision was swimming.

Cobb evaluated me with his careful gaze.

"I'm turning in," he said.

I nodded vaguely, bending to the manuscript. Cobb's hand covered the typed page in front of me.

"You're exhausted." His voice was as near to gentle as I'd heard it. "The words have waited a long time. They'll still be here in the morning, like the view."

"I don't know. You could change your mind. Run off with the thing."

"Or you, with the treasure."

I must have frowned hard, squinted, made some negative gesture, because Cobb laughed. It was a harsh sound, metallic and sharp. "Come, now. Let's play out our hands. Each of us. I don't see the point in remaining coy."

I shook my head to clear the haze. I was still in the grip of the journal I'd read so often, but never with the confidence that it was in the Admiral's original voice. I had no patience for Cobb and pointed to the fax.

"You know what my piece of the manuscript says. It's right in front of your eyes. So who the hell's being coy? What else do you want from me?"

"This is one page," Cobb said. "You've got another. My translator in Massachusetts is standing by." His face was deadly serious, a grave and severe mask. "I really do despise pretense. Am I to believe that the end of the letter contains nothing I want to see?"

"Suit yourself." I had him where I wanted him as long as he didn't actually confirm that my ace was a deuce.

Again we faced off, ready to snap. Tiring, I settled back and pushed down on the arms of the chair. "I don't know what the game is, but the rules are screwed up. You bring me down here, whet my appetite, demonstrate that the document you have is real, and then deny me free access. Don't accuse *me* of being coy. The treasure *is* the manuscript, and now you have every page."

"You do disappoint me."

"What? You really take this crown stuff seriously? Every other word of this Diary is hyperbole."

He laughed. "The Diary is icing on the cake. When I locate the crown, the book will of course go on the block as well, page by page, perhaps word by word if there are enough wealthy private collectors. Not to mention the many German, Japanese, maybe even American corporations who would pay to have a souvenir of the log in the vault of their headquarters. Who's ever going to see Renoir's *Bal du Moulin de la Galette*? What's the difference?"

I shut my eyes. It was one of the most incredible know-nothing ideas I had ever heard. Break up the Diary. Fracture the unity. Lose the true intent forever. I could not let that happen.

"You don't have the right. This is humanity's legacy."

"Possession is nine points. And you're being disingenuous, purposely obtuse. Look at the page you brought—here." He pointed to a word on the copy of the original I had given him. "*Corona.*"

"Yes, *Crown*, capital *C*. It probably refers to Isabella."

"Please. Don't insult me."

"Even if there were an actual crown, that was then. What you want is information." In my own ears my voice sounded childlike and peevish, not at all convincing. I thought very hard. In the past I was always the last to figure out what lay before my eyes, the one who misinterpreted or simply ignored the obvious. Not this time. I was different. I kept my mouth shut.

"I offered you eighty-twenty," Cobb said. "Off the top."

He was out to screw me, no doubt about it, but I'd do him one better.

"All right. You win. The second page of the letter may lead to the crown—I can't tell without seeing the complete document. But it's yours—in exchange for *that,* intact." I pointed at the dial of his safe.

He stared at me and lost his poker face. I could see the relief, the greed, the eagerness. He was mine, even if he didn't know it yet. I could make up anything for the missing page, any red herring, and by the time he discovered the lie, I would be out of here. And if that didn't work, I still had the shells in reserve. He'd find them irresistible.

Cagily, suspiciously, we exchanged our offerings: he gave me back my copy of a single page and I returned to him the typescript of all the rest. I collected Violet, still conked out from her trip, and then Cobb led me down a narrow walk of poured concrete steps to a small beach house equipped with an actual crib and a bed that looked like heaven on earth.

It was one of those deep plunges into sleep that refresh completely. Four hours later I awoke almost preternaturally alert, and experienced what my Philosophy 1 professor used to call an "Aha!" reaction. With a kind of wheeling clarity, as though I had dreamed the missing parts and now they connected before me, engraved in the thick and lightless swell of air that poured through my window, I saw a possible, plausible shape to the story. It had to do with the crown, of course. That was the key. It had to do with Guacanagari, the native cacique who dealt with Columbus. He had entered my unconscious.

Gilded clouds lowered, glowing, and there was something I had to do, something I had to tell. It was all clear for a moment and then it shifted, dispersed in the sound of ocean waves threading the beach.

12

VIVIAN

The combination was vinegar and oil, Roger and anti-Roger. In their first glance Roger confirmed every suspicion he'd held about Cobb, and Cobb sensed the judgment made and formed an opposite and equally antagonistic response. The two disliked each other so thoroughly upon meeting that I was afraid Roger would inadvertently blow my strategy. Each man reluctantly extended a hand and shook, too long, each one squeezing a little too hard, pumping too vigorously. The duration of their competitive grip inspired Nash to roll his eyes in boredom to indicate that he was above such pissing contests.

"Well, hi," he said to Cobb, who had ignored him. "Glad to meet you, too."

Roger and Cobb gave up the struggle, warily relinquished physical contact, and when Cobb finally turned to Nash I lip-synched to Roger, "Be nice."

His mouth turned down at the corners and he jutted his chin.

"So this is your son," Cobb said to me, all phony hospitality and welcome. "Your other dependent." He smiled at Roger. "Or does your boyfriend count, too?"

"Come on." I took Roger's hand, which clenched in outrage. "You're going to love the guest house."

"Just a moment." Roger's face tightened.

"Oh, I'm joking. Don't take offense." Cobb made to wave away his own remark. "I know a good deal about you, Professor Williams—a dropout from the family business, a poet with a trust fund, all of these little experiments that so discouraged your father and your brother. I'm well acquainted with Bart, of course. Done a fair amount of business with the man over the years. I apologize if I've hurt your feelings."

"Roger, just look at this." I swept my arm around us at the lovely sight and ushered Roger down the path, away from the taunts. The palms clattered in the light breeze and a tiny lizard skimmed through the dry bronze of the undergrowth.

"It's paradise, Roger. *Don't spoil it.*" I underlined the words.

He came with me down the path, but the muscles of his jaw were bunched into symmetrical angles. He was suffused with irritation. Even Nash, straggling behind us, was sensitive enough to Roger's mood to refrain from any comment, and he branched from the walk toward the beach.

Once inside the house, Roger immediately crouched by the small dormitory refrigerator and busied himself with transferring the contents of his bright silver bag into the humming interior. When he was finished, he brushed off his hands and perched stiffly next to me on the narrow couch.

"So," he said. "What does the old fart have and what does he want for it?"

This was unusually direct for Roger, uncharacteristically cynical, and also disconcertingly on target. His perspicacity was the turning point: in order to deceive Cobb into believing I would consider his offer, I'd have to keep Roger out of the way. There was no room for overt enmity, so I'd have to steer the two clear of one another. I'd distract Roger, lie to him if I had to. He wouldn't approve of the steps I was prepared to take, but I didn't want to argue. In the end, I told myself, Roger would forgive me.

"Don't be so suspicious." I messed his hair, adjusted his collar.

"Cobb's a familiar type, not so bad." I kneaded the tense muscles of Roger's shoulders with my fingers. "He's like everybody else—he's got his own agenda."

"You don't know who you're dealing with, Vivian."

My hands dug harder into Roger's scalp and he jumped, rubbed his head.

"Don't be offended. If *I* can't even pinpoint—"

"What you see is what you get. I do not require your condescending protection, thank you very much."

He leaned back, weary, to look at me. "The thing is, you know, you do."

I ignored him. "Cobb has the whole Diary. I'm sure it's the original. Positive, Roger. I actually had it in my hands. Look. You've never seen this before."

I handed him a slip of paper upon which I'd written the line from Cobb's translation that had struck me most forcefully. "I knelt with the Crown and dedicated myself once more, Most Serene Princess, to finding the gold which will pay Spain's task."

While he read I went over to the crib, rocked Violet, who was fussing. I jiggled her a little too wildly and she opened her eyes in surprise.

"Am I supposed to believe that there's something to it? A real crown, perhaps?" Roger's voice was dry, with an undertone of instruction. "Vivian, assuming the charlatan did not simply manufacture this line, you *must* know that each section of the Rosary was called a crown. It's clear that he's simply reciting a decade. He did that often, you know."

I dropped the subject. Roger could be right. There were too many oblique references, too many situations in which a crown was mentioned. But on the other hand, why would Las Casas have so scrupulously excised all mention of the *Rosary*? It didn't much matter to me one way or the other. What mattered was that Cobb believed in it and that made him vulnerable. What *I* wanted was already found: the Diary itself. I rocked Violet more gently, left Roger to make his own explorations of the tiny cottage, and stepped outside to regain my equilibrium. At least the sea, golden green and transparent, was as advertised. It had completely tranquilized my son, who had waded barefoot to stand waist-deep, bobbing with each silken swell.

The dark was velvety and full of sound. Night had come down on us swiftly, throwing us so abruptly upon each other's company that Nash had accepted the invitation to sleep in one of Cobb's spare bedrooms. He said he preferred the privacy, but I hoped he wouldn't make good on his offer to try to snoop around Cobb's house. He hadn't mentioned that idea since Hanover, and I prayed his interest in Columbus was under control. One nosy move and Nash would find himself bunking on the beach.

Roger was exhausted—he had sat up on the boat most of the night—and I slept deeply until Violet's first low cry awakened me. Before she let loose with a yell that might rocket Roger through the ceiling, I slipped from the bed and returned with her nestled to my chest. After she had nursed herself back into slumber, I lay awake, aware of her slightest movement. Her body was small and marvelous, a comfort, a bridge of our intricate genetic possibilities. But most of all she was herself, whoever that would eventually become beyond this willful enigma, this sweet calm weight. I felt a pinprick, rubbed at an unseen spot on my neck just as Roger slapped the air.

"Sorry," he whispered. "I've been *bitten.*"

"Me too."

"The tropics." He turned toward me in anticipation, clearing his throat, his mood changed and softened. Then his hand encountered Violet.

"Occupied." He rolled back with a grumpy moan. I could see him in the silvery light, a banded silhouette taking stock of an unorthodox situation.

"Another one!" Roger scratched at his ankle. There was an edge to his voice, and abruptly he reached to the floor to rummage in his bag. I heard the pump of a spray, smelled an overpowering herbal pungence. "Feel free. I'll leave the bottle next to the bed."

"It smells disgusting."

"How nice of you to say so, Vivian, now that I'm totally covered with it." He maintained silence for a long beat, then continued.

"The wind has died, utterly died. That's when the bugs come

out. I do not intend to awake in the morning covered with bites, a nine-course midnight supper for the local fauna."

"Go to sleep."

I felt something on my arm. A crawling set of tiny legs? Maybe I was becoming hypersensitive, but I worried about Violet, small and juicy and helpless. Should I coat her with toxic chemicals in order to ward off malaria? Did malaria exist down here? It wasn't a question to ponder late at night.

"I wonder how much longer," Roger muttered, "until the goddamn rosy-fingered dawn." He pressed an illumination button on his watch. "Half past one! We've only slept a little more than two hours."

He was quiet for a moment, seething, accusatory. I tried to change his focus.

"The moon's just risen. Look." Through the window we could see sky, a patch of the ocean. The light gleamed like old silver.

" *'But as we, in our isle imprisoned . . .'* "

Roger, the expert, always ready with the apt John Donne line, allowed his voice to teeter on sarcasm. I tried again to divert him.

"Do you want to talk?"

"Why not?"

"Don't *endure* me, Roger. It might take our minds off the— whatever they are, these things."

"The flies. Good God. The repellent isn't functioning." There was a slight edge of hysteria in Roger's voice. An American failed by the consumer product he had trusted.

"I know you don't take seriously the stuff about the crown, but I need your opinion."

"Of the man? Cobb's dangerous . . . no fool." Roger was fading.

"Just listen, all right?"

I waited for him to agree, but instead I heard his breathing deepen, felt his body go slack beside mine. I kept Violet in bed with us, not daring to disturb her now, or to wake Roger. I needed to think, to examine my whirling ideas with more objectivity. So I let the images and coincidences and ideas flow uninterrupted into the dark air.

What we had was a triptych. A puzzle composed of three

pieces: the letter, the shells, the original Diary. Each one contained clues to understanding the other two. They constituted some kind of whole, but I didn't know how they fit together.

I began with the Diary. Las Casas had omitted all references to the crown when he transcribed the Barcelona copy, suggesting that there was something controversial about the object itself. But what? A few moments of free association turned up several intriguing possibilities: One, it was *Isabella's* crown, from Castile. The story, long considered by scholars to be fabrication, of how she pledged her jewels to finance Columbus's first voyage may have had a factual basis after all. Except this crown wasn't pawned—it had come along. Okay, second brainstorm: This particular crown had an unsavory history. Stolen, perhaps, or loot from the recent sack of Granada. Maybe it hadn't been hers to send. But why *had* it been sent? That led to idea number three: It was a crown of state, sent with Columbus as a gift of ambassadorial goodwill. Medieval rumor had it that Prester John, a Christian king with big bucks, was lurking to the south of Europe, somewhere off the beaten track. Maybe the crown was the hopeful first half of an advantageous trade, just in case he turned up.

Or the crown was intended as a tribute to the Grand Khan. Or . . .

The letter. And the oysters. Columbus had dinner with the cacique Guacanagari, that much I knew. Let's say that afterward the discarded shells were lying on his plate. In the letter, he had mentioned the odd markings in the mother-of-pearl interior. When Racine arrived in a couple of days, I would know whether or not these cryptic slashes conveyed any sense, and if there was a translation it could be the key to the conundrum, a link between the Diary and the crown. I could feel the logic of it, almost touch it, so I invented a story to fit the evidence, to make sense— Grandma's favorite pull-the-rabbit-out-of-the-hat device, the trusty oral tradition. Create a bridge between facts that somehow must be related. Night becomes day, every day: please explain in twenty-five words or less.

Okay, what new information had I gained from Cobb's treasure? One scene especially stood out, and Henry had made sure I noticed it. La Navidad. Christmas Eve, 1492, with the *Santa María* grounded and breaking up on the coast of Hispaniola, Columbus depends upon the local cacique to unload the ships, to shelter and console him, and later, to protect the thirty-nine men he must leave behind—since there is no room for them on the *Niña,* a small caravel, and Pinzón had deserted with the third ship.

Waste not, want not. Columbus plans to construct a fort from the remains of the *Santa María.* He orders that a few lombard shots be fired to impress the natives and also gives Guacanagari a pair of gloves and other presents—this I knew from the page I had found. That's not all, and this was the new information, revealed nowhere else: Columbus gave the cacique something much more valuable, something meant to ensure obligation and loyalty. In my middle-of-the-night imagination I see Guacanagari inspect a crown—the latest fashion from Paris.

So what happened next? This part I truly had to invent, but sometimes a sequence seems so right, so appropriate to the order of things, that it takes on an aspect more than fiction. This was like that. I could almost watch it unfurl.

When Columbus came back to the island a year later on his second voyage, maybe crowns were all the rage. Everyone's got one, made of palm fronds or shells. Still no gold. But that's not the worst thing the Admiral doesn't find. All the men he had left behind are dead—though there are more than a few café au lait babies. The original crown has disappeared too. Language was a barrier—Columbus had no proof of what happened, but he had unpleasant suspicion that destroyed something, some faith or idealism within him.

According to the letter, one of the sailors had managed to leave a last message for Columbus, and Guacanagari—knowingly or unknowingly—passed it along. I hoped it was a set of directions, etched on oyster shells, embossed in pearl. The directions back to the crown.

What then?

Violet awoke and cried.

The sun streamed through the huge glass doors. Roger was fidgety and tense beside me on the bed. He had been waiting, I knew at once, for my eyes to open. He was poised. He had been thinking too.

"Give me a minute," I pleaded. I was groggy. My head hurt.

"I'm worried, Vivian. This can't wait."

"Please. Caffeine first."

"*I* listened."

I shot him what I hoped was a withering look, then I buried myself under the pillows. Violet, roused by our voices, let out a sudden roar from the crib across the room. I didn't remember carrying her there, but I must have done so at the time of her last feeding, the four o'clock.

"I hear you," I called to her. "Cool your jets."

Roger took the fact that I responded to Violet and not him as an affront and began to bustle, to unpack his suitcase, to extract his swimming trunks and sunblock lotions and the various bits of paraphernalia that he had so scrupulously brought along.

"I'll be at the beach," he announced at last, in a reproachful voice. "When I come back I expect you to do me the great courtesy of hearing me out."

He stamped away and I dressed quickly, saw to Violet. Then I sat on the porch and drank my first cup of tea while it was still hot.

"Heaven," I told Violet wearily, "that's what this is." My ankles were bitten up and my back itched in unreachable places, but the sight of the sea that morning made me forget small miseries. The iridescent waves lapped in lilac bands, then platinum, as they caught the sun in glittering arcs. Next to the house, the branches of the palms rasped and filed at one another, stiff combs of leaves. A huge black hummingbird buzzed at the mouth of some exotic flower.

"Hibiscus," said Henry Cobb behind me, evidently following the track of my bleary stare.

I offered him the coffee I'd made for Roger. He accepted it, sat beside me, resting the cup on one bony knee.

"So? Conclusions?" he asked. "You've had a day and two nights to think the matter over. I've left you alone."

"There's a lot to consider." I shrugged.

He waited.

I watched Roger, who swam at a reasonable depth, about thirty yards offshore, his arms dipping and falling in precise hemispheres. I hoped that the salt water would create a temporary balm for his painful welts—the smelly herbal mixture, now completely used up, had proved to be perfume to the local bugs.

"I hope Nash wasn't any trouble."

"I hardly noticed him. I heard him prowling around the house in the middle of the night but he didn't bother anything. He probably had trouble getting to sleep in a new place. He went out with Elvis Greer early this morning. Something about snorkeling."

Nash Twostar, private eye. And thanks for asking about the diving, too. Now I got to worry all day.

Roger finished his swim, and as he walked back up the beach he scratched his elbows moodily. The sky was overcast and the waves held a suspension of sand. One, bigger than the rest, thrashed itself high on the beach.

Roger mounted the cement steps, stared at us, then settled uncomfortably into a scavenged-looking chair made of rough red plastic. His hair was slicked back and the skin of his face was glowing. His thin robe, a silky cotton, was carefully belted and complicated rope sandals shod his slender, gnawed-upon feet.

"Good dip?" Henry's voice was neutral. A nice, nothing-promised ante.

"Lovely," said Roger. "But I must inform you that your beach house is infested with fleas."

"*Must* you?" Henry was not the least apologetic. "What a shame. I'll have to do something about that."

I tried a sympathetic look toward Roger, nodded encouragingly at the coffeepot, but he had not missed the cup in Cobb's hand and spurned the offering.

"I would think that as host you might bear a certain responsibility to at least provide some anodyne. Some sort of insecticide that works."

Henry rocked back his chair. "The no-see-ums are a kicker," he chuckled, his voice cutting off as he sipped at the coffee. "Especially when there's not much wind, like last night. They gave the guest house its name, as a matter of fact. This mangrove area can be dreadful. Lights attract them. Do make sure that if you have your lamps on in the evenings you shut the windows. The insects here are so small they pass through the screens. They travel on the air—have only the most rudimentary wings. They're all mouth, actually."

"Nice of you to inform us yesterday." Roger stared at me in blame. We had talked and read for a few hours after dark, windows and doors luxuriously wide in an attempt to catch the faintest sea breeze. From a bug's perspective we must have looked like a McDonald's on a Friday night.

"Lights out at sunset," Cobb instructed brightly. "The first rule of camping. I would have thought you'd remember from your youth, Williams."

"Pardon me. I didn't know we were roughing it." Roger turned to look closely at Violet. "What's *her* secret?"

Violet's peachy skin was completely free of stings.

"Apparently," Roger answered himself, "she is less than appetizing."

I took a deep breath.

"To bugs, you mean." I had rarely seen Roger like this. One righteous grudge competed with another, all derived from the first full night we'd all three spent together in the same room, our little pseudonuclear family. Up until now I'd kept him blissfully unaware of how many times a baby needs to be fed. Between Violet and the no-see-ums, Roger had hardly slept at all for the second night in a row and he clearly resented that somehow, trained by months of practice and lulled by the crash of surf, I had managed to get more rest than he.

Nash approached from about a mile down the beach. I could see his small black outline, flung back from time to time like a question mark, as he tossed chunks of coral as high and far as possible into the surf. I draped Violet over my knees, absently settling into a monotonous rhythm that both occupied and calmed her.

Roger finally poured a cup of coffee, spooned sugar and, with the air of a man about to immolate himself, tipped in a few dollops of canned milk. He was in high sulk.

Cobb made a gesture of reconciliation. "We got off on the wrong foot yesterday, Williams. All my fault, I'm sure." He smiled—stretched the muscles of his face, anyway—and laced his fingers behind the back of his head. His glance traveled between us, sizing us up now that we were both under the microscope. What did he see? Pocahontas and John Smith go to Hawaii? Was I Tonto to Roger's Lone Ranger, the sidekick, the squaw? He and Roger might despise each other, but it was the antagonism of equals. Was I about to be passed over in favor of Roger Williams even though I was the one who had found the pages in the first place?

"I'm sure you would like to see the Diary," Cobb said to Roger. "Vivian tells me that you need some convincing. But I'm sure you can appreciate that I can't just go around showing it to everyone. The material is too sensitive. Vivian of course is free to discuss the matter—and I'm sure we will both appreciate hearing any insights that occur to you."

Call it ego, but I gave Cobb points. He knew how to press Roger's buttons, and he had sensed what I wanted to hear before I did myself.

"As a matter of fact," snapped Roger peevishly, "you may keep your hoax to yourself. I'm quite happy to remain clear of the whole sorry affair. Isn't this absurd latter-day discovery of the lost journal just a bit too convenient? The quincentenary? And let us not neglect the priceless crown, Federal Expressed from Columbus to your bank account. How very fortunate. Bart, your favored associate, mentioned something to me about a leverage problem in several of your businesses, so I take it the *New York Times* story did not exaggerate."

Roger put down his empty cup and ran both hands through his damp hair. He did this several times, frowning as though putting his very thoughts in order with the sweep of his fingers, then he got up and firmly tightened the cotton sash of his robe.

"Vivian." His voice was pitched so as not to draw Violet's attention, but he used the full intensity of his eyes. "You're intelligent. Can't you see through this? Don't you remember the absurd hysteria over Hitler's 'found' journal? Oh, your friend here is clever, I'll give him that. I'm sure he has somehow procured old ink, vintage paper, and employed a handwriting expert. This document will stand the tests of amateurs. But to throw in a treasure! It's really too much of a cliché."

Cobb was smiling, but I kept my expression noncommittal.

Roger had clearly been rehearsing this speech as he lay awake, and now there was no stopping him.

"He views this escapade," he went on, "as a quick route to make a lot of money, to satisfy the creditors before they break his back. And along the way, he's perfectly willing to sacrifice history—that's the part I can't forgive. To him the truth is just a cheap drama to be exploited. Christopher Columbus as Long John Silver."

"Look." Cobb addressed Roger. "What difference does it make what the man wrote in his notebook? That was five hundred years ago, for Christ's sake. The important thing now—"

Roger cut him off. "It matters that the *discoverer* of the American continent was a Jew. He was the son of forcibly converted parents, a man who for all his fame would not have been able to obtain that appalling document, the *limpiezas de sangre*, the certificate of pure, Christian blood to the seventh generation demanded by the Spanish authorities. A man who wouldn't be accepted today as a member of half the clubs you belong to."

"You certainly live up to your reputation." Cobb pinched the bridge of his nose in disgust. "I don't care if he was a goddamn Martian. I've got something to sell here and no time to waste."

Roger's mouth twisted in such sourness that I nearly blushed. He towered over the seated Cobb, spoke as if he hadn't heard him.

"Christopher Columbus, sprung of supposedly uneducated wool weavers, is cast up on the shores of Portugal, still clinging to a spar. A few years pass and suddenly this same Columbus is an educated man who reads Plutarch, Seneca, Ptolemy, Albertus Magnus, Ailly, and quotes Aristotle, Pliny, and bits of Apocrypha to prove his case. Does this sound remotely plausible?"

"Okay, fine. Columbus was a Hebe who majored in Classics. Now can we get on with things?"

Roger's finger jabbed at me and I moved slightly out of its direct trajectory.

"Tell him," he ordered, then did so himself. "Columbus sometimes signed his name with a series of dots and curves that resemble the two Hebrew characters *beth* and *hei*, *baruch hashem*, 'Praise the Lord.' I'd like to see if *that's* in your bogus Diary!"

"P.T.L.," I spelled. "The Jim Bakker of his day." I tried to lighten the mood but received in return only a mystified look from

Roger. He was a true pop culture illiterate and was unsure whether I was supporting his position or making light of it. Cobb, however, quite approved of my joke.

Roger noticed, and assumed a clinician's diagnostic coolness. He made a steeple of his fingers, rested the little church against his chest, and lectured.

"Columbus was a fox, even a bit paranoid, if you will. He had to be if he wanted to survive in those treacherous times. He knew the Zohar, the Book of Radiance of the Spanish cabala. He knew the Aggadah and through it he had a reverence for names themselves, for symbols, letters. He believed that when God was about to create the world by His word, His *word* mind you, the twenty-three letters of the alphabet descended from the terrible crown of God where they were engraved with a pen of fire. The letters stood at God's feet and one by one they begged, *Create the world through me!*"

"Did he say the *crown* of God?" Cobb twinkled his eyes at me.

"Columbus begged too," Roger went on. "Whoever he was before he became the man we know as Colón, before he took for his own the name of a discoverer and a Christianizer, he had to recreate himself."

Roger was winding up, gathering energy—for a finale, I hoped. Violet was mesmerized by the sound of her father's harangue, but the peace wouldn't last.

"So he converted, changed his name, Schwartz to Black, so what?" Cobb was patronizing, but then he got an idea, and it made him laugh. "But *Christóbal Colón!*" He looked to me for verification, and I nodded. "The *bearer of Christ.* Isn't the name a little much? Overkill?"

Cobb threw back his head, opened his thin-lipped mouth, and let out a series of barks that could have filled a cartoon bubble. He held up a hand, palm out, for Roger to stop.

"You're wasting your breath, Williams. I'm not going to show you the thing. This doesn't mean crap to me. All I want is the money, then you can put ten yarmulkes on Columbus's head for all I care."

"Don't lend this oaf the credibility of your position, Vivian," Roger pleaded "You have standards."

"How kind of you to say so."

"I'm sorry. But ask yourself: If there was a crown, why wouldn't Las Casas at least have mentioned it in his extensive paraphrase?"

"Because Columbus lost the damn thing, hid it for himself, wanted to keep the whereabouts a secret," Cobb proposed. "All of the above."

"Absurd. There's no possible scenario to explain it."

"Yes there is. You just didn't listen last night." I replayed my sleepless speculations, omitting naturally all mention of the shells—I figured that Roger was unlikely to bring them up. When I was finished, he shook his head.

"Why Vivian, I had no idea," he sneered. "You've missed your calling. You could be the queen of the costume dramas."

"Maybe I will yet. But meantime, Roger, you haven't had a look at the Diary. Don't be so positive. You may be surprised."

Roger sat on the arm of a metal chair, put his index fingers to his temples, rotated them gently. "Vivian," he said at last. "Don't take this the wrong way, but someone must be honest here. You're no real expert. You don't know incunabula or handwriting analysis. You could be easily fooled. This document can't be genuine. If it were, Cobb would not be afraid to show it to me."

"I beg your pardon," I bristled in exasperation. "You've already got the answers. I can't believe you and my grandmother don't recognize yourselves in each other. Neither one of you ever gets tired of being right." I could as well have been talking to a yucca plant.

Roger raised his head and almost smiled at Cobb. "You know, you're not the first to think of this ruse. There was quite a flurry in eighteenth-century England when an original journal of Columbus's was supposedly found. Written in English, of course."

I couldn't stand the look of satisfaction on his face.

"Oh, shut up, Roger," I let myself say.

That was Cobb's cue and he stood up.

"Maybe I'll leave you two lovebirds to talk this over." Then, to me, "We still have several days in which to come to terms."

Roger, trained to be polite no matter what, rose to say goodbye, but Cobb caught him by the shoulders halfway up and literally shoved him back down.

"Don't bother."

"You pushed me!" Roger waited, appalled, with no idea how to respond. Was this a serious challenge? Did it require some sort of in-kind physical retaliation? I could see the questions fly in and out of his head. What emerged from his lips, though, was a bland question. "Why?"

"Things haven't changed much at Dartmouth, have they?" Henry was full of contempt. "Pontiffs still pontificate, professors still profess. Not since I was an undergraduate have I witnessed such a display of pissing pomposity."

"Stop alliterating." Roger, still leaning forward, refused to relinquish command of the language. "I suppose you have some clever profit-based theory that you'd like to share with us, Henry. We're *all* ears."

"I'm delighted to have your attention, Professor, but as it happens, I don't have to hold you captive with theories. You see, my ideas are fact. Here's a translation of one of the mentions of the crown. I believe you read it, Vivian? Use it to conjure with. Just don't beg to see more. You can read about it in the newspaper."

He reached into the breast pocket of his shirt for a folded paper, stuffed it in Roger's matching pocket, and then, with a great, loose stride, he stepped off the veranda and continued down to the beach. Having noticed Nash's meandering approach, he now strode to meet him. The two stopped about a hundred yards down, their heads bent forward at the same angle, and conversed for a few moments before they seemed to reach some sort of agreement and went off together.

Violet needed her diaper changed, so I slipped into the beach house, fed her, cleaned her up and put her down in the crib. A small land breeze fluttered the leaves outside, but the air was already beginning to feel heavy and dense with the rising heat. I poured myself a bowl of Rice Krispies and tried to eat them before the noise of their snapping and crackling disturbed Roger's concentration. For of course he had followed me indoors and was already arguing with the words on Henry's translated page. I read them over his shoulder, and not only did they match my memory, they fit my plot.

. . . *hands, I set this greatest treasure in Christendom within*

Guacanagari's arms. I explained to him its holy history and he made upon his own breast the sign of the cross. Again, with slow emphasis I repeated to him the history of the Crown, and he understood me, I am certain, for without any prompting he again made the sign of the cross. I joined him in that moment, my own hand trembling as I raised it, as my eyes took in the circlet and saw what marvelous change was wrought, shining leaves. My men are sworn to secrecy. Most Serene Princess, who can say . . .

"Utter claptrap!" Roger shook Henry's page until the paper rattled, as though freeing it of clinging spiders. "I can't believe that we've come all the way down here only to endure this egregious fraud. The man is cuckoo, if you ask me."

I plucked the paper from Roger's grasp before he lost his remaining self-control and shredded it with his teeth.

"Tell me about cuckoo." I leaned over, coaxing at the beginnings of a smile, a tiny grain of good humor that had crept into his voice. "What exactly do you remember about last night?"

"I remember what didn't happen." He took a deep breath, then his eyes softened and he touched my cheek. "I guess I began to drift. Is she asleep now? Can we take up where we left off?"

But just as I relaxed my body toward Roger's through what seemed like a very great distance, Violet gave a loud unsleepy wail. Just one. Sometimes she registered protest like that, as if to alert the world in general. Then a lull. We held our breaths, but no, another and another cry emerged and her momentum built until she was pledged to a full-blown fit of self-perpetuating screams.

"I'm sorry," I said, as though she were some extension of myself, as though I were solely responsible for her demanding existence.

Roger tried to laugh, but the effort cost him. The sound came out warped and angry. "She's got some sort of . . . radar, hasn't she. Perhaps she thinks we're going to procreate a rival. Can't you reason with her? Show her your birth control device, something?"

"Why don't you take a walk on the beach? It looks gorgeous out there."

"Oh, it could be heaven. It could be paradise. But there's one thing lost."

"I know," I said in the sweetest voice I could manage, settling Violet against me. "Eve's busy."

Roger watched for a moment, shuffled morosely. "I know I should be more mature about this, do my part. If I were biologically equipped . . ."

He suddenly seemed so alone, standing there, so welded into his maleness, so indivisible, that I took pity on him. His body was firm and complete, incapable of doubling, of incubating, not to mention providing nourishment, while here I was, pure sustenance. I felt rich, wonderfully extended into this tiny being. I was, in fact, more than just Vivian. I was goddess! And poor Roger was mere mortal.

He was, however, a mortal free to go for a walk if he wanted to, and soon he strolled out the door, heading for the spot where we had last seen Nash. Resentfully, I registered that if *I* wanted to walk, I'd have to lug along the demigoddess. Due to my amazing powers, she was no lightweight. But after I debated the possible effects of a backache versus the romantic loveliness of the long stretch of empty beach, I decided it was worth the effort.

Half an hour later I, or rather we, began our hike, but in the opposite direction from the one the men had taken. I'd bought a bathing suit cleverly designed from the inside out with stretch panels that would mold me into the shape of Aphrodite. Violet was happy. Pinned against my heart, the crash of the sea enveloping the two of us, she rocked dreamily. Life was all throbbing white noise and foaming water, close as she had yet come to the primal oblivion she still craved. I found a place to sit and watch the sea, a ridge of packed sand left by the tide. From the pocket of my windbreaker, I pulled the page from Cobb that Roger had discarded.

There was one paragraph that had probably been the last straw, a mention that on board the flagship *Santa María*, Columbus had carried a gift so fabulous, so invaluable and remarkable, that he referred to it as "the greatest treasure in all of Christendom."

Cobb had done his homework. Stapled to the translated page was a photocopy of an entry from the encyclopedia describing various famous jewels lost just before the turn of the fifteenth century. The most promising candidates, now known only from a watercolor drawing, were four magnificent ornaments given in 1468 by Edward IV of England to Charles the Bold, duke of Burgundy, on the occasion of the duke's marriage to Edward's sister, Margaret. The priceless objects were then supposed to have passed into Spanish hands when Burgundy attempted to make a secret pact with Ferdinand and Isabella. The queen was a one-woman disappearing act: first the Diary and now the loot. The jewels were never seen again, though it was rumored that they had been soldered together into a huge and unwieldy, though fabulously valuable, crown of state.

No wonder Cobb salivated at the prospect of locating it.

I tucked the page back into my pocket, dragged myself up, cradled Violet, and continued walking. This Roger and Cobb antagonism was confusing stuff and left me uncomfortably in the middle, playacting, caught in a sort of Nancy-Drew-goes-tropical quandary. At age forty, I was the Girl Scout with half the missing merit badge. In a way it was all bluster, irrelevant to this lush but desolate, terribly poor island where the local people lived in bare board shacks and drew their water from a single well while the rich tourists, Roger and I among them, complained of biting insects. We seemed suddenly like predators, parasites—Cobb most of all, but each of us desired something. We had come to Eleuthera to steal away some fantasy of our own. Roger wanted local color, inspiration. I was after vindication. And Cobb . . . he was determined to strike gold. What did we have to do with the pulse of life in this place? Our important, earth-shattering comings and goings probably caused barely a ripple.

When I got back to the beach house, I found Roger immersed in a struggle with the new portable computer his brother, Bart, had advised him to buy last fall. He couldn't decide on the proper tilt for the screen, and somehow he had managed to lock himself out of his own file. He frowned into the ions as he maneuvered the keys and fiddled with the batteries, and finally began to experiment, heedless of my presence, still fuming into the purplish square.

"What are you writing?" I asked.

"I'm working on the syllabus for my winter course," he answered. " 'Suicide in Literature.' "

As I lay there, patting Violet, doing the nothing one was supposed to do on an island vacation, listening to the tide, watching the beat of the motorized fan above in the white crossbeams of the high ceiling, it occurred to me that this was the benign stereotype of family life—our future, should we choose to accept it: domestic little woman, man at his machine, wrestling with work.

No way. I began to resent the prissy tap of the keys, the intake of Roger's breath that meant a word had clicked into its proper order, and most of all, the fact that I did not distract him to any visible degree. He had simply hunched his back when Violet cried to be amused. Mother and child were totally blocked out.

I took a pillow from the pile and lobbed it at Roger's head.

"OOF!" The foam column knocked him at the base of the neck and his hands slammed on the keyboard.

"What? What was that? I've erased a week!" It was the second time that day that Roger had suffered bodily insult. I didn't improve his mood by laughing, nor did Violet make the situation better by crying out, surprised in her own right.

"Let's get out of here, go someplace. I've got to keep moving and put her back to sleep before I can do anything else."

Roger was aghast.

"Are you crazy? I'm in the middle of something."

"This is our vacation, Roger. We're supposed to be having fun. It's required."

"Fun? Fun?"

He rose, his spine straight, and cracked his knuckles. He wore a beautifully draped brown shirt of some soft material printed with tiny palms, and black drawstring pants. His hair was now meticulously combed and his skin shaved without a nick. I had initially thought his getup was for my benefit, but I was wrong. Roger had dressed to please himself.

"I've lost my train of thought, my rhythm. I was almost to Spring."

His voice was petulant, shot through with accusation at my selfishness. I was condemned in the sad light of his gaze.

I stood too, rocked *our* baby back into a fitful peace. So much for romance.

He came over to the couch. "Sit," he invited.

I did. His tone was grave, ceremonious. A pronouncement

was finally going to be made, but I didn't know what.

"We must come to an understanding between us, Vivian, if we are to dwell at close quarters."

I waited. He held me with the sheer magnetism of his repressed irritation.

"When I am engaged at the keyboard," he said carefully, "there must be no interruptions."

"Come again?" He was talking to me as if I were a wayward student and he the high school principal.

"No interruptions of any sort," he continued. "It's a quirk of mine, but when writing I require total and complete silence, and the knowledge that I'll not be disturbed under any circumstances. It is the only way to follow out a tortuous train of thought, the only—"

I boiled over, leaned across the small space between us, and for some reason that I didn't stop to analyze, I gave in to a sudden urge. Instead of making an outraged speech, I tweaked his nose. It was a hard tweak. I hadn't known exactly what a tweak was—I'd never tried it on anyone before. But once I did it, it felt right.

He put his hand where my fingers had been. A man can't project much dignity when holding on to the end of his nose.

"Now *you* listen," I said. "I'm the one who can't stand interruptions, remember? That's how we met. But let me tell you: From now on there will be *plenty* of interruptions. There will be cries of hunger and thirst. There will be demands to be entertained. When Violet is older, there will be questions, so many questions, and you'll answer them. If you're sitting at the computer, you'll remove your hands from the keyboard. If you're writing with your fancy pen—if she hasn't flushed it down the toilet by then—you'll screw on the top and set it down. If you're having a thought, you'll put it on hold or forget it. You're a father, Roger. Get used to it."

He rubbed his nose one last time, but did not meet my eyes.

"Roger?"

He sighed. He still didn't look at me, then he about-faced and moved to the lighted computer screen, sat, and began to type. His turned back said it all.

I walked out. If he wanted he could follow, but he didn't. The beach was miles and miles long, and splendid, but I wasn't in the mood for postcard beauty right then. I was in the mood to forget the existence of the progenitor of my younger child. Purvis hadn't been easy to get over, but it had happened. This would too. And so, when in the distance I recognized my son and Henry Cobb, I put Roger Williams out of my mind and walked forward to meet them, waving.

After only a few days away from Hanover, Nash struck me as somehow more open, less the bearer of teenage brooding and more mature. The black sunglasses that he usually affected, even on the dimmest afternoons, were pushed up into his hair. He'd lost his edge of self-consciousness, and gestured with his hands as he talked. When I got to where they were standing, he told me that Cobb had volunteered to take him diving at the reef.

Nash pointed. "Right over there."

About a hundred feet into the Atlantic, a small shelf of brown coral protruded from the waves.

"Just snorkeling," I said. "Yes?"

"Sure."

Cobb was enthusiastic, the most at ease I'd seen him. "As long as we avoid the strong currents at the very far end of the beach, we're quite safe. I've dived here many times, and there's plenty to see," he encouraged. "Angelfish, parrot fish. Rays. I've chased a few good-size barracuda."

"They're the ones with the teeth?" Alarm bells went off.

But Nash and Cobb were clearly of one mind, admitting to no fears or trepidations as they continued to discuss the advantages of various types of gear. Henry allowed as how sharks were common enough this side of the island, but the only time to worry about them was late afternoon. Feeding was at dusk. I made a mental note, and didn't ask about between-meal treats.

"They're only little nurse sharks," Cobb deprecated, responding to the expression that had crossed my face. "They circle if they get curious, but they're not man-eaters. Still, if it makes your mother feel better, we can take along a spear gun for protection."

"A spear gun?"

I wasn't handling this well. Nash was my son, yes, but he was also a grown man, or nearly so. I had resolved more than once to respect his decisions. His high school counselor was in full accord.

Nash, I had been told, might have to find his legs before he took responsibility for his own actions. But around here some hungry fish might find his legs first.

"Absolutely not. You have no experience with this kind of thing." I drew the enveloping shield of my maternal dignity around me and glared defiantly.

"Mom!" To his credit, Nash did not whine.

"Naturally"—Henry pointed to Nash's earlobe—"it would be wise to remove any obvious shining lures. Barracuda go for anything that glitters."

Nash quickly removed the tiny hot-red stone, and then went further, unsnapping from around his neck the flat necklace chain, the portents of which had cost Grandma a month's worth of Rosaries. Just like that, he dropped the jewelry in my palm.

"I want to do this," he said. Then from his lips emerged the magic word.

Perhaps it was the shock. I hadn't heard "please" for so long, years it seemed, that I couldn't register at first that it had actually been uttered. "Please" connoted reciprocal obligation, eventual gratitude. It acknowledged the right to refuse.

I gathered myself. I resisted the urge to be taken in by this sudden display of charm, this seductive ability that Nash had developed overnight, this disconcertingly unusual behavior, this . . . niceness. But it was impossible.

"Okay." My voice was meek, a little stunned. "Okay, honey. Be careful."

That was how I came to sit the rest of the afternoon on shore, on the beautiful veranda, with my heart thumping wildly every time I saw my son take a header from Henry Cobb's small yellow rubber boat into the navy-blue depths that concealed so many dangers. From inside the beach house, I heard the nagging cheeping of Roger's cursor, and the sudden bursts of muted typing. The vengeful side of me hoped for a power surge, something sent by the gods to wipe out the words he preferred to me. I had been wrong to anticipate, wrong to depend, wrong to amend my ways to accommodate Roger, and worst of all, wrong to fall in love again.

*　　　*　　　*

Depressed by the rift between us, hoping to elude the sand fleas and the no-see-ums and whatever else had feasted on us during the previous night, we turned off the lights as soon as we had eaten, and lay down early. Roger had drunk—a bit too much, I thought— of a local pineapple rum mixed with some concoction called Goombay Punch, a sweet, suspiciously scarlet drink. My hurt feelings had worn themselves down to a drowsy sadness and I was ready for oblivion. Not Roger. He wanted, I could tell, to share with me the fruits of his labors, the latest great thought I had nearly caused him to miss.

"There is this wonderful passage in Pliny," he said, "which I'm sure spoke to Columbus. One gets a feel for what the man would value, perhaps memorize, what ideas would attract him."

"Oh, does one?"

Roger pretended to be obtuse, ignoring my coolness and hoping that we could regain our equilibrium without mentioning the circumstances under which it had been lost. Fine with me. I only fought when there was something worth winning, and I was discouraged with the conclusions I had drawn about our future. I had decided that tomorrow I would concentrate on the matter at hand, somehow manipulate Cobb into giving me the Diary, and fly home with it. Once there, I would find the strength to dump Roger—for good this time.

I studied his dark shape, looking for evidence to support this resolve, and found no lack of it. There he reclined, two sheets to the wind, his back propped against the wall, yammering on as if he had an enthralled audience at his feet. He had brought a walloping portion of Goombay Punch to bed and had spilled some on his new shirt.

"In his chapter on sudden death, Pliny describes poor Diodorus, a professor of logic who experienced an interesting demise."

Roger waited for a reaction, but I did not indulge him.

"The poor professor succumbed to mortification. He could not immediately answer some question put to him by way of a joke."

"And it did him in," I said in a pointedly sleepy voice.

"Right," Roger agreed. "A kind of suicide, don't you think?"

"You're asking *me*?" I turned away, took long, even breaths.

"Sleep and fatigue," said Roger too loudly and emphatically, "have dimmed the deadly anger of the mother snake." Thinking he had captured my attention with this maternal reference, he went on.

"And then there was Aemilius Lepidus. As he was leaving his house he struck his toe against the threshold and died. Torquatus. Dead in the act of reaching for a cake at dinner."

"Williams," I said. "Put a sock in it."

"You're implying?"

"No," I mumbled. "You're boring when you're sober, too."

"If you must know," Roger said, "I'm conducting an experiment that may dissuade insects. I'm hoping that my excessive blood-alcohol level will make me distasteful."

"Hey, it works that way for me, but the bugs will probably bring their friends to the party. By now you're the equivalent of a spiked punch bowl."

Roger fell silent, slapped at himself a couple of times, then spoke again.

"You'll think me morbid, but my thoughts are fixed on death tonight. Donne's *Biathanatos*. Remember? Those lists of suicides—Demosthenes, from poison he carried in a pen. Terence, because he lost his hundred and eight translated comedies, drowned himself. And then there's Cato's daughter, Portia, who swallowed burning coals." Roger shuddered, beside me.

Then he tried a quote he must have felt was certain to win a response. "Donne cites Indians, too. Did you know, Vivian, that in order to escape enslavement by the Spaniards, Indians killed themselves in terrible numbers? They only ceased when the Spaniards convinced them that they, too, would kill themselves and follow the Indians with some severity into the next life."

"Yes, I knew that. Save it for the sophomores, Roger. Go to sleep." I turned over once more, fixed my thoughts on the fizzing blankness between each splash of surf, and promised myself that the rest of this week would be devoted to gaining distance from Roger Williams—in every conceivable way.

13

ROGER

I was talking to myself and I was drunk.

But let them sleep, Lord, and me mourn a space.

Vivian had deserted me, eluded by falling asleep my stupid prattle about Pliny. She didn't care about my poem. She had no interest in the historical Columbus, the object of my intense speculation for more than five years. She felt unapologetic for having dragged not just me but her children as well to this pathetic excuse for an island where we would be consumed alive while she played detective with that scurrilous Cobb. She was content to be manipulated, to be a pawn in some self-aggrandizing game. She always dreamed of the easy way, the shortcut. "I like to think on my feet," she once told me, as if the extemporaneous, the faith in inspiration, were a substitute for thoroughness and hard work. Her naïveté played into Cobb's hands. I could see it. I knew Cobb from the moment I met him. My family is full of him, his veneer of politeness that is meant to conceal his singleness of purpose. What did he want from Columbus? Fame? Fortune? "Truth," if it came, was immaterial, a disposable by-product of exploitation.

Oh yes. I looked at the Henry Cobbs and recognized myself as I might have been: a scion of capitalism gone rotten. He was all I had escaped, and when I saw Vivian—a woman I had come to respect for her instincts, her ability to see through the shallowness that surrounded us—fall for his act, I despaired.

My brain felt heavy in my head, a dead weight that needed to be put down. I was a nonentity, a stranger whose strangeness was not the slightest bit interesting. After years of research, after devoting a substantial portion of my professional life to the contemplation of Columbus's mission, I had become in learned circles the expert to whom complex questions were addressed. Now, I was at last sitting where the Admiral himself might have sat. I had plans to compose poetry on and about this place, and quite possibly my name and that of this island would become entwined in the mouths of arguing scholars from Madrid to Mexico City. Yet here I was anonymous, perceived not even as a smuggler, not even with hostility. I was a middle-aged white tourist, one interchangeable with a thousand others, forgotten as soon as I passed by.

I was propped against a foam rubber pillow, probably home to several colonies of fire ants, and all around me this brood of Twostars pumped their lungs, each intake and expulsion of breath the mark on a clockface. Alert in my inebriation, I was the hand that swept past, the night watch.

I rose from the bed, walked barefoot to the ineffectual screen doors, and stepped outside. On the northern islands I knew well, there was always the taste of salt in the brisk air, but here it was different. The thick fumes of rotting plants, overripe and dense, hung like fog. There was a half-moon, bright enough that I didn't need a flash, and I followed the path to the beach. The tide was out, leaving a broad plain dividing foliage from water, and in starlight I paced forward. As my eyes adjusted I began to distinguish details: debris washed ashore and left to dry. Someone had walked here before me, for there was a trail of footprints. I followed them less than a quarter-mile before I found their source. Nash lay curled in a sheet made white and brilliant by the moon. His mouth was open, his exposed arm flung to the side. I could see no particular reason why he had chosen to rest in this spot, but I understood his purpose. At least here he was not trapped in an enclosed space with a swarm of ravenous centipedes. Here there was at least the chance of a breeze, the hope of relief. I watched him stir, settle more deeply into the contours made by the angles of his body. There was nothing to fear here—Eleuthera was empty of major predators, of poisonous snakes, of bandits. I saluted his disdain for convention, his freedom. Its loss would come eventually with age and caution. I resisted the impulse to touch his hair or to rest at his side, to wake him and then only put him back to sleep with my rummed-up thoughts as I had his mother.

Was she dreaming of Henry Cobb and his fake Columbus, a jack-in-the-box whose key she would spring? How easy, how facile, to ignore context and devise a cardboard figure, a retrospect whose every detail miraculously pegged to some subsequent event. Problem, solution, one, two, three. Why did Columbus cross the sea? To get to the other side. How *neat* for him to have buried a treasure: film at eleven. How *perfect* for him to leave provocative clues, how *right* for me to be wrong. How well this emerging version reenforced Vivian's politics! And how beautifully the dates elided: five hundred years practically to the day. Millenarianism lives, by halves as well as wholes. The old order ends, the new begins, and Vivian Twostar, indigenous iconoclast, lights the torch. *Reductio ad absurdum.*

I had been walking fast, almost running, and suddenly I stopped, inhaled, shook my head. What was this anger about? Did I see myself in some competition with the yammering Cobb? Was I as bound to my Columbus as he to his cheap forgery—and who appointed Vivian the final arbiter, the judge of ultimate veracity? I believed in complexity, had based my life and my work upon it, but what if I was wrong? What if the tangle was not of knotted strands but merely of a single thread that, once unwound, dangled unhooked and straight?

I had strayed to my left and the finger of a wave touched my ankle. The coolness sent a tingle up my leg, cleared my brain. I craned my neck and above me rose the Milky Way. There was a formula some scientists had concocted, an algebra for predicting the total number of intelligent civilizations in the universe. Were we among them? And in each civilization, how many distinct centers of consciousness, how many competing points of view? I found my truths in a chain of events that moved forward, but I could not deny the possibility of a reverse direction. The present was but a floating, random dot, a dancing cursor, and the scroll moved both ways. Columbus, idea if not man, was before us and behind us and beside us. He was Nash asleep and he was Cobb's manufactured family ghost. He was my explorer and Vivian's nemesis. He was the capital of Ohio, and he was a country terrorized by drug cartels. He was the excuse for hundreds of federally funded quincentenary committees from which Indians and Hispanics and Italians were scrupulously not excluded, and he was the impetus for yet one more expedition mounted by officious agents of the National Geographic Society. Who he *really* was was at once irrelevant and crucial, an enigma that, if repeatedly solved, could never be allowed to disappear. He stands for the question mark of history, the loop of inevitability, the joker heading the deck of cards. He is Rosebud. He is the Walrus. He is the pane of glass.

This midnight insight, half alcohol, half loneliness, left me strangely weak, as if I had carried a burden and not realized its toll until I set it down. I hunched my shoulders, tasted the dryness of my lips, and turned back in the direction I had come. I hadn't walked all that far. Before I had formulated another thought, before I knew it, I stood outside the house. And then I heard my daughter cry.

The words of Pliny, on the newly born: "There lies the animal which is destined to command all others, fast bound hand and foot and weeping aloud." Clearly this Pliny must have been the Elder, a father present when his child grew teeth—except I wondered about the translation. "Weeping" was too mild a word for the aggravated rage that emitted from Violet's mouth. "Weeping" suggested a certain helplessness, perhaps entreaty, but the sounds that reverberated off the walls of the beach house were of another magnitude. Self-conscious and indignant, they were instinctively calibrated for maximum effect and followed a definite rhythm. Da-da-da-DUM, da-da-da-DUM. It sounded curiously familiar, and then it came to me: Beethoven's Fifth, without a doubt. Like a grand diva in miniature, Violet progressed, a cappella, in solo, into the second movement—a series of great plunges forward with echoes in a minor key.

I slid the screen and stepped inside. My eyes were sharp as a cat's as I nimbly skirted the barricade composed of opened suitcases, diaper bag, and Nash's enormous shoes, to stand beside the crib. My daughter and I were perpendicular to each other—she horizontal, I vertical, she latitude, I longitude—our beings conjoined only by our eyes. Her look was, in counterpoint to protest, measured, even curious. Was it shadow, or were her tiny eyebrows peaked in speculation, in measurement of the catch her vocal net had snagged? I was not the one she expected—my exegesis on the nature of death had acted as a potent soporific upon Vivian, and against all odds she was still asleep. Violet seemed to consider: escalation or compromise, all the while maintaining at a constant the timbre of the first four bars. Then, as if by telepathy, I knew what she had decided. I was *not* an acceptable substitute. She paused, vacuumed in a double breath for added volume, but before she could release it, move on to Tchaikovsky and the "1812" complete with cannons, I counterattacked. Into the dark O of her puckered mouth I plugged the tip of my little finger.

She blinked, contemplated further protest, was tempted to explore the strange intrusion with her tongue, applied tentative suction—and, miracle of miracles, she discovered it to be to her liking. A new flavor, a bit dry perhaps, but amusing, not overpowering in its aroma yet hearty all the same. Emboldened by success, but never withdrawing my digit, I leaned forward and cupped her body in the bough of my free arm. Carefully I drew her toward me until at last I had scooped her from bed, blankets and all. When I rose, she rose with me, cradled and preoccupied, her mouth busy with my finger as she tried to locate the button that would release its novel flow.

I felt the seat of a chair against the back of my legs, and slowly, carefully, I sank into it. Violet raised one hand, flexed its fingers. Noisily, she breathed through her nose while she recorded every detail of my face. Did she think of me—if "think" in fact was the word—as a nighttime incarnation of Vivian? Was there some primal sense that recognized gender or paternity? Was this for her a moment, never to be consciously recalled, in which her world expanded, doubled, became mysterious?

It was that and more, for me. Never before had I been alone with any baby, much less my own. Vivian always hovered close by, supervisory, ready to rush to the rescue, full of experienced counsel. When I held Violet, Vivian would often make minor adjustments, act as a safety net, but this time I was on my own, and there were perceptible differences. For one thing, there was the matter of my left arm, crooked akimbo, elbow pointed above my head to assure a proper angle of entry for my finger into Violet's lips. For another, there was the unaccustomed motion I had for some reason assumed, as if simply being at rest were verboten. I fairly posted on my chair, rode it as I might a trotting horse, rising on my toes in imaginary stirrups, then dropping back onto a saddle. This was no learned response on my part, but it achieved its purpose, soothed Violet's nerves, matched and met some inborn yearning. How did I know to do it? Was this collective knowledge, a proof of Jung?

I don't know how long we remained that way, bobbing and staring, but a sufficient time passed that Violet's weight, at first insignificant, became leaden. Both arms—one support, the other sustenance—fell independently asleep. My hips became sore and cramped in their continual bounce. I was struck by how this process seemed to lack a natural conclusion, how, from Violet's perspective, it could continue indefinitely for days, for years. We were at odds in our wishes, and we would each in turn and many times over disappoint the other. There was no avoiding it. We would give what we could, but compromise, no matter how generous, was bound to fail. There we were, generations united in our inability to fulfill expectations, to give peace and still get what we wanted for ourselves.

I was desperate to record these thoughts, if not for posterity in general, at least for Violet in particular, but I had no free hand with which to write. I longed for my computer, for its megabytes of unused storage. The last remnants of alcohol would soon leave my system, and a day full of mundane conversation would drum all insight from my brain. I had a secret to convey, but no tools for a map. I had uncovered truths I would forget. I was the tree falling in the forest with no witnesses, deprived even of oral tradition as a means of preserving hard-won understanding. I could speak to Violet, whisper my thoughts, and on some subconscious level, who knows, she might hear, but that was not enough. I needed Vivian. I needed her memory.

I cleared my throat, and waited. Nothing. I coughed, and felt Violet pause in her working of my fingertip. She was alert now, reminded to be wary. But Vivian's sheeted form remained inert, impenetrable. Wake up, I willed. Wake up. I scooted my chair backward and the legs fairly screamed along the floor. The only response from the bed was a sigh.

Where was our mystical union? Was there cotton in her ears? Was she not bothered by the same bites as I?

It sucked me first, and now sucks thee,
And in this flea our two bloods mingled be;

As if in answer, a gnat alighted on my hand.

Oh stay, three lives in one flea spare,
Where we almost, yea more than married, are.
This flea is you and I, and this
Our marriage bed and marriage temple is . . .

I had no choice but to fire Violet, to put into motion those forces I had only minutes before contained, to prove my ideas by frustrating her happiness. I extracted my finger, brought my body to stillness, and watched.

She was shocked. She was appalled. She was betrayed. Just when she had begun to trust . . . THIS! Her rage knew no bounds. Her torso shivered in fury, expanded, and became a single bugle. She didn't cry, she bleated—or was it "blate"?—the ram's horn at Jericho. And Vivian fell.

I sat frozen while mother plucked daughter from my arms. I said nothing, fearing to lose my thought, and the instant I was free I made for my laptop. Impatiently I responded to its opening queries: No, I did not want to change the time or date. What processing program? Let woʀᴅ be made flesh. I opened a new file. Its title? My keys tap-danced ᴛʜᴇ ʜᴜᴍᴀɴ ᴄᴏɴᴅɪᴛɪᴏɴ. The blue screen appeared, blank and receptive, and I strained to replicate in shorthand the skeleton of my thoughts. "Utopia," I typed, "occurs when one's desire matches that of another, when the call and the answer are the same, and neither an echo. There is no hope. There is no hope. There is no hope. Subjectivity is all, the guiding rule."

I paused, my fingers flexed like talons before the board. Tonight everything seemed profound, meaningful, even my Toshiba's options. Did I want to change the time or the date? And if I did, what then? Was there no constant? I could exit this file, return to start-up, and enter October 11, 1492. I could make this year 0001, or become Chinese and record 4688. It could be my birthday, every day. I could command the future, mix it with the past. 2000 ᴀ.ᴅ. or 200 ʙ.ᴄ. I could create impossibilities: the thirty-first of February, the ninety-ninth of December. I could relive a good day, skip a bad one. Mere convention kept our calendars constant. Some technician in Kobe had set a standardized norm, but these numbers were no law of nature.

I closed ᴛʜᴇ ʜᴜᴍᴀɴ ᴄᴏɴᴅɪᴛɪᴏɴ. Did I want to save it, yes or no? No, I wanted to get out quickly, back to the first option. Did I want to change the date? Each number blinked invitingly. All it required was the press of gravity. Even intentionality was moot— time could alter if the machine dropped onto the floor, if a bird alighted on the top row of keys. I could close my eyes and fumble and accept the results as fate. Did I want to change the date?

I stared at my hands, luminous in the computer's artificial light, and saw a stigma, and then another and another. Everywhere my skin was scored and blistered; welts as broad as scars decorated my arms. I stifled the impulse to shriek, to give way to the panic that swept over me. I knew these were but the marks of beings thirsty for my blood. Once aware of the wounds, however, it was impossible to ignore them. They burned across my back, swelled the lobes of my ears. At the base of my skull the lymph nodes were distended, legions of white cells fighting for my life.

I was a victim of plague, of pestilence. I required solace, but I sensed no sympathy from Vivian. She had nursed Violet, and now lay on our bed watching me. Her eyes were measuring, distant. She disapproved, but of what? Had I been too abrupt in my rush to record my thoughts? I could not summon repentance, not now. It was I who deserved some amends, some pity. The taste of pineapple rose in my throat, sweet and suffocating, tropical bile. I would never drink again. I would accept only Perrier with a bit of lime. I would put Vivian's needs before my own, even before art. I would tolerate the wretched Cobb, feign interest in his dupe. I would get into shape, jog the beach, change the baby, read Hawthorne, cease to snipe at the scholarly papers published by my colleagues. I would make a greater effort with Nash and have a vasectomy. I would call the painter about my chipped woodwork and I would become more familiar with popular music. Anything, everything, but not tonight.

I drowned in the blue field of my computer, vacuous and opaque, bereft now of either questions or messages. I was its master yet I had no commands. Experimentally, in my last gasp, I punched a key at random.

"Bad character" was the reply.

Somehow I pushed back my chair, stumbled through the room, fell face forward on the mattress.

"Vivian," I said. "I need you."

I have no idea what she thought but, mercifully, she responded. She bathed my fevered limbs with a soothing emollient, shushed my appreciations, wrapped me in a cotton shroud. I opened my eyes, and in the misty light that fell through the windows in geometric shapes—in trapezoids and parallelograms—I saw that I had turned as white as if the vampire gnats had drained dry my every vein. I made no protest. I accepted peace, even welcomed it, allowed Vivian to close my lids with two gentle kisses cool as pennies. I bade farewell to my important thoughts and became as Violet: receptacle of all, repository of nothing. A silken hammock. A severed leaf in a midnight breeze.

14

VIVIAN

Roger had awakened me from a sound sleep by scraping his chair. He was still drunk, and Violet was wailing from across the room. They sat together in a wicker love seat. He was a man of shadows. Clutching Violet, he seemed in shock, his face unreadable and hollowed.

"Are you all right?"

He said nothing.

I got out of bed. He lifted Violet carefully toward me, but still did not speak. When I took the baby, he rose and fumbled to the table. Moaning under his breath, he plugged in the computer, and it hummed to life. He sat before it, but did not immediately lift his hands onto the keyboard. I stood behind him for a few moments, ready to break his fall if he lost consciousness, but he remained motionless, the grim recipient of some interior bolt of lightning. When his fingers began to type, the effect was eerie. He was a zombie transcribing coded messages from the beyond, a flea-bitten Artaud with a computer hookup to the supernatural. The granite stillness of the rest of his body made me uncomfortable, yet I couldn't help but watch.

244 / MICHAEL DORRIS · LOUISE ERDRICH

I started writing scenes in my head, paragraphs from our future literary biography: *He had extraordinary stamina. I suppose you might say he was the Iron Man of Poetry, regarding it as a sort of triathlon. I recall vividly one night in the Bahamas when Roger imbibed a massive amount of rum and Goombay Punch and then insisted on sitting up in a chair all night so as to instantly receive the next verses of "Diary of a Lost Man," which came to him in the chill hours just preceding dawn, at which time he began to write furiously, ignoring all else . . .*

I crept into our bed with Violet, and lay there as the sky gradually lightened. From across the room, there were long bursts of furious thumping, and a few times, muttered expletives. In spite of yesterday's irritation with Roger, the sheer vigor of his attack on the poem intrigued and impressed me. I was beginning to think I should relent, go with the flow, be forgiving of a man with such a passionate inner life, when he stopped and rose.

"Vivian." Roger's voice was harrowed and hoarse. "Vivian, I need you."

He turned and shuffled toward me, his entire body drained-looking and feeble. When he reached the bed, he folded himself onto the sheets and lay completely still.

"This has been a night beyond all nights. It has been indescribable. I haven't slept for days."

I must admit that I felt something like awe. I had never witnessed such a fire storm of inspiration. I hadn't realized exactly what the poem cost Roger, in physical terms, or how grueling the process of writing was for him. My voice, as I comforted, was hushed.

"Was it important? Was it the part you've needed for such a long time?"

Roger's features were radiant with suffering. He closed his eyes wearily under my hand as I stroked his brow, then waved the air away from his face, as though it were suffocating him. He strained for the words to describe his travail, and found the strength to raise himself on an elbow and gasp his answer.

"Vivian, you lay there so peacefully, oblivious, while I . . . it was terrible. *Earth, ah, earth, what is this agony that crawls beneath my ribs!*"

Roger's voice was low, scratchy, traumatized. I looked at him closely. There was enough light now to see that he was covered with raised red bumps. One eye was swollen nearly shut.

"I was eaten alive. I suffered alone. Orestes did not endure worse, tormented by the Furies."

"He killed his mother. He deserved it."

"No, dear. Think contextual justice."

"You're in no shape to argue." I nestled Violet against him, got up and went over to the kitchenette. Baking soda poultices were Grandma's remedies for just about any sort of skin condition, so I mixed a handful with water in a cup, formed a paste of the stuff, and brought it back to bed.

"Lie still."

I began to plaster Roger's arms and legs, patted carefully over the bites on bites. As I did so I felt such raw sympathy for him that tears burned my eyes. In a moment I regained control, didn't let down my guard entirely, and made some weak joke. I was not going to make the mistake of forgiving him without a confrontation. Too much empathy is a woman's mistake, a problem of our gender's conditioning. If I was to raise a daughter who would not become one of those women who love men too much, I was going to have to start putting a brake on my own feelings. I suppressed the urge to sing Roger to sleep, to massage his feet, to scratch his bites.

"Try and nap," I ordered, draping the sheet over his torso. Within my halo of nurselike firmness, I was able to ignore the agonized look in his eyes, the aura of pleading. I cut off the words he longed to say—for I had a sense of there being much unspoken: he probably wanted to apologize for his afternoon behavior, then to read his verse to me, and I was unwilling to hear him out. I was afraid I would capitulate and tell the truth: that his work was good.

"I'll take Violet outside so that you won't be disturbed."

"Where are you going?"

I shrugged. "I guess I'll sit on the veranda awhile, or go on over to Cobb's and wake him up, see how Nash is doing, have some breakfast."

Roger gripped my palm with surprising force, kneaded my fingers as he stared at me bleakly. He was asking me to forget Cobb, to forsake his document, to accept it as a lie. But it wasn't a lie. I kept my hand limp, cool, absolutely neutral and unresponsive, not returning his grip as I usually would, not overpowering his fingers with the strength of my own. I played no games, but out of pity I didn't explicitly deny Roger's plea. We just wouldn't talk about the Diary anymore. At last he dropped his gaze and then, slowly, loosened his hand. He brushed the backs of my knuckles gently, then let go.

Cobb was out and Nash was probably shadowing him. When I returned to the beach house, I found Roger, red-eyed, groggy, trying to shave. A clouded mirror hung at an inconvenient height and he peered into it.

"Let's get out of here," I said. "Explore. We've got hours before Hilda and Racine arrive."

Roger agreed. He was low-key, embarrassed about last night, and I took advantage to keep him out of Cobb's way. I couldn't help but soften toward Roger a little, though, as I watched him struggle with a canvas bag of beach supplies. His hair stuck straight up where he'd slept on it. He had a small boy's vulnerable cowlick.

As I strapped Violet into the baby seat of our rented car, I told myself to ease up, so we talked of inconsequential things while we drove along. It was surprisingly simple to keep my unanswered complaints in a locked compartment, to let the smooth current of conversation mask my own deceptions.

Cobb had given me directions to a seldom used beach, and it was a beauty. The reef-ringed bay was absolutely clear and we could wade out for half a mile, the water was so shallow.

"Here we are with no chaperon," said Roger. "At last."

Violet dropped into a deep slumber in the floating shade of an acacia tree, and Roger turned, touched my chin, and guided me toward his kiss.

No other person was in sight. There was impassable brush behind us. Untrammeled sand on either side and empty water ahead expanded for miles. I was almost shocked to find that at this moment of what I considered our greatest estrangement, Roger and I were capable of making love. And not just capable. I don't know how to describe us—it was *From Here to Eternity* without the modesty panel. We were synchronized swimming. We were perfect. I gave way a little, then I gave way entirely, and then after a long while I began to come back into the world, to pick out the soft greens of the palms again, the hazy burlap-barked trunks, the calm depth of sky farther down. I rolled halfway over onto my side. The sea was a mirror of stillness except for the slap of small waves.

I turned to Roger. Sand stuck like sugar powder to his shoulders. His eyes were pure. I lay my head on his chest. I could feel his heart, efficient as a Swedish motor, throb against my temple. I traced the swimmer's muscles, long and taut, in his arms.

"It's really something," I said. "Together like that."

"I know."

"At the same moment."

Roger took a breath, let it out in a long, lazy sigh, and spoke with a smile in his voice.

"Not that we can ever really experience the *same* moment."

I gently strummed my hand across his ribs. "Oh no? What would you call it then?"

He gave a short laugh.

The laugh. There is no precise description I can attach to it, for it was changeable. Part hearty, part knowing—there was some element to it, though, something distinct, a tiny core *that did not take me seriously.* I knew the inflection well enough to not pursue and push it, but I did so anyway. I couldn't help myself.

"What's funny?"

"It's nothing."

"It's something. You laughed."

"It was nothing. Honestly. I'm sorry."

"Roger . . ."

"Do I detect a note of threat?"

I reared over him and looked him in the eyes. I could *see* the laugh. It was in there, percolating.

"I merely want to know what it was you found so funny."

"Can't I laugh to myself?"

"Not at a time like this. You broke the spell of intimacy."

"Now Vivian, don't accuse *me* of breaking the spell of intimacy, *you're* the one demanding to know why I laughed."

And then he laughed again.

"Roger!" There it was! The same damn snicker.

"Pardon."

He looked at me, but he wasn't sorry.

"Come on, Roger."

"All right. It's just that . . ." His face all innocence. "It's just that . . . as wonderful as it was, you know, it wasn't simultaneous. *Nothing* is simultaneous."

"Well, I wasn't implying, of course, in a world measured in picoseconds, that we shared orgasms of the exact duration. All I was saying, celebrating really, was the fact that for once we experienced the same thing."

"Uh, the *same* thing?" He gave a soft groan of disbelief.

"Oh, what now? The egocentric predicament? The mind's inability to transcend its own experience? Okay. You had yours and I had mine, but you can't deny that it occurred at roughly the same time."

He pondered my concession.

" 'Roughly.' How do you mean, 'roughly'? And what is this 'it'? I only mean to say, Vivian, that since there is no adequate language to describe what we feel at such moments, and since whatever syntax we do use misrepresents the reality of our respective sensations, we should simply remain mute."

"There. There!" I rose to my feet. I kicked sand on Roger. "Now you're really accusing me of breaking the spell!"

He brushed himself off with broad strokes of his hands. "I'm only saying—"

I began to shout. "You're saying that sex should take place in that realm beyond language, and remain there. That the direct experience should not be defiled with words, especially my words, because I do not use them with the ideal precision you require."

"You're raising your voice," Roger pointed out.

"I'm yelling. That's the word for what I'm doing."

We glared at one another, our faces hard, exposed against the brilliant sand and sky.

"I know words are messy, Roger, full of connotations, old desires and memories. I know no word has the identical meaning to two people. I know there is no way to absolutely describe what just happened to us, but to give up on language, to give up on what we have, no matter what a rag box it is—that is an act of cowardice. I love language, I give it its peculiarities, its old bones, its failings. I love words in my mouth. I love to spill them and I don't really care how every one of them fits. I love the fluidity and ripeness of talk, the forgetfulness of it, the way it vanishes into thin air, or how a sentence sags with meaning, laden like a piece of dry bread sopping up soup."

I stopped, confused by my own runaway image.

"Bread. Soup." Roger smiled, but he also looked hungry, clearly ready to move on. "A seafood bisque, a gumbo, some sort of spicy local chowder. And a crusty loaf, French or Italian, even stale."

"What a coincidence, Roger. We're hungry at exactly the same moment." I grabbed my beach sandals, knotted my thin towel around my waist.

"There's a little hole-in-the-wall café where we could stop on the way home," said Roger.

He seemed invigorated, almost cheered by our argument, and without any fuss or self-consciousness he picked up Violet from the shade. For once she did not fully wake, just wedged herself against him. Roger's literalness infuriated me, perhaps because it bespoke a reverence for truth, a candor that I usually admired— but not today. Today I was playing a double game, and I didn't like the role.

We drove to the airport and waited until the small commuter plane touched down. The hatch on the side opened and first Hilda, then Racine descended the small ladder and walked quickly across the tarmac. Hilda's pink scarf was interwoven with vibrant golden threads, her face shone with curiosity. Racine advanced more slowly, a bit suspiciously, as though he was wary of all warmth and dazzlement, but as he neared the gate his step lightened. He was ready to be seduced, and shrugged off the gray shackles of the northern winter, squinted eagerly at the sun.

I looked at Roger. Dark glasses concealed his swollen eyelids, his arms were covered with long sleeves to the wrist. He was not visibly twitching, scratching anywhere. He looked all right but I knew he wasn't, and yet he was so self-contained and uncomplaining that I had one of those sudden surges of affection, of irrational tenderness toward him. I wanted to hold on to my irritation, but it was shifting sand compared to the ground of my feelings.

"So how *is* everything?" Hilda wanted to know, after they had passed through customs and we had exchanged formal hugs and greetings. "How is the wheeler-dealer? How is paradise?"

"Guarded by demons," said Roger in a flat, vehement voice.

15

ROGER

I despise a clutch that slips. A vehicle is the extension of oneself, the four-wheeled face one presents to the world, the ectoskeleton upon which one depends both for attracting others and for protection, if necessary, from them. A car announces its occupants. The medium is the message, the means that justifies the end. When air travel deprives me of my vintage Saab—understated, elegant, secure—I don't begrudge the extra money spent for a quality rental. Nothing flashy, of course, nothing with a movable roof or that must be entered from a crouched position. I ask for midsize and hope to be bumped to full. I actually like leasing, the variety of exploring the gadgets of each new model: cruise control, electric mirrors, the random-scan button on the radio.

When Sydney Clock had quoted the steep fee he charged for one of his "Island Getaway" fleet, I hadn't blanched. Anything for mobility, for an air-conditioned refuge with a door that closed. Or so I had thought, not counting on the corrosive powers of salt air, on the results of casual maintenance, on the fact that when the winds of change, of catalytic converters and gasoline conservation, had swept the landmass of North America, a detritus of enormous, Detroit-made clunkers had been blown to the islands off shore.

Late on the afternoon of our arrival, Clock had presented me, in exchange for my substantial check, with a twin of the car in which I had ridden to my girlfriend's public high school senior prom. It was vaguely Chevrolet, tan and broad, with treadless tires as smooth and inflated as inner tubes. The upholstery of the bench front seat—odd how antique phraseology lay in wait at the back of one's mind—told tales of melodrama and passion, of passengers carrying sharp objects in their back pockets and drivers who ignored the ashtray when they smoked. The glove compartment was closed with a complicated twist of coat hanger, and the odometer read an incredible ninety-seven thousand miles.

"One thing," Sydney was conscientious to point out. "You can't open the hood and the trunk at the same time. They both require a prop." He produced a stick of driftwood and demonstrated the efficiency with which it could prevent either of the car's fore and aft mouths from snapping shut. "The spare's in the shop," he went on to lament. "If you break down, feel free to call me."

He was carried off on a friend's motor scooter before I turned the key, before I heard the roar of the pockmarked exhaust pipe, before I attempted to shift the car into drive and watched it slip, ever so slowly, into a category of forward motion labeled simply "2," where it grindingly remained.

This 2, I soon discovered, was ill suited for ordinary terrain—I assumed it was intended for mountain climbing or steep descents. On Eleuthera's level plain, 2 was undertaxed, and thus the engine constantly felt as if it were on the verge of hysteria. It whined and wheezed, exhaled in exasperation, and generally called attention to itself, even at rest. At least the racket seemed to hypnotize Violet.

Now, as we proceeded like a demented calliope through the small settlements on the way from the airport, the interior noise level prevented me from participating in the eager conversation of my friends. I was left to my own thoughts. In light of Vivian's and my current contretemps, this was something of a blessing. Personally, I hoped that Hilda's and especially Racine's presence would add a leaven to our mix. To enact our domestic comedy, we needed a more attentive audience than Nash, and certainly than Cobb. A divisive force, he brought out the worst in us.

It had taken little time for me to tire of Vivian's sadistic jokes about bugs, and for her to lose patience with my insights regarding our duplicitous host. There are few published anthologies of prison humor—incarceration without the possibility of parole is not funny—and in this Alcatraz our sentence lasted ten full days. As the grim realization of our circumstances stretched before us, we had found it harder and harder to make light of the deteriorating conditions. Sarcasm became accusation and was answered with defensive reproach. Complaint was a pointing finger, and any minimal admission of unhappiness on my part was enough to turn Vivian into a veritable booster for the island's delights. Being with her in this mood was like dining with the chamber of commerce of a small, depressed mill town: everything wrong was *actually* right. The problem, if there was one, lay in my snobbish interpretation, my inadaptability, my Puritan boorishness, and in my refusal to buy into Cobb's scheme. "Loosen up, Roger," she had dared to say last night. "Make the best of things."

What was the "best" to make of my inflamed skin? Should I challenge Cobb to a friendly round of shuffleboard, winner gets to define history? Vivian wouldn't even allow me to work in peace, almost as though she were jealous of my poem, threatened by my absent muse. I had tried to patiently explain my habits, my occasional retreats into an interior communion from which I should not be disturbed. And what was her response? Sympathy? Compassion? Respect? On the contrary. She as much as told me that her obsession with raucous give-and-take would ever supersede my yearning for solitude. She had looked to me at that moment, this woman whom I loved, who had borne my child, like the most fiendish of jailers, the kind who raked the bars of one's cell with a billy club in the middle of the night for no purpose other than to disrupt the flow of dreams.

I was overreacting, I knew it. I was maddened by sleep deprivation and the torture of small stings. I hated everything equally, everyone, every future: with Vivian, without Vivian, both intolerable. I despised the bright sun, the heat, the oppressive verdure, the incessant reggae renditions of traditional Christmas songs that

254 / MICHAEL DORRIS · LOUISE ERDRICH

assailed my ears from the radio, which, missing a critical knob, could be turned neither off nor down. "Silver Bells" did not lend itself to a limbo beat. "White Christmas" grated when rattled out on steel drums. The chorus of "Jingle Bells" sounded positively demented, a jazzed-up band of carolers transported from Carnival in Rio. In between tunes the disc jockey broke the news that a group of contestants in the local Junkanoo celebration—whatever that was—was the Harlots of Babylon.

At least it was December 23. I would only have to endure this racket for two more days. I refused to cha-cha-cha to "Little Town of Bethlehem." Vivian, however, tapped her foot. Well, that was the difference between us. So be it.

As if Eleuthera did not have enough unpleasant surprises, the kitchen facilities at the ill-equipped beach house were barbaric. The refrigerator sang a constant medley of tunes, from a slow rumba when the door had been long closed to a polka allegro when its Freon was recharged. It didn't exactly "cool," this busy machine. Rather, it froze all contents into a uniform, solid block that had to be chiseled free of the bottom at least two hours before use.

The gas stove was a complete waste. The burners didn't burn and the oven was a useless, tepid box. The first evening, I had assumed there was a simple trick to lighting its pilot, and so had prostrated myself on the floor and peered into its inner mechanisms. I sniffed cautiously for gas before striking a match, and even when the air registered nothing I approached my task with all the reckless abandon of a bomb squad expert who expects a maiming explosion at any moment. No protuberance proved flammable, and only the mounting evidence of a pile of charred matchsticks finally convinced me that the reason my nose detected no gas was because, quite simply, there *was* none.

"What shall we do?" I had asked Vivian, who stood above me, hands on hips, the foreman to my crew. "What about the meat?"

I had transferred most of our mainland cache into the arctic depths of the refrigerator—where the constant subzero temperature would preserve it indefinitely, if left alone, like some Siberian mammoth carcass. But there was the matter of supper, and toward that end I had reserved the small but nicely marbled sirloin roast. It was too late to refreeze without incurring a damaging burn.

Vivian reached over me to the counter, moved one of the bags of groceries we had purchased at the store in Savannah Sound, and plugged something in.

"Thank God," she said. "At least this works."

I craned my neck to see. "But that's a toaster oven," I pointed out. "Meant for slices of bread."

"So? It's better than nothing. Improvise, Roger. Where's your spirit of adventure? If we had wanted hi-tech we would have stayed in Florida."

Or New Hampshire, I might have added, but didn't. Or gone to Boston, browsed the Cambridge bookstores and sampled a Sunday brunch at the Ritz. Vivian absently tousled my hair, actually scratched behind my ear, then walked away in response to Violet's restless murmur before I had the chance to lick her hand. Or bite it. I stood and faced the neat bundle of the roast, now at room temperature. Obviously the question of dinner was mine to solve. What had happened to the division of labor? In traditional societies the man brought home the carcass and the woman turned it on a spit—a perfectly complementary arrangement. Now a modern female need only throw up her hands, say "Oh, you're better at this than I am!" and be absolved of all subsistence responsibility. I examined the dial of the one working appliance. The highest setting optimistically read "Cake," and I had no choice but to select it. While the single electric coil changed from black to a glowing red I sliced the roast into eight thick slabs. Over the interminable course of the next three hours, I toasted them two at a time.

Hilda and Racine had not stopped talking since they got into the car, though the sense of their words disappeared into the din. When together, they generated a kind of magnetic force field that defied all shifts in external context. Within the dynamic of their couplehood they remained impervious, immutably themselves. Now, dropped from the sky into Rahita's Native Food Hut, shed of the sweaters and coats in which they began their journey and facing me across a linoleum-topped table, they seemed completely at ease. The sum of their collective experience, of the individual years when each had been a refugee, an outcast, an immigrant, had rendered them immune to culture shock. Their home had become each other, not some boundaried piece of real estate. There was a rather daunting quality to the oblivious way in which they traveled, moving around the planet as casually as some people rearrange their furniture or change the color scheme of their rooms. Expatriate Europeans in America, aggressively American in Europe, Hilda and Racine were everywhere foreign and therefore everywhere equally content. They were citizens of their marriage, their united state, and in contrast I, as usual, felt a mixture of awe and deprivation. They even tended to speak with plural pronouns.

"We *hoped* you'd feed us," Hilda said, smiling. "We had a sandwich on the flight from Hartford, but nothing since. What do you recommend?"

Rahita herself stood behind the counter, a vat of bubbling oil at the ready. "Fried" was the adjective preceding each dinner listing on the menu: chicken, conch, steak, and grouper. In this late afternoon, we were the only customers.

"Believe it or not," Vivian confided in a loud, traitorous voice, "this is the first time we've eaten out. Roger brought down enough meat to feed an army of carnivores and we've been chipping away at that. Of course, Nash won't touch a bite!"

"Do you recommend the grouper?" I called over to Rahita. "Is it fresh?"

The woman blinked before replying, "Yesterday's."

"Then I'll try the conch," I decided. "With a small green salad."

"We'll have the same," Racine said.

Rahita plunged her arm into a bucket of seawater and brought out a handful of medium-sized conch shells, which she placed on a wooden butcher's block. With a sharp awl, she smashed a hole in each one and extracted the solitary inhabitant, then struck it with the edge of a plate. I couldn't watch when she picked up a rubber hammer. You'd think that coming as I did from a region famous for boiling lobsters alive and swallowing clams fresh from the surf, I would have lost my sympathy for crustaceans, but my heart went out to the queen conch and I castigated myself for my choice.

"Roger, what happened to you?" Hilda demanded.

I assumed she was referring to my haggard appearance, to the red welts that covered my arms and hands.

"You noticed it too?" Racine asked his wife. "Vivian, you are a tonic for this man. I've never seen him look so healthy, so in the pink."

Both he and Hilda had a fondness for using what they considered to be American colloquialisms, outdated or not.

"The pink you see is blood poisoning," I answered. "You'll find out tonight. You have a horrible surprise in store." I was annoyed—how dare they fail to recognize my distress!—and the prospect of the discovery that awaited them gave me a twinge of pleasure.

"The bugs *are* terrible," Vivian was forced to agree. "I hope you brought some spray. There's no keeping them out once the sun goes down."

"But our hotel is air-conditioned," Hilda said. "Surely we will rest in peace."

"Air-conditioned?" The words were almost too painful to enunciate. I glared at Vivian. "I didn't know there existed such amenities on this hellhole."

"Life's too short." Hilda shrugged. "These days, we require just a touch of deluxe. Yes, we would like to sleep with the sound of the waves in our dreams, but . . . one cannot have everything. We have become old fogies with no appreciation for adventure. It's different with new love."

"No, it's not," I insisted. "Do you think they have another room available at your hotel?"

Racine shook his head doubtfully. "The travel agent had a dickens of a time getting one for us last week. They are booked solid for the holiday."

"Well, you can't beat our price," Vivian said. She was being overcheerful again, a sure sign that she read my mind.

"Whatever you're doing, Roger, it certainly agrees with you," Hilda interjected. "Racine is right. You're blooming. You, too, Vivian. How is Nash? Where is he?"

"Nash is in his element," Vivian said. "He's made friends with some local people, gone snorkeling, the works. I guess all he needed was a change of scene."

"And my little Violet." Racine smiled at the baby in her car seat on the chair next to him. "*Ça va, ma petite?*"

"She's exhausted," I said. "The poor child was up all night."

"Ah, a carouser!" Hilda approved, and winked at me. "Just like her father."

"Roger has turned into a regular beach bunny," Vivian said without a trace of irony. "I think he must have always been a surfer at heart." She squeezed my forearm, sending off tingles of pain from my wounds. I hated to be discussed in the third person. It made me feel like one of those men on television, endlessly patronized by their cute, precocious children.

"I am no stranger to the sea," I explained to Hilda and Racine, who rolled their eyes at each other in response to my serious tone.

"Speaking of the sea," Hilda said, "what's new with Columbus? Is this Cobb a character?"

"Out of *The Jungle*," I muttered.

"He's fascinating," Vivian said, overriding me. "Obsessed, of course, but very well-versed."

A look passed between the two women, a signal from Vivian to Hilda as unmistakable as the flash of a lighthouse: time for private communication. They pushed back their chairs and without explanation headed for the ladies' room. I turned to find Racine smiling upon me, his face open and hopeful.

"Why do they go in pairs?" I asked in annoyance. "Are their bladders governed by the phases of the moon?"

"Girl talk." He shrugged. "They haven't seen each other in a week. There's a lot to catch up on."

We sat in silence. There was no "boy talk," no confidences to exchange. Racine and I, who shared no interest in sports and had no common ground of departmental politics, had long counted on Hilda to propose topics and direct the traffic of our conversation. We were friends in that mute, shoulder-punching way of most adult males who know each other through work. Having rarely been left alone unsupervised, we were somehow embarrassed at the forced intimacy of being one-on-one. We existed in that familiar masculine gray area—too long acquainted for chitchat and yet never having crossed the bridge into private revelation. My pairing with Vivian had made things easier. I was no longer a solitary wild card, an ambiguous predator or challenge, an unexplained bachelor, a man whose status proclaimed either that he couldn't get along with a woman or that he didn't choose to do so.

I glanced at Racine and to my dismay saw that he was beaming at me with concern and even affection. I had heard him proclaim in various faculty groups that men must learn to talk to one another, to not shy from physical contact, and I had the uncomfortable apprehension that he was going to turn his theory into practice. Luckily, a female came to my rescue. Violet, roused by heat and by lack of motion, made a quick visual scan for Vivian.

It was a long time since Racine had held a baby, yet he was famous as a man who was in touch with his emotions, who was active in the ad hoc feminist literary criticism seminar. I enjoyed his dismay, the dilemma presented to him by my about-to-be-seething daughter. If he picked her up and she wasn't satisfied his reputation was shot, but if he appeared helpless in the face of her demand his cover was blown. I let the agitation build for a few more seconds and then, fabricating the practiced ease of a professional—I had at least the precedent of last night to go on—I scooped Violet from her car seat and held her up to face me.

"It's all right," I said firmly. "You need not worry. You are among friends."

At the sound of my voice, Violet blinked and there passed between us the ubiquitous moment of judgment. Would she or wouldn't she accept me as a substitute? And then, where I held her tiny back with the support of my cupped hands, I felt her muscles relax. She kicked her feet playfully, almost flirtatiously. She stuck out her tongue and she made a raspberry sound. Amazed and proud—Racine would report this to Hilda at the first opportunity, and she in turn would tell Vivian—I returned it. Violet gave it back. We were talking. We were engaged in our first conversation, and it was a private joke.

Eventually Violet was content to doze in the nook between my arm and chest, though every so often she would startle into wakefulness and stare at me intently before relaxing once again.

"You've become very adept," Racine approved in some relief. "I'm impressed."

"It's quite simple," I responded modestly. "A baby has the same need as anyone else for reassurance, for a stable environment."

"Is that what you and Vivian have created? How wonderful.

The attraction of opposites is one of those adages that often prove true, even in the least likely of cases. I have to hand it to Hilda. She saw it coming."

Hilda, I realized as the minutes passed, was undoubtedly right now getting an earful on the degree of our oppositeness. The amount of time women could consume once behind the doors of a rest room never ceased to astound me. It seemed a universal trait. When as a child I traveled with Mother, I invariably found myself loitering outside the women's lounge in airports and train stations. It had been the same ever since—with dates and acquaintances, at the theater, in restaurants, at gasoline stations along the highway. Was it biological, one of those female mysteries, or was it learned behavior? Among hunters and gatherers, I wondered, did mothers and grandmothers and little girls disappear behind a bush, only to reemerge unapologetically hours later, long after the game had fled? Vivian, to her credit, fell at the short end of the scale on this matter. Once, she had even been waiting for me, and I, a neophyte in such a situation, had felt compelled to explain.

"Roger, please," she had said. "Spare me the details. Your toilette is your own affair."

But let her reconnoiter a powder room with another woman, especially with Hilda, and she immediately devolved into the worst of her gender. Whatever the transactions that took place, they were conducted with deliberation. The chess match was played without clocks.

"What could they be doing?" I finally asked Racine. Rahita had produced our food, and my hunger was such that I knew I could not endure a long wait before eating. The conchs, fried to a golden crisp, looked delicious. Their aroma was at once briny and buttery, and even the salad, which turned out to be a mayonnaisey coleslaw, was inviting.

" 'Now if you're ready, Oysters dear, we can begin to feed,' " I addressed my plate. With my free hand I dredged a conch through the little paper basket of tartar sauce and took a bite. It was warm, firm, quite resistant as a matter of fact. My upper and lower jaws seemed to spring apart after every clamp, as though I were munching on part of a breaded tennis shoe. I dented the mass more than masticated it, and when I swallowed I could follow its progress through the first several stages of its journey.

"Tough," I commented, and Racine nodded.

"All muscle. They have to be, to pull those big shells around."

Each individual conch strip required several minutes of chewing time and thus imposed a silence at the table. Racine and I fed like cattle on the range, grinding our teeth up and down, side to side, mute and stupid. Violet was content to watch us graze.

Hilda and Vivian were still sequestered, but a peal of laughter floated from the lavatory. I could not help but believe that I was the major topic of the debriefing. I had not passed muster, of that much I could be sure. Vivian would describe me as rigid, a complainer, as drinking too much, and as having been rude to Cobb. She would despair of my relationship with Nash and accuse me of paying more attention to my work than to her. I closed my eyes: she might confide my insistence that our orgasms had not been simultaneous. To be involved in a modern relationship was to sacrifice all privacy, to open one's inner sanctum to public scrutiny. First the son posts my diary, then the mother entertains with tales of my inadequate performance.

If men could talk freely among themselves, what would I say to Racine? How did I "feel"—the operative word of the late twentieth century—about being with Vivian? To her I was clearly disappointing, but was I equally disappointed? Her distractions were often aggravating in the extreme, and she stampeded pell-mell through the established order of my existence. There was no area of my life or my thoughts that she and her family did not invade and try to dominate. She had opinions about everything to do with me, and she expected that I would reshape myself to conform with her requirements. She regarded me with no deference—absolutely none. Forget my record of professional accomplishment—to Vivian Twostar I was simply the man in her life, the object she sought to mold, the problematic father of her daughter, the troublesome unknown that preceded her future. Ultimately, she didn't give a damn about my family, my work, my aesthetics, or my possessions. Whatever she saw in me was something else, a factor that did not appear on my curriculum vitae, an essence to which no one else had ever paid attention or given credit. The criteria that mattered to her were basic and primitive:

in her eyes, I succeeded or failed to the extent that I was desirable, by the degree to which I was capable of reciprocating love.

Across the room, the bathroom door opened. Hilda and Vivian, their hair brushed, their public faces securely in place, walked toward our table. Vivian glanced at the empty baby seat and a worried frown tensed her features. Then she saw Violet, asleep in my arms. She touched Hilda's elbow, pointed to me, and she smiled.

There was a quality in that look that instantly transformed—without changing a single detail—every negative emotion I had been feeling toward her to positive. What had been bad became good, what had been oppression became grace, what had been complaint became jubilation. I pushed back my chair, stood, and met Vivian halfway to the table. I held Violet slightly to the side, and with the fingers of my other hand I touched Vivian's arm. Her smile broadened.

"Your ears must have been ringing," she said.

"What about this big news flash?" Hilda asked, once we had all gnawed our way through the conchs. "It's burning a hole in Racine's pocket."

"Save the details for later," Vivian replied rather quickly, and looked at Racine.

"I haven't grasped the whole picture," he said deliberately, "but I can report that the letter appears to be real. I had the ink carbon-dated and it's definitely fifteenth, sixteenth century. A graphologist confirmed that the script could be that of Columbus, though there are some variances."

"Due, no doubt, to the slap of the ocean waves as the *Pinta* teetered on the edge of the flat earth." I could not resist. Why not validate the whole fairy tale?

Vivian silenced me with a glance.

"Does this Henry Cobb have more scraps?" Racine asked. "Have you made any headway with what you do have?"

"That's a sensitive issue," Vivian answered. "But yes, a lot more than scraps, though he's got his own agenda in all this, and plays his cards close to his chest. I'm supposed to show my hand first, then he decides how much to tell me."

Rahita called from the kitchen, inquiring if we wished her to fry us some bananas for dessert. We did, and momentarily the now-familiar crackle of hot oil sounded from behind the counter.

"Vivian, you're not in his league," I said. "This isn't your penny-ante kitchen table poker. He's playing to win."

"Roger is jealous, can you imagine?" Vivian smiled at Racine and Hilda, then regarded me as if I were some lovesick adolescent. Like the flick of a light switch, her condescending expression had the effect of changing all my recent positive feelings back to negative. Who did she think she was talking about?

"The man is an ass," I said to Racine, counting on our burgeoning male solidarity to produce a loyal reaction. "He operates outside the law. As for Vivian, he's stringing her along."

"He won't show Roger the Diary," Vivian explained. "And Roger is unhappy with our accommodations. There are certain inconveniences."

She actually seemed bemused, causing the adrenaline of indignation to prickle through my veins.

"The place is not fit for human habitation," I stated categorically. "We might as well be sleeping in the sand, cooking our meals on sticks over an open flame."

"He actually toasted a roast," Vivian confided. "My cave man. My hero."

Hilda and Racine looked at me with frank curiosity, so I had to explain.

"I used the only appliance available."

"*Delicioso!*" Vivian pronounced, and kissed her fingertips for emphasis. "Roger is a whiz . . . in the kitchen."

Racine, ever the gourmet cook, was interested. "Didn't it dry out?"

"Forget the roast," I said. "Forget the bugs and the plumbing that doesn't work and the brackish water. The point is, we are on this island at the mercy of an indicted criminal and all Vivian can do is bat her eyes at him." This wasn't entirely just, but then she had not been fair to me. "You should see the two of them together, quite prepared to negotiate away established history to suit their own purposes. Anything goes. Let's make Columbus this, let's make him that. Abandon context, oh yes. 'The first modern man,' full of self-contradiction and existentialism. Why not turn him black? Or gay? Perhaps he was actually a she? And did I mention the buried treasure? The lost jewels of Burgundy, or is it Babylon?"

The table fell silent after my harangue. I realized that Rahita had been standing at my side for some time, waiting to place a plate of crisp banana slices before me. I glanced up at her apologetically, and found that her brows were knit.

"Columbus was gay too?" she asked, more to herself than to me, and then broke into a wide grin. "Wait till I tell my brother in Miami. He's always saying Alexander the Great, that Michelangelo, movie stars . . . He'll be jolly happy to hear it."

When the woman had gone back to the kitchen, still smiling, Hilda leaned close to me. "I've never seen you so animated, Roger. What is it?"

Vivian, of course, answered for me, providing her expert psychiatric analysis.

"Roger can't stand that someone knows something about Columbus that doesn't fit with his research. It might screw up the meter in his epic poem."

I glared at her, but she continued. "I'm not saying Cobb isn't difficult. He enjoys getting Roger's goat and baiting me. But he's nothing I haven't met a hundred times before, and we have one great advantage. He needs what he thinks we've got."

"I can't stand it any longer," Racine said. "Look at this. He may not be entirely off base." He handed Vivian a white envelope. "Naomi was able to translate those inscriptions. I was right, they were Hebrew, but neither of us could make any sense of them."

"What inscriptions?" I demanded.

"They really mean something?" Vivian asked, her voice amazed. "Those are really words? You're sure?"

"What are you talking about?" I insisted on knowing.

She shook her head. "Later."

In supreme exasperation, I clamped my overworked jaws together so hard on a banana that my teeth hurt. Enough of this puerile exercise. Secrets, hidden messages, lost diaries. Next would be the Fountain of Youth. We already knew enough of the past to adequately reconstruct it. There was a direct line from any then to any now, a chain of linked logical consequences that did not depend on science fiction for their interpretation. That was the province of the armchair historian, the dilettante who pretended it was unnecessary to pore over daunting, dusty documents—inventories, court reports, census records. Real history was a science, not a maze. It was the delineation of the facts of one day that remained pertinent in the next. The relative importance of events and ideas could be assigned only in retrospect. Columbus, like any other figure, was essentially the accumulation of his causes and, more important, of his effects through time. He was who he has become. The narrator of my poem, which Vivian lately seemed to regard with such disdain, was the man who fit the evidence of his life, not some specter who ran in counterpoint to it. My basic Columbus had endured for five centuries and, reinforced by my careful work and by that of others like me, he would become even more himself in the future.

I kept these thoughts private, consoled myself with them, while Hilda and Racine devoured their bananas, while Violet dreamed in peace, while Vivian, oblivious to the insult she had inflicted, used a butter knife to slit open Racine's white envelope and read to herself—once, twice, a third time—the rows of typed lines that marched the length of a single unfolded page.

16

VIVIAN

In his copy of Ptolemy's *Geography*, Columbus wrote: "Wondrous are the tumultuous forces of the sea. Wondrous is God in the depths." Before leaving Hanover, I had copied this exalting observation onto a sheet of my thick vellum stationery to convince Nash that Columbus had his points. I carried it to Eleuthera with me, but wound up keeping it. When I wanted to torture myself about the meaning of the shells and the rest of the journal, I took out this scrap, sealed in a Ziploc bag in the side pocket of Violet's diaper tote, and read the lines over and over. Talismanic words. In good moments, they proved Columbus capable of true poetry. In less optimistic times, I felt mocked by their innocence, by the man's zeal, by the ultimate cruelty of his design and of his ignorance. Five hundred years later I was anxious to get the better of him somehow, and it seemed that with the inscriptions he had given me a tool.

Except I didn't know how to use it: where the phrases from the oysters fit, what they meant.

The first thing I did, after Racine gave me the translated

Hebrew, was to memorize the lines. Now they were stored in my head, invisible and safe. In a fit of paranoia, I had burned the envelope and paper and crumbled the ashes into the sand beside the porch, where shy lizards ran and tiny birds hopped, pecking seeds. They pecked at the ashes, too, scattered them. The lizards traced them with their rapid feet. There was no evidence left, and I was glad that Racine had brought along no second copy, that I hadn't even told Roger about the discovery. Cobb had his eye on me and, I was pretty sure, he had used the period of our absence yesterday to thoroughly search the beach house. He'd done a good job of putting everything back where it was supposed to go, and I wouldn't have noticed if he hadn't run afoul of a private compulsion of mine, one of those small personal habits that, once you start, you can't relinquish.

Like Roger, like any academic, I have my particular ways of organizing papers and methodically alphabetize even casually collected articles. So, when I looked through the material I had brought and noticed that the *National Geographic* special issue on Columbus had forged ahead of some Xeroxed pages of Morison, that Molander's interesting arguments about Eleuthera were mixed up with Rose's ethnohistorical research article on the Lucayans, I knew they had been disturbed. On such idiosyncrasies hangs the exposure of careless spies. I should have been outraged, but somehow I wasn't even surprised. Once I realized someone had reshuffled my papers, I saw other small disarrangements in the chaos of my suitcase. They told me something important.

If Cobb would go to the length of searching my personal belongings, he was even more desperate than he let on, and less scrupulous than I had assumed. This was pertinent information, but he had been looking for the wrong thing. He lusted after the second page of Columbus's letter—believed, as I wanted him to, that it would lead him out of bankruptcy—but I knew its cryptic mention of the crown would only increase his frustration. What he truly sought was preserved in pearl, its enigmatic clues lodged within what I assumed was the idiom of its time. The sole transcript lay buried safely within the circuits of my brain. If Cobb agreed to let me take the Diary, maybe I would tell him what he wanted to know. Or maybe not.

Meanwhile, the actual shells were in my freezer at home. Over and over I repeated their words under my breath—sometimes when alone I even tried them out loud. I was becoming in my own way as obsessed with locating the treasure as Cobb, though I told myself that I wanted the crown for humanitarian, for political reasons—to prove an initial recognition of native sovereignty, to raise awareness, to produce incontrovertible evidence that would return at least a fraction of the much-ballyhooed discovery back to the discoverees.

Although all this was quite true, in my heart I knew that there was another reason—age-old, inglorious. I couldn't help it. Stars flashed in my head, the facets of precious stones; the gold gave off the gleam of greed. I wanted it. Not to keep it, mind you, just to *find*. Hypothetical moments of climax played out in my imagination, haunted me. The crown rested on an altar, blazing, magnificent. I approached it, or dug it up, or kicked over the right rock and saw it glitter.

I mulled the words on the shells—one way and then another—but I got nowhere, or at least no further. I assumed that I was on the right island. According to Cobb, I was possibly on the right beach. I had the directions, but not the sense. I was a would-be safecracker standing before a massive door, and all around me, everywhere, in the very movement of the leaves, the push of breeze and tide, the sun's passage, the combination to the lock was encoded, staring me in the face.

The Hebraic lines were my constant mantra. I tried to organize them into a logical sequence, but who could be sure? Were they meant to guide or to confuse?

When the sun is the crown of heaven.

Noon obviously.

Over sand like old glass.

Eleuthera's famous lavender-pink beaches. From walking in the desert and picking up bottles, I knew the color handblown glass could turn with age. Lavender-pink was not far off the mark. So far so good, perhaps, but then came the stumper.

Weave a ribbon through a sea of clouds.

And I was lost. I took the sea of clouds to mean a mist, the ribbon to be the wake of a sailing ship, but that was little help.

After all, mists are not exactly stationary and a ship's passage is instantly obscured. I tried to free-associate, got nowhere. Could he mean an actual ribbon? A string of cloth used as a marker, a guide back through a labyrinth? I always ended up leaving the line for later and moving on to the next.

To the hollow spear of breathing rock.

I had more to go on here. I imagined a kind of temple, erected of stones, a marker. Or perhaps a native-built altar of some sort. Pointed, certainly, and hollow, so that it could contain the crown within. As for the "breathing" part, there were almost too many possible explanations. Coral was a living rock, though I was not certain that Columbus knew this. Or the rocks could have been encrusted with barnacles, with mussels or land snails. Or there could have been a species of tough grass, a form of lichen, covering the sides.

Enter the tip through the inner channel.

Another blank, since what came to mind were only the eighth-grade mimeos that Nash had once brought home to memorize, diagrams of the male reproductive system. Try as I might, that was about all I could think of, although "channel" must have meant that the crown's repository was set near water, perhaps at the end of a stream, if there existed such a thing on this narrow island.

It rests in the pool of light.

At odd moments, I would find myself shuffling through the litany of lines and stopping at this fragment, hoping that it would jostle loose a new thought that pulled the other bits together. But nothing happened, nothing shifted, no crevasse opened, not a hairline crack. I was at an impasse, just as I sensed was Cobb. Perhaps the Diary made greater mention of the crown, but if from his source Cobb had a better notion of what we sought, mine apparently held the only hope of determining its location. He needed more and I needed more, yet we did not trust each other enough to meld the last cards in our hands. We stalked each other in a tight circle like two wrestlers looking for an opening. There had to come a breakthrough, a leap, but neither one of us was ready to dare the stretch.

Or so I thought. But Henry Cobb took me by surprise. His

lunges had previously been so obvious that when he made a lateral gesture he seemed the very model of subtlety.

Late on the fifth morning of our visit, he rapped lightly on the frame of the screen door and then let himself into the beach house. For the last hour I'd been sitting by the window in a round wicker chair, watching the waves break hard over the reef and the clouds roll in. Violet, curled on my lap, slept with sensuous, gusty breaths. I'd been alternating the lines from the shells on a mental tape loop, hoping for a penetrating inspiration.

"Tomato," proclaimed Henry Cobb. He displayed a round red globe in his hand. "They're more precious than blue-chip stocks on this island. Impossible to buy. But I have connections to a garden."

"I'll bet you do."

Roger glanced up from his computer, sighed, and ejected his floppy disk. As usual—he was such a creature of habit—he slipped it into his pants pocket.

Henry ignored him, addressed me. "I hardly dare inquire if you will come up to the house and share a salad."

"I'll pass," Roger replied.

"But I will see you later?" Henry asked. Roger nodded. This was news to me, but what did I care? Maybe they would work out their differences in private. Fine, though I did hope that Cobb would stick with his refusal to display the Diary. Roger's skepticism was convenient and made my course easier to follow. As long as he didn't believe the document was real, he didn't take my actions seriously, but once he got a load of what was in Cobb's safe, Roger wouldn't let me out of his sight and would try to take over.

Cobb's invitation was a perfect chance for me to talk to him alone and I decided to take him up on it.

"Lunch sounds great," I said. "Salad would be terrific."

I rose carefully, keeping Violet asleep against me. The day was slightly overcast, but the night's rain was no more than mist as I followed Cobb up the path to the big house. Above the clouds, I could feel the sun heating up to burn away the moisture. By this afternoon the air would lighten, the breeze blow, the sky turn brilliant and smoky blue.

* * *

272 / MICHAEL DORRIS · LOUISE ERDRICH

"I can't claim any relation to the Cobb for whom this salad is named. I take no resspsonsibility." He had clearly made an effort. The bowl before me held an arrangement of lettuces and cold chicken, vegetables and crisp bacon. For the first time since I'd arrived, Cobb asked me about myself, and I was surprised to find him capable of careful listening. In turn, he volunteered information of his own—a failed marriage, children grown distant and uncommunicative—he seemed so earnest I congratulated myself on drawing him out. We were getting somewhere, I was sure of it. The trick was to keep up the exchange of confidences, to prolong the mood of trusting rapport.

"It's a crime," he said when we had finished lunch, "for you to visit this island and not view it from its most pleasing vantage."

"Which is?"

"Discovered from the sea, it rises like a green jewel. My afternoon is free, and your son has approved the motor of my little cruiser."

I considered. Offshore, Roger couldn't show up and break into the conversation, which was finally going so well. I wanted to get this over with, settled. I had the feeling that we were on the verge of a breakthrough. I couldn't say no.

Cobb carried the glass plates to the sink. "Meet you in an hour," he offered, escorting me to the entrance of the walk.

Back at the beach house, Nash had returned from another morning of diving with Elvis Greer. I heard him talking to Roger and didn't announce my presence. This time they were arguing about the fate of the earth.

"The biota," Nash stated in a superior, lecturing tone. "You don't know a thing about it, Roger, and you should, because if we stay high on petroleum, continue our addiction, we'll throw the entire climate out of sync. We'll poison ourselves, like dying of our own bad breath."

"So what does this *biota* have to do with it?"

I heard, in Roger's reply, both contained boredom and something like patience. I sat just inside the door. Encouraged by an audience, they didn't stop.

"A biota is one unit of the biomass. Total life. It is what you get oil from. Fuel. See, Roger, if we converted our vehicles to run on seed oils we'd have more than enough, a renewable nonpolluting source of energy."

"You mean"—now Roger was straining to take this seriously—"that one day my Saab could be converted to use extra-virgin olive oil?"

Nash had warmed to his subject, the way he always did when talking apocalypse and salvation. I knew, of course, that the plant upon which Nash believed the future of the entire planet depended was none other than the stuff he'd gotten wrecked on the night of my last class. I was curious to hear how Roger would react when Nash began to advance the many unique properties of marijuana.

"The hemp plant," revealed Nash euphemistically, "is the answer. Take deforestation. Do we really have to clear-cut our old growth, the Tongass, the Amazon Basin, for wall studs and computer paper? We wouldn't—if we planted hemp. A hemp plant can grow twenty feet in one year, and actually makes better paper than wood pulp. Babies' diapers, the disposable kind like Mom uses, could be made from hemp."

"Where would we plant this hemp?"

"Anywhere. Take the millions of acres that the feds pay farmers not to sow. Tons of hemp could be harvested on that land."

"Isn't hemp . . . ?"

"Yes, it's pot, okay, so what? Liquor and tobacco companies don't want it available. That's the thing. Two of the most dangerous drugs in our society are completely legal, and hemp isn't. Why not? Because anybody can grow it and use it. Not good for the old balance sheet."

"I see your point."

Nash was taken aback. He never expected to convince someone over the age of twenty of anything, and in the rarefied air of this new communication plateau he cast about for a topic to try next. It didn't take him long.

"So what do you really think about this Diary stuff?" he asked Roger. "I mean, what gets me is how much we don't know—aren't allowed to know. There's a lot that's not explained. Like, who did those Indians think the Spanish were, anyway? Rich or poor? Human or extraterrestrial? Wouldn't they have wondered why there were no women on the boat? No children? No babies?"

As if summoned by mention of the name, Violet began to fuss, and I bounced her. The interruption, however, served to bring Nash to his senses: he had momentarily lapsed into vulnerability in the presence of adults, had spoken in a mode that was neither oblique nor condescending, had asked a sincere question—and he looked shocked at himself.

"You seem to believe that everything *is* knowable." Roger was unaware that Nash had already retreated behind an adolescent mask that admitted to no beliefs whatsoever. "That if we simply had all the facts they would spell some absolute kind of truth. An optimistic posture. Personally, I think the whole is greater than the sum of its parts."

Nash did not respond, but I jumped in.

"Wait a minute," I said. "You're the one who doesn't want any new facts. You won't even consider the possibility that Cobb's Diary is legitimate because if it is, it blows—or at least it might alter—your nice, tidy construction of the past."

"Hardly tidy, I think," Roger answered. Now he, too, shrank back into the shell of his official, public self: the full professor, above all questions. The authority. It was the side of him I found least attractive.

The one-room house suddenly seemed very small to all of us. Roger glanced at his watch.

"I'm off," he announced. "I'll eat at the club, where it's air-conditioned." At the door, he perfunctorily inquired if Nash wished to join him.

"I can't," Nash said. "I'm supposed to do something."

"Right you are." Roger nodded, clearly relieved, and left. He couldn't be meeting with Cobb. I was.

"How did you know I needed you to baby-sit for a couple of hours?" I asked Nash, once we were alone. I tried to make a joke of my request, but the ploy didn't work. Nash's face clouded, full of the plans he would have to cancel.

"Don't start," I said. "I haven't asked another thing of you the whole trip, and this is important."

"Right," he grumbled. "Nothing *I* do is important."

"Glad we're in agreement." I put my arm around his shoulders. "You're in luck. Violet is in a good mood, though she was up all night while you were comfortable on Cobb's couch."

Nash looked at me as if to contradict what I said, but then gave a noncommittal shrug.

"I'll be two hours at the most." I waved from the door.

Outside, the world was suddenly hushed. All the surf sounds abated at once, as if the sea drew breath, and in the suspension everything seemed to float out of time. I stopped where I was, oddly content, watching Nash and Violet through the screen. I remember, because I later thought that if I had been more receptive, had peered into the silence, read the air, I would have turned around at that instant, put my children into the car and headed for the airport.

But I was blind.

A boat is a boat is a boat as far as I'm concerned. As long as it floats, it's the same to me, and one of the tedious aspects of Columbus research was the deadly apathy that automatically overcame me when faced with the subject of boats. Okay: Ships, caravels, ketches, yachts, tubs, take your pick! Tears formed in my eyes as Cobb began his seaman's spiel one step beyond the gangplank of the *Cobbler*. Give me a break! It—whatever it was—was long and fairly roomy, had a cabin, a mast, a sail. There was a motor for emergencies, a wheel by which it could be steered.

He kept the thing anchored in a deep, mangrove-infested lagoon a mile down the road from the houses. From there, a man-made leeway led to the open sea. We followed that canal, then abruptly were sailing due east. The sky was placid and the ride was not bad, though the surface of the sea had seemed smoother from the shore. By the time land had receded far behind us, I began to feel odd. Nervous. And something else: I regretted the salad.

"Okay, it's beautiful," I said, catching a quick glimpse of the island. "Now turn back." I'd had enough. More than enough. We could just as easily converse at the dock.

Cobb ignored me, let down the sail, and fiddled with some loose ropes. He undid a small hitch that whined, then released a length of chain to which I assumed was attached an anchor.

"Now we won't be disturbed," he said. "Let's get to it."

"Let's get *back* to it. Terra firma."

He unfolded a low chair.

"You might as well make yourself comfortable. We're going to be here until we get this matter settled to my satisfaction."

I'd walked right into this, down the proverbial gangplank.

"No fair," I said, attempting humor.

"Fair's for amateurs."

Cobb's expression was suddenly hard, different, shed of pretense. He was again the man he'd been the first night, the blanket trader. He tossed me a can of ginger ale from a small ice chest, popped a beer for himself, and drank.

I dropped my head in my hands.

"We can go back anytime you want," he said. "As soon as you give me the second page of the letter. This is no exercise. You're not in a classroom, Professor Twostar, and neither of us is eighteen."

I regained a measure of control and studied him through one squinted eye.

Cobb's face flushed with excitement, and he regarded me as he sipped at his can. He wore a Panama hat that shaded his eyes, so I couldn't read their expression, but what did it matter? The way he crossed his bony legs, settled back and looked prepared to wait, said it all.

We remained silent for ten minutes or so while my queasiness got worse. Once we were at anchor, the sea seemed rougher.

Cobb did not miss its effect on me.

"I've heard the way to a woman's heart is through her stomach," he said.

"You're going to find out for sure in about two minutes."

I felt hollow. Yellow spots swam before my eyes. I tried a weak bluff.

"So, Mr. Cobb, you're not one for finders keepers?"

"On the contrary. I *am* a finder. And I've always believed in winner take all."

He looked down into the keyhole of his beer can, then lobbed it overboard.

"And you," he went on. "How do you feel about losers weepers?"

"If I had the page with me," I managed to say, "you would certainly have found it. Your search of my belongings was pretty thorough."

He didn't even feign embarrassment, so I tried another tactic.

"I told you: the page is in my memory. The only way you get it is if I choose to tell you. And I'm not easily coerced. Psychology is not how to get what you want."

"All right."

He rose and made for the back of the boat in a loping crouch. I was still too secure in my own notions of what was possible and what was not, so I didn't turn with his movements, I didn't watch him, I was not prepared when my arms were wrenched from behind. He held me fast and pinned me, whirled a piece of thin rope quickly around my wrists and in and out of the weave of the chair. When I was trussed, he knocked out the aluminum legs and collapsed me on the deck. Then he leaned down, spoke into my face.

"Better?"

My balance righted. My vision cleared and the knot in my stomach untied itself. Lo and behold: I was cured.

17

ROGER

I hurried back to the beach house, my mission firmly in mind. Even during the few hours I had been away, the ferny plants that bordered the path seemed to have grown, deepened, and needed to be brushed aside. The lushness of this place was oppressive. The scent that hung in the air a throbbing mix of rot and bloom that befuddled as much as it pleasured. A profusion of oversize red flowers yawned and gaped from a bush and made me think of snow, clean and neutral, the annual drop cloth over the furniture of the land where I grew up. As my eyes were assaulted by deep greens and pinks and yellows, I thought how much better I enjoyed the muted rusts, the dusty golds and browns, of New England's late autumn. Nature made her brief statement with the foliage and then retired, permitting contemplation and even regret. Full palette was on view for weeks only, and thus more precious than this tropical orgy. Every modern decorator agreed: a white interior properly set off a select item of furniture or art. One didn't find museums with garish wallpapers. As in fashion, too much jewelry detracted from the overall effect.

If I decided to humor Vivian and fake rapport with Henry Cobb, this might be one area in which we could agree. Yankee blood, even when kept at the constant boil of these latitudes, would tell. Not for nothing had generations of the man's forebears remained north for education and culture, and Cobb himself, still untanned after a year of exile in Eleuthera, was testimony to the immutability of genetic stubbornness. Loath as I was to admit it, he and I emerged from a common pool and so could understand and appreciate each other on some basic level. The glances we exchanged above Vivian's dark head, though hostile and competitive, were knowing. We were on the same geographic frequency, and so I was confident that we could come to terms on whatever proposal he wished to make—if I found it in my interests to do so.

His note, delivered to me by a waiter at the club along with the prepaid bill for my luncheon buffet, had been terse: "Change of plans. My treat. Meet me on my yacht at three. Use the rubber raft and I'll anchor off shore. We have matters to discuss in private. Cobb."

It was no surprise that Vivian was to be excluded—because of her gender and her background, she was a cipher between Cobb and me, an auxiliary chasm of subtle contention quite apart from our intellectual disagreement. This was something Vivian refused to credit, which was typical of her often naive approach. She tended to actually believe what she asserted to be true, as if the variables of sex and class could be banished simply because in certain arenas they oughtn't to matter. During the past few days' arguments and conversations, she behaved as though we were all panelists, identified only by our initials, in a debate published in *Harper's*. Cobb, and to a greater extent I, adhered to the same fiction, but *we* were not fooled by the formality. Vivian was. Her loyal allegiance to liberal theory, her insistence upon the match of substance and form, alternately charmed and irritated me. She would be furious when she learned that Cobb and I had engaged in a closed caucus, but perhaps she would never need know.

I was still unclear as to the degree to which the man had indebted himself on the Street. His placation might be something I could easily, invisibly arrange, once our jousting over Vivian's approval was eliminated. As far as I could tell, Cobb and I each wished to emerge from our discussions with egos intact, ideally strengthened. He demanded his lucrative Columbus and I insisted upon my heroic one, but perhaps they could yet be squeezed into a single outline. Well, why not? Personality was complex, even in the fifteenth century, and European history was broad enough to accommodate a paradox or two. It was Vivian's Columbus who was the destabilizing element. She sought a villain, a pillager, an obtuse spoiler, a foil for her derisive pride. Her Columbus was personal, while, though at odds, Cobb's and mine were both abstracts.

A cry intruded upon my thoughts, a howl really, that seemed to combine warning, distress, and boredom. There was no question of its source: my daughter's voice escaped the screened windows of the beach house as deftly as the nightly no-see-ums entered. I paused on the driveway to calibrate her tone—I had become rather proud of my ability to distinguish the coda for hunger from that which signaled dampness, but this bespoke neither. There was a plaintive note I had not heard before that on some primal level connoted shocked abandonment. "Here I am," Violet seemed to convey. "Find me."

Who was sitting her? I assumed it must be Nash, for Vivian would never allow hysteria to progress so far, but when I entered the baby was unattended. She lay in her crib, her face red from exertion, her eyes squeezed tight in denial, her body rigid in condensed fury.

"What is this? What is this?" I said soothingly, and picked her up. "Where is your brother? Who is in charge of you?"

In answer, Violet's volume increased. She was encouraged by any hint of empathy, and simultaneously excoriated and entreated me until I lulled her into quiet by practicing the alternately rocking and jiggling gait that had worked for me before. To remind her that it was my presence and not some faceless earthquake that came to her assistance, I kept up a stream of conversation.

"Dreadful," I said. "How could a baby be so wretched? I don't blame you, truly. I've felt the same way on more than one occasion. No, no, don't repress. You'll only have to explain it to your analyst in twenty years. That's right, vent."

My blanket permission finally caught her attention, and as

was her practice she peeped through an eye. I knew I was winning.

"Right you are, you're saved. The prince has come to your rescue."

There was one problem: in Violet's world there were still but two inhabitants: Vivian and not-Vivian, and I was not-Vivian. At the sight of me, she screamed her preference.

"Be reasonable," I admonished. "I am not nothing. I am not worse than nothing. You liked me yesterday. Compromise."

The word struck a chord that resonated to my previous thoughts. I would propose the same thing to Cobb—some modus vivendi that would take cognizance of our situation. I would make him see how damaging this whole business could be to Vivian's fragile career. If he really had anything else, I should be the one to examine it. My reputation was intact. It could withstand controversy, scrutiny, if there was indeed something new to publish. Thus, I was encouraged when even Violet responded to the logic of my suggestion. She was visibly calming, slowing like a pendulum turning into a plumb line.

"Whom do you wish Columbus to be?" I asked her. "You are after all the ultimate contract between your mother and me, the splice of our DNA, so whom?"

Violet blinked, engaged at last.

"As a modern young woman," I addressed her, "does it matter all that much to you? Are his intentions, whatever they may have been, relevant? Well, certainly yes, to an extent. You are the product of history, after all, more completely than any Virginia Dare. Maybe this was all leading up to you, maybe you're the point."

My daughter yawned. Dissension was exhausting, her eyes pleaded. Such a mood could be sustained only so long without intermission. I understood, and in that understanding sensed that we had arrived together at a breakthrough event, captioned slightly differently for Violet and for me. Her version would be labeled, "Somebody else but Her is acceptable," and mine would read, "A father soothes his infant daughter." As she shifted in my arms, searching for a more comfortable assignment of her limbs, I experienced an emotion that can only be described as thrilling. I felt light-headed, progenitorial, and I searched for some word to encompass the sensation. I had browsed through stacks of books about "Baby's First Year," and so it was only an instant before the proper definition presented itself. What we were doing, I suddenly and absolutely realized, was bonding.

Once Violet was on to other matters—in this case, a close evaluation of her own fingers—and I had recovered from the shock of immediate paternity, I remembered to be incensed that the baby had been left alone. It had to be Nash, but this was irresponsibility at a level of which I had thought even he was incapable. No doubt he had wandered to the beach, convinced himself that he was in earshot of the house, and then forgotten his sister. The boundless extent of his self-rationalization was amazing to me: there was no situation in which his culpability exceeded his victimization, but this time he had gone too far. Desertion was a self-evident crime, and unless he had been kidnapped or rendered unconscious, he was unambiguously guilty. His absence was unforgivable and, I fumed, impossibly inconvenient.

I was scheduled to meet Cobb in less than twenty minutes, and as I looked out the window I could see his yacht already stationed just beyond the reef. In vain I scanned for signs of Nash, but the shore was empty. I could scarcely call out and shock Violet back into her former mood, and yet this was a rendezvous I did not want to miss. The opportunity for a secret rapprochement might not soon again present itself, and I was sure that Cobb would take unkindly to an excuse that included childcare.

The tide was coming in, but still out far enough so that the distance to the yacht was manageable. An idea occurred to me, based upon my years of observing young colleagues at Dartmouth who arrived at faculty meetings with their sleeping offspring bound securely to their chests or backs. They seemed to dare anyone to object, these proud contemporary custodians who were smug and boastful about their shared responsibilities, their dexterity with a pacifier, their skill at combining career and parenthood.

Why not? I thought. Carefully so as not to perturb her, I wrapped Violet in her baby life jacket, slipped a suncap upon her head, pulled her blanket from the crib, and headed toward the door. As an afterthought I recalled that Vivian never went anywhere with the baby without also bringing the infernal diaper bag, so I hooked that monstrous, deceptively heavy article over my arm.

The yellow rubber raft had been left at the point of the last high tide, and I dragged it behind me until the water was deep enough for it to float. It was a small boat, but its sides were satisfyingly plump with air, and it was easily maneuvered with the single oar that rested in its well. I noticed in amusement that some adventurous soul had secured a spear gun to the side. The weapon was attached to a long coil of nylon line, just in case a catch needed to be drawn back in. There was a small plastic bucket for bailing as well as an assortment of abandoned beach paraphernalia scattered on the floor. These I pushed aside to make a nest for Violet. She stirred, but did not flail, as I set her down, and I was proud of her, proud of me, content with the concessions I was prepared to make as I wedged the paddle into the wet sand and launched the raft.

I was used to the Atlantic in Maine, and in contrast this southern ocean was deceptively benign. All rocks were visible, both above and below the clear surface, and there was no danger of hypothermia if the boat overturned. On the other hand, as I rowed toward Cobb's yacht I occasionally encountered unexpectedly strong streams that seemed to flow quite independently of the ocean's general drift. These, too, could be identified by sight as they formed smooth, swift highways cutting through the otherwise rippling terrain. Whenever I traversed their paths I had to cut perpendicularly with my oar, to use it as both rudder and motor, and invariably I lost some ground.

But it was nothing I couldn't handle, and the afternoon sun gave bright illumination, scattering sequins of reflection on every side. The generally good weather was forecast to hold for the duration of our stay—less than another week—and if only it would be punctuated with a stiff, cleansing evening breeze it would be perfect. I had used a corner of the blanket to rig a loose awning above Violet's head, and she basked unconcerned, trusting, as I closed the distance to Cobb.

He watched our progress through binoculars. Against the overall glare I could make out the bean of his head, made insectlike by the dual mirrors trained upon the raft. I saluted a greeting but he was immobile, perched high in the bow and drawing us as if with the intensity of his gaze. Let him gloat for now, I thought. Elevation is relative and temporary, and his yacht is no larger than Bart's, than any one of a number I could have had if I had followed in the family tradition of business and finance. You and I are afloat in the same sea, I thought. Don't make too much of who summoned and who responded. The conversation is what will count, and there I will hold my own.

At hailing distance, Cobb called hello.

I maneuvered close to the larger craft and indicated Violet. "I'll need a hand with her. She's happy. You won't know she's there."

"Did you bring her diaper bag?" Cobb asked, surprising me by his familiarity with domestic necessity. I had pegged him as part of my father's generation, from a time in which men knew next to nothing about the plumbing of their children. Cobb's concern oddly humanized him to me, made me less suspicious of his motives. Perhaps we would exchange joking small talk about night feedings and precocity, thus creating an atmosphere in which a meeting of the minds on other matters would be enhanced.

"Right here," I shouted, holding up the satchel for him to see. "Don't leave home without it!"

Cobb smiled approvingly. "Lift it over first," he instructed. "Hang it from the end of your oar so I can reach."

"Good idea." I did as he suggested and stretched as I extended the dangling object toward the man's reaching hands. He grabbed the base of the paddle to steady the connection, then slipped the bag free.

"Got it," he announced, as much to himself as to me.

"Let go," I called, tugging gently on my end of the wooden paddle. "Lower the ladder."

But instead, Cobb pulled back, jerking so hard that I lost my balance and let go in order to steady the raft. It was an annoying joke and could have imperiled the baby. My good feelings for the old bastard instantly dissipated and I frowned up at him. But he had vanished behind the rail.

I heard the whine of a rising anchor. The yacht's motor roared to life, and faster than I could mentally process what was happening, the boat began to pull away, its propeller churning a buckling wave that threatened to capsize my raft.

I watched, shouting above the noise, repeatedly demanding an explanation, as the boat raced away from us until its edges began to blur. The furled sails seemed to dissolve in the mist of clouds, and finally the hull, a jaunty silver, darkened until it could not be easily distinguished from the line of the horizon. There was no option but to head for shore by sculling hard with my hands. I have no great rapport, no understanding with the sea, have always been an indifferent sailor, though all Williamses are carefully instructed in the art. At this instant I actively hated it. The line of waves was sickeningly irregular. The rubber boat did not steer easily but swayed side to side. Equilibrium required a dexterous shoulder maneuver that sapped my energy before we'd half begun.

"We're going back," I told Violet, who looked mildly interested. "Hang tight."

She'd managed to anchor three fingers in her mouth, and sucked them experimentally. My heart surged with a sudden pride. She was not helpless! She had invented a form of comfort, an interim gratification. We were getting somewhere.

"Good girl!"

She contemplated me, and I gave myself over to the task of getting us home. The spear gun, strapped onto the side of the craft, created an uneven haul for which I had to compensate. In every way the flimsy boat was so thoroughly unsatisfactory that I promised myself I would kick it when we beached, but for the present we had important business to attend, and we made slow progress. I scooped and struggled until my arms ached. Things couldn't get much worse, I thought, but as it turned out, "things" were just beginning.

Before attacking its dinner, a shark may circle. It's a sizing-up maneuver, a formality, a kind of decision-making flourish that can be compared with the reading of a menu in a restaurant. I saw him in the water, large and sleek and gray, and felt a shiver of recognition mixed with excitement and, of course, fear. Then the top fin broke just off starboard and he dived beneath the boat. I recalled—as if the sight had opened a file titled "Shark Facts"—every bit of trivia I'd ever stumbled across.

Shark attacks on people are rare, and even if attacked, only a very few victims are killed. More men than women. I was sure about *that*. Sharks don't like the taste of human flesh, or was it that they preferred humans over all else? I could not remember.

I plied my hands with a will, churning my own waves, all exhaustion gone, adrenaline flooding every muscle. I thought surely the splashing, the effort I was making, would frighten off the shark. They were shy creatures, really, weren't they? Or was it the other way around? *We* were shy—*they* were bold. But it wheeled, almost playfully dipped under the flimsy bottom of the craft, and sheered off like a torpedo making a run. Then a return. I forgot everything. Its shadow—its speed—was sharp, evil, a death-dealing instrument. It looked to me like hunger, the shape of hunger incarnate, of greed and desire. Land was still out of reach and the current blunted my strongest efforts.

Surely, I thought, surely we don't resemble prey. Surely it will leave us alone. But no, the shark came on. Plowing toward us, rolling through the water, the thing flung itself our way. In my mind I saw the tipped-back nose, the rows of ugly teeth, the triangle of the mouth, and then it swept under us again.

War! Blood left my arms, my legs, and as in a dream my fingers fastened on the ties of the spear gun, but so weakly that I could hardly maneuver it from the Velcro holster mounted on the side of the craft. Once I gripped the stock, though, I seemed to imbibe a kind of intestinal firmness from its sleek and lethal design. Violet was quiet, apparently caught along with me in this strange aura. I did the thing I had always done as a boy when faced with a bully, a fight, a difficult rite of passage. I inserted myself into the scene as an actor. I pretended I was doing the correct, the manly, thing. I breathed long and slow, made myself calm as I waited for the next charge. I cocked back my arm.

I fired the spear too, only I'd forgotten to unlash the safety cord. To my unbelieving eyes the barb, instead of singing out and finding the shark's small black heart, plunged through the edge of the inflated gunwale and left a ragged hole that hissed as the air exploded through it.

The make-believe abruptly ceased. There was no place to hide. My brain raced. Violet's weight was so slight that the pressure might equalize at some point, or perhaps there was a double wall, a lining, an inner tube–like compartment that would keep the craft marginally afloat. With my weight aboard, though, her chances were gravely reduced. If I didn't move, the boat would most certainly sink, flatten out completely.

And so I threw myself overboard.

I saw the arc of my leaving, the shadow under me as I sank. Then I was one with the shadow, alone with the hunger.

The water was tears on my tongue, the warm salt I had not tasted since childhood, but it all came back, primordial and strong. Grief, the cause now lost, swept over me and into me and I floated limp and supple, the offering, Abraham changed places with Isaac. Every sense was alert, in competition to be heard. Where would the beast strike first, and how painfully? I willed the attack to be fatal, instant, merciful. Let the thing not have fed for days, let it view me as both appetizer and entrée, not some snack to be prolonged. Every joint relaxed even as each muscle tensed. I imagined myself as seen from below, my dark shape marring the blue, my torso the eclipse of the afternoon sun. I must be as irritating as I was delectable, a blot who cried to be eliminated. My eyes were closed and the only sign that time still moved was the push and lift of waves against my skin.

The human head is heavy, the heaviest part, and yet my lungs were buoys. In the ocean, man's natural state is to stand erect, and so, passive and unresisting, I assumed that pose, a fruit suspended from a tree, ripe for the plucking, but the instinct to survive did not altogether retreat. Imperceptibly my arms and legs began to tread, to argue with the water. I felt absurdly polite, as if to remain fresh and breathing was the preferable marinade for steak tartare. What was taking so long? I rode my bicycle impatiently, pumping faster against the blackness, my teeth gritted but still allowing air in and out along with the whimpers and cries I finally identified as my own calls.

I felt it graze against my toe, gentle as silk, and then again, always at my farthest reach. It was toying, and I pictured it stationary beneath me, mouth agape, waiting for exhaustion to drop me in. It would consume me like a banana, a nibble at a time, and gravity would be my hanging rope. From some other place and era, from some stockpile of accumulated impatiences—waiting in a long queue at the dry cleaners, watching the mail for an editor's reply, listening to a bore, sitting stalled in highway traffic, put on hold by a telephone-answering machine, standing at the bathroom door while Nash examined his complexion—from the accretion of wasted inaction came an overwhelming emotion I barely recognized: indignation. I refused to wait a moment longer for my own demise, and like a lifter preparing to jerk more weight than ever before attempted, I placed my arms at my side and then raised them with a mighty thrust that made my body a harpoon aimed true.

The jolt was abrupt and absolute, the pain in my toe excruciating. After the continual rock of the sea I was suddenly inert, run aground in the shoals, my head a post just above the surface. I slid one foot as far as it would reach and discovered a rising slope, then shifted my weight and took a step. Another. Air surrounded my face, my chest, my waist, and at last I opened my eyes. From the point where I protruded, water, some dark blue, some an aqua green, ran toward the distant shore. There was no sign of the shark, no telltale approaching ridge among the uniform waves, only a beating wind so strong that its vacuum blocked all other sound.

I turned left and right, squinting for sight of the raft, until I saw it, caught in a current, disappear around the next peninsula. My impulse was to swim after, but there was no point. It was beyond my reach, moving too fast, in the tow of my daughter's own fate. At least it was still afloat, I told myself. At least, marooned as I was, I had been granted that much knowledge, enough to justify a plan of rescue. If I could find a two-way radio, a telephone, surely the authorities could be alerted, patrol boats dispatched, helicopters summoned.

I could not remain still for too long—if I did, the ground collapsed in swirls around my feet. And yet I seemed rooted to the spot, to my own island of safety. Leaping from the raft was one thing—impulsive and spontaneous—but leaving this providential sandbar was a more demanding choice. My brain performed simultaneous calculations: the odds that I would make it to shore unconsumed, versus the chance that someone would notice Violet without my sounding the alarm; the risk that we would both die if I attempted to swim, against the guilt of never knowing for sure if I stayed. The balance swayed, beyond my control: me or her, or neither, or both. The shark swam from one side of the scales to the other, removing any chance of balance. Numbers and percentages infused my thoughts—fifty percent, twenty, thirty-three—each one meaningless and yet on some level taken seriously. It was as if Gallup were polling some anonymous statistical sample of opinion and I would follow his estimate. I wanted to be intelligent about this. I wanted to be right. I wanted. I wanted. I wanted. I wanted . . . Violet, and I took a breath, dived toward the nearest land. My body surged into that flow of things that tumbled forward or backward, governed by the pull of the moon, by the hidden algebra of magic and magnetism.

I was stronger than I expected, than I had any right to be. For a good long time I pulled resolutely toward land, maintaining a constant rhythm to the intake and expulsion of oxygen and stretching my arms with every forward reach. I followed the instructions I had first been given by my Red Cross teacher, making bowls of my palms and flutter-kicking with my legs close together. I concentrated on pace, on completing one movement before thinking of the next. I resisted the impulse to rush—"Slow and steady wins the race" had been drummed into me during those many practice laps in the Harvard pool as I matched Bart's progress in the adjoining lane. And I counted to one hundred before I paused to assess my progress.

The sight was worse than a disappointment. I had drifted far to the right of my intended destination, and seemed to be even farther from shore. It was as if I were following in my daughter's wake, caught on the satin train of her gown as it snaked into the distance. In fact I was approaching the vicinity of the very promontory of coral behind which her raft had disappeared, and rather than attempt to regain lost ground, I altered my course, kept my head above water, and breaststroked toward the very place. This time the current was with me, a hand between my shoulder blades encouraging me forward. I scissored my legs, forgot the shark, and rode the crest of a large swell. I would save my fight for dry land, when it counted more, and with the compliance of the ocean I fairly lunged with every pull of my arms.

As I approached the craggy jut, however, I suddenly learned a fact about which I had never previously even wondered: it is impossible to break momentum in rushing water. No frontal resistance is comparable to the inertia of sustained forward motion. I was propelled toward the beach much too fast for caution, and my skin tightened with the physical dread of sharpened rock. But, dropping my legs as I fought to neutralize my trajectory, I felt a new and much stronger force come into play. From deep below a suction grabbed at my ankles and locked around my knees. The razor shore became in that instant my heart's desire, the most acceptable of havens, yet like so many recent changes of my mind, this one came late. I was too tired and the tug was too insistent. Fueled only with a last gulp of air, I was yanked into the earth as surely and as swiftly as if I had fallen over a precipice.

There are unexpected disadvantages to being a film buff. Other people's imagined sights and sounds invade your thoughts at the most private and critical of moments, and as I was swallowed into the undertow this happened to me. I saw myself clearly through a camera's eye: My skin was white. My hair, static straight, formed a halo around my face. A trail of final bubbles escaped my lips and raced toward the surface. My limbs moved in slow motion, as much a product of the whims of passing fish as they were directed by my starving brain. Shafts of light radiated through the aqua depths, and from some distant speaker the theme music from *Jaws* throbbed insistently. I waited for my life to flash before my staring eyes, but all I got was a double feature of *The Blue Lagoon* and *Das Boot*. It seemed a gratuitous insult to learn—the last piece of the puzzle—that I was so shallow. I begged for a suitable quote to occur to me, some apt epitaph that I could append to forty-four years of ambition, but when I opened my mind, a single thought rushed in: Violet, adrift and unprotected. My final curtain was failure.

Out of habit, I held my breath for as long as possible, and seemed to ride on a track that cut through the surrounding sea with growing acceleration. I banged against rock, my toenails were packed with sand, my nostrils filled with the water that blew against my face. A stark wall rose to meet me, and I assumed I would be pounded there, tenderized for my shark. Then I was swept beneath an overhang that blotted out all remaining light, and into a long, narrow cave, a rough-sided esophagus that added—as if I needed still another route to madness—claustrophobia. Within this capillary, the dragging force that had snagged me grew even stronger, matching almost, but not quite, the frustrated expansion of my lungs. It wedged me ever more securely into the funnel until, at last, I stalled, trapped at the hip. I knew what lay in store: my chest would burst and I would fill this compact tunnel, the cork against its lip, the ball to close its open faucet.

Instead, I cleared the mouth, undamming the channel, and propelled by the released pressure, I shot into an open pool. Released from their confinement, my arms flailed instinctively, climbing the water, clawing it out of my way.

"He fought to the end." The phrase came to me like a benediction, and I was grateful. It was, though prosaic, what I had been holding out for, and I opened my mouth to the water and breathed.

18

VIVIAN

Shame made it worse. Hypnotized by my own self-assurance, I had believed things would be the way I wanted because I wanted them to be that way. Will is blind. The truth was, I was trussed and bound by my own nearsightedness, helpless and stupid.

Then there was another factor, beyond me.

That's it, I fumed as Roger drew near the boat, as I heard him hail Cobb from a short distance, *we have no mental connection. We're through.* Cobb had stowed me on the far side of the low cabin. When he sighted Roger, he had also tied a red bandanna tightly around my mouth. For the past ten minutes I had been sending a barrage of extrasensory Mayday signals. I was incensed that Roger hadn't received a single one. *Call the Police,* my neurons shrieked. *Go Back!* But on he came, his eager progress narrated by Cobb, who made officious adjustments of the sails and tidied up the boat as if to welcome him.

He bent low to speak, thrust his nose against mine.

"I always have at least one backup plan—that's why I invited your boyfriend to the party. I doubt he's as obstinate as you. Care to reconsider? We're still quite a distance offshore. That's a long swim for Roger if I capsize him."

Poor Roger. I was nothing but trouble. For the second time he didn't know what was going on, didn't know he was getting in over his head.

When Cobb loosened the bandanna, I yelled. He clapped his hand over my mouth, then drew it away slowly. "Leave Roger out of this," I said. "He doesn't even believe you have the Diary, and besides, we're in sight of land. Swimming is no problem for him."

Cobb tightened my gag and returned to his station. Within a few seconds he was back.

"Roger may be Mark Spitz," Cobb's voice was gloating. "But what about the little one?"

Perhaps it was self-protection, the mind's inability to recognize a killing fear, but at first there was simply no computing what he said. I did not process his words, except to let them pass me by without hauling them in.

Cobb put his hands on his knees, crouched near me, a boardroom expression on his face. "Now, Professor Twostar, tell me. Where is the page? Or recite it, as you prefer."

His eyes became grotesque, sharp with threat. He bent over to loosen the knot of the gag, and his breath was hot and beery on my cheek. On the one hand, Violet couldn't be in the boat. Whatever Roger was doing, he'd be alone. On the other hand . . .

"You're bluffing," I said over the loosened material. "Tell me what she's wearing." I'd changed Violet's clothing just before I left the beach house, and there was no way Cobb could know what she had on unless she was in eyeshot now.

Cobb stuck his head above the rail. "Blue and yellow stripes."

Then I caved in. The sky whirled and there was nowhere to touch down, nowhere stable. I rocked myself back and forth so hard the small aluminum chair frame buckled under me. Cobb leapt back, pushed me down, and held me still.

"Let them go."

"I'm listening," he said. "But I've got it narrowed down. It's either on one of you, or in that bag you never let go of. That's where you carried the page from the Diary. And what do you know? Your boyfriend's even got it with him."

He was smart all right. I was out of red herrings.

"Bull's-eye. It's in the bag. That's all you need."

I had one advantage left, and I needed all the bargaining power I could get. I remembered that he couldn't read old Spanish. The translation he was so desperate to get didn't contain what he wanted, but I'd make up something, claim I had left out the best part when I wrote the thing down in English. I closed my eyes. He wouldn't buy that. I was kidding myself. More likely he'd just get angry, crazier in his frustration to reach one more blind alley. And another thought: He wouldn't let me go after pushing matters this far.

"Leave them alone," I said. "When we're all safe I'll tell you about the oyster shells. They're what you're really after."

He cocked his head to the side, smiled, but didn't believe me. "We'll see."

He reknotted the bandanna behind my ears so tightly that the only sound I could force past my tongue was a thin whine. I heard Cobb on the other side of the boat again, shouting to Roger. Roger's voice rose, clear and unsuspicious. I strained for Violet's cry but . . . nothing.

I chafed my wrists within the ropes, but Cobb had left no slack in his double hitch. I drummed my heels on the deck, but the thunk of waves covered my attempts to warn Roger. No matter which way or how violently I moved, I remained firmly bound onto that chair. I was lying at an awkward angle, my hips higher than my elbows, so that actually getting onto my feet was impossible. I tried to bite the bandanna apart, but the cloth was tough and new. I began to inch across the deck like a mechanical toy, but Cobb kicked me hard.

The blow landed in my stomach. I hadn't felt physical pain since labor, and it all came back. But this was different. The last time, pain had led to life. This time, clearly, it was just the opposite.

Roger shouted. I heard him distinctly. "Stop fooling around and give me the paddle!" It was a simple, no-nonsense command from a man accustomed to having students obey him.

"Give it to me!" Roger insisted again. The motor in the back of Cobb's boat revved. The slick boards throbbed beneath me and we began to turn.

"COBB! THROW IT OVER!"

Roger's voice now competed with the engine noise, yet still its timbre held the same reasonable expectation, mixed with pique, until it was gone, the syllables lost at sea.

Cobb opened the throttle and the boat surged through the swells, throwing up mist and spray. It was a rough ride and I was tossed by the pitch and roll of the deck. I struck my head hard on the side of the cabin, and from deep within me, a dark and comfortable cloud seeped up, a cushion. A place to rest. Oblivion. It was very close, very tempting, and I closed my eyes.

I was looking at a blackboard. A thought scrawled itself across that space in perfect chalked script.

Follow the Way of the Empty Hand.

I was, at first, confused by the intrusion of the sloganny *do-zen* from Nash's karate class. But then it made absolute sense. This was my interior voice of survival. I was in a life-or-death situation. By abandoning Roger and Violet to make their own way to shore, Cobb had demonstrated how serious he was, and his vicious kick was the punctuation. The most frightful killer is the civilized one. The man or woman who can think ahead, premeditate, plan and even take into account a victim's fear or pain, is the one with no excuses. Our laws note the furor of passion that can lead to violence, to a temporary loss of control, but the murderer who commits a sober and even polite execution is beyond forgiveness. To a naive observer, also beyond comprehension. Even bound and gagged, I found it almost impossible to understand that Cobb actually intended to do me real harm. It took an effort, a suspension of disbelief—until Cobb cut the motor.

Mind of Water. To confront Cobb, I must clear myself of hatreds that could distort the surface of the mind, just as ripples on a stormy lake make the bottom impossible to see. Put aside anger, vengeance, put aside fear or avidity for the moment. Maintain eye focus. See. There he was just to the left.

Then Cobb disappeared from view. A cut over my eye stung and I could feel it bleeding. Good. If he thought I was helpless, I could summon the spirit of *sen,* or ahead-of-ness. I could take Cobb by surprise. The thing was, though, lying down I was incapacitated, and could not rise by my own efforts. I had to get on my feet so that I could find the sixth essential component of my actions. Balance. With my arms tied back, I'd have to locate my center quickly, and hold it. I concentrated on the spot where Grotz had insisted my source of strength and even my psyche resided. That wasn't hard to do: my stomach still hurt like hell. But I put the pain away from me, breathed from the source, breathed from nowhere, as I heard Cobb return.

He was above me, his shadow cold, a dark negation. I struggled toward the moon. *Mind of the Moon.* I visualized the circle, absorbing and reflecting the blue light of his gaze, the indifference of his smile crisscrossing me, laid over like a grid. If he really meant to commit murder, Cobb would have to throw me overboard, but to make it look like an accident, he would first have to untie my wrists.

My calm was deep, primal. I pretended to be unconscious, and he checked my pulse. Too fast? Too unsteady? His fingers were warm and dry on my throat and I tried not to swallow. I tried to slow the tripping of my heart. As he stooped next to me, as I heard his knees creak, I felt him busily working at the chair, untying me, I thought, although he didn't loosen the ropes around my wrists. He would, though—I counted on it. He dropped something heavy behind me, maneuvered it along the deck as he jerked at the webbing of the chair. Then he was in front of me, standing again and lifting me to his chest. I smelled his sharp sweat, the warmth of sun on cotton cloth, the garlic in the salad he had eaten. Beneath my limp weight, he staggered, and I let my head fall to his shoulder. As he pulled me toward him, I realized that we were dragging something.

Dragging something! I'd imagined the wrong scenario, but what was this one? He stopped, pulled an object along behind us. Panic fizzed up my arms and legs, slow bubbles that left me weak. He had tied something heavy to the chair. He didn't intend to fake a drowning accident. When he threw me overboard—and he was going to, no doubt about that now—I wouldn't have even the slight-to-moderate chance of swimming to shore. With my arms bound to the chair, I'd be dragged down immediately and anchored. The sea would cover me. The sea would leave no clues.

Now was the time to act. No fear. No hesitation. *Sen.*

I lifted my head and looked him in the eye, fixed him. Screamed.

There are stories from the old days, around where I grew up, stories of how the enemy is entered by his victim, possessed by her soul, and with that scream, hurled from my center, louder and more resolute than any sound I'd ever made, I entered Cobb. As he stepped back startled, I was already part of him. The slate-blue of his eyes held my reflection. It was a terrible intimacy. Grotz had not prepared me.

Cobb staggered, lost his balance, set me down hard on my feet.

Center. Stance. Kick.

In the instant Cobb was off guard, I used a front lateral to the groin. Illegal, yes, in tournament action, for good reason. Cobb folded up so violently that I thought the match was over. He flew backward, hit the deck gasping. The hat tipped off and he sprawled on the varnished wood. There was enough time for me to position my torso, to plant myself in a minor straddle stance, before he squinted at me, groaned, and staggered to his feet. Without a word, he swung toward me, arms wide to grapple. I managed to turn him aside, using the arm of the chair to catch him across the throat. He stumbled a bit, caught his ankle, tossed hard over the rope that tied me to the—

I was tied to a latched bucket of sand.

I lost composure, lost timing. Terror squeezed them from me, sealing my lungs like plastic bags. The thing was flare orange, signal orange, hunter's orange, an eye-stopping death orange. For a moment, I could take in nothing but the sand bucket. It was made of metal, with a top that fastened with a thick clasp, and it was so damn heavy. Cobb circled me, his fingers spread, trying to get behind in order to pin me against him again. I forced the bucket from my mind and replaced it with a single word. Focus. I looked straight at Cobb and circled too, keeping him before me, stepping over the rope every time I rotated around my new point of gravity, the thing that now defined my existence. I had to protect the bucket from Cobb's reach, yet make it work for me at the same time. If he got to it, if he managed somehow to hoist it up and to throw it over, I would be completely immobilized by the weight.

That's when I had an idea. I'd have to use both my centers, to enlarge my clarity and use gravity. We couldn't keep circling one another, because eventually Cobb would win, find an opening. With each pitch of the waves I rocked down slightly, and the bucket stayed a little higher. I would use my position, use the rope, use the bucket that was supposed to anchor me in nothingness, as another aspect of *sen*. Next rotation, I didn't step over the rope. I let it bind me once above the knees. Cobb caught this. His eyes narrowed and he took the meaning that I wanted from it. He decided I was tired and he circled again. The rope bound twice. I was four feet from the bucket. I executed a tight pirouette. The rope bound again, again, and Cobb moved as I expected, straight in to complete the task.

I whirled my hips, and as I did the rope tugged sharply. The trick was to get the bucket up and then, by dint of quickly mobilized centrifugal movement, keep it in the air at the end of the rope like a bola while I attacked.

Thank God as a girl I'd mastered the Hula-Hoop. By madly, and I do mean with the most convulsive swivel I had ever mustered, hulaing, I managed to plant myself the moment the bucket started moving and unwind it from me in one tremendous arc. And it would have worked. It really could have. The damn thing was, though, Cobb jumped. And once the bucket missed and kept swinging to the end of its trajectory, I was yanked so swiftly off my feet that I pedaled in the air. I landed still standing, with my back to the cabin and Cobb in front of me.

I had only one weapon left: the kick.

I would now see if it was true, as Sensei Grotz insisted, that it was not the number of techniques learned that counted in the Way of the Empty Hand but how perfectly one technique was mastered. The only piece of *kata* I had practiced was the repetitious snap-thrust kick. Nothing else. Hundreds, maybe thousands of snap thrusts, at least, not one of which had satisfied Grotz. While Nash had learned to stand on one foot like a crane and use the chicken-head block, I'd been stuck with a bag of sawdust. Around me, others swirled and punched. Others tumbled. I kicked.

I was wearing nonskid sneakers. Keds. They cushioned the

blow a little. Still, when Cobb took the heel of my foot in his chest, he coughed. I'd done damage. I advanced, knees bent for balance, resumed my stance and struck again. This one went straight to that core of wind and light, the solar plexus. Cobb's mouth opened. He tried to breathe in, couldn't, and went down. He looked stunned as he scrambled up again. I dragged the bucket forward, stayed prepared. Kicked and stepped aside when he lunged. I heard a rib snap. Cobb bounced backward to the rail of the boat and paused a moment. Then something passed over his face, a look of dismay, decision. He feinted away from me and desperately rummaged in Violet's diaper bag.

I was not supposed to think about the outcome of the fight. *Mind of Water.* I was not supposed to give in to distorting hatreds. Carefully, I put the image in my mind's eye of Violet safe on shore with Roger. They were all right. I had to take care of Cobb. He ripped open the side pocket of the bag and, ignoring the envelope that contained the photocopy of his precious page, he chose the wrong thing. With furtive speed he removed the little Ziploc sack that held Columbus's exhortation, the words I used for encouragement. Then he staggered to the rail of the boat.

"Come any closer and I'll drop it," he said.

I took one step, another, and his face grew long in resignation. I was fully in range now, and I had to remain calm. A hoisting kick to his stomach and chest. Another when he turned, and then I had him over the edge. He went in, backward, still clutching his prize.

When I heard the splash I shuffled, crablike, banged the latch off the sand bucket with my foot. It overturned and I made sure the sand spilled out. The thing clattered on the deck as I went back to try and figure out the motor. Impossible. I had to free my arms. And of course, it was Violet who came to my rescue. I sat down beside the diaper bag, felt to the bottom with my bound hands, and came up with her baby lotion.

From below, I heard Cobb's voice. He was taking the same understated approach to disaster as had Roger. Was this a part of their patrician training?

"Vivian, I know you can hear me. Be reasonable. You're not going to do this. The sun is going down. I'm not sure I can make it to shore."

I unscrewed the top of the bottle, let the fragrant oil flow onto my wrists, make them supple and slippery. It would be a long process but it would work. Cobb kept talking, reasoning, insisting that he knew what I would do, and then the waves pounded him one way and the boat another, or perhaps he decided it was best to swim for shore. At any rate, by the time dusk thickened, the two of us were alone with the night before us, divided by the will of the sea.

19

ROGER

Air caught like fire in the pockets of my lungs. Coughing and gasping, I fixed my entire concentration on their flex and squeeze. Oxygen flooded into my brain and filled my cells. I expanded, light and pure as a bubble, and skimmed above myself, stunned by beams of physical pleasure. The air was rich, voluminous, and breathing was a sensuous act. Was this some illusion, some unheralded psychological balm that softened the moment of death? If so, so what?

I opened my eyes. Nothing.

I put my hands to my face. Yes, my eyes *were* open. I could feel my eyelids move up and down. Either my brain had somehow shut down all auxiliary systems, including sight, and I was now blind, or I was looking out into a blackness so deep I had never experienced anything like it. In most darknesses there are areas of greater density, there are reflections, there is texture. My darkness was utterly blank.

I seemed to float in a bowl of unclear dimensions, and I swam tentatively forward to explore. Within a few strokes I reached a ledge, rough and dry. Its flatness extended at least as far as my arm could reach, and with the last of my energy I pulled myself upon it. I lay on my back, still incredulous that I could breathe, and tried to remember the direction of the tide. If it filled this chamber, my refuge might be short-lived. Was the vault high enough? Low, I had sailed at low, and the tide was washing in. I had to attain higher ground.

Disoriented, I slowly waved my arms over my head, then tentatively to each side. Space. Yet the darkness pressed evenly upon me. It held me in my skin as water holds a diver. I rested on sand. I felt the grains shift beneath my hips. Without a visual reference, my body seemed huge, then small. The space around me was first enormous, then tiny, as in the feverish dreams of a child.

I became aware of an overpowering sensation. My throat seemed to close and my tongue burned as though swabbed with ammonia. Tears leaked and ran along the side of my nose. They dripped to my chin, my throat. I found that I could stand, and did so, slowly, and as the sensations lessened degree by degree, it came to me that I was in the presence of an awful stink. I hadn't known before how thoroughly a bad smell could affect the body or the mind. I tried holding my breath, but that was impossible for long. I breathed, gulped down acrid musk. It had an undertone of something long dead, a bacterial strain of old socks left too long in a closed closet. There was a hint of acetylene, a vigorous irritant that left my tongue raw.

Yet I was standing, I was alive, wasn't I? I opened my mouth. "Violet," I called. Her name brought everything back in a flood, formed the unbearable image of the fragile boat.

I was answered. The walls vibrated. *Vio-let-et-et.* The cave was huge. In the hush I repeated her name, just to hear it. And then I called for Vivian. I spoke every name I could think of. I called my mother, called my father, called Bart, cursed Cobb. And every name reproduced itself in echoes, met and joined in a susurration of whispers, as if the ghost images of those I loved and hated, summoned by their names, met in the air and disputed among themselves. I sat down, listened to the last murmurs fade, and began to rub my skin for warmth.

It was then I heard another subtle sound, like the rustle of maple leaves in autumn.

"Get a grip on yourself. Get a grip," I said aloud and heard ricochetted back. I knew very well that the worst thing would be to lose self-control. By giving in to the irrational urge to cry for help, for comfort, I had almost relinquished my mental hold. And I wasn't the only audience. The frightful Pandemonium I raised had in turn roused something alive and vast all around me. I'd brought the cave to life. I'd awakened the bats.

They were the source of the sound. They were the authors of the smell. I was sitting on an island of bat dung.

Most of us struggle with a phobic horror of some creature—snakes, mice, and spiders are the most common objects of fear. Vivian hated the rat. Bart was deathly afraid of tadpoles. In my childhood, at my sleep-away camp, I had been introduced to my own nemesis: the bat. They were numerous, and nested in the chimneys of the old wooden cabins. Above the circle of the big campfire where we held our sing-alongs, they swirled and dove among the rising sparks. For two summers, they held me hostage beneath a Red Sox baseball cap, until I came to terms with them, as I ultimately coped with many other terrors—the fear of death, the futility of experience—by transforming them into an object of study. Though I never quite lost my boyhood uneasiness, by demystifying bats I came to appreciate their magic.

And so now it was with a mixture of atavistic loathing and excited respect that I accepted the idea that I was not alone. The "excited" part was this: if there were bats, there must be an exit to this place. They had to get in and out, didn't they? Which meant that I had a chance of escape, too. I could help Violet only if I alerted others and gathered an immediate rescue mission. And so, for minutes that seemed like hours, determination drove me, even though any misstep might have been the beginning of an endless fall. I touched the blackness with my fingertips, felt my way nowhere. Once, in exploring, I encountered a strange formation, a smooth bump I traced until I encountered a slight depression, then another, as if where a second eye had been. I could not help but wonder whether others besides me had swum into the current at the wrong moment and been sucked into this rock. None escaped to tell the tale, I thought, then firmly suppressed the notion. I had always been different, and would be again. I would measure the limits of this prison with more boldness and ingenuity than any precursor. I would find my way out even with no visual assistance.

As if in reward to my will, there came a kind of guidance.

It appeared at first to be an eerie white tower standing upright before me, its manifestation so sudden I thought at first it had to be a hallucination. I approached the column, and passed through it. It was light, its particles reaching up for fifty feet into the solid darkness.

There was a single Cyclopean eye far above which was probably both exit and entrance for the bats; through it there stared down a translucent, hazy shaft. I sat within this column on a hummock of stone deeply covered with guano and tried to take it all in, to find an advantageous use for this ghostly spiracle. Strange solutions flew at me, in and out of my mind.

"De-energize," I muttered, thinking of Nash's television show. When nothing happened, I imagined unraveling my swimsuit thread by thread. I imagined constructing a thousand bat harnesses and saw myself, as the night fell and they commenced their migration, hauled up by frail membranous wings. I saw the light as a helix of pulsing stairs. But my fantasies quickly exhausted themselves and I was left with the frustration of the impassable elements: Water I had come from, air I could not ascend. Fire I needed, for I was cold. Earth to which I would return.

Did I have any tools for survival? I emptied the pockets of my shorts. Three soaked Bahamian dollars. A half-melted mint. One paper clip. A small Japanese carrier shell I had found for Vivian. My ubiquitous computer diskette.

I unwrapped the mint and put it in my mouth. The taste was sweet, reassuring. I needed sustenance for what came next. I turned the disk over in my hands. It might be completely ruined, and yet I extended it out into the light, as if to dry it. Ludicrous. What I held was useless, a plate of dried bone. I had relied on a blue square of memory, a small silver clip, a technology within the plastic. And yet I no more understood how my thoughts and words were stored there than I comprehended the workings of my own brain.

I pressed it to my head, and willed Violet's yellow boat to drift toward land, toward fishermen, toward any human being along the narrow coast of the island. I willed what I saw in my mind's eye with such concentration that I fell from my low perch onto the ragged ground. It was there, surrounded by blackness so absolute that it absorbed even thought, that my brain went blank, too. Washed clean by seawater, simplified by loss, erased by fear, my life was cast briefly on a fizzing pool. It was a small life, I now observed, a small life and a smaller death. My brain was unique among the billions on the planet, but it was just another storage unit, no more interesting in itself than the blue disk. I was a photon of light in the well of radiance. I was drifting.

I was never so alive as when I woke from that nap, never so charged, never so amazed at the things I could do. I seemed to encompass everything. Each sense was knife keen. Joy filled me to the fingertips, or not joy, exactly—something more focused than that. Call it clarity. All the useless little mental tics and tremors had vanished. Truth communicated itself instantly. I slept moments, I slept hours. The light went, yet I did not fear darkness. I trembled with cold, but danced to keep warm. That I was a different temperature than my surroundings was a good sign. My body was doing the job, shivering to generate heat. Without water, I would cease to function in only a few days and become the same as the dung of the ages. What of it? Flesh become stone, I would vanish. I would be covered. But right now each breath was a gift. Another and another entered and filled me and was expelled, and there were more to come. I didn't number them. Why should I mourn?

I had thoughts, such thoughts. My past brimmed over and filled with faces. My mother peeled a pear at a table of rich cherry-wood. She cut it into slices for me and I ate them one by one. My father caught a fish, then looked into my face, took the hook from its jaw with a pliers, and threw the fish back into the ocean. I knew how the fish felt, returned to grace. I, too, had been hoisted into a burning element and held by monstrous hands. I, too, had been released.

Donne perched on my shoulder.

> For love, all love of other sights controls,
> And makes one little room, an everywhere.

Let sea-discoverers to new worlds have gone,
Let maps to other, worlds on worlds have shown,
Let us possess one world, each hath one, and is one.

Against all the expectations that I might have demanded out there on the surface of the earth, down here was not so bad. Only hours ago I could have died, been eaten up. I could have swallowed water in a tunnel. But I was alive, and the knowledge that only days might remain seemed beneath notice compared to the sumptuous river of seconds and minutes I now possessed.

Of course, I was not the sole consciousness. Ten thousand ears cocked in my direction. Yet even in heightened apprehension, I couldn't picture it—their world defined by sound. The void was filled with noises so high in pitch I couldn't hear them. The human range is narrow. From the planes and cups of their delicately sculptured, gargoyle faces, my companions skirled ultrasonic beeps, deploying them the way we use vision, building up and changing and reviewing a moving panorama.

If a word formed on my lips, if I spoke, I would add to their sonar view. And there was so much I could add. My brain held everything I ever knew. Its capacity was unimaginably vast, bigger than the air around me. I remembered the alphabet backward, the states, their capitals. I remembered long conversations with friends and enemies, the plots and stars of old movies, recipes; the periodic table from eleventh grade was still there, and Kubla Khan, Emerson, the complete Donne, hymns I'd heard in church, jingles, ads, articles I'd read in the bathtub, instructions off the backs of cleaning product boxes, the fine print to warranties, the rules of games, insurance clauses and gardening hints, the particulars of every woman I had not loved well enough.

Vivian.

I reconstructed her in living detail, from the beginning to the present. Every word she uttered and every expression that had crossed her face, I now realized, had been captured by an interior reel. I replayed the precious film to myself, again and again. I reexperienced blue afternoons, and then the pull and tug of days. I put Violet in her arms. I put her there and kept her there and would not let her go.

There was no stopping the endless outpouring of details, the esoteric along with the mundane. I remembered letters I had written. I remembered whole years. I saw there had been no need to keep a diary. It was all available to me, every experience, detailed and filed, and then, besides the scholar's brain, dry and organized, there was another brain that entirely fabricated its *own* world— imagined it—a poet's brain filled with interior rhymes and luscious syllables.

Again, I took from my pocket the disk that held my poem. A useless amulet, a mere mnemonic device. Impressed, wound tight and coded in some synthetic pattern, my work was drowned. Intentionality versus time. I had composed my poem according to the shifting context of my recent life, but its purpose had remained clear. To illuminate, to shed light by the flash of art, to give shape where none was apparent—that had been my persistent goal, the most honorable of my motives. My mind, my imagination, was the equipment I relied upon, and if these were to be my final hours, let them be my companions. The human brain is like a megachip, and in its RAMs upon RAMs of memory there resided the soft copy of each neural connection, the product of each closed circuit of my past thought. The diskette was the duplicate made for safety, but I was the original. I could call up anything, raise from dormancy every phrase, every insight, retravel each harmonious pathway, recite every last recorded line. It was a challenge, but it was not impossible. It was all there, waiting, and if I could discover Columbus just once more, trace his path to nowhere that now seemed so parallel to Vivian's and to mine, I could save a part of myself by making sense in this place of emptiness. I had no hope that the block would yield. If it was not my fate to sail with Columbus all the way across the sea, at least I could retrace his overture. "Diary of a Lost Man." It was all I had to do, and I said it.

> I do not know myself. No more than the thread
> woven in the field of cloth
> knows the pattern. No more than the pattern
> apprehends the mind that devised it, or the hand
> that threw the shuttle or the strength

that bent and pegged the wooden loom.
No more than the garment
knows its purpose, its maker,
do I know Columbus.
Fragments of song reach me, chants,
my son's voice raised to question. La Rábida's
lost summer light stills the blood.
I spread my packets, my arguments
and exhibitions across the table.
I cannot eat them, nor can Diego
who by the kindness of Juan Pérez
is kept and schooled.

Talavera doubts because Saint Augustine doubts.
The high court will do nothing while Granada stands.
What hope I muster lies along the margins of this page
as the night comes on, in which our prayers are isolate.
            The wick grows. My candles are bought at
the cheapest dealer, but I am expert. Snuffing, retaining,
even stealing old tallow occupies me. Thus the mind of
Talavera nags and quibbles with the flame.

In the thirtieth year after the ruin of the city,
I was in Babylon, and lay troubled upon my bed
and my thoughts came up over my heart.
So said Esdras, who was answered as I am answered
by the signs around me. Brothers,
I read cracks in the wall. Did not Our Lord
command the shoulders that raised and secured the timbers
and the hand of the mason who fit the stone, mixed these
plasters and mortars? Did not Our Lord send the rains
and blast the winds and fletch the sun's arrows
so that in its own time the wall might split
in no random design, but in the very image
of the world? Six parts dry land, one part water.
I read the map of *what is* in the wall.
Etched as though by the hand of my brother, Bartholemew.
That skilled, that firmly attentive,
the lip of the world bleeds white
at the promontory where Columbus sits,
nursing a feeble stub of light, watching his shadow
devour the map.

            Esdras, said the Lord,
I shall light a candle of understanding

in your heart, which shall not be put out
till the things be performed which you shall begin
to write.
     So I begin.
Columbus, Christoforo, son of Domenico and
of Susanna, brother to the ghost of Giovanni Pellegrino,
husband to Dona Felipa Perestrello, now ten years dead,
and cherishing one sister, Bianchetta,
who has married a stinking cheesemonger.
I, Christoforo, repudiating former ties, still seeking union
 with
my brothers, have come again in this season
with my motherless son, Diego,
to the cliffs of La Rábida. I have begun
this poor journal in the room behind the chapel
which is dedicated to Our Lady of the Madness.

As a boy with Bartholemew
I pulled and twisted raw wool
that our mother spun to thread upon her wheel.
One hand upon the mast, eye fixed, she would not have
 looked
had the earth yawned wide beneath us.
The texture of her yarn was of such evenness we bragged.
So, too, my scrawl, learned at Lisbon,
strung above the bleak ravine, this most anxious hour
preceding lauds, when the luminate brain shuns
 unconsciousness
to weave frantic argument, counterpoise, proof,
as the body drifts along the warp of sleep.
   And when you have written, the Lord directed Esdras,
some things shall you publish, and some
things shall you show secretly to the wise.
So this kept book bound against me, bound for no eyes
but of believers, those of my brother Franciscans
who have in this year 1491 saved me from despair.

October. I have sold a small map for fish,
bread, and candles. But tonight
we have no need of candles as the fire steadies its glow.
Fray Juan Pérez and Columbus plot.
The first, confessor to the Queen, the second,
the Queen's beggar, outcast, poor moth
chewing on the hem of her cloak.

"We can do no more." Pérez tips the earthware cup.
The wine of intrigue dances on his tongue.
He says, laughing, "I've attempted
Her favor through light penances. You the *via dolorosa*.
Your approaches to the Queen's companion are
    transparent,
clumsy. Painful to observe."
"Why should my poor seductions pain a Franciscan?
Your office is to forgive.
Your burden is your freedom.
Homo homini lupus. Man to man is a wolf.
Man to woman also."
"Simple foreigner. Amateur. Marquise de Moya is the
    wolf."
"Yes."
I'm an amusement. My awkward tricks replicated
for the idle and the weary,
those court hangers-on
who each month stuff themselves, their hidden pockets,
with twice the cost of my requirements.
Too many outstretched hands. War makes beggars
by the hundreds. I have other plans.
Bartholemew's at Fontainebleau, I tell Pérez.
There's madness in the French royal line. I shall appeal
to madness then, as reason's failed.

Six years. The sheep follow their shepherds,
the King, the Queen. In their wake the skilled dogs,
the watchful advisers and tax-farmers, the court
physicians and the squinting astronomers,
the wise, the narrow. Maldonado, Ferdinand
de Talavera. Outside the flock, in the woods,
just out of the keen range of dog's view
sulks the unfed wolf. Moving like a mist
through the low scrub,
Columbus follows. But enough.
I was not born to make a pretty mouth, speak
like a trained bird, however rare. I was not hatched
within a rooftop coop to wrap my feet in messages.
I did not throw off my apprenticeship to limp and cower
in the tracks of the gray-eyed Queen. Columbus did not
    hide
his cursed blood nor was he tossed a spar
to ride on off *Bechalla*

when the cries of drowning men
flew toward unanswering heaven.
He was not dragged from the spume to waste on land.
He was not baptized in the sea,
fed and clothed within his brother's house,
he was not shown the signs and wonders
in order to keep mute.
                        Men die. The soul is retrieved
to serve its maker. Waking deep in the night I gather,
as do my brothers in their office, scraps of courage.
Yet Pliny's complaints, silent-furred and sharp
of tooth, haunt my sleep. *Of what substance
is the soul? Of what material does it consist?
Whence is the seat of its thoughts? How is it
to see, or hear, or how to touch? Of what
use is it? Where, too, is its residence, and
what vast multitudes of these souls and spirits
must follow the lapse of so many ages?
Figments of childish ravings! Of mortality
so anxious to never cease to exist. Out
upon it! What utter delusion is it to suppose
that life is to recommence after death?*
                        Therefore in life, of life, in this short time
are we chosen to complete our task,
pursued by grace, driven to it, thrust
from the boat by fire and delivered to the shore by water.
In the year of my salvation in Portugal,
I was plucked in mercy from the salt.
I was shown the map of Toscanelli, the book
laid open to the heart, to Esdras, the proof
scattered here and there to gather like odd-colored wool
until the surety, the knowledge, the *gnosis*,
became the weaving of myself. Pattern.
I botch with words. Simple truth.
Fact so unbearably manifest I cannot prove it.
The shore lies here. The shore lies there.
Between the two lines I have marked my voyage—
endlessly—with twigs, quills, fingers. Shall I
go on feebly tracing with an old man's stick
until I can no longer grasp the cane?
The shore lies here. The shore lies there.
The wind's fair between.
My tongue clacks in the emptiness and I am bound for
  France

or was, until the news. Granada fallen.
Pérez caught the wind like a fox and fled
to his desk for instruments, from there to the dark
confessional's secrets, or perhaps to some other persuasion.
He wrote all evening. Sebastian Rodríguez went out at
  dawn
bound for Seville, where the court of locusts settled.

My son and I climb to the roof
after the day's heat lessens, and we sit.
No word passes between us as the sun descends,
spreading its cloak upon the water, fading
into dusk like a dye set unevenly into the fabric
of the sere waves. Darkness
overcomes us and we are more at peace
than in the house. God is tangible
again within the stars and I am home
in the predictable heavens. "I'll show you
navigators' tricks," I tell Diego.
"Heaven is a clock. Time is a man
whose soul is the unmoving star.
Draw lines through the figure
and count the hours as he points."
And so we sit watching the guards,
Kochab and Pherhad, until Diego leans against me,
his breath warm and ragged on my sleeve.
He has a brother, a half brother. I've not told him.
Beatrice shadows my thought
even though I have offered marriage.
None can say you have abandoned me now, her answer came.
All is as you would have wished.
Take this money. Leave.
I have my son and you have the Marquise,
whose favor will advance your cause.
This from her lying-in, a note written only days
after the birth of the child, when a woman
is still dangerous to men.
Her look dims mirrors and blunts
the keenest swords. In her presence
bees die in swarms, iron rusts, dogs
turn mad and gnaw their paws and tails.
Columbus was a dog. I chewed my own hands
and begged Constanze and Diego de Harana
to make a strong appeal to Beatrice.

Set me as a seal upon your heart
as a seal upon your arm
for love is strong as death
jealousy is cruel as the grave.
But I received no absolution in her arms
and then the Marquise moved on to Granada,
with her husband, de Cabrera,
who smiles and recommends my request to the Queen,
as he believes that I will not return.

So I sit, my son's form eased onto my lap,
until the guard stars move head to foot
and it is morning. I have slept
but known the whole time
that I was sleeping. That is the rest of a true sailor.
Three varieties of men—the dead, the living,
and those who sail the ocean—
populate the earth.
I know that my son Diego
is of the last sort
for he wakes and looks upon the calm expanse
with troubled eagerness, and then, as the wind and the sun
rise together, as the waves swell and throw themselves
    forward,
as they rise and smash the rocks, Diego shouts,
hunger moving in his slim frame.
So it is.
                          Longing shakes Columbus also.
Desires fade. Flesh cools. Even the mind
loosens in our captor, time. Land
sifts through the fingers,
stone is ground to dust, dispersed.
Even mountains are conquered, their slopes plowed and
    sown.
Only the sea resists, filling in its own
constant furrows, swallowing cities and towers,
grinding the bones of ships and men
as one to sand.

Pérez received the summons and sets out. He will
    champion
Columbus. I would join him but no invitation
has been proffered and Fray Juan Pérez smiles.
"I've honed my tongue in argument while you
have kissed of life too deep. Take no offense,

my dear friend, but yours is a blunt instrument,
good only for knocking sheep. Mine is a razor
sweet enough to cut the lilting song from a bird's throat,
and leave the bird in flight."
I do not laugh at the image, but drink more wine,
picturing the bird in air warbling
its excised tune,
puzzled by the lack of sound.
It is Pinzón who pounces on these words,
repeating the subtle boast.
His brothers roar, as they are meant to do. Martín Alonzo.
He has wealth. He is bold.
He knows the sea and Toscanelli.
But I recognize in him ambition the twin to mine.
Ambition only. None of the passion
that humbles, that drives a man as I am
driven to this far extension.
If I were Pinzón, if I were not Columbus,
I, too, would wear red.
I recognize the cast on his wool cloak,
the double weave, what increase
that variation cost when woven in the hem.
The stuff of his overgarment, so fine it shimmers.
No. I would rather walk naked into court
and remain Columbus, he who knows, chosen to bear the
    word,
ordained to walk the sunken ground until the Moor
prays. I would rather be Columbus, mocked,
than Pinzón, smiling, as he tilts
the bottle overhead, tears apart the loaf.

Dark night. Strange news that sets me about myself.
Rumor that comes from the Queen's table.
Once Boabdil surrenders, Spain will purge
of the Hebraic fallacy.
Thoughts whirl, the God to whom Esdras appeals
shifts and buries his face in heavy garments.
If you did so deeply hate your own people, yet
should you punish them with your own hands?
I breathe the darkness into myself and out again,
the dark that is laden with images and questions.
I enter the small compartment where my mother's father
dons his shawl, language like sticks in his mouth.
I know none of it. I don't recall.

A bite of honeycake. Taste of bitter herb.
Nothing in man is of so frail a nature as
the memory. I drift through these difficult nights,
lateen-rigged in the uneasy ocean.
Often the memory appears to attempt
to make its escape from us, even while the body
is at rest and in perfect health.
When sleep comes over us, it is cut off
altogether, so much so, that the mind
in its vacancy is at a loss
to know our place.
                In this cell, thin-strawed pallet,
or tossed along the cold beach of Thule,
brought up in Guinea, the torrid zone,
or perhaps again the house at Porto Santo, waiting,
until my wife's breath ceases to cloud the glass.

March of the year. In haste, I write from the Alcazar
where I have come in the fine new clothes
the Queen directed me to buy. What words
shall I choose from those I've gathered?
What looks? What patiences? What weary
proofs, and what evidence? Tomorrow,
in her presence.

He who digs a pit will fall into it.
He who quarries stones is crushed by them.
He who builds a tower of proofs
is annihilated when they fall.
So I am fearful, unlike myself, frantic with hope.
I am stirred through with desperate impatience
and must hold my tongue. *For in a multitude of dreams*
there is futility, and ruin in a flood of words.
So I will keep them dammed and loose them singly,
calculated for effect. Her face will register
the depth of water, how swift a current will sweep
objections past and leave her standing firm
with me, with me as the doubters chafe and quarrel,
with me as I lay not *their* demands
but *mine* before the court.
Admiral of the Ocean Sea, my title. Viceroy
and Governor General of lands I claim and no less
than a tithe of all bought or sold or found thereon.
All titles, all powers, inherit. I have sons, two,
and claims of the heart I've laid upon myself.

I have claims of friendship, and of fond duress,
brothers of the blood and brothers of the spirit
who have not for one day ceased to lend me sustenance.
I have left a trail these past six years of creditors,
debts of gold, debts of passion.
There is Beatrice
who gave her dowry fortune
to my eager hand for food and rooms,
when I was wretched in Córdoba.
There is Fray Juan Pérez who stumps my case now.
If I am to sell a life, the price will not be cheap.
For six years I've spun boredom like a hoop
to mesmerize myself.
For six years I've offered a cheek
to those who mocked. *A fool
folds his hands and eats his own flesh.*
I've had no comfort. For six years I've scraped my chin
   smooth
every morning, first the red hairs
then the half-red and now the gray
stubble of a man who's aged with one idea
caught in his brain.

These long years advance me, legless tedium
has its purposes. Over time I shaped my words
to fit the sovereign will.
Greed is simple. Religion, not.
But the second can be made to serve the first.
"To free Jerusalem, to one day
return the Temple to the hands of true Christians,
to bring home the honor of that deed,
an act which in history Spain will possess,
Castile and Isabella,
Aragon and Ferdinand, to thereby shine forever
as the greatest of rulers
requires . . . gold."
The Queen, so well regarded in the streets,
with the pure complexion
of a woman who has fasted for her sins,
with her gapped smile, the teeth
an apothecary's nightmare, with her lovely neck.
The Queen, her lips, a blushing pink,
open and she speaks.
Her eyes, the pale gaze of a Jew-hater,

rest on me, grave as bones, blue as my sister's,
sweetly gathering refusals.
"Well said, well done, your case, though . . . is difficult."
I have been advised not to press
my expectation, not to speak
strong words or force my luck.
So for a time I compose myself
with desperate meekness,
while the bargains flash lip to lip,
candles extinguished with each breath.
My titles and percentages
All that should be mine! My voice escapes.
All that should be mine!
And the Queen turns, her eyes the gray sea withheld.

I soar in rage. They call it flight
when the soul storms out of self, when the spirit
is uncontained. I puff with wind
until my fury twice fills the room
and they are small things
waving their hands and twisting their mouths
and bending as saplings
double over before the hurricane. Fray Pérez,
appalled with me, jabs a finger in the air.
"What is the worth of my friendship and faith:
an Admiralship? She scorns us,
scorns you.
Greed has overcome your purpose."
I am tossed to farther shores
and cannot reckon.
If they'll not have me at my price then France,
then King Henry, then anyone.
But Fray Pérez had rushed to repair the damage,
his face a lathed mask.
It was Santángel, the court treasurer,
who stopped me in the hall.

In this country, it is said that in three cases
water has flowed in vain: the water of the river to the sea,
the water in wine, and the water at a Jew's baptism.
Santángel is saved, but still of the damned?
It is impossible to know as his hands
shape the cross.
"Brother in Christ," he dares say to me.
                    I could be a man proud and boasting

of the dagger and the olive branch,
emblem of the informer
who watches rooftops for the smokeless
chimneys of the Sabbath. But I'm Columbus, who has eaten
his secret. My heart stills.
The keeper of the sovereign purse
has greeted me as an Inquisitor gently addresses his charge
whom he has just disjointed like a chicken.
"Brother in Christ, stay," Santángel urges.
"You are closer than you think.
You're a sailor, can't you smell it?
The odor of wind that has passed over land,
the smell of earth and leaves."
You're a Jew, cursed by edict
to handle gold,
can't you feel the fever of it, can't you feel the flame?
"What do you mean?" The Grand Inquisitor
confesses Isabella and no one
states the truth by word or sign.
Our gazes level. Our breath moves together.
There is no trust.
There is none needed.
Santángel offers from his own fund a million,
and urges me again to stay. "I will describe
before the King and Queen a wealth beyond imagining.
All yours to find."
                    Yet, I leave the castle of Santa Fe,
perhaps in pride,
perhaps because Santángel's look,
sharp with the unbearable intelligence,
reminded me of what I had seen in holy Seville,
one day in spring
when the green wood smoked
and would not burn the woman
so that the crowd, in its impatience,
took up stones.

Atlas and map of the Christian faith. Defender.
Tonight in this crooked inn my own fears bloom.
It happens that in the eyes of the converted
my image, upended, breaks and whirls
or advances in the white robe of the purified
in the white paper hat, bearing toward the square
the lit taper I will use to ignite my own death pile.

If a man does not abide in Me
he is cast forth as a branch, and withers.
The branches are gathered, thrown into the fire
and burned.
So said Saint John. So quote the Inquisitors.
Oh my beloved
how shall I name you?
As I stood outside the gates of the convent school
at the window, *kissing iron.* As the ornate grille
shook in the pound of hooves. As the rough light
  sharpened.
"There was a man," you said, "a young man
in love, in secret.
In secret he crept into the house
of the girl his heart was made to match.
In secret he watched as the Seder meal was laid.
He understood. His dove was crow.
She was spawned by a family twice damned:
maranos, *swine,* washed but not reborn.
He went back, as he should, as anyone would,
as I would do. He denounced them to the Tribunal."
She was silent. I traced the smooth curve
of metal with my hand and found hers.
"Felipa de Moniz," I said. "I am not that man.
I am a Christian, but I will not betray you."
Her fingers were cold as the iron bar.
Her voice was hard.
"You are neither one nor are you the other.
Therefore, so says my mother, I may love you."

Stain will not bleach from linen
nor blood from wool,
though the sun of a thousand and a thousand days
beats down and scorches the rocks.
There are monks who practice
ritual, circumcised monks.
There are Jewish informers,
there are Jews brought to bay
for showing too ardent
an outward Catholicism.
Friends, dear brothers who would devour me,
how should I tread?

            "The question." Juan Pérez' voice lowers—
he will say anything to me. "The question is this:

Do we live in a world redeemed?
What do you think?"
In another man's presence, he could die for the
    uncertainty.
And I for the answer, though it is from Ecclesiastes'
    mouth:
"The race is not to the swift, nor the battle to the strong,
nor bread to the wise, nor riches to the intelligent,
but time and chance happen to them all.
Good friend, is this a world redeemed for justice?"
Fray Juan's laughter shakes the bench.
"Casuistry. Cleverness.
When will you take the vow?"
He means that I should become a member
of the Third Order, lay order, bound so closely
with the First Order of Franciscans
that there is little difference
except for one large difference.
"When sons are born to celibate fathers
then I will wear the robe of a Franciscan."
"Sweet Innocent!" Fray Juan's voice is gentle.
"Whole monasteries
now consist of the bastard sons of begging monks."
"That is rich begging, Father."
Again, Fray Juan laughs.

On the rough road to Córdoba, the Pinos bridge,
as I am tracing the route in mind,
the route to France and Bartholemew,
a shudder takes my body and I turn to the rider
knowing already.

> The tide has turned.
> The wave runs and swells powerfully
> beneath me.
> I am walking on the sea.

Night in Palos. Cool night
of sauntering breezes
in which my three daughters
lie flank to flank in the river's lock.
Pinta, sleek and quick as the joke of her name,
a jest on Quintero, her owner, the stumbling lout who
    fears
no one but his wife of the Pinto House,

will be Martín Alonzo's to command.
She lies calm in the river Tinto
aside my square-rigged ship, *La Gallega*,
which I have named for the Mother of Our Lord
that she should spread her blue cloak
upon the waters, that her gaze
should level the clouds.
She is round-built and stout enough to carry
two hundred pipes, enough wine to have kept my father
singing for a month of nights.
Niña's smaller but she's nimble
and balanced like a star.

Day of halcyon, the sea
gray and dull as the flat of a sword.
No breeze stirs, no wind. Into this calm
comes dawn, the sun a hammer
beating the sea's blade thinner.
Earth a forge on which the waves spread their metals
to a reflecting glass, a tide of images
on which we quit the harbor.
Cries of women, weeping in the stillness
as boats of Jews are expelled
down the Río Saltés.
They float in their tubs, already the children bailing
for their lives. That boy
could be Diego, or that one.
I turn and lead the chants
as the men brace rigging.
Groan of oars. Here, now,
begins the account of this voyage
which I shall keep alongside
the one I shall direct to the eyes of these men—
loyal not to Columbus, but to Pinzón—
or shall until the turrets of the moon,
wealth of silver, mines of gold, more increase
fills their hands than they could dream.
Down the Tinto, passing beneath the fortress walls
of La Rábida, at the hour of prime.
I force my men to kneel with me,
to beg the Virgin Mother's mercy,
she who smiles on the mad,
who strokes the brows of fools,
whose hand trembles on the shoulder

of the impetuous man, restraining him,
slowing as he passes between the sand slopes
and twisting black pines
along the canal of the Holy Father,
Her sign: Look, the seabirds
choose the day of the glass wind
to weave their floating nests.
Strands of maidenhair, drowned filaments
and leaves pliable as eels.
Watching them, I praise Him who showed
them the art. Who set
the perfect loom of habit
within them. Who defined them.
It is in these details that the Maker's genius
is shown. I rise to greet Him
and a favorable wind unfurls the sails.
Before us, Pliny's Fortunate Islands, the Hesperides,
across the gulf of mares,
south and by west.

In Pliny's time, the stinking bodies
of monsters were tossed in the wrack,
and fouled the beaches.
Lizards as large as caravels infested Capraria,
and two-headed dogs were rampant.
Also birds, fruits of every kind, date palms,
honey and papyrus.
Our need is for dried meat, an ironmonger,
fresh water and a final load of sea provisions.
Also, I have heard Dona Beatriz de Peraza,
the young widow governing Gomera and Ferro,
Fuerteventura and Lanzarote
has very beautiful white shoulders.

San Sebastion. Day twenty.
Time slips from us as the wind turns rough.
Yet we've made good the repairs on the *Pinta*,
rudderless and floundering.
Two graceful gentlemen who wait on Beatriz
report that they have seen
land, land blue in the west, shimmering at dusk.
Their tongues are light and their hands
soft and pink as those of girls, it is strange
to encounter such fine musicians
so far from court.

She arrives, and the shoulders were true.
No one mentioned her arms, her throat,
arch and curve
gleaming in the stuff of her dress,
like pearly shells
pulled from stones
in the ocean's floor.
No one mentioned her satin face, her skin
the flesh of winter pears, nacre, black foam of her dress
filtering the light of waxen tapers.
It is well the vow to Fray Juan remained unspoken.
Pay what you vow. It is better that you not vow
than you should vow and not pay.
I am a free man, unquestionably welcome, or so I gather
from the bounteous ease with which my ships are
   resupplied.
We lack for nothing. I burn all night.
You are stately as a palm tree
and your breasts are like its clusters.
I say I will climb the palm tree
and lay hold of its branches.

Morning. I have addressed my lords,
and repented of my sins. I have leveled
the ground between Beatriz and Columbus
but neither of us has set foot upon the smooth terrain.
Portuguese spy ships are said to hug Hierro's coast
and in avoiding them we now
begin this voyage.

20

VIVIAN

Roger had left a note neatly folded and taped onto the door of the beach house. *I have Violet, if anyone cares! We have gone to meet Cobb and will be back for dinner. Please refill the ice cube tray and remove the milk and turkey from the freezer/refrigerator. Yours, etc.*

"What does this mean?" Soaking wet and half in shock, I waved the paper at Nash. 'If anyone cares?' What's he talking about?"

I couldn't get my brain to work properly, to tell me when the note had been written. Before? Yes, it must have been written before Roger took Violet out to meet Cobb. He must have used the raft. Cobb had taken Roger's oar, to slow him down. But by now, Roger and Violet should have made it to shore. The two should have coasted in on the high tide. They should have been here, waiting, Roger aghast and outraged, Violet hungry, Violet safe.

They had to be here. I strode through the little room, wrenched open the closet, stared at the stacked towels in the quiet interior. Nash shuffled uneasily in the doorway, and combed his hands through his hair, pulling it back tightly.

"It's my fault. I was at the big house—you know, looking for the thing. When I got back here, I saw Roger take her out in the boat. So I went down the beach, ran into a couple kids working with their parents in the place next door, bleaching off the steps with Clorox. I hung out with them for a while."

Suddenly weak, I knelt down in the middle of the floor. Nash couldn't stop explaining, so I held up my hand. A roar built inside my head, in my ears.

And then the circuits fused and I was crying into my palms. But I stopped myself. There was really nothing to worry about with Roger. Even if swamped by waves, he was a strong swimmer and could easily carry Violet in one bent arm. Not that the boat would have capsized. Of course not. It was a fat, heavy, stable raft. A life boat, built to endure much bigger waves. I was worried over nothing.

I lifted my hands away from my face. At this very moment, Roger and Violet were most likely sitting up at Cobb's house, waiting with the police for the man to return. I didn't know how I felt about what I'd done to Cobb, and I wasn't going to think about it. Roger might be standing outside on the porch. Perhaps he had just noticed Cobb's boat, rocking and tumbling with each breaker that hit the reef—for I'd cut the motor and let the thing drift in as close as I could, then swum to shore, an eighth of a mile maybe, not far.

And if Roger wasn't at the house . . . He would perhaps have been troubled by the wreck. Being a responsible person, he perhaps had gone to the club to phone the authorities about it. The car would be gone. He would of course have taken Violet. I hoped he'd strapped her in her car seat. He would be worried. *He* would be looking for *me*.

I pushed my hands across my eyes, wiped off the tears, got some dry clothes from the closet, dressed in the bathroom.

"Let's go to the big house and see if Roger's there with Violet," I called to Nash.

His voice was quick and earnest in agreement.

As we broke into the dusk I looked first at the sea, but the waves washed in, pale gray and steady, and there was no human in eyeshot. Rushing up the path to Cobb's villa, the whole story of what had happened pulsed through me. I yearned, with a need almost physical, to tell it to Roger. Words pushed behind my lips, formed on my tongue.

But the house was entirely quiet, the deep, tall windows reflecting the sunset, the shadows already springing from beneath the trees. Moths wafted silently along with us, stirred by the wind of our passing.

The rented car was in the driveway.

I fought for control. "We have to form a search party."

"There was a phone at that place I was helping out," Nash said, and I now followed him down a narrow, dark lane. My arms ached, stretched and sore at the shoulders. There was no breeze within the dense brush of the interior. Nothing moved. Then we heard the sound of voices.

"Yes, she did. That's right. Just like Moses."

A Bahamian woman with a spray bottle full of yellow liquid worked on the moldings, talking to a man perched on a ladder next to her. At our approach the man came down. He was portly, smiling.

I walked past him, directly into the house. Outside, I could hear Nash telling our story. The huge living room was dim and the last light fell through the rectangular windows that faced the sea. I located a phone on the kitchen counter, and a list of important numbers was attached to a humming refrigerator. "Police" was third down. I dialed. The phone rang, and rang. I hung up and dialed again.

"You can call"—the man stood in the doorway, his face concerned—"but the police won't be there. They're both gone to keep order at the Junkanoo carnival."

The woman shook out her cloth and came to stand beside me. "You're looking for a man and a baby?" she asked. "Well, I told your boy here they *got* a baby. Just found a baby over in the sound." She paused, then went on. "Little baby girl. Little tow-haired girl."

I looked at Nash, but couldn't form the words. He didn't make me wait.

"She's okay." He made it a flat statement, but then his voice shook with its own question. "And the man?"

The woman glanced from one to the other of us. "Was no man." She saw my face, tried to soften the blow. "Well, I guess the baby's hale, anyway. I hear she's crying up a storm over to the settlement. I hear there's no one who can rule her, even Eunice Clock, and she knows babies."

I closed my eyes. Nash asked where this Eunice lived.

"She and her girl are right in Savannah Sound. Anyone can direct you. But they won't be home. Tonight is the blessing of the children, so the church is where you'll find them. That Clock girl who found the baby, they say she's the Pharaoh's daughter. Listening to the Scriptures might calm that baby girl down."

Out of reflex, the woman squeezed the spray bottle when I grabbed her and held her arms.

"You said the church. Where?"

"In the sound as well."

I let her go, then turned and ran down the path back to Cobb's house. Nash followed. I heard the woman's eager voice, the man's baritone seconding her.

"She your baby, then? She the one you're looking for? She'll be all right, don't worry, lady. Eunice Clock knows babies."

The keys were in the rental car, and we pulled out. As I drove the six miles to the town I told Nash to go to the hotel, get Hilda and Racine, and then track down the police. I'd find Violet, and the woman who had discovered her. Wait until I get hold of Roger, I kept thinking. How could he have let this happen to her?

But there was no Roger to tell me.

St. Margaret's Church was a small stucco building set amidst the lush foliage and small wooden houses of the settlement—a poor place, but carefully kept. The whitewash outside was fresh, and inside, the walls were unmarred, new and still smelling faintly of lime. The Stations of the Cross looked as though they had been painted by number.

Nine people, the entire assemblage, looked at me expectantly as I walked through the door and stopped. I searched their faces for news, but they were only curious. A thin woman in a white turban frowned over the piano behind the pulpit.

"Eunice Clock?"

"Eunice," the priest explained after a moment, in the kind of voice that's used to calm a wild dog, "has chosen to worship elsewhere."

"Show me. She has my baby."

My words were electric. Everyone in the church began to talk. The woman left the piano and came down the aisle. She grabbed my hand. The talk of Violet clearly had circulated, and I suddenly was a valuable exhibit, a new and dramatic piece of the story, the unfit mother who had left her child to danger.

"It wasn't my fault," I told them. My voice was a torn cloth. "Please."

"I'll guide you. Eunice is my cousin." The piano woman took command, led me out the door and up a road that snaked randomly around the little dwellings of the village. Her high heels buckled beneath her stride. As I followed I listened for Violet, prepared to dash at the first hint of a baby's cry, but a deep, Christmas stillness flowed over everything. Normal people were safe in their homes or gathered in a church. A few bantam chickens flapped out of our way, then clustered to scratch companionably together. A scrawny cat lurked hopefully in our wake. We passed a ruin overgrown with vines, caving in to vegetation. A store made of cement blocks, the door secured with a thick padlock, sat solid under a single porch light. Red tinsel hung off a lintel here, a green paper bell was pasted in a window there. Some houses had no windows, just shutters, the glow of candles flickering between the slats. As we entered farther and farther into the village, down trails scraped from coral, then along tracks that could barely be discerned, the buildings leaned into each other, less steady, the bare boards surrounded by pulverized rock.

Before the thick brush began, there was a final, feebly sputtering electric yard lamp. A hand-lettered sign was nailed to its wooden post: HOME OF THE LIVING GOD. We turned into the walk, picked our way over ruts and potholes to a bluff above the sea, and there was a chapel—no more than a rude shed—leaking light and music. The service was just over, and people had begun to straggle out, some still singing.

I quickened my pace. I flew. The voices rose to hit a high note, then fell, but one voice stayed up, soared in a grating soprano yodel. I passed my guide. I could have leapt through walls.

*　　　*　　　*

Nash had succeeded in summoning help. When I returned to the beach house, there was a policeman down by the water with a flashlight, a small jeep, and a bullhorn. I held Violet close, listened as the jeep drove a few yards, stopped. The driver raised his megaphone and addressed the black ocean.

"Roger Williams?" he asked. "Are you there?"

He waited a moment as the sea hissed and drew, then drove a few yards, braked, repeated his call. A mile away, off the place where they said the girl had found Violet, a boat with a searchlight made slow progress. It would cross and recross the area all night.

I spent an hour with the investigator, explained all that I could explain. The whole story unraveled in such a complex and surreal tangle that at long last he dropped his chin to his chest and held up both hands, palms turned out. Later, I sat on the beach, Violet wrapped in a blanket in my arms. The night swirled around us, alive with stars and breezes. With my gaze I drew a line to true north.

I had turned on every lamp in the beach house, left the place blazing, a beacon teeming with insects. If Roger was out there, swept past sight of land but still swimming, he might see the flicker of light and pull for it.

The policeman came back, exhausted. A call had come in from Governor's Harbour, a car accident, and he had to go. He had seen a lot of people drown, he said, but none had ever been found at night.

Hilda and Racine found the drowned man at dawn, except he wasn't drowned, and he wasn't Roger Williams. Henry Cobb had washed onto the beach directly in their path as they patrolled with Nash. In a way I felt relieved that I hadn't killed Cobb, but at the same time I would have traded his life for Roger's. He had almost strangled himself on the plastic bag he stole from me, and the policeman—my story still fresh in his ears—was not gentle when he placed Cobb under arrest for attempted murder. The only question was where he would first stand trial: in Nassau, or in Manhattan federal court.

As the morning dragged toward noon I curled around Violet on the bed. I even dozed for an hour or two. Nash came up from the beach and stretched out near us on the couch. When I woke it was to the sound of his murmuring in sleep. Warm air. The simple sunlight. Then the memory lurched over me with all its weight and I gasped for breath.

It takes forever to absorb loss. It takes no time at all. On the second night that Roger was missing, I left on the lights again, positive that since Cobb had been found, no fate could be so unfair as to save the aggressor and doom his victim. I prowled fitfully in the guesthouse of the murderer, then took Violet with me into bed and dreamed that her father slogged along the ocean floor and brought us home a grotesque array of coral. Bones of the sea filled his hands, white and harrowing. Brain coral. Arms of lime. Sea fans like maps of veins. I woke. I slept again. I dreamed whole years in minutes. An ordinary life together passed. A marriage. Time dissolved, day came, and the world was bare.

He had come here because of me.

The third night, rain falling, I insisted on burning the lights once more. Hilda and Racine tried to argue with me, tried to make me grieve, but gave up. The lamps would blaze. Tonight at least, Roger would not be alone.

When I slept this time—it got no easier—my dreams were of walking, driving, moving. No matter how I traveled, Roger blocked my passage, waited around every corner. He stood insistently beside the road signs that the headlights of my car illuminated. If I ran, he loped along with me. He was the bend in the trail, the ground under my feet. He was the path itself, and I knew one thing when I woke: I wouldn't leave him here.

On the dawn of the third day, the search boat was deployed elsewhere and ceased its rounds before my windows. The police videotaped statements from all concerned and Roger was declared officially lost.

After that, Hilda and Racine treated me with shocked care, but I did not feel stricken. I took "lost" to mean something other than the worst. It implied the ability to be found, and that gave me irrational hope. I grew impatient with Hilda's tact and Racine's solicitude. I found it maddening when they hovered.

I had bought a pack of cigarettes—just to have them. I lit the first one in nervousness, but could not quite put it to my lips. Racine regarded me with worry all the same, so I blew out the match and put the book in my pocket.

"It's not like I'm still pregnant," I snapped.

The thing was, their concern tried to close a lid. I refused to be a woman in grief. I was a woman searching, in all the suspense that implied. I sought. I didn't conclude anything.

After breakfast, I turned to Hilda.

"Will you look after Violet? I need to be alone." She started to protest, but stopped herself. She took it as a good sign that I could let the baby out of my sight, and nodded sympathetically. I stifled the urge to slam the door.

A boat slowly putted past the reef, heading south. It was not looking for Roger, but the sight of it gave me comfort all the same.

As I walked along the shore, I talked to Roger as if he were in step next to me. I promised constant attention, no criticism, the bed made in the morning. I promised to listen to Bach. I promised three-minute eggs boiled by a timer, and not to lose my temper. I promised hash brown potatoes on Sunday, and that I would raise Violet to appreciate National Public Radio. Nash would love Roger too—I'd make sure—and I would bend Grandma to my will. Alternately, I promised never to bother Roger again and to stay with him forever.

But the blame. The blame wouldn't loosen its grip.

I examined my conscience, tabulated my crimes: pride, deceit, pride again. In my consuming rush to change, to seize control of my future, I had taken too much for granted, assumed that time was infinite, that every rash, expeditious act could be someday undone.

"Don't ask for what you want because you might get it." An adage Grandma never tired of repeating.

I had the Diary—or at least it would not now be lost. Housed in some museum, poured over, analyzed, dissected and debated, it would cause a flurry. Its secrets would be revealed and, eventually, if they were important enough, they would be absorbed into that body of common knowledge that people accept as naturally true. History would change by becoming more accurate. I had saved the past.

And lost a future.

Columbus wasn't worth Roger Williams. Standing on this shore I wasn't an Indian, wasn't a scholar, wasn't even a mother. I was pure lonely. My mother. Purvis. Now Roger. What was it about me? The waves beckoned, and I thought about it. I considered it. I turned the idea over in my mind. Death was a mystery whose solution I could discover just by walking forward, just by giving in, letting it overtake me. I waited, opened every sense.

Nothing happened. The blue waves lapped at my ankles. The beach stretched on for miles. The sand was the color of old glass.

Over sand like old glass.

Old glass. The refrain of the shells' messages penetrated. I remembered them so clearly I could not drive them out. I had come this far, but there was more I could do. The sun blazed gently above and I looked at my watch. It was noon, *when the sun is the crown of heaven.* Ahead of me, the retreating waves left a glossy plain striped with shimmering bands that reflected the sky and fleecy clouds.

Weave a ribbon through a sea of clouds. I stopped.

I was the shuttle. The mirror in the watery sand was exactly the image of a sea of clouds. I looked to my right and saw how the point of land at the end of this beach jutted into the sea, flat and slim, tapered at the end. I turned, moved toward it. The clues arranged themselves in my mind and my heart beat faster in anticipation. Maybe this was all my delusion, maybe my brain was thinking fast to save its life—but I couldn't stop before I found out for sure.

The wind picked up and clouds scudded overhead. Staring at the spit of coral overgrown with low hummocks of plants, the scrub of water-strewn seeds, I saw a plume of smoke. The thin, dark line of ascension flickered, dispersed, meshed again, whipped in the breeze, and disappeared.

I was drawn toward it, fascinated, squinting, trying to fit what I saw into some reasonable explanation. A fisherman's fire. A religious sacrifice of some kind. A hot springs. A tiny volcano. But nothing worked, nothing translated the sight into an ordinary event. It was discordant, out of place, wrong—the opposite of common sense—and so I raced for it, my running feet stumbling but never tripping on the rocks and residue left by high tide, my hands fists held close to my chest.

The next time the gray cloud rose, I was close enough to tell that it was not smoke, but a dark stream alive with tiny erratic shapes that moved so quickly they were sucked into nothingness before I could identify them. Were they a flock of birds? Were they locusts?

I faltered, my steps slowed. I felt my resolve, my interest, weaken and fall behind me. The continual presence of Roger in my dreams could foster any hallucination to keep me from coming to terms with the truth: that there was nothing to find, that nothing would make a difference, that I should go home.

But not yet. At the outcrop's base I began to climb. I didn't move quickly or with hope, just with curiosity. A hypothesis, an encyclopedic notation, had formed somewhere in my thoughts, an incongruity that fit: the smoke had actually been a cloud of bats. Bats, but during daylight. An odd fact. Didn't bats feed only at night?

The stones were sharp. I skirted jagged furniture and cracked lime littered with shards of seashells, the pits of shallow holes, coral chimneys. The air was still now, my scramblings the only sounds. Perhaps if I sat quietly I would again witness the sight of bats emerging in midday. There must be, somewhere below, a cave or tunnel that they inhabited.

I kicked over bits of glass, twigs, sea refuse. The highest tides, hurricane gales most likely, had thrown a few buoys and other large objects in among the snags of rock. I upended a broken red milk crate, sat on it, played with the tag end of a huge dry fishing net, tough and new, that had blown in filled with a catch that had been picked clean by crabs and gulls. I tugged at a star-shaped bone. It disengaged from the twined plastic and rested in my hand, bare as a wish. I closed my eyes, waited.

The hollow spear of breathing rock. I was sitting on top of an underground cave, with an entrance from which bats emerged. I had no doubt that I was near the end of the search. Somewhere below me, the object of Cobb's desire, the focus of generations of Cobbs, intensified in its importance in every cycle, "the greatest treasure of Europe," was probably buried. The question was, did I feel like digging it up?

"What do you think it is, really?" I had asked Cobb only two days ago as I sat across a wooden table from him at the jail in Governor's Harbour. He was dressed in blue scrubs, like some hospital orderly. He was clean-shaven, his ribs taped, but otherwise physically none the worse for his ordeal in the sea—though he lacked his familiar energy, that humming drive that had seemed to light him from within. He wore no shackles on his feet, yet there were fetters, visible to all who knew him before defeat. Now, briefly, his eyes lit.

"You have to put yourself into their minds," he said. "What was treasure then, greatest treasure, might be nothing now. A philosopher's stone. But of course, the Diary itself would still be of considerable worth to a scholar."

"You're rationalizing. You didn't sabotage Roger, try to kill me, for some . . . junk."

"May I remind you," Cobb said—but the heart was out of him again—"that I did nothing directly to your Roger. I didn't touch the man. If he had stayed on the raft with your daughter he'd be alive. I merely relieved him of his oar. And as for you . . . yes, we had an unfortunate incident. I lost my temper, for which I've apologized."

"You tried to drown me."

"And you, me. Rather more successfully, I might add. It might be said that we canceled each other out. And if Roger's body isn't found . . . He was, after all, less than stable—he abandoned his own daughter. Who knows why he jumped?

"If you would concede to my interpretation concerning certain unpremeditated aspects of our misunderstanding, I would be most grateful. It seems clear that I will be a guest of the federal government for some time to come. Perhaps it could be arranged for you to take charge of the Diary. Papers to that effect could be drawn up."

Cobb sighed, turned away. The story he had worked out in a phone call to his lawyer was unconvincing and he needed my corroboration. I neither agreed nor disagreed. I had come in hopes that he would reveal some additional detail that would lead me to Roger. But Cobb had been advised of his rights—anything he said could be used against him—and I was not about to admit that Roger was lost. Not then. Not now.

Perched on this razor-edged rock, alone with my thoughts, enveloped in the sounds and sensations of the natural world— wind, salt, sun—I pictured myself the center of a compass. To the east, Ireland and Spain. Equidistant to the west, the reservations in New Mexico and Idaho. Water to the north and south. Columbus's gift lay at the crux, the fulcrum of balance. There were five hundred years of questions, too many for any single answer, too much sadness and loss for any repayment. If I looked directly into the ocean, grave and blurred, I could see as much and as little as any Lucayan might have seen from this same vantage a thousand years ago. Timeless, beyond language, it was immutable in its constant flux. But if I glanced to the right or left, it would all be changed, particularized: a clubhouse, a road, houses feathered with television antennae.

"What do you think it is?" My question to Cobb, asked a second time, echoed in my mind as I squinted, dazzled by the lights reflected from the choppy water. If I could rekindle his greed, he might be motivated to help me in my search.

He hadn't answered right away, and when he did, his voice was low.

"I thought it was my salvation," he had said. "The thing that would pull me out. Now it doesn't matter."

And he was right. It didn't. The secret sadness, the secret of the secret: when it could be unlocked, it didn't matter anymore. It had been hidden too long. The past its presentation was supposed to precede and influence had unfolded without it, crushing, making impossible every future but this one, and now the lure of this . . . thing had, as its final contribution, deprived me of Roger Williams. It was a gift of poison, a treasure fit to be dug only so that it could be put away. Like so much Columbus had carried, it was a curse.

I sensed rather than heard a motion in the air, saw the smoke regather, form a plume, and, like a film run in reverse, disappear back into an open hole not thirty feet away. The army of tiny bats twirled and spiraled and then were gone, leaving no trail.

But now I knew where it was.

I didn't move for more than an hour, weighing the benefit of forgetting versus the closure of discovery. It was not that I feared to spend my life plagued by a sense of not knowing: I knew enough. If I were to find this "greatest treasure" and it indeed had value, what could I do with it? Would I use it, together with the Diary—the Diary that Cobb was now willing to trade, one truth for a lie—for justice, for good? That had been my naive intent, the justifying story I had told to Grandma and to myself—but would I have the strength? Without Roger, would I have the will?

And yet, it came to me that I was the appropriate agent, armed with research, purified by grief, stripped of hope. I had become as uninterested in Europe's gift as any twentieth-century person was likely to be—as dispassionate as Guacanagari himself, so secure in the belief that he knew all that was important to know. A king accepts tribute and remains aloof. He has no need of a foreign crown. I was like him, but also his opposite. Like Columbus, seeking anything except what he found, I had no need of crowns because I had no country.

By the time I saw Nash walking down the beach, following the tracks I'd left, I had decided what to do. Now I wouldn't have to attempt it alone.

Nash's gaze was averted in order that he not be caught staring at me. His concern for my welfare—something that would have seemed claustrophobic an hour ago—had become a kindness: empathy was an unfamiliar offering from Nash, and I didn't take it lightly. He wended through the wrack and flotsam, elaborately intent on his footing, deliberately mindful to check his handholds. To save him the pretense of discovering me, I called his name when he was finally near enough to hear. He peered into the sun, directly up at me.

What a coincidence, his expression seemed to say. He reached into his jacket pockets and brought out candy bars, wrapped pies. Popcorn, my favorite. Along with meat, Nash had publicly sworn off anything that contained processed sugar. His preferred snacks were politically correct, environmentally approved. This food he had brought for me was therefore more than food. It was goodwill.

"You must be hungry, Mom."

"No fair." I smiled. "Okay. Come up and help me find something. It's been waiting a long time."

Relieved to hear the blame, the accusation, gone from my voice, he climbed agile and strong until he reached my side. The circle was new once again. Whatever lay buried here, whatever it turned out to be—diamonds or fool's gold—it would now be known to Nash and all who came after him. I'd be the last one who ever had to wonder.

21

ROGER

I had driven the bats crazy. Batty. My recitation had begun tentatively with a search for each word, a whisper, but as my confidence in memory had increased, so too had my momentum and my volume. By the third recitation I was booming, broadcasting to the universe, creating echoes of echoes of echoes, and all around me, high above, the swarm of bats beat their wings and careened in confusion. Sound came from every direction but there was no substance. They had lived their lives—basked in the collective experience of generations of ancestors—according to one set of sonar rules and suddenly here was another. The cave was their sanctuary and now it was transformed into a nightmare chamber. Physics itself became their enemy, their tormentor, and I, a dark presence in the lower darkness, vocal cords aflame, was the invisible cause. Overstimulated, confused, they found escape only into the dimension that normally they loathed. For in the course of my performance the planet had rotated on its axis once more and now full-faced the day. The single eye was ablaze with light, and into that alien environment the bats fled. It blinked with their departure, closed and then reopened. I pictured them, blind and pro-pelled without destination, flitting black stars against the blue Caribbean sky. The world was turned upside down. Day had become the only night, and night, too brilliant to endure. My poem destroyed their tranquility, and I exalted. Man prevailed. *I* pre-vailed, even if that triumph left me, at the end, alone.

When the last of them had gone, when the air was still, the pillar of light became again distinct. Now Herrick's lines all came back.

> Fame's pillar here at last we set,
> Out-during marble, brass, or jet;
>   Charmed and enchanted so
>   As to withstand the blow
>   Of overthrow;
>   Nor shall the seas,
>   Or outrages
>   Of storms, o'erbear
>   What we uprear;
>   Tho' kingdoms fall
>   This pillar never shall
>   Decline or waste at all;
> But stand for ever by his own
> Firm and well-fixed foundatión.

My pillar moved with the sun, a traveling spot that traced a path through the rubble of the floor. I saw the pool from which I had emerged. I saw my own hand. I saw just beyond the perime-ter of illumination the pedestal upon which I had sat as oracle and seer. Its geometry was arresting, for crusted as it was with guano, it betrayed a cubelike core too perfect for natural origin. There was a perpendicularity to its roughened angles, a Euclidian plane to its top, and with nothing else left to think about I gave its incongruity my full concentration.

It was not as though the edifice was high enough to use as a stool to reach the top. In height it was only about two feet, and it measured about the same in breadth. The base was obscured by petrified droppings that sloped on one side at a diagonal to the floor. It was a kind of altar really, a bench, and as the sun arcked across the sky and the sword of its light moved closer and closer to impale the strange object, my curiosity increased.

But the process took too long. When I set a pebble only an inch ahead of the light, it seemed forever before it was lit. The progress was inexorable but pointless. A shit-coated square bore no relation to my redemption. I moved to a recess of the cave and ran my palm over the walls. Even an expert spelunker, a rappeller with years of experience and a belt full of specialized equipment, would be hard-pressed to scale the sheer convexity that led to a natural nave. I had not a prayer. I tapped the surface with a rock, moving at random from one spot to the next in hopes of betraying some variance in the thickness. But it all sounded equally dense, as if the stone were an abutment of some fixed plate, an outcrop of Gondwanaland itself.

If I could not go up, perhaps I could go down, return by the route I had entered.

Dar'st thou dive seas and dungeons of the earth?

The face of the pool was calm, but I was not deceived. My body still bore the fresh scrapes and bruises where the sea had shoved me through the narrow, curving channel. I stood, composing myself to dive, and calculated my chances of success. As mentalists so often counsel, I visualized the experience: the shock of cold water, the utter blackness, the search for the fontanel and the pulsing rush of pressure, the competition for dominance at the point where sea and land confront. I would use my arms for levers, pull myself forward by fingers turned into claws. My lungs would cry for air. . . . And suddenly, the terror of entrapment came rushing back. Better to stop moving and die of hypothermia, better to starve slowly, better to scratch some message of farewell on the blasted cube—surely the first thing that would catch the eye of any future visitor to this place—than to become a bag of bones snagged against a protuberance of coral until dissolved by salt or consumed by hungry fish.

My resolve collapsed, my legs sagged beneath me, and at the sharp recognition of my impossible situation I was enveloped once again in an emotion very much like relief. Helplessness was seductive. No exertion, no matter how arduous or painful, would make a difference, so I might as well spare myself further agony. I turned from the water and into the plodding light, closer now to the puzzling rhombus, my only furniture, my subterranean Strato-lounger, my perch, my nest, my stage. I sat, waited to be lit, close to the faint warmth the sun cast. In unhurried time the tracking rays caught up to me.

You would think in such a dilemma that I, especially I, would become preoccupied with plans, and for a while that had happened. Could I invent fire, convert water to steam for warmth? Could I train a bat to be a homing pigeon of the night and send a message clipped to its wing? Could I make a camp here, become Robinson Crusoe marooned in a volcano? Were there edible fish to be caught in the pool, and if so, how? I had always been a man distinguished by his ingenuity, famous for it, and never was I in greater need, but nothing came to me. I tried to recall statistics: How long did it take for an adult human male to starve to death, to expire from thirst? And when had I taken my last food and drink? What was the starting point of my ordeal? Without water, perhaps days before madness set in: quite a lifetime, really. How to use it productively, to maximize my remaining potential? The question of *why* to do so skipped briefly across my mind, but I did not give pursuit. To go intellectually insane before I went genuinely, biochemically haywire would be to jump the gun. I was not a religious man—I was technically Christian, of course, but restrainedly so—and yet I did believe that existence was governed by some underlying sense of purpose. If that was true—and in extremis seemed too late and too convenient a moment to revise my theoretical perspective—then there was a reason I had not died in the undertow, a plan of which I was still marginally a part, a role I had yet to play in my own drama.

But what? I had said my poem, several times, and by rights that should have been a climax. Lightning should have struck, or rescue appeared, just as the last triumphant verses rolled off my tongue. There should have been applause, at least, or a falling curtain, but the minutes after my recitations were remarkably like the minutes before. My poem, my life, was a parenthetical phrase, an insert into the silence, and nothing more.

I had wasted little time in the contemplation of death, except for those few morbid undergraduate years when every act seemed to have heightened significance. I assumed I would die—why not?—but not soon, not before I was fulfilled. In my vague forebodings I had seen myself, frail and tucked into clean sheets, gentle music playing, slipping away without discomfort or regret. I was not prey to melodramatic fantasy, and so I found myself signally unprepared for the prospect that now seemed imminent: a hooting lunatic digging his fingernails against the walls of a pitch-black prison. Quite unseemly, so much so that I rejected the idea. One did not die so differently from the way one had lived, and I had never, never completely abandoned restraint—except for certain moments with Vivian.

The thought of her was a punch in my chest that left me winded. I was, I realized with dismay, more lonely than frightened. What would she do without Violet? Would she ever find out the truth? Would she know enough to blame me? Would she know enough *not* to? I pictured her face, contorted in grief, and me not there to hold her. How would she explain my disappearance when she returned to Hanover? Lost at sea? Whisked off the face of the earth? My colleagues would have private hypotheses: that I had been murdered, that I had been kidnapped by drug runners. Would anyone imagine that Roger Williams, well-known compulsive and responsible committee member, had been so lulled by the balmy sway of the palms that he chose to drop out and become a beach bum? One heard of such instances—college presidents who became forest rangers, executives who forsook their businesses in order to tie fish lures—but would anyone think *me* capable of such a step? I had to conclude, no. In all those cases there would have been something, some minuscule but recognizable spark of iconoclasm or perversity, and I had none. I was—and I had always rather prided myself on so being—proper, staid. Dull, if you will. Dullness was the one badge of my class that I wore with aplomb.

But how, within my present context, did I succeed in *dying* dull? With dignity, even irony, that most valued of aristocratic attitudes? I deserved a boring death, I had earned it. It was my entitlement, my birthright, and it now became my quest.

At last, at least, I had thought of a worthy question, a challenging task with which to occupy my remaining tenure. After the aberrations of the previous day—the leap from the boat, the near drowning, the frenzied declamations—my goal would henceforth be to return to normal. To compose myself in preparation for whatever afterlife was in store. To die the way I had consistently endeavored to live, up to the intrusion into my carrel of Vivian Twostar. To manufacture a boring end, even in this absurd circumstance.

Not surprisingly, my thoughts turned to food. I was hungry, I accepted that, but I took control of the menu. I thought of pot roast, boiled ham, a full Thanksgiving dinner. I concentrated on pudding, visualized its dull gleam, the way it built in layers within specially designed dessert dishes. Brown bread, a simmering pot of beans spiced only with chunks of salt pork and a touch of maple syrup. Cottage cheese. I absolutely refused to think of those outrageous concoctions Vivian so delighted in serving me: stuffed grape leaves, Indonesian satays flavored with coconut and cardamom, garlicky pestos and lime-guava cream pies. I evicted the entire cuisines of Thailand, Korea, Yemen, and Nigeria—the cookbooks she had recently dabbled in so deliciously—from my consciousness. I admitted no sauce thicker than gravy, no chocolate except in chips, no item whose total caloric content exceeded five hundred.

But damn it, I snagged on her infernal Navajo chili with jalapeño corn bread. It stuck in my head the way the cursed melody of certain songs can't be cast out. I saw its rich bubbling brownness, tinged with red, in high contrast with the flaky, crumbly squares of yellow. I smelled it, even above the bat odor. I tasted it on my tongue, rolled it around my mouth, swallowed in disappointment. It eclipsed the familiar turnip, it banished cod, it obliterated chowder. I wanted chili.

All right, forget food. Push away the plate. Instead, I would make a thorough review of my accomplishments, a kind of living résumé. I marched out grade school prizes, Latin awards, honor rolls—rolls, steaming from the oven!—sit-up competitions. I congratulated myself on successful term papers and forgave myself youthful folly—in the greater scheme of things I had not done so badly. Not like some who for all their brashness were still struggling for a promotion, someone like Vivian, willing to go to any length to discover new and improbable facts about a well-established historical figure. Someone with—God, it was true—the courage to take a chance, even if it meant ridicule, failure. And if she was right, she would in one swoop rise above all the rest of us, leave us in the dust. Dust to dust. Dust never found. Another set of anonymous bones.

And thus I passed the days, three orbits of the sun. A pendulum of unwelcome emotion, I swung from sorrow to joy, from regret to congratulation, from chill to fever, from hunger to satisfaction. The bats came back and I gathered the energy to disturb their slumber. Why should they resume their accustomed routine, my outburst forgotten or absorbed by them on some instinctual level as part of the vagary of existence? On the second night it had rained. Drops had poured through the hole above me and collected in the small natural pools that pitted the floor. It tasted sweet, slightly salty, impossible to resist, though its empty nourishment could only prolong my ordeal. Eventually I passed some boundary, some built-in marker usually not cleared before great old age, in which the anticipation of final peace superseded the tenacious impulse for more of anything new. I grew placid, studied my passivity with detachment. Awake, I watched the hourglass of light traverse my chamber, waiting for transcendence or oblivion, but still dreaming, when I slept, of Vivian's chili.

I don't know when it was that I finally lost track, when I ceased to tabulate my incarceration. We tend to move through the days the way, as a boy, I once tested my muscles on a jungle gym, crossing a horizontal ladder gibbonlike, one rung at a time. Normally we progress in highlights, befores preceding afters anticipating yet more befores, but now I seemed permanently mired in an endless middle, suspended between the sum of my memory and the end of it. Forward motion slowed, a music box winding down even as deliria accelerated. I was dizzy from starvation, sharply attuned to the most minute variation in temperature or visibility. Everything mattered because nothing did. I settled myself into a state of watchful torpor, of numb deterioration. Strangely, I made no protest, carved no epitaph. Nonbiodegradable, my dried diskette would last unaltered for millennia. When I dozed I kept it tucked secure beneath my arm so that it would be umbrellaed by my very skeleton from all future bat droppings. Someday, if this cavern was ever penetrated and mined by archaeologists, my verse would become a recovered voice, vivid, its blue shield a precious artifact as honored for what it revealed about the current state of technology as for the tale so compactly preserved. Egyptian potentates were sent on their long journey with urns of food, with golden chairs and murdered slaves, but they could not talk back to those who disturbed their tombs. I could. Silicon, not myrrh, conferred immortality.

I was in a relative state of flux, having just awakened or just dozed off, when a shadow passed overhead, and almost immediately afterward a rock fell from the sky and struck the floor not six feet from where I lay. Then another. Had the bats determined to bomb me out of their domain? Was the cave about to collapse? I curled further into the deep shadows, roused and crouched, then took cover behind the cube. In less than a moment, a huge bristly snake began to slither through the hole in the dome. Thick in silhouette, it descended in straight rhythmic jerks. It was as long as a sea serpent, long enough to finally stretch the distance from roof to floor, and in panic I tried to think of a weapon with which to defend myself. I had never read or heard mention of such a creature—yet the existence of a twenty-foot worm on such a small island would seem impossible to conceal. Was I hallucinating? Had I dropped to another plateau of confusion? Was this some Freudian prelude to complete madness? A vision of myself, Odysseus armed with an unbent paper clip confronting a giant cobra, flashed into my imagination, but before it could jell and be dismissed, the reptile checked its fall and hung suspended, a swaying bridge between day and night. Once more the opening was capped and then, as I strained my eyes against the gloom to see, something—someone—began to slowly climb down the length of the snake. Hand under hand, legs wrapped tightly, the room was filled with the sound of ragged breathing. I had no impulse to announce my presence, but rather remained a mute witness, stunned by a level of surprise unlike anything I had previously experienced. I had lost all familiar bearings, all comparative measurement, all normal standards of expectation. What happened, happened. Prediction was gone.

Feet touched the floor, a long sigh was exhaled, and a tiny light flared, drawing a radius around the walls as the body turned. Eventually it shone into my hiding place and stopped. Exposed, I stood in its flickering revelation, a soul at the Last Judgment, naked and ready to be counted.

I bent my elbow, raised my palm to shield my eyes.

"Roger," cried the startled voice of God. Cried Vivian Two-star, who stumbled toward me in the darkness and wrapped my shaking body tight in the strength of her arms.

Which of us touched more insistently, more incredulously, the face of the other? I say it was I, who after all was the one found.

Even when the shock was over, we could not disengage but spoke mouth to mouth, the ache of grinding bones made nothing by the miracle of human contact. We could not get enough of touching.

"I thought you were dead," Vivian said. She grasped the snake, which turned out to be a fishnet, for support. "They're looking for your body, but I left the light on so you could find your way."

"Violet," I said, but couldn't ask.

Vivian did not falter and that alone told me enough: the baby lived. I barely listened to how she had been rescued.

"But what are you doing here?" Vivian demanded when she had finished. Her voice was laced with annoyance, even anger, as if my torment were some practical joke at her expense. She went so far as to punctuate her words with a definite jostle, and I stiffened.

"I could ask the same of you," I countered, disappointed somehow that she had not come intending my rescue. Then I felt ridiculous. Who cared about motive? She *had* saved me. The idea was just sinking in. "How did you know where to look?"

"The oyster shells," she said. "I finally figured them out."

"Vivian, snap out of it. Did someone above ground hear my poem?"

"Your poem?" She was genuinely confused, and stepped back. "Roger, can the goddamn poem. I figured out the shells."

"You figured out the shells," I repeated, and pulled her to me again. "Oh good. And one of them had a pea underneath."

"The shells, Roger. Remember? From the library. From the feast on Hispaniola. Racine got them translated. It's too complicated to explain, but they brought me. It's here, Roger. *Here.*"

"Are you saying . . . ?

But first she finished filling me in on the recent past. Violet was safe with Hilda and Racine. Nash stood at this very moment on the surface, ready to help pull us out. When Vivian shouted up the news of my discovery, he replied with a whoop of what sounded to me like joy. It bounced off every wall, sank into the floor, was reflected off the water, redisturbed the bats. He didn't ask why or how, not yet—though he would no doubt devise some occult explanation, some fatalistic cause with which mere fact could ill compete. Who could say he was wrong?

Cobb, the villain, had been cast into the sea . . . by Vivian herself. What satisfaction that news brought me.

"We thought it was murder," Vivian said. "But now I guess it's just assault."

"*Just!*"

"Attempted murder," she corrected. "Second degree at least."

"Are there degrees of intent?" But enough of him. I wanted to know more about Violet. What had happened when the raft had drifted off?

"It's a long story," Vivian said. "Something to tell your grandchildren about."

My grandchildren!

"Your skin is freezing. You're all bones and eyes."

"I'm fine." And I was, amazingly, restored. Mind over matter. Life over death. When given half a chance. It was as though the promise of food, of warmth, of return, was temporarily enough. My blood was a spring brook fueled by the melt of snow. I had the energy of a man back home from a long trip, determined to visit each familiar sight before he rested. I wasn't ready to leave my cave, now that I knew I could. There was something we had to do first, and I persuaded Vivian to try.

She lit another match and played the light over the speckled walls, the pool, the floor. If she had read her clues correctly, somewhere here in this cave, here with us in this ammonia heart, reposed the crown of Columbus. I was prepared to believe anything was possible.

But where? Vivian held her wrist before her eyes, checked the illuminated face of her watch.

"It's almost three," she said, shaking out the match. "Vespers. The sun should do it."

Our eyes adjusted to the gloom, and the now-familiar shape of the pillar slowly coalesced. It formed a cone, a pointed finger, and its aim was true. There was only one thing besides us that did not belong in this place and, as it had been each cloudless afternoon for five hundred years, that object was now bathed in burnished light. My throne.

"Eureka," Vivian whispered.

Bat dung is white when it dries, ivory when it calcifies. Layer upon layer had been applied over the centuries to every inch of the floor, and the pattern effect was not unlike a monochrome canvas. Eventually, in a hundred thousand, in a million years, this cave would fill to the top and the bats would have to find another haven. Eventually the ice caps would melt and this whole island would be submerged. Eventually human beings would forget the particulars of their past, or cease to exist altogether, giving way to ages of insects or amphibians. Eventually, but not yet. We were in time.

We knelt before the raised square and Vivian struck a match against its surface. Whatever it contained was long sealed—completely, hermetically, provided with a second skin impervious to the elements and wonderfully camouflaged by nature. No pyramid's secret room, no lava pit, no laser-equipped museum was safer, more permanent, more impenetrable. Whether by provident design or, more likely, by accident, the treasure of Europe that Columbus had transported to the Indies but never successfully delivered had remained the safest, the most secure cargo of all the many voyages since. If this was truly a crown as Cobb insisted, if it had once represented the hope for equity and respect between worlds, if it had been meant to symbolize a new beginning, a kingdom free of past mistakes, then its hard organic casket was indeed a fitting storage.

"Right here, all along," Vivian's voice was quiet, oddly resigned.

"All we need is dynamite," I said. "I don't suppose you brought along any."

Vivian patted her pockets and came up with only one implement: the silver Cross pen I had given to Nash but which she forever borrowed and never returned.

"I wasn't exactly expecting Mount Rushmore. I thought . . . I don't know what I thought. I had given up looking, except for you. And even when I did imagine finding the crown, I guess I pictured one of those comic book pirate chests. You know, strings of pearls looping over the side, diamonds galore, and nestled among them, the fabulous *corona* of Burgundy. I guess I expected some sense of the man, that the artifacts would be his final signature, not . . ."

"Shit?" I offered.

"Not shit." She smiled. "But what better? What more appropriate jewel box? So there it is, used oyster shells plus guano equals the treasure of the Indies."

"Try the pen," I suggested. This was, after all, my right to grant since it would probably be ruined.

Vivian pushed the Cross into a slight indentation and, using it as a lever, pried off a flake, revealing more below.

"Mom," Nash called from above. "Did you find it? Are you all right?"

"I don't know what I've found," Vivian yelled. "Save your questions—time is precious. I'll explain everything when we get out of here. Go get Hilda and Racine. Tell them to bring the car. Roger is too weak to walk back."

"I'm gone," Nash said.

"Wait," I demanded. "Do you have any food up there? I haven't eaten for . . . I don't know how long."

"Just a sec."

I waited, my neck craned back, looking for manna from the sky. And then it came, in the form of potato chips, of Cheez Doodles, of Mars bars and Snickers. It rained inflated bags of popcorn, sticks of chewing gum, a package of Twinkies. Last to fall, rewrapped in haste, most precious because a bite of it had been already taken and hence it was a gift literally yielded from the boy's own mouth, was a Hostess cherry pie. I picked it up from the ground, peeled back the paper. It was broken and bleeding, and it was quite the most beautiful sight I could imagine.

"Back in a flash," Nash called. "Don't anybody move."

"Don't move," Vivian laughed, and I said, "Not a chance."

*　　　*　　　*

We had no notion what it was we were finding, and so we were careful. Probably we should have left it for experts to unstick, as Vivian noted mournfully from time to time. All her anthropological training about establishing exact provenance and not disturbing sites argued against our actions, and yet we didn't stop. The object, the crown, did not belong to us—that was clearly understood. It was the property of the Vatican or of the government of Spain on the one hand, or of the Bahamas on the other, depending on whether one accepted that delivery had been made five hundred years ago.

"Actually, if we're talking about intent," Vivian pointed out, "it should be turned over to Japan. Cipango was where Columbus thought he had landed. He claimed to believe that until he died."

In any case, ownership was to be determined and we were not in the running. But somehow, without ever saying so explicitly, we agreed that the *discovery* belonged to us alone. We had both—without meaning to, I will concede—risked our lives in order to reach this spot. We had a stake in being the first to know. Cobb too, certainly, but he had forfeited his claim.

The deeper one got into the guano, the more brittle it became. A few inches down and a blow turned it to powder, to chalk. The shape of the frame began to assert itself, a perfect square, and within two hours we were able to brush away the accumulated cover using just our hands, just the strength of our fingers. I found a depression, rubbed into it with my thumb, and encountered something below so smooth, so uniform, that I held utterly still.

"We are there," I said, and Vivian nodded.

"I know. I felt it too."

Reverently, a grain at a time, we picked away the dust.

"Let's clear off the whole thing," I suggested. "Maybe when we get it out of here we'll be able to see."

Vivian lit her last match.

"It's glass," she said softly. "It's a glass box." She directed the light into the excavated opening, but the surface was opaque, clouded from within.

FOUR
RETURNS

22

1.

December 27, 1990
Eleuthera, The Bahamas

NASH TWOSTAR

My mother emerged from the mouth first, blinking at the sunset. It was late, close to dusk, but the sky was tremendous. The clouds down here are what do it. They act as barricades, letting the colors pass on the sides, intense at the edges, but blocking them out in the center. They look like *National Geographic* pictures I've seen of Stonehenge, big watery monoliths, dams almost, against the light. It's refraction, and I understand the principle, but the name is too tame for what happens. The rays get bent and the spectrum turns strange. I've seen oranges here, true purple, once a sort of peach. This late afternoon the major shade was blue, but shifting from nearly black to the mildest turquoise. I had been watching it happen for an hour, letting it wash over me. Photographs never print as vivid as the real thing. They can dilute your memory, make it ordinary. I captured this experience with my mind.

Mom was covered with cream-colored dust of some kind, which made the inside of her mouth and her eyes look especially dark. She reminded me of those Japanese Noh actors, very remote, who don't beat you over the head with what they have to say. Roger was next out of the ground, Mom's male twin, a tall, skinny yellow chalk ghost. No, that wasn't it. He was a larva, so weak you'd think the wind would send him back below until he was ready to fly. When he saw me, he shook his head. Both of them were dazed and disoriented, like they had forgotten the world, like they had been buried and returned to life. They smelled like it, too. I held my breath. I reached out to Roger to steady his arm. It was trembling from the climb.

"Cherry pie," he said, and his tongue when he smiled was pure bright number-two red. "Best I ever tasted."

He could embarrass me, Roger, and he knew it, but I wasn't sure that was it this time. He had never completely quit trying for revenge, not since that night I blew his cover with his diary, but he'd never admit it, even to himself. He was supposed to be so mature, so good for me. It was only a matter of time before he would want me to call him "Dad." I never called anybody that and probably never would. Dads were for other people. I had troubles of my own.

"Do you have it?" I asked, though I didn't know exactly what they'd found down there. I had squinted through the hole but all I could hear was scraping, tapping, little bursts of conversation that rose like bubbles and broke into the air.

Mom sat on an outcrop of rock and stared at the sun. Her skin showed through in a hand print when she wiped her forehead. She was as captured by the clouds as I was. The sky was one of those things we had in common, as though it was in our family genes to look up whenever we were outside. She took a while to answer and I didn't rush her. The sunset was in no hurry.

"It's wrapped in the net." Roger was watching the waves crash against the rocks, and a kind of shudder squeezed his thin shoulders. "Waiting to be reeled in."

He made no move to do it, and I handed him my jacket.

"Okay, I give up," I said to him. "Mystery of the universe. How did you get in there?"

"It is the destiny of Adam," Roger answered, all phony dramatic, then laughed at himself. "No, seriously. It was only fair that I get to Columbus's box first. I started my research before your mother did. There is justice after all."

A wind blew from the water, strong enough to billow our shirts and ruffle Mom's hair. She stood up and put her hands on her hips. "So then of course you know what's under the glass," she said. "Enlighten us."

We all heard a car at the same time and looked down the beach to see our tank of a rental approaching slowly over the hard sand and pebbles. As it got closer we could make out that Hilda was driving. Obviously they had gotten the message I left for them at the store. Racine was pointing to us, and then stuck his hand out the window and waved furiously. The baby carrier was belted in the backseat, and at the sight of it a rush of weakness passed through my body. Would I once, in all the rest of my future, look at my sister without experiencing this surging gratitude and relief? She was my reprieve, the commutation of my sentence of guilt with no parole for good behavior. By turning up, she had rebegun my life as surely as her death would have been the end of it. She had returned to me what I had every right to lose and I was more than in her debt. What happened to her, happened to me. I was in her power.

"The witnesses arrive," Roger said, but I could tell: all he saw was Violet. He looked ridiculous—gaunt and storklike, his hands clasped together in front of him so hard that his fingernails turned rosy. I still didn't know his story, didn't know what had happened to drop him into this cave, but one thing was certain: he had believed the baby was dead and he thought it was his fault. I could read him loud and strong because he looked exactly the way I felt.

"Hey," I whispered to him low, so only he could hear. "It's okay. She's fine."

He turned to me and our eyes connected. More than our eyes. We couldn't have looked at each other for more than a second but somehow it seemed a long time, the kind of pause that first you think, "Oh my God, we're looking at each other," and then you think, "Yeah, we're looking at each other, so what?" and then you don't think at all, you just do it and it's all right. I read the words from his lips.

"You're welcome," I answered under my breath.

I don't know my father well. A telephone call here, a summer in California once or twice. He's got a whole other family and I'm a complication, a thing that happened to him before he settled

down and became the person he was going to stay. A school counselor asked me once if I had buried a lot of anger toward him, and
though I denied it at the time, I thought about the question now
and then. How can you be mad at someone you don't know? All
it means is that you're pissed at the idea of them, at who they aren't
and never will be. I sometimes thought of going back to that shrink
and explaining how dangerous that kind of question can be. It gets
stuck in your head and you have to answer it, and the thing is, you
don't want to. The answer's meaningless. What did it matter if I
was angry at my father? Would he care? Would he change his life
around to make me happy?

I talked about it to Grandma. "They think I'm mad at my
father," I told her. "That's why I act out."

She snorted, rocked her chair a little faster.

"Excuses."

"It's not an excuse," I protested. "It's psychology. You don't
understand."

"I'm mad at my father, so I'm not going to do my homework,"
she said, mimicking a falsetto singsong voice. "I'm mad at my
father, so I'm going to smoke a cigarette." She raised her eyes to
the ceiling, then shook her head. "*I'm* angry at your father. *You*
have no idea what to blame him for."

That conversation came back to me, instant recall, while the
long windy moment with Roger stretched longer.

"You're welcome," I said again, only this time out loud, and
just like that he forgave me. I saw it in his eyes. The wariness lifted
and there he was, served on a silver plate.

Oh shit, I thought. Now I've done it. Now I'm responsible for
this guy, too. But the funny thing was, I didn't really mind. The
funny thing was, I was glad.

I hoped they put Cobb away for good. I hated the guy for
what he'd done, for what he'd tried to do. I hadn't worried about
Mom because I hadn't known she was lost. And then with Violet
I was crazy for two hours until Mom found her safe in that little
church.

But the next morning when I saw Racine bending over Cobb,
washed up on the beach, I hoped the sucker had drowned.

Roger was Mom's second chance, and she deserved it. He

cared about her too—that much I knew from his diary, though it had made me mad at first. And Roger was Violet's father. I was an expert on what it was like to grow up without one around. And Roger was . . . Roger was somebody I couldn't hate. He did stupid things. He had his head up his ass half the time, and the off-the-wall stuff he said—it was not to be believed.

But I would have missed Roger Williams. I would have thought about him a lot. As we stood there, Mom watching him, his gaze fixed on my sister, I felt—I don't know—whole.

Hilda broke the spell. It was not hard to get to where we were standing if you knew where it was you were going. Otherwise the little hole we stood around seemed like just another pit among thousands, with no indication that it led anywhere deeper than a couple of feet. Hilda was a strong climber and quickly outdistanced Racine, who was more naturally careful, especially since he was carrying Violet. While Hilda mounted the rocks as though her sneakers were soled with suction cups and grappling hooks, Racine tested each foothold before putting his weight on it.

It was fairly typical of Hilda that once she hugged Roger, she went over and asked Mom what his story was, where he had come from. Tell me about female solidarity after living with Mom and Grandma for ten years. It seems disloyal now to admit it, and I don't feel that way anymore, but I had hoped for a brother. When I was little it wasn't so strange for me. I was let in on the gossip, a part of it really. Nobody, myself included, paid attention to the fact that I was a boy. I looked out at the world and saw these normal married families, one of each of everything, and they didn't seem so much better off than us. Usually worse. Most of the time the parents were so wrapped up in each other they ignored their kids. Not at our house. Grandma and I were the allies and Mom was the one we worried about. Had she done her homework for school? Who was this guy she was going out with? Had she been to church on Sunday?

Grandma taught me to cook. That gave us a lot of time together in the kitchen, and we made the most of it. We had our private jokes and she talked to me like I had a brain, told me things I was maybe too young to hear. She never would answer questions, though. She had this theory that if you didn't understand right off you weren't ready to know. "You'll remember this," she would tell me, "and someday you'll figure it out on your own. I can't tell you how to think." That left me with long lists of unfinished ideas in my head, and the thing was, she was right. Every so often as I got older I'd see or hear something new, something that stretched me one way or the other, and the next minute I'd remember some story of Grandma's that fit the situation perfectly.

The first time that happened I ran home all amazed and told her about it, said, "You know that story about my great-uncle in the war and what he wouldn't do? Well, I think I know why." I don't know what I expected her response to be. I mean, she obviously must have understood the stuff she told me, but you'd never know it from how she acted. "You explain it to me," she insisted, and I did, and then when I was finished I asked her, "Is that right?" She just shook her head, her eyes open wide and serious. I can still see her as she was that day, frying beans, standing by the stove. "Is *that* it?" she wondered aloud. "It could be. It *could* be."

That drove me crazy, but I liked it in her too. It seemed as though she was always ready to change her mind, accept a new theory if it was logical enough. Nothing, not even an event that had taken place before she was born, was fixed in its interpretation. Truth was all in the story, in the way it was told and in who was doing the telling. It could change in a minute or remain the same forever. A truth lasted only until a better one came along and replaced it. Or sat alongside it, an equally plausible alternative. Try to explain *that* to a physics teacher. I did once, and it made him angry. He thought I was bullshitting him because I hadn't read the assignment, but I had. I had just made the fatal mistake of discussing it in Navajo with Grandma.

But then, as I got older, doors started getting closed. Mom and Grandma teamed up, though they still fought over the usual subjects, and half the time they treated me as if I were a member of an alien species: interesting, potentially hostile, somebody to be skittish of. All right, I started it. I tried to be mysterious and told them they didn't understand a thing about me. But I didn't expect them to take me so seriously. It began as a game, me pretending to be grown up and distant, and then it stopped being a joke and turned real. They *didn't* understand me, and so they started making rules and I started having to break them. That hurt their feelings, I could see it in their eyes, and those times I wanted to go to Grandma and to Mom and say, "Let's stop this now. Let's go back to before,"—but I didn't.

So here we were, on the top of a hollow rock at the edge of a skinny island, Hilda and Mom conferring on one side, and Roger and I tongue-tied on the other. The third couple finally made it to the summit and gave the mix another stir. Nobody seemed to have told Racine how to behave—I always attributed that to his being foreign. Back in New Hampshire this lack of restraint could be a major cringe—you try walking along the street with your friends and have this smiling dude kiss you on both cheeks!—but it was what we needed at this moment in Eleuthera. He came at Roger and me with his free arm held wide and somehow he managed to pull both of us together. His expression held no questions—they would come later and they wouldn't stop for a long time—just a kind of gratitude. We formed a tight four-sided square—me, Racine, Violet in her car seat, and Roger—and let the wind find its way about us, like the clouds did the light.

Mom had wrapped and tied the end of the net around whatever it was she and Roger had found in the cave, and before the day failed we all worked together to bring it up. We pulled slowly so it wouldn't swing and hit the sides, and as the webbing collected in a growing mound I couldn't help but be curious. Nobody talked. Every year at my school the seniors bury a time capsule—yearbooks, top forty charts, predictions, a newspaper. They plan to open it at their twenty-fifth reunion, then to bury it again until their fiftieth. After that I don't know what happens. Maybe nobody cares anymore. Maybe the past is only important to people who can remember it firsthand.

There are different ways of feeling like an Indian for me. There are moments in Hanover when it sets me off from everybody around me, for better or worse, and times, like when we're back on Mom's or Grandma's reservations, when it makes me be at home. Mostly it's just confusing or irrelevant, one disguise among the many I put on. Except it's not a disguise, it's skin. I know enough about what happened—how smallpox and measles and all those other diseases wiped out most everybody who lived in North and South America—to know that statistically I'm an improbable exception, a survivor of survivors of survivors. Memory fades, identity gets blurred, as fast as blood gets mixed. When this thing we were hauling to the surface got buried Eleuthera was an Indian place, and now there wasn't a living soul who could trace back a connection or descent. They were gone, anonymous and invisible as if they had never existed.

Except for Mom and me. That sounds likes bragging but I don't mean for it to. It was no thanks to us that we were here, breathing the same salt air, watching the same sky as those long-ago people. It was pure chance, yet . . . yet it mattered. It was another one of Grandma's stories that finally clicked. We were the proof.

We had reached the purse of the net, and the prize it contained finally appeared: a square gray-crusted box, the size of a small typewriter or a big telephone. We had been careful, and the web now formed a bowl that capped the opening. As we each stepped back it flattened, caused a slow-motion eruption, and the object was presented as if on a spider's hammock. The strings looked so frail, so thin a support, but of course they weren't. They were green nylon, high-test, strong enough to drown a dolphin, to catch and kill anything that the ocean might throw against them. Their knotted diamonds had not even stretched at Mom's full weight, and not one link had broken as Roger clawed his way up. They would hold, and we let them. We stood, each of us planted like the points of a sundial, and waited.

"*Omphalos,*" Racine said.

"What do you mean?" Mom asked. At first her voice was barely audible in the wind, as though she didn't want to break the mood, and then she changed. She tried to break it with a joke. "If this is a navel, it's an outie. The thing must be pregnant."

"*Omphaloskepsis,*" Racine went on. "A mystic order in the fourteenth century, the Hesychasts, had a monastery on Mount Athos. They were quietists, believed that if you stared long enough at your own navel you'd be able to see the uncreated divine light. That contemplation was called *omphaloskepsis.*"

"You mean like you could know a baby that hadn't been born

yet?" I glanced down at my stomach, wished I could see through my shirt. I loved the idea that a body could answer its own questions.

"Something along that line, but more in the sense of the infinite potential. These were celibates, after all. They had no real children. Their future generations were not fixed because they never happened. Anything was possible."

Mom was thinking in a different way. "Quietists," she repeated, and we all became quiet, thinking of the idea.

"You could say that," Racine eventually agreed. As we talked among ourselves our eyes had never left the mystery box in the middle. We hadn't planned in advance how to reach the thing without dropping it. Some of us would have to play out the net while the others brought it toward them. But which way? Who?

Mom glanced at me. I knew what she was remembering. In karate, *tan-den*, the source of physical strength, is located right below a person's navel. It's the place of balance, and that made me think of Grandma and the prayer she had made me memorize that Mom and I spoke in the car before each of the lessons we took together. Karate was *do-zen*, the moving zen, and this was the correct Blessing Way. I recited the shortened version of the chant now, and she listened.

> Earth's feet become my feet, thereby I go through life.
> Its legs become my legs, thereby I go through life.
> Its moving power becomes my moving power, thereby I go
>   through life.
> Its body becomes my body, thereby I go through life.
> Its mind becomes my mind, thereby I go through life.
> Its voice becomes my voice, thereby I go through life.
> Its speech becomes my speech, thereby I go through life.

I stopped, not sure what to do next. I was suddenly afraid that Hilda and Racine and especially Roger would think I was weird. Maybe they did, but they didn't say anything and Mom . . . Mom was smiling. After a pause, she sang another part of the chant, one I didn't know by heart but could translate to myself easily enough. I had heard it recently: it was the Blessing Way that's used for a woman during her pregnancy.

ᵉ *ne ya* . . . a beautiful one came into my hands, a
beautiful one came into my hands, ˏ*a* ˏ*a* ˏ*a.*

Now I am long life, now happiness as a beautiful one came
   into my hands.
Before me it is blessed as a beautiful one came into my
   hands.
Behind me it is blessed as a beautiful one came into my
   hands.
Below me it is blessed as a beautiful one came into my
   hands.
Above me it is blessed as a beautiful one came into my
   hands.
Around me it is blessed as a beautiful one came into my
   hands.
My speech is blessed as a beautiful one came into my
   hands.
My surroundings are blessed when a beautiful one came
   into my hands.
A beautiful one came into my hands.

Things come together sometimes, they connect, and when
that happens it feels right. No Navajo had been anywhere near
Eleuthera long ago, but somehow these were the words that should
be said. They came back when they needed to. Roger hadn't understood a bit of what Mom spoke, but he stood with his head bowed,
the way you do in a strange church when you want to show
respect. Hilda looked fascinated, as though she couldn't wait to
know more, and Racine . . . it's funny but he looked like he was
praying himself. His lips were silently moving, forming words I
couldn't read. Violet, for her part, had the decency to stay asleep.

Before Mom was done she had made a strategy, and took
charge.

"Feed it to me," she instructed Roger and Racine, then reeled
in the net as their grips retreated across it. The heaviness of the
box made a depression in the web, but as long as we kept the
tension even, there was no way it could fall through. And we were
careful. In the process each of us retreated a few steps onto firmer
ground. The circumference got wider, and we didn't let go until
what had been the center was moved to the edge. Watching all
those circles in circles of circles was like looking down the mouth

of a telescope while the focus got more and more precise and every sight but one was funneled out. By the time it was safe, the box was all we saw. Before it touched the ground I said the two lines of the "Way" I liked the best because sometimes they seemed to describe better than anything else how I felt.

> Now I am the boy-reared-at-the-interior-of-mirage, I found
>   mirage, *ni yo o.*
> At the center of the mirage I found mirage.

It was glass carpeted with dung and there was something inside its walls. We knelt and squinted our eyes to see within, but the angles of vision were tight and narrow. From one vantage I made out part of something straight and from another, the curve of something round. Roger picked it up, held it like a prism to the disappearing sun. It turned his face red, but still he couldn't decipher the contents.

"Murano crystal, I would guess," Racine observed when Roger set the box down. "Very old and made by a master. It's a treasure."

"It's just a *container,*" Mom corrected. "Inside is what we came here for, what Peter Paul, that long-ago Mohawk at Dartmouth, hid for me to find."

"There are no seams." Roger examined the box slowly, looking for some point of entry. "It's as if it were blown whole around . . . whatever."

"A ship in a bottle," I said. "But no cork."

"So the question is, what do we do?" Hilda was practical. For her, there were always choices. Either we took the thing unopened, or we found a way to penetrate it here.

"It should be studied under optimal conditions," Racine argued. "Each step should be documented, photographed. It should go to the Smithsonian or to the British Museum."

"One could make the case," Hilda went on, "that it belongs to Cobb. I've read about these suits of ownership. Persistence counts in a court of law."

"Or to Spain," Racine said. "She funded the voyage. Presumably she still holds legal title. Or to the Vatican, since it is religious in nature. I'm sure the government of the Bahamas will make a claim. The Mexicans will want it for their conquest collection in the anthropological museum. And then of course there's us. The United States will undoubtedly base its position on our discovery."

Roger was silent, still dazed, lost in his own thoughts, but Hilda nodded. She and Racine were scholars. Their duty was clear. They could wait. They were objective, removed from the message.

Mom was different.

"What we have here is Europe's gift to America." Her words were paced, calm, and I recognized the tone. It was her voice of preparation, the gathering of her forces. "What we have here was the promise, the pledge, the undiluted intent, the preconceived idea before any fact was known. This little nothing, this box anyone can lift, was the bond, was supposed to be a fair trade. And Columbus left it unopened. Never given. Never accepted."

Roger caught my eye. It took me a moment to tell what was different about him, but then I knew: he was listening. Usually when someone else was talking, Roger could hardly wait for them to stop so he could weigh in—agree or disagree, it didn't matter. He was always impatient for his turn to express an opinion, to argue his point of view. But not now. Now he was simply tuned in to Mom, as though he had something to learn.

While she was still speaking, Mom reached across to Violet's car seat. My sister was awake now, a neutral observer as the voices tangled in the wind. She watched as Mom removed the one clean diaper stored behind the cushion. She watched as slowly, deliberately, Mom wound it like a bandage around her stiff right hand.

"Europe got America, everything and everybody in it and on it, and in exchange we were supposed to take . . . this." Mom closed her eyes, concentrated her strength. Her next words were a whisper.

"We've waited long enough."

I saw the chop coming. Like every perfect movement in *do-zen* it broke from nowhere and yet from everywhere at once. It arose from the inner self, from a long procession of subtle decisions, links in a fine chain, that finally translated into action. Mom *became* her white-wrapped hand and fell with it into the glass.

*   *   *

There must have been sound. Glass makes noise when it shatters on rock. But sometimes one sense overpowers all the others, blocks them out, and this time it was sight. Our eyes registered and recorded the event, not our ears.

There, framed by a halo of shards, was a twisted brown circle, a few pointed sticks.

There must have been sound. Five people breathing, a baby at the end of her patience. And yet all was still. Even the wind seemed to pause, to draw into itself.

Like Cobb, I had expected jewels. Diamonds, rubies, emeralds. I had expected gold, the most valuable thing, the object that in and of itself was supposed to so dazzle the people Columbus found that they would welcome all those who came after.

"It was a crown after all," Mom said.

And it was a crown, no mistake. I recognized it from the picture over Grandma's bed: It was the Crown of Thorns.

Metal lasts. Plastic never disintegrates. And in an airless vacuum, even the stalks of plants can be preserved for centuries, though their moisture evaporates to mist. The Crown looked brittle, dust arranged in peaks and pathways. When no longer shielded by the walls of our bodies, would it blow away?

The world has become a small place, all parts connected, where an Indian using an ancient Asian art can break into an old European box, witnessed by someone who grew up in Australia. Whatever happened next at least was new, at least had never happened before.

The wind returned, found its way between us strong enough to move the smallest piece of glass. Before we could react, the Crown was lifted, set down again, but its circle didn't separate. Only the thorns fell off, every one.

It was too dark for us to descend from the rock, too dangerous for the baby, and so we waited for dawn. We made a tent for the Crown with our jackets held down by stones, and rested against one another as we watched the night. The stars were bright enough to count.

Racine of course had an explanation. "It must be some natural preservative," he decided. "Painted over the entire surface as a coating. That's why the thorns didn't hold. Their connections were internal. There was nothing to keep them attached once they hollowed."

"Do you think this is the real thing?" I asked Racine, to draw him out. I had read that archaeologists had carbon-dated Veronica's veil and the Shroud of Turin and found that they were fakes. I remembered from Grandma's *Lives of the Saints* that Saint Helena had gone to Jerusalem and carried back pieces of what she claimed was the True Cross. But I hadn't heard a thing about the Crown of Thorns.

Racine was silent. He had not forgiven Mom. In the first heat of the moment he had called destroying the box "a crime against history," and had collected every splinter of glass in a careful pile. "Reconstruction is the only hope," he had commented before the failing light forced him to stop. I had never before seen him angry, and his mood made me nervous. He was waiting for Mom to apologize but she didn't, so he couldn't absolve her.

"Tell us," Hilda prodded her husband. She was bored with her role of peacemaker. "You know you want to. Don't sulk."

There was a rustle in the dark as everyone leaned forward to demonstrate an interest that was meant to appease, and Racine relented. "The tradition goes," he began, "that the Crown was kept in Jerusalem until it was brought to Byzantium in the eleventh century. Two hundred years later the emperor Baldwin the Second gave it as a gift to Saint Louis of France, who built Sainte-Chapelle to house it. One thorn is supposed to be in the cathedral of Barcelona, Mary Queen of Scots eventually brought another to Edinburgh, and a few were given to various German knights."

"Sir John Mandeville saw it in Paris," Roger added. "According to his *Travels,* it had come from Genoese sailors and rested in a vessel of crystal."

"Genoese," Mom repeated. She sounded more tired than I had ever heard her, tired the way Grandma sometimes got.

"Let me take her," Roger offered and reached for Violet. Of us all, she was the one with energy, ready for action. Despite the cool night air she refused to keep a blanket around her shoulders.

"So what do you think?" Hilda asked. "Did they fool the king and keep the real one, those Italians? Is that where Columbus got it? And why did it wind up here, inside this rock? How did you know where to look?"

"The answer was obviously in the shells." Racine waited for Mom to explain to him, as she had to me when I joined her this afternoon on top of this outcrop. "In the Hebrew inscriptions," he prompted.

"She was amazing . . ." Roger began, but when he spoke Violet raised an exploratory note of protest and he stopped, shook his head.

"She was a fool," Mom said to him, then spoke to Racine, or was it to herself?

"Maybe those Indians were expecting something better and got insulted. Maybe they thought the Crown was dangerous and so they never opened the box and buried the whole business where no one would mess with it. Maybe they put it in a safe place until someone came along who could explain how to use it. Maybe they just pure and simple didn't want the thing and didn't know how to give it back."

"It explains so much," Racine said slowly. "The continual voyages of return, the unending search. Columbus came to wear the habit of a poor monk, a Franciscan. Was he trying to atone? Perhaps what he lost was more than what he found."

There was the suggestion of light far to the east, just beyond the edge of the sea. It defined the bottom of a cloud with a narrow stripe of gold, but the morning star was still the brightest spot in the sky. My sister had dozed off, content in her father's quiet arms.

I thought of Grandma. What she would say about all this, how she would explain what had happened as though she had known it all along. This would drive Mom crazy at first, but she'd eventually give up like the rest of us. Grandma wouldn't change her mind. Facts fit into the answers she gave for them or they weren't worth wondering about.

I liked that about her, how she never let anything go.

2.

COLÓN

I tem: *You will tell their Highnesses, that the welfare of the souls of the said cannibals, and of the inhabitants of this island also, has suggested the thought that the greater the number that are sent over to Spain the better, and thus good service may result to their Highnesses in the following manner. Considering what great need we have of cattle and of beasts of burthen, both for food and to assist the settlers in this and all these islands, both for peopling the land and cultivating the soil, their Highnesses might authorize a suitable number of caravels to come here every year to bring over the said cattle, and provisions, and other articles; these cattle, etc., might be sold at moderate prices for account of the bearers, and the latter might be paid with slaves, taken from among the Caribbees, who are a wild people, fit for any work, well proportioned and very intelligent, and who, when they have got rid of the cruel habits to which they have become accustomed, will be better than any other kind of slaves. When they are out of their country, they will forget their cruel customs; and it will be easy to obtain plenty of these savages by means of rowboats that we propose to build. It is taken for granted, that each of the caravels sent by their Highnesses, will have on board a confidential man, who will take care that the vessels do not stop anywhere else than here, where they are to unload and reload their vessels. Their Highnesses might fix duties on the slaves that may be taken over, upon their arrival in Spain.*

> —Memorial of the results of the Second Voyage of the Admiral, Christopher Columbus, to the Indies, drawn up by him for their Highnesses King Ferdinand and Queen Isabella; and addressed to Antonio de Torres, from the City of Isabella, the 30th of January, 1494.

. . . God is just, and He will in due time make known by whom and how it has been done. Let them judge me, as a governor who had been sent to Sicily or some province or city under regular government, and where the

laws could be executed without fear of danger to the public weal or subjection to any enormous wrong. I ought to be judged as a captain sent from Spain to the Indies, to conquer a nation numerous and warlike, with customs and religion altogether different to ours; a people who dwell in the mountains, without regular habitations for themselves or for us; and where, by the Divine will, I have subdued another world to the dominion of the King and Queen, our sovereigns; in consequence of which, Spain, that used to be called poor, is now the most wealthy of kingdoms. I ought to be judged as a captain, who for so many years has borne arms, never quitting them for an instant. I ought to be judged by cavaliers who have themselves won the meed of victory; by knights of the sword and not of title deeds; as at least, so it would have been among the Greeks and Romans, or any modern nation in which exists so much nobility as in Spain; for under any other judgment I receive great injury, because in the Indies there is neither civil right nor judgment seat.

Already the road is opened to the gold and pearls, and it may surely be hoped that precious stones, spices, and a thousand other things, will also be found. Would to God that it were as certain that I should suffer no greater wrongs than I have already experienced, as it is that I would, in the name of our Lord, again undertake my first voyage; and that I would undertake to go to Arabia Felix as far as Mecca, as I have said in the letter that I sent to their Highnesses by Antonio de Torres, in answer to the division of the sea and land between Spain and the Portuguese; and I would go afterwards to the North Pole, as I have said and given in writing to the monastery of the Majorada.

✝

I know, assuredly, that the errors which I may have fallen into, have been committed without any intention of doing wrong, and I think that their Highnesses will believe me when I say so; but I know and see that they show mercy towards those who intentionally do injury to their service. I, however, feel very certain that the day will come when they will treat me much better; since if I have been in error, it has been innocently and under the force of circumstances, as they will shortly understand beyond all doubt: I, who am their creature, and whose services and usefulness they will every day be more willing to acknowledge. They will weigh all in the balance, even as, according to the Holy Scriptures, it will be with the evil and the good at the day of judgment.

—Christopher Columbus

November 25, 1992
HANOVER, NEW HAMPSHIRE

ROGER

In the quietly ticking peace before dawn, I rise from the warm nest of our bed, leaving Vivian folded silently in private dreams, her body oriented by our lovemaking. I put my arms into the sleeves of a huge goose-down robe and tie it around me so that I resemble a walking sleeping bag. I trace my way downstairs, into the low hum of the kitchen. I press the button on my coffee machine and am answered by an obliging gurgle, then a thread of steam, then the aroma of brewing Tanzanian.

In those mornings when the tilt of the earth erases the moon's radiance, when by reason of a heavy cloud cover no stars appear, no light, it is in the blue of my own kitchen that I sometimes remember that vast depth where I found my own darkness. As I feel for the stair rails, the way to my office, as I tap my hands along the walls, I think of that world below.

I was lost, but now am living in the daily heaven of an unexpected life. I was a stranger to my family, to my daughter, but now am found.

I prefer working at this hour, especially now that I am on to other things. The first, and only, section of "Diary of a Lost Man" was published in a fine literary journal, *Caliban*, early in 1991—shortly, in fact, after we returned from the island. With that behind me, I'm free to pursue whatever comes to mind, and so these mornings I sing of canned goods and door hinges, vegetable stews, pitted roads, the whorled bark of butternut trees, the faces of those I love. I sing the body electric instead of the stranded mind. For I've changed.

One *can* change. I've learned that. One can accommodate the habits of others. We have built a house together, Vivian and I, with a room attached where her grandmother's furious rocking and her imperious pronouncements will not disturb me, just as my need for silence won't hamper her enjoyment.

I suppose that I've fallen into the public shadow of Vivian Twostar. Her televised testimony against Cobb—now serving a ten-year prison term—followed closely by her publication of the unexpurgated, annotated version of Columbus's *Diary*, has gained her much attention from many quarters. The messages on our answering machine range from Nash, studying ethnobotany at the University of Washington, to requests from Valencia and The Hague for keynote addresses and papers.

Vivian found, within the text, material for a plethora of legal approaches under international law, issues of aboriginal claim and sovereignty, of premeditated fraud. The prospects for victories— here, in Brazil, in New Zealand, in Mexico—appear better than anyone would have expected. The demands upon her time are many and important, and she must be away more than we'd like. There's not a great deal I can do to assist in her endeavors, but I offer help where I can—such as completing the alumni magazine piece on the historical Columbus, an article which now bears both our names as author.

Proprietorship of the Diary itself is still in dispute, and is likely to remain so for some time, but meanwhile it is scheduled for display in the central hall when the new Smithsonian Museum of the American Indian opens in Washington, D.C. As for the Crown, after a brief barrage of media attention, few serious scholars became persuaded of its authenticity or remained interested in the question. One thorn was tested. The results were inconclusive. It could have been real. It could have been only very old. The Church, officially proclaiming that the Crown of Thorns was more important as metaphor than as object, cast no vote, and for the time being, it reposes in the Museum of the Discovery in Nassau. A postage stamp has been issued bearing its image superimposed upon the Bahamian flag.

Human nature is no different now than it has ever been: the present is a sponge that sucks history dry.

As for me, it may seem to some that I've vanished, drawn into myself, or even that I've undergone a pedagogical or artistic crisis, but nothing could be farther from the truth.

Now I live simply. The cave both vindicated and gave closure to all the choices I had made in my life up to that point. I continue to maintain a polite, firm distance from family demands that so distressed me as a youth, and I chart my own way within the academy. So far, I have avoided the heart attack that took my father's peace of mind. I don't so much live *through* Vivian as complement her. I am satisfied in our differences: She hungers and thirsts for future justice, and I strive to bring forth from the past what is good. We meet in the present, in this house that holds the treasure.

Violet glows at the center. The other day, I found her, just over two years old, smoothing with her plump hands the coverlet in her crib, making her own bed. Unmistakeably my daughter. Ours. What stories we have to tell her. What games and what thoughts. What experiences and what poems. What a world to prepare.

Sometimes I take out the scrap of paper Cobb pressed into my hands on that Eleuthera beach. I read again of the "shining leaves," "what marvelous change was wrought" by the king's hands when he touched the brittle circlet. What *was* the miracle? When his fingers traced the dry brambles, did the wood tremble with life for an instant? Did it sprout green shoots?

I have lost my certainty, gained doubt. Before I begin my work on these dark New England mornings I often return to John Donne's holy sonnet "La Corona."

I keep trying to understand.

> *Deign at my hands this crown of prayer and praise,*
> Weaved in my low devout melancholy,
> Thou which of good hast, yea, art treasury,
> All changing unchanged Ancient of days;
> But do not, with a vile crown of frail bays,
> Reward my muse's white sincerity,
> But what Thy thorny crown gained, that give me,
> A crown of Glory, which doth flower always;
> The ends crown our works, but Thou crown'st our ends,
> For, at our end begins our endless rest;
> The first last end, now zealously possessed,
> With a strong sober thirst, my soul attends.
> 'Tis time that heart and voice be lifted high,
> *Salvation to all that will is nigh.*

4.

It was finally the least likely of the two women who broke the spell of astonishment and plucked the baby from the raft. Valerie Clock held the girl bent-elbowed, right in front of her, and clicked her tongue until one of the baby's eyes squinted, blinked open, and focused. She was four months old, discovering the delights of other humans, and at the sight of Valerie's long-jawed sullen face, so near, both the baby's green eyes widened. She burst into a smile and held it, entranced, waiting to be fed.

"Mama, she's a pretty one!" said Valerie, jiggling the baby up on her shoulder as she picked her way ashore.

Eunice, pulling the sagging raft into the scrub yard of the beach house, did not answer. She stared suspiciously out to sea, sweeping the empty horizon, and then, just as suspiciously, she regarded her daughter, who was holding the baby as if she'd already had one, as if she knew how.

No one was home during Christmas week up at the big house, but this was no matter, anyway, for those folk. This was a tan-colored baby, light-haired, mixed by God, maybe drifted from near Governor's Harbour where the Club Med ran buses and hired girls to watch the wealthy tourists' children. Maybe one of those girls had this baby and cast it out for shame, or maybe she had been rocking her baby in the surf and shifted her eyes away from the raft to roll at some boy. Wherever the little one came from, it was clear to Eunice that she would have to go ask her brother, Sydney, what to do about the child.

Sydney Clock was a preacher who moonlighted as a mechanic, fixing taxis and rental cars. On the day that Eunice came looking for advice, he was behind his house under the spread of some acacia trees, swapping a couple of fan belts.

"A baby." He stroked his chin and brushed sand pickers from his shirt. Sydney was large, and made a tight squeeze under cars.

"You inquire around," instructed Eunice, her voice adamant.

377

She knew that the best source of information was the taxi-men's circle, for they drove up and down the island's length all day, wasting expensive gas.

Valerie sat on Eunice's front porch in the shade of the darling plum, hung with red, yellow, and fluorescent orange fishing buoys. The girl was having no luck in getting the baby to take a bottle—a goat, that's what they needed, Eunice thought. A goat's milk was best for weaning. She'd weaned off Valerie on goat's milk, though the girl even then had been too dreamy to care about insisting on the breast, indifferent in her feeding as with all else in life, except this one thing, which was making Eunice annoyed.

"Come away from there," she ordered, "or it's going to get around how you're showing off your own baby."

But Valerie just smiled. Even parting her lips was usually too much trouble, and here she was coaxing the baby onto cow milk and had even changed the soaked diaper for a clean cloth.

As much as the life jacket it was that original diaper, the one the baby was wearing when they found her, that bothered Eunice. It was no cotton piece, no rubber pants, no type of thing many island girls could afford to use. It was the kind they threw out by the dozens up at the big house during the week the nephew and his wife took their vacation last year. Eunice had disapproved then. She disapproved now. It was the United States diaper that made this mystery complicated.

The Home of the Living God Church, an oblong board building, contained plank benches that had once been painted brown and now were worn tan, in places to cream. On this night it welcomed a record number of worshipers: not only for the Christmas Eve celebration but because everyone was curious to see if Valerie Clock would bring the baby she had found.

Sydney, driving to the airport and back, had spread the news. By the end of two hours it was known that there was no baby, white or black or in between, reported missing on Eleuthera or on any of the island stops from Fort Lauderdale. At least, the pilots who made the trip twice a day reported nothing to the mailwoman who greeted them coming and going. Lounging against the Club

Med limousine, a battered Country Squire station wagon with real planks replacing its missing fake wood-grain siding, Sydney discussed the matter with other drivers, gestured with an imaginary cigarette.

"I'll be consulting the Scripture tonight," he'd promised, handing out one of the Bible leaflets he kept stacked in the glove compartment. In that way, Sydney took advantage of providence to summon the most impressive congregation of his career, and now, in the long and waning light, he greeted each of them at the doorway. Outside in the cooling dusk, in the grove of palmettos, the money-bats flapped—huge moths with gold coins on their wings. Sydney felt the power swell in him as he walked up the center aisle. There was Eunice in the front row, head down, eyes shut, lips moving in prayer. There was Valerie beside her, the fat little baby ready to yell in her arms.

Sydney felt it proper to pay special heed to this niece whom he'd never much liked, and didn't like now, either. He smiled forgivingly as he stopped before her, opened his arms to invoke the Redeemer, then pressed his hands on either side of her brow. Maybe he squeezed her head a little tighter than necessary, or maybe it was just Valerie's unpleasant nature coming out as it did so often. At any rate, instead of closing her eyes while Sydney prayed over her, Valerie looked up at him. In the pupils, which she had made black and hard as marbles, Sydney read refusal.

He was surprised. He had thought Valerie would have loved to be the center of attention. Later, to his annoyance, during the chorus of the first hymn, when he happened to glance Valerie's way so she would shush the baby, the girl responded by sticking out her tongue. So swiftly had she flicked it that no one else in the congregation, not even Eunice, seemed to notice.

Pride goeth before a fall, Sydney reminded himself. The girl was certainly no fit mother, no example of the blessed, to behave in that fashion toward her uncle. Therefore, he decided that in the text of his homily he would emphasize the serious troubles that the Pharaoh's daughter had caused. After all, for the good work of saving the bulrush baby, what did the Egyptians get once the child reached its growth? Their rivers turned into blood, frogs swarmed their homes, then died and raised a stink. Their dust bred gnats and other bugs, then flies. All their animals pitched over dead. The people got boils, then fever plagues, then a rain of hail. Locusts, darkness three days and three nights, the death of each firstborn son.

They were sure in a poor fix before they let go of those Israelites.

When the meeting concluded, Sydney again stood by the door, chatting with and embracing members of his departing flock. The first shall be last and the last first, he thought, as finally the first row's occupants stood before him at the straggling tail of the churchgoers.

"That sure was fancy talking," Eunice said, taking Sydney's one hand in both of hers with a stern look, but it was clear that she agreed they should give the child over to the police.

Beside her mother, Valerie kept the baby's head covered. In the light of her glare, Sydney thought he'd wait for a more private time to tell Eunice about the girl's misbehavior. For now, feigning kind interest, he bent toward his niece.

"You been taking good care of that baby?" he inquired in his most soothing voice. "Feeding the child milk and honey at the palace?"

"Only difference . . ."

Valerie was uncommonly quick with her retort. Her brows lowered, her lips pursed. For the first time, Sydney saw something of Eunice in her.

"Only difference, Pharaoh's daughter, *she kept hers.*"

Valerie would have said more had not Eunice, with a scandalized yank at the girl's thin waist, taken and propelled her down the crushed coral walkway.

They crashed straight into the arms of a tourist woman who was running up the path, making a display of herself. Well, she had a right to, Eunice said later, didn't she? It was her baby, lost at sea and drifted in to shore, not a great distance mind you, just around the point down from the Cobbs' big house.

While the woman wept and held her Violet—that was the baby's name—and talked on and on and hardly looked at Valerie, who stood like a pillar of salt, struck speechless, Eunice began to think how she could do a favor for a friend. One of her closest lady acquaintances had cooked for the Cobbs one whole month and had never been paid. When the commotion cooled, Eunice mentioned the money to the woman.

But it was no good. They never heard you right. The woman's face was swollen red, and she couldn't seem to grasp the justice of the complaint, so Eunice gave up. Instead, she and the woman walked back to Sydney's car, followed by a small crowd of Eunice's neighbors, all eager to see the baby and the mother reunited. They would tell the story, become a part of it. Later on, each would bring the telling to the point at the end of the path where the woman put her baby in the car, then, gripping the hands of this or that surprised person, began her other questions.

"Have you seen a man?" she asked. "Have you seen a man around forty? Tall? A white man? Was there a man in the boat too? Did a man drift in?"

That was when everybody turned around to look for the one who had greeted the boat, for Valerie. They cast their eyes to the church steps, where they had seen her last, and saw that she had disappeared.

Valerie walked out behind the church, through the scrub, to a sand bluff above the sea. She sat there for an hour, then two hours, thinking. Everything was different now, everything was changed, but if she went back among the crowd or into her mother's house, Valerie knew, the difference wouldn't last. And so she continued to sit. In all her fourteen years, she hadn't noticed the sea before, hadn't really taken it into account. The waves were just a sound she could always hear, a noise in the background. Now Valerie looked at the dark expanse and opened her thoughts. The water was alive, breathing, full of fish. People died out there, lured to the bottom. Boats sank. And sometimes a marvelous thing washed up on shore.

She had been the one to receive the sea's mercy. She was also the one to give the mercy back again, but the mother had just snatched the baby away with no thanks.

Valerie's throat hurt when she thought about that. Her shoulders still ached from rocking the baby to sleep that afternoon. Her fingers were still clenched from letting go. The fact remained, though, that no matter what had happened in the end, she had been chosen in the beginning. This meant that other things might happen to her, too, she was sure.

It was a while before Valerie started to think of the sea as a place to cross, but once she did, she couldn't stop.